Patricia is the million-copy bestselling author of the Lottie Parker series. She very early learned to be ... by ... her full-time work ... or commitment to fulfil that ambition. However, tragedy was to intervene which caused a major shift in her life.

In 2009, after her husband died following a short illness, Patricia had to retire from her job and found that writing helped her cope through her grief. She then started to write seriously. Fascinated by people and their quirky characteristics, she always carries a notebook to scribble down observations and ideas. Patricia lives in the Irish midlands with her children.

www.patriciagibney.com

LV 60107618

LIVERPOOL LIBRARIES

ALSO BY PATRICIA GIBNEY

The Missing Ones
The Stolen Girls
The Lost Child
No Safe Place
Tell Nobody
Final Betrayal

TELL NOBODY

PATRICIA GIBNEY

SPHERE

First published in 2018 by Bookouture, an imprint of StoryFire Ltd.
This paperback edition published in 2019 by Sphere

13 5 7 9 10 8 6 4 2

Copyright © Patricia Gibney 2018

The moral right of the author has been asserted.
All characters and events in this publication, other than those
clearly in the public domain, are fictitious and any resemblance
to real persons, living or dead, is purely coincidental.

All rights reserved.
No part of this publication may be reproduced, stored in a
retrieval system, or transmitted, in any form or by any means, without
the prior permission in writing of the publisher, nor be otherwise circulated
in any form of binding or cover other than that in which it is published
and without a similar condition including this condition
being imposed on the subsequent purchaser.

A CIP catalogue record for this book
is available from the British Library.

ISBN 978-0-7515-7753-2

Printed and bound in Great Britain by
Clays Ltd, Elcograf S.p.A.

Papers used by Sphere are from well-managed forests
and other responsible sources.

Sphere
An imprint of
Little, Brown Book Group
Carmelite House
50 Victoria Embankment
London EC4Y 0DZ

An Hachette UK Company

www.hachette.co.uk
www.littlebrown.co.uk

For my friends, old and new

PROLOGUE

The smell of smoke from the chimneys in the housing estate clogged her throat. She hurried on, and tried to keep a tally of the seconds and minutes as they passed. But she became confused and lost count as another pain pierced her abdomen. She fell to her knees, her hands gripping her belly.

Street lights directed her along the desolate lane that ran behind the terrace. Her jeans were saturated, and she wasn't sure if it was blood or water. She hoped it wasn't blood. As another pain ripped through her, she bit her lip to stifle the scream that threatened to erupt from her throat and escape out into the smoggy air.

Rain pricked her skin like pellets from a gun. She was surprised by the feeling. Because before the shower had started, all she could feel were the sharp twinges in her lower body. It was pelting down and she had no coat. Her thin T-shirt quickly became saturated like her jeans and shoes.

Turning left, she headed for the football pitch, but the lights were on and a crowd stumbled around the side of the clubhouse. Must be a party, she thought. As she headed back the way she had come, another shooting dart of pain creased her in two.

'Not yet. Please!' she cried at the rain-laden sky.

The shower passed over. Within five minutes she had reached the tunnel snaking beneath the canal. No, she couldn't go towards town. Someone would see her, and she didn't want to be seen in this state. People gossiped enough as it was. She climbed the slippery slope towards the water. On reaching the gravelly footpath, she started to run along the edge of the canal, surrounded by reeds and cans and dirt. She thought she heard someone behind her. She hadn't the energy to look back. There was no one there, she told herself. It was only the rats in the waters of the canal.

And then there was another pain. And everything changed completely.

SUNDAY

'Goal!'

Mikey Driscoll thumped the air as the ball landed in the back of the net. He was immediately engulfed by his teammates. Yes! He was a hero. At last. For the remaining five minutes of the under-twelves match, he played with a smile spread across his face.

The referee's whistle sounded, and whoops and cheers chorused through the air as the crowd filled the pitch. Mainly parents and families of the victorious boys. Mikey was hauled up onto someone's shoulders. He no longer felt the smallest on the team. Now he was a giant. Yeah!

He spied his friend Toby smiling up at him from the crowd, and he grinned back. As he was carried towards the gable end of the clubhouse for the presentation of the cup, he scanned the crowd for his mother. His heart dipped slightly. Of course, she wasn't there. She'd never come to any of his matches before; why would she now? But it was a *final*. He'd sort of hoped … He gulped down his disappointment.

Sliding to the ground from the unfamiliar shoulders, he sought out his teammates. Mikey might have scored the winning goal, but Toby was the captain and he'd get the cup. Mikey rushed to his side. Toby was taller by a good head, and Mikey had to look up at him, shielding his eyes from the setting sun with one hand.

'Great goal,' Toby said.

'Ta,' Mikey said. 'Is it okay if I stay at yours tonight?' He crossed his fingers. He'd already told his mother he was going to be staying over at Toby's. Please say yes, he prayed silently.

Toby hesitated. 'I'll have to ask my ma.'

'Sure. Don't worry.'

'Why d'you wanna stay anyway?'

Before Mikey could answer, he and Toby were jostled to the front of the crowd by the team coach, Rory Butler.

'Come on, lads. Presentation of the cup and medals, then I'm treating you all to a McDonald's!'

A cheer went up, and Mikey was swallowed up by the rest of the team, quickly becoming separated from Toby. He was sweating from the exertion of the game and the evening heat. Should he run home for a shower first? No. He'd told his mum he'd be staying at Toby's, so he better not put in an unexpected appearance. Ah well, he thought, all the lads would be smelly, not just him.

He took his medal from Rory Butler, and then Toby raised the cup. The crowd dispersed, and some of the parents sat in their cars waiting to bring the boys to McDonald's. The team mini-bus was also ready to ferry whoever needed a lift. Mikey followed the team into the dingy changing room.

'That was the best game of the season,' Rory said, clapping each of them on the back as they entered.

Mikey liked their coach. Rory was maybe the same age as his mum. Thirty-something she always said when anyone asked.

'I'm so proud of you lads. No more team talk, it's time for celebration. Grab your things and I'll meet you all at McDonald's. Nuggets and chips are on me!'

The boys cheered again before collecting their bags, then, still in their jerseys and shorts, and with their medals hanging on green ribbons around their necks, they set off with a cheer.

*

Toby felt bad. Yeah, they'd won the final, and yeah, they were all sitting eating their nuggets and chips, and yeah, they had the coolest coach of any team in the county, but …

Mikey was eyeing him across the table with his big, sad brown eyes. Shit, Toby thought. Maybe he could bring him home to stay tonight, like he'd asked. After all, Mikey had often stayed over before. But Toby didn't want him there tonight. His big brother, Max, would be home, and Toby didn't like how things felt in his house when Max was around. None of his family had come to the match, but that didn't bother him. He was better off without them.

He pushed his fair hair out of his eyes, his special cut, shaved all around with a mop on top, as his ma described it. Mikey had tried to keep up with him by getting his mother to put blonde tips on his. Looked shocking. Awful. But Toby never told Mikey that.

Stuffing a chicken nugget into his mouth, Toby chewed hard. He'd known Mikey since junior infants; they'd been in the same class right through primary school. Now they were growing up. Moving on. Would Mikey still be his best friend once they were at secondary school? He hoped so. He felt sad now when he saw Mikey gathering his food wrappers, his medal swinging proudly as he went to put his rubbish in the bin.

Laughter and chat surrounded him, but all Toby could hear was the silence between himself and Mikey. He kept watching him. Mikey was chatting to Paul Duffy, the team physiotherapist. Well, he wasn't actually a physio, but he was a doctor. Next best thing. Everyone was here. Barry, the doc's son, always tagging along and giving orders like he was the boss. He's only fifteen, Toby thought, not the boss of me! Paul's wife Julia, who washed the kit sometimes. Creepy Wes, the bus driver who brought them to away games. Bertie

Harris, who thought he was the coach but was really only the club caretaker. And of course, Rory Butler. The real coach. Toby liked Rory and grinned over at him when he smiled his way.

Stuff it, he thought. Mikey *can* stay with me. Max can piss off. His whole family could piss off. He gathered his empty nugget box and the remains of his fries and was heading to the bin when he felt a hand on his shoulder. He swung round.

'Toby, you played so well today.'

Toby shimmied out from under Bertie's grip and grinned uneasily at the caretaker. 'Yeah, thanks. It was a good match. Great fun.'

'You played a stormer.'

'But Mikey scored the goal.'

'Great goal it was too. Young Driscoll doesn't score too many, but that was an important one. Don't forget the celebration party next Saturday night.'

'I won't.'

Toby picked up his bag and looked around for Mikey. The place was packed and noisy. He was tall enough to see over the seated heads, to search and scan. But there was no sign of his friend.

'Shite,' Toby said. Just when he had decided to let him stay over. Ah well, it was Mikey's loss.

*

Mikey remembered that his mum would be at bingo, and anyway, she wasn't expecting him home. But he had a key to the house. And Toby was being a dick.

He hitched his bag on his shoulder, one hand on the medal around his neck, and talked to himself as he walked. So, first he'd have a shower, then he'd update *FIFA* on his PlayStation, and while that was running, he'd see what was on Netflix. One of the lads had mentioned a series called *Stranger Things*. It sounded really cool. He knew his mum would never allow him to watch it, but she'd be out, wouldn't she? Yeah! He punched the air and began to jog. With the rest of his evening sorted, he felt a lot better.

He crossed over at the traffic lights and headed towards the tunnel to take the shortcut home. He hated the tunnel under the canal. Yuck. He was always thinking the walls would crack and he'd drown in the muddy water.

He kicked an empty beer can, and as it echoed back at him, he heard a vehicle rumble up alongside him. He kept walking. It kept pace with him. Turning around, he peered in through the side window. When he saw who it was, he smiled.

'Hi,' he said.

'Jump in. I'll give you a lift home.'

'Ah, it's okay. It's not far.'

'You must be knackered. I'm headed that way.'

'Okay, so.'

Mikey walked round to the passenger side and opened the door. He sat in and snapped on the seat belt. He heard the click of the automatic locks sliding into place.

'Good Lord, Mikey, you stink.'

'I do, don't I?' Mikey laughed nervously.

'I can fix that.'

'What do you mean? I'm nearly home. Plenty of hot water there,' he said, though he knew he'd have to wait half an hour for the immersion to heat up the tank.

The driver took a left when the traffic light turned green and headed up over the Dublin Bridge.

Mikey looked out of the window, confusion knotting in his chest. 'Hey, *that's* the way to my house. Back there.'

The driver stared straight ahead. Silent.

'You're going the wrong way.' Alarm spread through Mikey's body.

'Oh Mikey, this is the right way. Don't you worry your little head. Trust me.'

Mikey slid down in the seat, his feet resting on his bag, and risked a look sideways at the driver. Trust me? No, Mikey did not, but there wasn't much he could do now, was there?

DAY ONE

Monday

CHAPTER ONE

The flight from New York arrived into Dublin Airport early. It was exactly 4.45 a.m. as Leo Belfield waited in line at Passport Control. He wasn't nervous. He had nothing to hide. Nothing to declare. He was a captain in the NYPD, after all. But he knew that the secret of his birth, and the secret of his family from this country, where he had never before set foot, were things to be kept quiet. He had found out a lot in the last six months. Ever since Alexis, his mother, had suffered her heart attack, he had discovered things about his family he was sure she'd never intended telling him. But he didn't know it all. Not yet.

I am here now, Alexis, he thought. In the country you tried to leave behind. The country you never wanted me to know about. Looking for the family you denied me.

He smiled at the passport control officer and answered the mundane questions.

'On holiday, sir?'

'Yes, I am on holiday.'

'Travelling around?'

'I'll be staying in the Joyce Hotel in Ragmullin.'

'Ah, yes, Ragmullin. Down in the midlands. Lots of good musicians hail from that neck of the woods.'

'I wouldn't know,' Leo replied. 'This is my first visit.'

'Hopefully the first of many.' The officer stamped the visa and handed Leo back his passport. 'Have a nice stay.'

'I'm not so sure about that,' Leo muttered to himself as he pocketed the blue passport. 'Not so sure at all.'

*

Detective Inspector Lottie Parker flicked the ash from the butt of her cigarette and watched it sizzle in the cracked concrete at her feet.

'They're bad for you.'

She looked over her shoulder to see Detective Sergeant Mark Boyd standing beside his car, leaning over the roof, dragging hard on a cigarette of his own.

'Pot and kettle,' she said, and turned her head to continue staring at the ruin that had been her home until five months ago.

She sensed him moving nearer.

'Staring at it won't help,' he said.

'My life has gone up in smoke.'

'You're still alive. Your kids are okay. It's a sign that you have to move on.'

She sighed, and dug her hands deep into the pockets of her jeans. 'I know it's just concrete and clay.'

'That's a song, isn't it? I seem to remember my mother mentioning it.'

'How would I know, then?' She shook her head. 'And please don't attempt to sing it.'

'I won't.'

'What brings you here anyway? Surely not to join me in wallowing in misery?' Her house had burned down in February. She'd thought it was arson, but it had turned out to be an electrical fault. She still wasn't convinced that was the only cause, though.

She glanced up and found Boyd staring at her. Long and lean, his ears sticking out a little, more grey than black in his tightly cut hair and a light shimmer of stubble on his chin – very un-Boyd-like.

'McMahon is looking for you, as usual,' he said.

'What time is it?'

'Just gone nine.'

'Can the super not give me five minutes of me-time?'

'Lottie, you've been coming here every morning for months. It's not going to turn into a phoenix and rise from the ashes.' He held up his hand as she opened her mouth to protest. 'Your house of memories is no more. Like I said already, you need to take this as a sign, and move on.'

Biting her lip, Lottie thought of her husband, Adam, now five years dead. This was the house they had lived in from the day they'd got married. The house in which they'd reared Katie, Chloe and Sean, their three beautiful children. Burned to the ground. Gone. All gone. Was Boyd right? Was it a sign? She didn't know. She didn't know anything any more.

'Fancy a drink?' she said.

'Jesus, Lottie! It's nine in the morning. Come on. Where's your car?'

'I walked.'

'From your mother's?'

'Thought it was a nice morning for a stroll.' She looked up at the inky blue sky and noticed the warning clouds gathering momentum, despite the lazy sun. She knew Boyd didn't buy her lie. 'Car wouldn't start, so I called Kirby for a lift. He dropped me off on his way in. He's in a jolly mood today.'

Boyd said, 'Must be his woman. Gilly O'Donoghue is like a tonic to him. Anyway, you should have rung me. I'll give you a lift to the station.' He made for the car. 'Are you coming, or are you going to stare at that boarded-up ruin for the rest of the day?'

She kicked at the butt of the cigarette, took out the packet and said, 'Got a light?'

He raised an eyebrow.

'I'm not going to set fire to the rubble, in case that's what you're thinking. I want a cigarette, and Kirby lit the last one because I'd no lighter or matches.' Tears threatened. Jesus, she thought, I'm a worse wreck than the damn house. Bricks and mortar. That's all it was. But it had been more, much more. It had held all her memories, and now it was nothing.

'Get in.' Boyd opened the car door for her.

Lottie shrugged and did as she was told. She was in no humour for a row. Then she remembered why he had come looking for her.

'McMahon sent you? Why does he want to see me?' Acting Superintendent David McMahon was keeping her on a tight leash. Paperwork and then more paperwork. She was sure he got off on it.

'Guess.' Boyd switched on the engine, reversed, then drove out of the estate.

'Trouble,' she said.

'Probably.'

CHAPTER TWO

Lottie dallied in the station yard after Boyd had parked the car. 'Go on ahead. I just need a bit of fresh air first.'

'You'd better hurry up. I'm not making any more excuses for you.' He strode into the building.

Why was she feeling so low? Maybe it was the overcrowded situation at her mother's. With twenty-year-old Katie and her son Louis, seventeen-year-old Chloe and fifteen-year-old Sean, it was a tight squeeze. But Rose had opened her house to them after the fire, and Lottie had accepted the offer of a roof over her family's head.

It wouldn't be for much longer, though. She had it sorted. So what *was* the problem? She took a deep breath, knocked away the longing for another cigarette, vowing to quit. She found a Xanax in her jeans pocket and swallowed it. Hopefully it would calm her.

She walked inside, letting the door swing shut behind her. In the reception area, she nodded at the desk sergeant, Garda O'Donoghue, and went to key in the code for the inner door. Before she could enter the second number, she heard a shriek from behind her.

Turning around, she came face to face with a teenage girl with wide black eyes, damp hair criss-crossing her cheeks, expression wild and feral. Her jeans were ripped, zipper undone, feet bare. Her T-shirt, once white, looked like it had been tie-dyed in blood.

Involuntarily, Lottie took a step back, banging into the door. She opened her mouth, but words refused to form.

The girl spoke.

'I think I killed him,' she whispered.

Lottie pulled herself together and stepped forward. 'What did you say?'

The teenager raised her voice. The sound was guttural, animal-like. 'I killed him.'

And then she fell in a faint to the floor.

The duty doctor insisted the girl needed to be hospitalised. The ambulance arrived within ten minutes, and Lottie travelled in the back with her.

'Shock and hypothermia,' the doctor had said. As she watched the pale face beneath the oxygen mask, Lottie wondered how the girl could be suffering from hypothermia in the warm July weather. But that was the least of her worries.

The paramedic studiously monitored blood pressure and other vital signs.

'Very low heart rate,' he said.

'Who are you?' Lottie whispered to the girl.

'Don't think she's able to answer you,' the paramedic said. The name badge on his green uniform told Lottie he was called Steven.

'I'm not stupid,' she snapped. Seeing his eyes dip, she added, 'Sorry.'

'No problem. What did she do?'

'I have no idea.' She checked the plastic evidence bags she had hastily fastened about the girl's hands, preserving the evidence of a crime she knew nothing about. 'Do you know what's wrong with her?'

'Not being smart with you, but I've no idea.' Steven shook his head and checked the monitor. 'Blood pressure is dangerously low.'

'Keep her alive,' Lottie said, 'please.'

He nodded.

The siren waned and the engine stopped. The doors opened and Lottie jumped out, then stood back to allow Steven and the driver to extract the stretcher. They pulled down the wheels, and as the hospital doors slid open, they ran inside. She followed.

'Keep her alive,' she repeated as a porter slid the girl from the stretcher onto a trolley bed in the A&E cubicle.

When the curtains were discreetly pulled tight, shutting Lottie outside, she called Boyd.

She bought a Diet Coke from the hospital shop and stood outside the main door to have a quick cigarette, only to realise there was no smoking allowed anywhere on site. She'd no lighter anyway.

Boyd parked on double yellow lines. 'Any news?'

'They're working on her.'

'Do you know who she is?'

'Jesus, Boyd. She appeared at the door covered in blood, said, "I think I killed him" and then collapsed.'

'So you have no idea what happened?'

Lottie snapped her head around. 'I've told you all I know.'

'Hey, keep your hair on.'

'For feck's sake, Boyd.' She turned on her heel and walked back into the hospital. Some days he wound her up like a spring, and today was one of them.

She sought out the consultant who had taken command of the teenager.

'Dr Mohamed,' she said, flashing her ID badge. 'What can you tell me?'

His eyes were tired and his skin sagged, though she estimated he was only in his early thirties.

He said, 'She lost a lot of blood. We may have to give her a trans-
fusion. I'm monitoring her progress and will make a decision soon.'

Lottie scowled. She hadn't noticed any visible wounds. 'In what
way is she injured?'

'She is not injured in your sense of the word. Do you not know?'

'Know what?'

'She has given birth. Quite recently. The placenta was still in
place, adhered to the womb, and that caused the haemorrhage. It's
been removed now.'

Digesting this information, Lottie wondered where the girl's
baby was. How and why had she arrived at the station uttering those
guilty words of admission? Feeling Boyd's presence at her shoulder,
she hoped he would ask sensible questions of the doctor, because all
logic had fled her brain and she was speechless.

'What are her survival chances?' he asked.

'We got her in time. I believe she will be fine. However, if you're
thinking of interviewing her, it won't be today.'

'If she says anything, let us know,' Lottie said. 'And if you find
out who she is …'

'I will inform you.'

With that, the doctor walked away down the narrow corridor
lined with helpless patients on trolleys. A uniformed officer arrived
and Lottie instructed him to keep guard outside the room containing
the girl's cubicle.

'We need to retrace her steps,' she said.

Shrugging his shoulders, Boyd asked, 'And how do you propose
we do that?'

'Old-fashioned police work.' She pushed through the double
doors. 'I need a lift back to the station.'

CHAPTER THREE

Fifteen-year-old Sean Parker was happy for the first time since the school holidays had started. He'd been at the soccer match last night, and congratulated young Mikey on a great goal. He knew Mikey from when the youngster used to play hurling, not that Sean played much any more. He had even helped coach him at one stage.

A schoolmate, Barry Duffy, had been there as well and had texted him this morning to see if he wanted to go fishing. They had only become friendly when Sean had moved to live at his gran's house, which wasn't too far from Barry's.

Sean glanced at the canal water, where the odd ripple moved the reeds to and fro. In the distance, he could hear the hum of traffic. The cathedral bell chimed. Fumes from the sewage works filled the air with a sickening smell. It happened every summer. Must be the warm weather, he thought. A slight breeze rustled through the trees. The water undulated with tiny waves as a moorhen swam across.

'I like your fishing rod,' Barry said. 'Where'd you get it?'

Sean followed Barry up the bank and onto the pathway that ran along the edge of the canal. 'It was my dad's.'

'I thought all your shite got burned in the fire?'

'The stuff in the shed survived.' Sean hoisted the old green army bag onto his shoulder and held his father's fishing rod with both hands. 'Where do you want to set down?'

'Just a bit further on. Caught a trout up here yesterday.'

'Liar,' Sean laughed.

The path opened up in front of them once they had crossed the Dublin Bridge. Sean caught up with Barry and they walked side by side until they reached the section where the canal was joined by the supply river.

'This is the best place,' Barry said, and dropped his bag.

Sean decided not to argue. Barry handed him a can of cider. Shit, his mother would kill him. But she wouldn't know, so he took it, flipped the tab and took a sip. He looked at the sun, creeping up the sky.

Yeah, it was going to be a great day.

CHAPTER FOUR

Hope opened her eyes. She was lying flat on her back, staring at the ceiling. She could see dots of blood peppered in a V directly above her head. She glanced at her arm, where the line of an IV ran from her bloodied wrist up to a drip bag.

The baby was gone. She knew that. The little body that had grown in her belly for the last nine months, twisting and turning, was no more. The pain had eased but she could feel the child's shadow as though it had refused to let go even after the last contraction and burst of pain. And after *that*? She could not recall.

'Oh, you're awake.' A nurse in a white tunic lifted Hope's wrist, jiggled the drip bag and tightened a blood pressure monitor around her upper arm.

The hiss of the expanding cuff pinched Hope's arm but it was nothing like the pain she had experienced a few hours ago. Or was it days? She had no memory of what had occurred. Why not?

'How long … how long have I been here?' Her voice sounded raw, not like hers at all.

'You were brought in by ambulance about an hour ago.' The nurse wrote notes in the chart at the foot of the bed. 'Can you tell me your name?'

'What? Why do you want to know?'

'For one, I can't keep calling you "the girl in cubicle three". And two, we need it for our records.'

Hope toyed with the idea of giving a false name, but she knew she would be found out. Eventually.

'Hope Cotter.'

'Address?' The nurse was scribbling on a clipboard.

'Fifty-three Munbally Grove.' Hope waited for a reaction as she gave the address from the wrong end of town. But there was none. And how come she could remember those details but not what had led to her being here?

'I'll get a doctor to come in to have a word with you. No more talking for the time being, and don't go back to sleep yet, do you hear?'

'You said something about an ambulance? How ... Who ... I don't understand ...'

'Now what did I say about not talking? Rest yourself. The doctor will answer all your questions.' The nurse made to leave, then turned. 'The gardaí want a word with you too.'

'What?'

But the door had already swung shut, leaving Hope alone with her fuzzy memories and a knot of fear tightening in her chest. Why did the guards want to talk to her? She didn't know what was going on.

But there was one thing she knew for sure.

She had to get out of here.

And soon.

CHAPTER FIVE

'Who *did* she kill?' Sitting at his desk, black hair flopping over his forehead, Acting Superintendent David McMahon was staring at Lottie like he wanted to laser her in two.

Lottie stuck her hands into her jeans pockets and leaned back against the wall of his office.

'That's a bit presumptuous, sir.'

'I don't think so.' He folded his arms and leaned back in his chair.

If he starts to swivel, Lottie thought, I'll swing for him. But he didn't move.

He continued. 'She appears at the station, covered in blood, announcing, and I quote, "I think I killed him." That sounds to me like there's a body out there waiting to be found.'

'According to the A&E consultant, she had delivered a baby and the placenta was still intact, so it caused a major haemorrhage. It's probable that the blood was her own.'

'And you're a doctor now, are you?' he grunted. 'Have blood tests been run yet?'

'Being analysed as we speak.'

'So you don't actually *know* whether the blood on her clothes is her own or someone else's?'

'Not yet,' Lottie admitted. She clenched her hands into fists inside the pockets of her jeans. She was sure McMahon knew he was infuriating her. As usual. But she had to admit he was right.

'Therefore, you must treat her as a suspect in a murder. This is top priority. Go and find me the body.'

'With respect, sir—'

'No more is to be said on the matter.' He stood, swiping his hair from his eyes, two pinpricks boring into her. He smoothed down his double-breasted waistcoat and buttoned up his jacket. 'Get to it, Parker.'

'For feck's sake,' she said under her breath as she pushed herself away from the wall and left his office.

McMahon had been gunning for her from day one. He had yet to hit the mark, but he was getting closer with each passing day. Lottie had got the better of him in a case last October when he'd been drafted in from the drugs squad. But when her superintendent, Myles Corrigan, had had to take sick leave, McMahon had secured the acting job ahead of her. As further punishment, he was continually bombarding her with paperwork, which she hated, and the pile was rising as high as his temper. Every morning he called her in to check on progress. At least this morning he'd had a different tune.

She headed for her own office, situated at the back of the main area. It was little more than a cubicle, much like the space their unknown girl was occupying in the hospital at the moment. But at least Lottie had a glass door rather than a curtain. Where was the girl's baby? And was it dead or alive?

Detectives Larry Kirby and Maria Lynch were seated at their desks and neither raised their head as Lottie made her way past them.

'Where's Boyd?' she asked, noticing his vacant chair.

Two sets of shoulders shrugged in answer.

'What's up with everyone?' She knew it was a rhetorical question, but all the same, it bugged her when neither detective replied.

'Have it your own way,' she muttered and slammed her door. Sinking into the chair, she wished she could escape to a desert island. But that wasn't going to happen. Not with three kids and a grandson to take care of.

She clicked on her computer, scrunched her eyes trying to remember her password, then shoved the keyboard away.

Her phone vibrated. *Mother* flashed on the screen. She rejected the call. Could the woman not leave her alone while she was at work? It was bad enough that Lottie had to live in her house and spend the evenings with her. At least she was in the process of decorating a rental house, with the help of Maria Lynch's husband, Ben, but the day she and the children moved out couldn't come quick enough. Hopefully it would happen early next week. She knew the kids needed their own space too. And soon. Otherwise Katie was in danger of murdering her younger sister. And Sean? Well, he was no bother—

The desk phone rang. Surely her mother wasn't that insistent? But it was a nurse from the hospital. With news.

Lottie took down the name and address of the bloodied teenager and hung up. Just as she was about to leave, her mobile vibrated again.

'Look, Mother, I'm busy,' she said without checking the caller ID.

'Lottie, are you okay?' It was Father Joe.

'Sorry. I thought you were … oh, you know.' She felt exasperated and flopped back on her chair. 'Anything wrong?'

'Can you come over to the cathedral for a couple of minutes? I want to have a word with you.'

She really should be checking out Hope's address before returning to the hospital to get an interview with her.

'Sure. Where will I find you?'

'I'll be inside the main gate.'

As she finished the call, Boyd stuck his head round the door.

'You were looking for me?'

'Fancy a walk?'

CHAPTER SIX

The A&E department was chock-a-block. Doctors and nurses frantic. Orderlies and porters rushing to and fro. Hope found her clothes in a blue plastic bag on a steel rung under her bed. She tore off the IV and the hospital gown and slipped on her blood-soaked elasticated-waist jeans, still damp. The pain in her abdomen protested, but she got them on. Her T-shirt was a mess but she pulled it over her head anyway. There were pads jammed between her legs, and she found it awkward to move. The nurse had told her she'd been brought into hospital from the garda station. Why had she been there? Had she done something awful? Whatever it was, she felt with an unnatural certainty that she had to get out of here.

There was no sign of her hoodie. She had no idea if she had been wearing it or not. And no shoes. Where the hell were her shoes? She would have to go barefoot.

Slowly she dragged the curtain to one side and sneaked out behind a porter pushing a patient in a wheelchair towards a side door marked *X-Ray*. To the left she saw a fire door with a sign in big red letters warning against opening it.

She ignored the instruction and pushed down on the emergency handle. No alarm sounded. Once outside, she let the door swing shut behind her.

The ground was hard beneath the soles of her feet, but she had to keep going. Keeping her arms across her chest, hugging herself, hiding her bloody T-shirt, she headed for the rear exit out onto the main road. She knew the canal snaked around here somewhere. She just had to find it. And then she should be able to make her way home, relatively easy and unseen.

As she mounted the stile that led to the canal footpath, a cramp assaulted her abdomen, followed by a screeching pain. But she kept going.

She couldn't remember a thing since just before the baby slid out of her womb.

And then she was struck with a horrible thought. Where *was* her baby?

*

The sun dipped behind a cloud and the water darkened.

'This isn't much fun,' Sean said.

Barry flung his empty cider can into the centre of the canal and picked up his rod as a rat scuttled through the reeds. 'You're some moaner. You can piss off back home if you want.'

'I didn't mean it like that.' Sean wasn't sure what he meant, but he didn't want to annoy Barry. It was cool to hang around with someone other than his friend Niall. Wasn't it? And Barry was popular. He was different. Sean took a swig from his own can and threw it, still half full, into the water.

'Let's see if there's any more vermin ready to attack,' he said, forcing bravado into his voice. But his laugh died in his throat.

'What now?' Barry asked.

'Do you see that?'

'What are you talking about?'

'That … that thing over there … what is it?'

'I can't see anything. Anyway, I don't like the four-legged yokes.' Barry began to stuff his fishing gear into his bag. 'Let's go up further.'

'Okay so,' Sean agreed, even though they hadn't been here long.

As the clouds shifted, a gentle breeze rose and the reeds swayed. Sean felt his eyes widen and his mouth open in protest. He dropped his tackle bag and picked up his fishing rod, leaning forward and poking through the reeds.

'What the …? Jesus Christ, Barry. Look. Not there. Over here, you eejit. What is it?'

Barry shuffled up to Sean's shoulder.

'It looks like … Is it human?' he said.

'I need to see more of it.' Sean prodded with the rod. 'Jumping jack shit, Barry. We need to call the guards.'

'What for?'

'Whatever that is, it … it's d-dead,' he stammered. 'And it looks very small.'

'Might be a dog or something?' Barry said.

'It's not a dog, you moron. It hasn't got any fur.' Sean had his phone in his hand.

'You don't even know the number for the guards.'

'My mother's a detective.' He tried her, but she didn't pick up. 'I'm calling 999.'

'What'll we do with the booze?'

'They're hardly going to search *us*.'

When his call was answered, Sean gave the details and then hung up. He continued to poke through the reeds with the end of his fishing rod. Suddenly, a rat swam along the edge of the bank and he dropped the rod just as he prodded the *thing*. He was only just quick enough to save it from sinking.

Barry turned and started to run.

'Hey!' Sean shouted. 'What's up with you? Come back.'

'It *is* a body,' Barry yelled. 'Only … only it's a …'

Sirens sounded up on the bridge.

'Too late now. You'd better wait. I told them there were two of us here.'

When he saw the pale hue of Barry's face, Sean turned to look into the water once again.

'Fuckity-fuck,' Barry said, and promptly vomited.

CHAPTER SEVEN

The air was crisp despite the July sunshine, and for a moment Lottie thought she should have grabbed a jacket on her way out. She took the lit cigarette from Boyd and inhaled.

'About time you bought your own,' he said.

'Why would I, when you're so generous?'

'Where are we going?'

They stood on the bottom step outside the station. She stared over at the cathedral and thought about Father Joe. She had to keep him on her side. He'd be good to have as a confidant now that Boyd was making a circuitous route around her on the personal front. She couldn't blame him. For too long she had distanced herself from him, and when he had asked her for commitment, she had baulked. It was her own fault. But she knew her life was too complicated to share with anyone other than her children and grandson. And her mother, Rose? Now *she* was a different problem altogether. A distorted family history that Lottie had no desire to tackle at the moment.

She spotted Father Joe Burke just inside the main gates. She felt Boyd stiffen beside her. She threw down the cigarette and crossed the road to greet the priest.

'Nice day,' she said. 'You had something to tell me?'

'It might be nothing, but there is something I wish to discuss with you,' Father Joe said. 'In private.'

Lottie turned to Boyd. Shit, now he would have a face on him all day.

'Would you give us a minute?'

'First you want me with you, and then … I take it that's not a request,' he said. He blew out his cheeks, then ground out his cigarette with the sole of his shoe and stomped back inside the station.

'Sorry,' Father Joe said.

'Oh, don't mind Boyd. He'll get over himself,' Lottie said. 'You look worried.'

'Let's walk and talk.'

They moved into the cathedral grounds.

'How are things at your mother's?' he asked.

'Cramped,' she said, with a laugh.

'How long do you have to stay there?'

'Not long now. Against my better judgement, I accepted a house for a nominal rent from, of all people, Tom Rickard. You remember him, don't you?'

'Of course I do. He was involved in the failed St Angela's development.'

'And he's Louis' grandad.'

Lottie's daughter Katie had fallen pregnant by Rickard's son Jason early the previous year, just before Jason was murdered. Louis was now nine months old. Tom Rickard was residing abroad. He knew better than to return to Ragmullin, and that suited Lottie. But following the fire that had destroyed her home in February, he had offered her the use of a vacant house he owned on the outskirts of town, and no matter how proud she wanted to be, she couldn't turn it down.

'I should have called you more often,' Father Joe said. 'To see how you were doing – you know, since the fire – but …'

'Don't worry. I know where you are if I need a chat.'

'Good.'

A warm silence sprang up and Lottie snapped away the urge to link her arm through his. No, they had never become that familiar, but she liked the younger man's company. Even though he was a priest.

'Are we going to walk around in a circle, or are you going to tell me what it is that has worried a furrow so deep in your brow you could sow potatoes in it?'

He smiled, and they turned right and walked towards the large black cross with the crucified Jesus hanging there.

'I heard you had a young woman present herself at the station this morning,' he said.

'Where did you hear that?' Lottie cursed the grapevine that meandered its way out of the station and wrapped itself around the community so quickly.

'Doesn't matter, but I think I might have seen her. Day before yesterday.'

'Where? How do you know it's the same person?' Lottie stopped walking and eyed him suspiciously.

'I was coming out of the cathedral and I noticed someone sitting at the grotto.'

'Show me.'

Lottie followed as he led her to the partly enclosed space that she had forgotten existed. Trees and bushes circled the mound of moss-covered rocks, on top of which stood a statue of the Virgin Mary. A narrow stone seat was situated at the entrance.

'There. She was sitting there. Staring up at the statue.' He sat down and patted the warm stone for Lottie to sit.

She remained standing. 'Did you speak to her?'

'I sat with her. She was like a statue herself. Pale as alabaster, unmoving except for her lips. A poor damaged angel.'

'Was she praying?'

'That's what I thought. But she turned to me and I saw she was crying, with her hand resting on her stomach. She was pregnant. I don't know much about these things, but she must have been eight or nine months.'

Lottie joined him on the seat, their knees almost touching. 'Tell me what she said.'

'I'm not sure I can.'

'Jesus, Joe, it wasn't confession, was it? You're not bound by any heavenly rule.'

'We didn't speak within the confines of the confessional, you're right there. But I believe what she told me comes under that seal.'

Lottie jumped up. 'Ah, for feck's sake. You and your man-made laws protected by unseen gods.'

'Sit down, Lottie.' His voice was so calm and reassuring that she sat, despite her annoyance. 'The poor girl was distressed. Her hands had been torn to shreds by her own nails. Even though it was a warm evening, and she was wearing a hoodie, she was trembling uncontrollably. But there was something about her that held me back from comforting her. Can you understand that?'

'No, not really.'

'And then she spoke …'

'Go on,' Lottie said carefully.

'She said, "Your God can't keep the evil away from me." That frightened the life out of me. Her words … it was as if they were spoken by a much older, world-weary woman.'

'Jesus, Joe. That's weird. What did you do?'

'I was dumbstruck. I couldn't do or say anything. Then, without warning, she laughed at me. She was sort of crying and laughing at the same time. Next thing I knew, she'd jumped up and rushed off. Or more like hobbled. Clutching her stomach like the baby was about to fall out of her.'

Lottie looked up at the statue, its white paint peeling in places, the sun forming a halo about the head. A white feather floated down from the sky and landed on her knee.

'Did you see where she went?'

Joe turned and pointed behind him at a pathway through the trees. 'Down there,' he said.

She got up and stared through the leaves, shielding her eyes with her hand. 'Did you follow her?'

'No, I let her go.' He stood up and gripped Lottie's elbow, twisting her round to face him. 'I think she might be the young woman you have in the hospital.'

'How could you know that?'

'Covered in blood and has just given birth. It has to be her.'

'I'd like to know how you're in possession of this information.'

'I'm the hospital chaplain. I heard about her from one of the nurses.'

'So where do you think her baby is then, oh knowing one?'

'No need to be sarcastic.'

'I'm sorry,' Lottie said, seeing the hurt in his eyes.

Someone was calling her name. She snapped her head around. Boyd was running towards her.

She said, 'What is it?'

'We found a body.'

'Where?'

'Down by the canal. A couple of boys fishing. Jesus, Lottie ...'

'What is it, Boyd?'

He wrung his hands together. 'It's a baby.'

'Oh no. Shit.'

'And one of the boys who found it ... is your son.'

'Double shit.'

CHAPTER EIGHT

The two boys were huddled together under the watchful eye of Detective Maria Lynch. After ensuring that Sean was okay, Lottie took a deep breath and moved to the edge of the water.

'I can't see anything.'

Boyd handed her a fishing rod. 'Here, use this.'

She got down on her knees and leaned in over the reeds, parting them with the wooden handle.

'What the hell?' She pulled back, almost dropping the rod.

Tangled in the mess of empty drink cans and muck and reeds, she saw it. The purple-grey skin. Tiny bare buttocks. Little hands and fingers. Entwined in the detritus. Dumped. Abandoned. Murdered?

'Dear God in heaven,' she whispered. 'Do the boys have a net? Fetch some plastic sheeting.'

'Hey, Lynch,' Boyd said. 'Call in for sheeting.'

'Kirby's getting it.' Lynch pointed to the burly detective rushing down the path with the sheeting rolled up under his arm. She handed Lottie a net.

Lottie pulled on a pair of nitrile gloves.

Lynch said, 'Let Boyd do that. I really think you need to comfort your son.'

Glancing at the teenagers, Lottie said, 'I'll be over in a minute. Keep them occupied. I don't want him to see this.'

'He already did. He called it in.' Lynch moved back to the boys.

Lottie nodded at Sean to stay put and waited as Kirby rolled out the thick plastic.

'SOCOs are on the way,' he panted. 'Shouldn't we wait?'

Lottie shook her head. Kneeling on the sheeting, she grabbed the long handle of the net, took a deep breath and reached it out over the body. She turned it underneath and dragged it back to the water's edge.

'Maybe you should take the boys to the station, Lynch,' she called over her shoulder. Her heavily pregnant detective shouldn't have to see this. Nor her son, who was standing a few metres away. She wanted to run and hug him, to reassure him that her job wasn't like this every day.

'I will,' Lynch said, her voice just above a whisper.

When she was sure Lynch and the boys had moved away, Lottie dragged the body closer and, with Boyd's help, lifted it onto the plastic sheeting.

Falling back onto her buttocks, she looked up.

'The poor little mite. Jesus, Boyd, what happened here?'

He just shook his head. No words could describe what they were looking at.

*

The heat of the sun was making her dizzy. But Hope kept walking. Stone and grit cut into her bare feet. She could only feel the pain in her stomach. The emptiness. That hollow feeling. The one you know is there but can't put your finger on. Her baby. It was gone. But something else was flowing freely in her blood, and it terrified her. What was she going to do?

As she rounded the bend in the river, she noticed commotion up ahead. At the place where the river linked into the canal. She paused. What was going on? She hunched down among the rushes and long grass. Two boys and … No! The guards. Twisting to look behind her, she knew she hadn't the energy to double back and find another way home. To her left was a high bank with a boggy field beyond. There was no way out. She was stuck until whatever was going on up there died down and fizzled out. She hoped it was just young lads caught drinking or smoking dope.

Sitting at the water's edge, she let her bare feet dangle in the cool water, soothing the cuts. She was no one. A nobody. But there was one person who needed her. And that was the reason she stayed where she was. Waiting until the path ahead was clear.

She lay back on the grassy bed, and was soon asleep.

*

Jim McGlynn, head of the SOCO team, arrived with perspiration forming on his forehead and dripping down his nose. He'd suited up before making his way along the path, his forensic case weighing him down on one side.

Pulling up his mask, he knelt beside Lottie.

'I won't mention the fact that you've compromised the scene.'

'It was already compromised by the boys who found the body.'

He had a look and said, 'An infant boy. Umbilical cord was cut with a sharp implement, probably a knife. Maybe scissors.' His gloved fingers hovered over the stomach.

'How did he die?' Lottie whispered.

'No visible sign of any wounds.'

'Was he born alive?'

'Won't know that until the state pathologist does her post-mortem.'

'Has he been in the water long?'

'I've no way of telling that. And to pre-empt your next query, I don't know how long he's been dead either. Yet.'

'What's your gut telling you?' Lottie persisted. The sun was beating down on her back; her hair stuck to the skin of her neck. Her shirt felt like a damp dishcloth, clinging and sweaty.

McGlynn took a deep breath and exhaled into his mouth mask. 'My gut has nothing to do with this. But you and I can both see that this baby has been in the canal. He was either already dead, or he drowned. There are marks on his neck, but that could be from the birth.'

Lottie said, 'This is awful. The poor little thing.' Her stomach heaved and she was glad she had left home this morning without having eaten any breakfast. 'Jane should be here soon,' she said. The state pathologist was based forty kilometres away, in Tullamore.

'We'll erect a tent. Not much evidence to collect, but I can see lots of loose wild flowers caught up in the reeds. Might be something. Might be nothing.'

'Maybe I should call in the sub-aqua unit,' Lottie said.

'I'm waiting for the pathologist. You do what you have to do.'

'Thanks.' She rose and turned to Boyd.

'What are we dealing with?' she said.

'Probably a young girl unable to cope with an unwanted pregnancy. Came down here to give birth. And the baby was either born dead or she … you know. Killed him.'

She thought of the girl who had arrived that morning at the station covered in blood. 'What did she use to cut the cord? I can't see any sign of a knife or anything sharp. Can you? The vicinity needs to be searched.' She swept her hands around, indicating an area to be cordoned off. Then she thought of Sean. A rush of panic sped through her chest. 'Did Lynch leave with the boys? And what were they doing down here in the first place?'

'Fishing,' Boyd said as he picked up the discarded bags and tackle.

Lottie watched as he handed them over to a uniformed officer. 'That's Adam's old army bag.'

'Come on,' Boyd said. 'You need coffee. You look like hell.'

'I could do with something stronger.'

It had taken the state pathologist, Jane Dore, very little time to assess the scene, and once she had examined the baby's body, she'd given the okay for it to be moved to the mortuary. She'd informally classed the death as suspicious.

What was Ragmullin coming to? Lottie wondered. The town was dying on its feet, caught in a mire of corruption, murder and abuse. She'd just about had enough of it. And she worried now more than ever for her children having to grow up here.

The incident room back at the station had one photo on the board. The unidentified newborn baby. Lottie glanced at it before seeking out her son.

Lynch and the boys were in the canteen. Lottie rushed over to Sean and hugged him tight to her chest.

'What happened? Why were you at the canal? Who found the body? Are you okay?'

'I'm fine, Mam. Honestly. Me and Barry were just fishing.'

Glancing over at the other boy, she said, 'And who is Barry?'

'Barry Duffy,' Lynch said. 'We're waiting for one of his parents to arrive.'

Barry slumped in the red plastic chair, his pale cheeks flushing. His blonde hair was stuck to his scalp with perspiration. Why was he hanging around with Sean? Lottie didn't think she'd seen him before.

'I know Barry from school,' Sean said quickly, as if reading her mind.

'How old are you, Barry?' Lottie asked.

'Fifteen.'

Same age as Sean. 'Where do you live? Is it your mum that's coming for you, or your dad? We need to finish up here as soon as possible.'

'Finish up what?' the boy asked.

'I have to find out exactly the course of events that led to you finding the baby.'

'Can't Sean tell you that? We were together.'

'He will, but I want to hear what you have to say too.'

'We were fishing and then … then Sean saw the body and rang 999. End of.'

'I'm sorry, but I need a parent present in order to conduct a formal interview.'

'I don't need them here.'

Lottie noticed the colour reappearing in the boy's cheeks, and with it, some of the bravado she associated with a cocky teenager. No harm in getting basic information, she thought.

'Had you been there before? On that stretch of the canal?'

'That's where I fish. When I fish. Not every day.'

'When were you last there?'

'I'd nothing to do with that baby, if that's what you're thinking.'

'I'm not thinking that at all. I just want to get an idea of how long the body might have been in the water.' Lottie paused and looked at her son. 'Did you see anyone else around? Before you arrived at that spot?'

Sean reddened. 'We walked up and down the path and did a bit of fishing. We were just getting ready to move on when we noticed the body.'

As he spoke, she caught the whiff of alcohol on his breath.

'Have you been drinking?'

'No,' Sean said.

'Yeah,' Barry said.

'Just the one, that's all,' Sean said hurriedly. 'When I threw the can into the water, that's when I saw the little … the body.'

Lottie thought he was going to cry. She gave him a quick hug. He slithered out from under her arm. Embarrassed in front of his friend? She'd have to talk to him later.

Turning back to Barry, she said, 'So when were you last there, at that particular spot?'

'Two days ago, maybe. I was on my own. Not much fun alone, that's why I asked Sean along today.'

'Why him? You're not best friends or anything, are you?'

'Mam!' Sean said.

'I know he plays sports and I heard him say once that his dad used to fish.' Barry picked at the skin around his short nails, his head lowered.

'We meet up now and again,' Sean said.

'Okay. That's enough for now.' Lottie realised she wouldn't get anything more. 'Barry, you need to wait for your parents before you can leave.'

'I don't need to wait for them. I can go home on my own. Don't need any guards either.'

'You've been through a traumatic experience; it's best to wait until someone comes for you.'

'They don't like to be disturbed. My dad will be at work.'

'I think they'd like to know you're okay. Have you phoned them, Detective Lynch?'

'I called Barry's mum. She said she'd contact her husband. Didn't seem in much of a hurry,' she added.

Barry took out his phone and tapped his finger on the contacts. He handed it to Lottie. 'That's my dad's number. Paul Duffy.'

'The doctor?'

'Yeah. He won't be happy having his day disrupted.'

'And your mum?'

'Julia. That's her details beside Dad's.'

Lottie wrote down both numbers, then asked Lynch to stay with Barry until he was collected. 'We can do the formal interview later today or tomorrow morning. See what his parents have to say.'

'Right,' Lynch said as she wrapped a bobbin around her long fair hair and went to fetch soft drinks from the vending machine.

Outside the door, Lottie gave Sean another hug. 'How did you hook up with him?'

'Barry? Like he said, he called me. Asked me to go fishing. I'm so fed up at Granny's house with the girls fighting all the time and Louis screaming. Anything's better than that.'

'And was it Barry's idea to drink beer?'

'Cider,' Sean said with more than a hint of insolence.

'You know what I mean.' Lottie led him down the stairs and out to the front reception.

'Only had one can. Not even a full one, so don't go all Holy Mary on me, Mam. Where are we going now?'

'Home.'

'We don't have a home,' Sean said sulkily. 'Are you coming too?'

'Yes.'

'You don't have to. I'm fine. You need to find out what happened to the baby.'

'I can get a squad car to drop you if you like. Is that okay?'

'That's grand. Honestly.'

She studied him, his blue eyes, his fair hair falling over his fore-head. His chin showed an attempt at beard growth, but it was losing the battle. More fluff than stubble. Pale skin and bright eyes betrayed his youth. But she had to admit he was the image of his dead father.

He smiled up at her, and she could feel the warmth, the sincerity of it bleeding her heart dry. He was her son. She knew every hair on his head but had no idea of the thoughts that careened through his mind. He wouldn't want her to know. But as his mother, wasn't she entitled to understand what he was thinking? How his mind worked? Or didn't work, as was the case when he suffered from anxiety and teetered on the brink of depression.

'You sure?' she said.

'Was the baby murdered?'

'I don't know. It might just be a tragic case of a child dying as it was born and then being abandoned.'

'Find its mother. Because I don't think I'll be able to sleep until you do.'

'You and me both,' Lottie whispered into his ear.

She kissed his cheek before he escaped down the steps and into the waiting car. She was sure that the girl in the hospital was most likely the mother of the dead baby. As soon as she was ready to be interviewed, the interrogation would begin, but first she needed to build up a picture of Hope Cotter.

CHAPTER NINE

Their mood darkened further when they entered Munbally Grove housing estate, where Hope Cotter lived. The location of many disturbances and call-outs, its reputation preceded it, and it was far from a good one. If you were born here, it was unlikely that you would travel far; indeed, only the gifted few made it out in one piece.

'We should be wearing stab vests in this place,' Boyd said.

'You're more of a drama queen than my Chloe,' Lottie told him.

She had left the team working to try to establish the circumstances surrounding the death of the baby and decided to follow up on the name and address that she'd received from the hospital before she attempted to question the girl. Hope Cotter was under guard there and wasn't going anywhere, was she?

They entered the estate from the wrong end and drove through the warren of roads meandering around the three hundred or so houses. At last the terrace containing number 53 loomed up in front of them. Dark red brick on the bottom half, and on the top, what had once been white pebble dash now appeared scuffed, patchy and discoloured.

'Are those aluminium window frames?' Boyd asked.

'The original estate was built in the seventies,' Lottie replied, not sure if that explained anything. 'And more and more houses were added as time went by.'

'That's definitely a song.'

'Don't start.'

'They were built to last,' he said.

'What are you talking about?'

'The houses. Oh, forget it.'

As she walked up the footpath to number 53, Lottie noted that the windows of the house to the left were enclosed in wire mesh, padlocks on either side keeping it in place. The door had a steel outer panel guarding the interior.

'No chance of breaking in there.' Boyd again.

'We don't need to go in there. Shut up, Boyd. You're giving me a headache.'

She searched the door for a bell, then, not finding one, pounded the wooden frame with her fist.

'This is a wild goose chase,' Boyd muttered.

Lottie counted to five and hammered again, trying to drown out his complaints.

'There's no one in,' he said.

'I've a good mind to leave you here and let you make your own way back to the station. You're acting like a spoiled brat today.'

The door creaked open slightly and a child of no more than four peeped through the narrow slit.

Lowering herself to eye level, Lottie said, 'Hello, sweetie. Is your mum or dad in?'

The brown eyes widened and the mouth formed an oval. 'No.'

'Are you on your own?' Lottie had no idea if the child was a boy or a girl. All she could see was the face, and thin brown hair in need of a wash.

The child's eyes dipped, and milk teeth bit into its bottom lip.

'Can we come in?' Lottie said.

'Get away from the door,' a voice roared. The child disappeared.

Before she could rise, Lottie found herself looking at a pair of hairy white legs dressed in Bermuda shorts. She got to her feet and came face to face with a man about her own age. He emitted the dry smell of stale cigarettes and beer. His craggy face and bloodshot eyes gave credence to that observation. With his bald head, he looked like a caricature, and his stomach protruded over the top of his shorts, causing his black U2 T-shirt to roll up.

'I'm Detective Inspector Lottie Parker and this is Detective Sergeant Mark Boyd. May we come in?' Lottie said, regaining her composure.

'No, you can't come in. Now piss off, the pair of you.'

She stuck her foot in the gap just before he slammed the door. Pain shot up her leg but she managed to keep the wince from her face. Bastard, she thought. 'I think you need to let us in.'

The door opened wide so quickly she almost lost her balance. Boyd steadied her and they followed the man down the dimly lit hallway.

There was no sign of the child as they entered the kitchen. To her surprise, Lottie noted that the room was clean and tidy. The man stood with his back to the sink, arms folded across the expanse of his chest, waiting.

'We've introduced ourselves,' Lottie said. 'So who might *you* be?'

'Robbie.'

'Robbie Cotter?'

'None of your business.' He hawked mucus back down his throat and Lottie feared he was going to spit at her.

'Who's the little one who opened the door?'

'None of your business.' He unfolded his arms, spread his legs and secured his hands on his hips. 'Are you going to tell me what this is about?'

'Can we sit down?' She pulled a chair away from the table, but his hand slapped down on top of hers. She wasn't going to be intimidated by his manner.

'Take your hand off mine, right now.'

He obliged, but said, 'Leave that chair there. I'm giving you to the count of three. One—'

'Okay, okay.' Lottie held up her hands. 'We're here about Hope.'

'Hope? I haven't seen her. Left me with her young one. What's the wagon done now?'

'You can confirm she lives here, then?'

'You're here, so you know that already. Don't be asking me stupid questions.'

'Are you her father?'

'You're still asking stupid questions, lady.'

'You're not her father then.' Lottie bit her lip. This was torture. 'So who are you?'

He ran his hand over his bald head and sighed. It was like his whole body deflated in an instant.

'I'm Robbie Cotter. Hope's uncle. Her father's brother. Her parents are dead. I was left to care for her, and now I've to look after her brat too.'

'Her brat being the child who opened the door?'

'Ah, Lexie's not really a brat. She's a good kid. Now, are you going to tell me what Hope's done to bring the guards to my door?'

Lottie paused, wondering how much information she could divulge. 'I'm not sure yet. I thought maybe you could help us.'

'You're like a fucking crossword puzzle,' he said, pulling out a chair and plonking himself at the table. 'Look, I haven't seen Hope since yesterday evening. She hasn't been home since then. Probably out whoring around. Though what with her being up against having a baby, I'm not sure anyone could get a leg over, if you follow me.'

'So you can confirm that Hope was pregnant?'

'Yes. Wait a minute,' he said, realisation dawning. 'Was? What do you mean?'

He was quick at connecting the dots, she had to give him that. 'Mr Cotter. Robbie. Hope arrived at the garda station this morning covered in blood. We brought her straight to A&E. According to the doctor there, she had given birth, but we don't know where the baby is.' She cringed inside, thinking about the body found in the canal. It was more than likely that it was Hope's baby. Likely that she had killed him?

Robbie's ruddy face paled. He clenched his hands into tight fists and kneaded them into his eye sockets.

'Are you okay?' Lottie asked, placing a hand on his arm.

He swiped it away and glared. 'Hope is only seventeen. She had Lexie when she was thirteen. I've kept social services away from our door because I'm her legal guardian. I've tried my best to keep her right. The two of them. On my own. But it's hard. Damn hard. Don't get me wrong, Lexie's no trouble. She'll be going to school in September. Goes to the community crèche at the moment, three mornings a week. But Hope … Now, she is a troubled girl, I can tell you.'

'In what way is she troubled?' Boyd asked.

'I don't think she ever got over her parents' deaths. Her father hanged himself when she was just eight years old. Then her mother, she did the same not a year later. I think it was all too much for Hope.'

'Did she get counselling?' Boyd said.

Robbie glared at him. 'What do you think? You with your fancy suit and your giddy smirk. No, she didn't get bloody counselling. Hard enough to get food on the table. I do my best by those girls. Honestly I do.' He stood up and filled a kettle with water and switched it on. 'Tea?'

'If you're making it,' Lottie said. 'Does Hope attend school?'

'High notions for one so low down the pecking order. She wants to be a hairdresser. Made an attempt at doing a beauty course at the community college. Dropped out after a few weeks. Started a cleaning job and then got pregnant for the second time.' Robbie was rinsing mugs under the sink, the water gushing out over the edge and down the front of the cupboards.

'Do you know if Lexie's dad is the father of Hope's baby?'

He glanced over his shoulder, his big face sagging with dejection.

'She never told me who Lexie's dad was and I have no idea who she's been whoring around with. She's as quiet as a mouse when she's at home, then she goes out and gets pregnant again.' He returned his attention to the sink.

'Is she into drugs?'

'Not that I'm aware of.' He turned off the tap and put the dripping wet mugs on the table.

A scream caused him to crash out of the room. 'Lexie!'

Lottie and Boyd followed.

The little girl was sitting cross-legged on the floor. *Peppa Pig* was on the television, the sound low.

'What happened?' Robbie whipped her up into his arms.

'Peppa crying. Daddy Pig left her on her own.'

'Now, pet, I'm here. You're okay,' he soothed the child.

'I want Mummy,' Lexie sobbed.

'I'll take you to see her right now.' He looked up at Lottie. 'Is that okay?'

'I'm sorry. I don't think it's wise at the moment.'

'Why not?'

'We have her under guard.'

'What on earth for? She's just a girl. Only harm she ever did was to herself. I don't understand this.' He sank into an armchair, cradling the child, rubbing his large hand softly over her hair.

'Robbie, I don't want to say this in front of Lexie …'

'She won't understand. Go on.'

Lottie took a deep breath. 'Hope ... well, she told me ... she told me that she killed someone.'

After Robbie had comforted Lexie and switched channels to *Ben & Holly's Little Kingdom*, they went back to the kitchen and he made the tea.

'I think Hope must have been hallucinating. She'd lost all that blood. You said so yourself.' Robbie's head shone with sweat and his big hands gripped his mug.

'I don't know the full story,' Lottie said. 'We're heading to the hospital shortly. I wanted to get an idea of what was going on before I spoke to her.' Despite herself, she felt sorry for the big man sitting in front of her.

'Hope's a good girl,' he said softly, the hard-man act abandoned. 'But since she got pregnant with this one, she's been different. Going on about evil spirits. The devil and such shite. I wanted her to go and talk to a priest, but she wouldn't. Told me she knew a good person who would listen to her and she didn't need no kiddy-fiddlers near her. And she was so protective of Lexie. It was a bit unnatural, if I'm to be honest. But then again, she lost her own ma and da at a young age, so you know ... But this is the thing. I wondered from time to time if she was ... you know ... interfered with by some paedo. If that's what happened, I'll string the bastard up myself.'

'You say she never told you who the father of the baby was?'

'Nope.'

'And she looked after herself during the pregnancy? No sign that she might harm the baby?'

Robbie stood up, brought his mug to the sink and rinsed it. His broad shoulders wrinkled his T-shirt. 'No. She wouldn't do anything to hurt a baby.'

CHAPTER TEN

After they'd finished speaking to Robbie Cotter, Lottie rang home to make sure Sean was okay, then they headed to the hospital to interview Hope. She was their number one suspect in relation to the baby found in the canal.

'Go easy on her,' Boyd said.

'I will.'

'You don't know the baby is hers.'

'Boyd, don't keep telling me things I'm already aware of. We need to get a statement from her.' She also wondered if little Lexie was in the best hands. A call to Child and Family Services might be needed.

She pushed open the door and headed towards the treatment room, where she asked to see Hope.

A harried-looking nurse set off amidst the chaos, but returned immediately. 'She's gone.'

'What do you mean, gone?' Lottie rushed into the room, tugging at curtains, stripping patients of the little privacy they had. 'She has to be here.' She turned on her heel and headed out to the corridor, where the uniformed officer was running his hands through his hair.

'I never saw her leave, honest to God. She never came out the door.'

Turning to the nurse, Lottie glanced at her name badge. 'Lucia, is there any other way out besides this door?'

'Follow me.'

Back inside the twelve-bed treatment room, the nurse led Lottie under an archway and down a corridor.

'This is the way we bring A&E patients to the X-ray department.' She pointed to an emergency door. 'She might have got out that way. Her clothes are gone; the bag they were stored in was shoved under the bed. She didn't even have a pair of shoes.'

Lottie pushed open the emergency door to a blast of heat and blinding sunlight. 'How did you not miss her before now?'

The nurse dropped her eyes. 'We're rushed off our feet. You can see for yourself. The department's overflowing. Patients on trolleys, and the waiting room is full. It could be an hour, maybe more, since she was last checked on.'

'Jesus Christ,' Lottie said. But she knew it wasn't the staff's fault; it was the failing health system and that dumb guard she'd left on duty. She called him over. 'I want you and as many uniforms as you can muster to search the grounds. Try to establish where she's gone. I want her found. Do you hear me?'

'Loud and clear,' he said, stepping around her and escaping out into the fresh air.

Boyd was standing behind her. 'The patient in the next cubicle says the porter brought him to X-ray about two hours ago. He's sure the side door opened just as he was being wheeled around the corner.'

'Two hours?' Lottie dug her nails into the palms of her hands. 'The girl could be anywhere by now. Call it in. Give her description to Traffic Corps. To everyone.'

'Will do,' Boyd said. 'Then we'd better deliver the news to Superintendent McMahon.'

Goddammit, she thought. McMahon was going to fry her.

*

The silence woke her.

Hope had no idea how long she had been asleep. She pulled her feet out of the water and swiped her hair from her face. Her feet felt better, but pain shot through her as she kneeled. There was still some activity on the bridge. A group of people in white suits moving about. And what was that strung across the path? Blue and white tape. Why? What was going on?

There was no way she could walk up there covered in blood, but she had to move soon. The only option was over the bank and through the fields. Hopefully the white-suited people would be too busy to notice her.

She dried her feet on the grass and headed for the steep bank, crawling on her sore belly like she used to as a child. A million years ago. At the top, she could see a sharp dip in the field and a ditch lined with barbed wire.

She slid down the embankment and came to a stop at the ditch. Warily she squeezed between the gaps in the wire, hoping it wasn't electrified. It wasn't. The ditch was full of cow shite and muck and mud. But at this stage, she didn't care. The wire snagged her hair and took a lump out of her T-shirt, but she wriggled through to the other side. At last. She could see the housing estate in the near distance.

Walking quickly, the mud drying hard on her feet, she made her way across the field and towards something akin to freedom.

But Hope Cotter knew she would never be free.

CHAPTER ELEVEN

Alphonsis Ahern stroked his goatee beard. He was happy with it now that it was growing quicker. Made him look older than fifteen, he thought.

Taking out a can of cider, he balled up the plastic bag. He liked it down here, at the side of the soccer clubhouse. You were out of sight of the housing estate and you couldn't be seen from the road; when there were no summer camps or training sessions taking place, you could be virtually invisible.

'I'll have another one, Fonzie,' Kylie said, flicking her fringe away from her eyes and putting her hand out for a can.

'Ah, bollocks. It's my last one. I'll share it with you.' He eyed Chan and Malia, lying on the grass behind them, tongues halfway down each other's throats. He edged closer to Kylie. 'Any chance of a kiss?'

'Piss off, Fonzie,' Kylie said, taking the can and flicking open the tab. She took a long drink before handing it back to him.

'Ah, go on,' he said.

'I've to leave soon,' Chan said, standing up.

'Sure, we've not been here that long,' Fonzie said.

'All the booze is gone and I have to go to work.'

Fonzie looked around at the cans littering the small grassy enclosure. He didn't even feel drunk, and he knew he had downed the most alcohol. If Chan leaves, he thought, Malia will too, and then Kylie won't want to stay without her friend. Trust Chan to feck it all up.

'That father of yours is a slave-driver. He should invest in a proper dishwasher instead of having you doing the donkey work. He must make a fortune in that restaurant.'

'At least I get paid.' Chan stuffed his hands into his pockets and smiled as Malia linked her arm through his.

'Spoilsports,' Fonzie said, standing up.

'Better pick up all our rubbish,' Kylie said, gathering the cans. 'Or Bertie will know we've been here.' She pointed at the CCTV camera on the side of the clubhouse wall, just under the gutter along the roof.

Fonzie looked squarely up at the camera and gave it two fingers. He'd forgotten it was there. The caretaker, Bertie Harris, was a nuisance. Was he spying on them? Fonzie wondered. He got the plastic bag and held it out for the empty cans. Kylie filled it up.

'Hey, I haven't finished that.' He grabbed the last can from her hand and swallowed the dregs. 'Where are the bins? I'm not carrying this junk home.'

'You're such a wally,' Kylie said, and took the bag from him.

Fonzie watched her tight butt clad in skinny white jeans as she walked around the corner to the recycling bins. Chan and Malia were already at the gate.

'Hurry up, Kylie!' he yelled.

And then he heard her scream.

CHAPTER TWELVE

It was hot enough to roast a pig in McMahon's office.

A pewter statue that Lottie hadn't noticed before stood on the window ledge. She concentrated on its angelic face while she related the news to her increasingly red-faced boss.

'Why didn't you bring the girl straight in for questioning?' he said, once she had finished.

'She was too ill.' Fingers crossed he wouldn't explode.

'Christ, Parker, she had a baby, not an elephant.'

'That's a bit unfair.' Lottie glared at him.

'You lost our number one suspect for the death of that baby.' He swept his hand through his fringe and exhaled loudly. 'Find her. I want her in an interview room in the next hour. And charge the little slut with murder.'

'Hey, just a minute.' Lottie felt her mouth drop open. 'We don't know how the baby died yet. We don't know that she killed anyone. We don't even know if it's her baby.'

'Don't tell me what you *don't* know!' He marched round his desk and stood in front of her. 'How many young women are wandering around Ragmullin dropping babies and appearing in the station claiming they killed them? Eh? How many?' He held up his hand. 'No! Don't answer that, because you and I know she's the only one. Find her and charge her. Murder or manslaughter or something. Jesus Christ, Parker, I want this closed.'

'I don't think that's wise.'

'I'll tell you what's wise and what's not. Follow my orders. That's what's wise.'

As a smug smirk creased his face, Lottie had to dig her nails into the palms of her hands to stop herself slapping it right off his jaw.

'And bring that uncle of hers in too.'

'But there's her little girl. Lexie. Robbie Cotter looks after her.'

'That's why we have Child and Family Services.' McMahon shook his head. 'Can you not take a direct order?'

Lottie exhaled loudly. 'Hope can't be far away. She lost a lot of blood.'

'There will be blood spilled here too if you come back without her.' He strode to the door and opened it. 'And then get stuck into those court reports and paperwork. You're dragging down my KPIs.'

Lottie marched out of his office and down the corridor.

'Bastard,' she said.

CHAPTER THIRTEEN

Larry Kirby walked slowly, puffing on his cigar, with Maria Lynch muttering beside him.

'I wish you wouldn't smoke around me. I am pregnant, you know.'

'How could I not know?' Kirby said, pinching out the embers and shoving the cigar into his pocket. 'You remind me every five minutes.'

'You can be a right arsehole when you want to be,' Lynch said, picking up pace and passing him by. 'Don't know how O'Donoghue puts up with you.'

Kirby slowed to a stroll. He wondered that same thing himself a hundred times a week. Gilly O'Donoghue was at least ten years younger than him. A beautiful girl in his eyes, with a world of young men to go out with, and she was dating him. He shook his head in wonder that their relationship had lasted this long. He was divorced, overweight; he smoked, liked a few pints – a good few – and still she was with him. Maybe this was his second chance to make things right in his personal life. He hoped so. He really liked her. Thinking of Gilly put a hop in his step and he caught up with Lynch as she rounded the side of the clubhouse.

A group of youngsters were standing in a huddle, one with a mobile phone in the air. Filming something?

'Now, children, make way,' Kirby said.

'Who are you?' A tall teenager with droopy eyes and a goatee beard stepped into his path.

'Detective Larry Kirby. Are you the one that called us? Something about a body. Hope you're not wasting garda resources bringing us out on a wild goose chase.'

'Yeah, I called you.' The lad stood to one side, the others clustered around him. Two girls and another boy. 'Back there. By the wheelie bins. Kylie was dumping a few cans when she saw him. I had a look, then called 999.'

'Wonder why uniforms aren't here?' Lynch said to Kirby under her breath.

'Everyone's out looking for the suspect in connection with the baby's death,' he muttered in reply.

He watched the youngsters' eyes as he walked by. They all appeared spooked. 'This better not be a dead dog, or you'll be answering to me. What's your name?'

'Fonzie.'

'Like the guy in *Happy Days*?'

'What?'

One of the girls piped up. 'His name is Alphonsis Ahern.'

'And who are you?'

The girl was very pale. There was dried vomit around her mouth. 'Kylie.'

Kirby scratched his head and moved towards the industrial-sized bins.

'Where is it?' He had been convinced when he got the call that the kids were taking him for a ride. Now he wasn't so sure.

'Round the back.' Fonzie moved forward. 'On the ledge. In the flower bed.'

'Stay there. Leave this to me.' Kirby pulled on a pair of nitrile gloves. Lynch joined him.

'Don't think you should look,' Fonzie advised her. 'Being pregnant and all.'

Lynch gave him a withering look and continued to glove up.

'Put away those phones,' she said.

'We've got it all videoed anyway,' the other lad said. He was Chinese, a head smaller than his friend but sporting the same goatee beard. For a moment Kirby wondered if they were a gang, but decided they were just trying to blend in with each other.

'No more filming. And I don't want to see any of this on YouTube. I'll have to take your phones.'

The boys laughed. 'Grandad here knows about YouTube.'

Kirby took a step towards them. 'If I do see it, I will personally smash each and every one of those fancy iPhones. Got it?'

Fonzie said, 'You don't even know what's over there. Are you going to look or not?'

With a sigh, Kirby edged between the bins, Lynch squeezing awkwardly in behind him.

'Stand back, Lynch.'

She didn't need telling twice. Her face was green.

With one hand clamped to his face, covering his nose and mouth, Kirby held his breath, wondering if the smell was from the bins or something else entirely. He looked at the grassy bank, which was edged with flowers in full bloom and littered with discarded cans and bottles. Feeling his stomach contract, he turned away and exhaled a long, soft breath.

'Told you so,' Fonzie said. 'Can we go now?'

'Stay right where you are. All of you,' Lynch ordered.

'Call the boss and get SOCOs here. Quickly,' Kirby said, once he had recovered his voice. 'And confiscate those phones.'

'What's up there?' Lynch asked.

Kirby took a deep breath and looked again. 'He's dead. After that, you really don't want to know.'

*

Once the teenagers had been taken to the station for questioning, and uniforms had a cordon erected and the main gates guarded, Lottie suited up and approached the scene with Kirby and Boyd.

'Not a pretty sight,' Kirby said.

'Never is,' Lottie pointed out.

She fastened her mouth mask in place and pulled the hood over her hair, then stepped up onto the small ledge.

'Jesus Christ, Boyd, look at this.'

'I see it.'

'Told you it was bad,' Kirby said.

She looked at her detectives, then climbed the stone steps to the flower bed. Lying among the bottles, cans and plants, face up to the blue sky, the boy's body was so white it was almost transparent. His only clothing was a pair of football shorts. A halo of plucked wild flowers surrounded him.

'What age do you think he is?' Boyd said.

'Maybe ten or eleven.' Her voice was low, her heart racing and her stomach reeling as she studied the body.

'Shit.' Boyd took a deep breath. 'Wonder how long he's been dead.'

'Hard to know. It's been very warm over the last few days. We'll have to defer to the state pathologist for exact time of death.'

'Right.'

'But I bet he hasn't been here long. Someone would have noticed.'

'There was an under-twelves final played here yesterday evening,' Boyd said. 'There would have been a big crowd around. So he must have been killed and left here later than that.'

Scanning the area, Lottie noticed small black cameras nestling in the eaves of the clubhouse roof.

'Kirby, see if you can locate the caretaker. We need that security footage. Boyd, we need a tent to protect the scene. And where are the SOCOs?'

'Still at the canal,' he offered.

'Call McGlynn,' she said. 'Get him to assign a team over here. And phone Jane Dore. We need to get this body into a cold room soon.'

Two bodies in one day. What was happening? At least they had a suspect for the baby's death, even though they had lost her. But this boy? Who was he? She sighed at the final indignity of being dumped in an area for rubbish bins, despite someone's attempt to beautify the area by planting flowers. She wondered then why flowers had been placed around his head.

She went to the bins and with gloved hands lifted the lids. Rubbish and recycling.

'Someone needs to search these. There might be evidence dumped in them.' She hadn't much hope of that, but at this stage you never knew what you were dealing with. 'He was left out on display, Boyd. No effort made to hide the body.'

'His killer wanted him to be found.'

She looked up into his eyes, dancing nuts of hazel. 'Is the killer sending us a message?'

'I hope not, because if they are, there may be more deaths like this poor lad.'

CHAPTER FOURTEEN

'You little bastard,' Kirby said under his breath as he sat down in the interview room. As usual, there was no air in the confined space, and he felt the effects of his cigar-smoking creaking through his arteries. Fonzie Ahern sat opposite him, his mother by his side.

'Excuse me, Detective,' she said. 'No need for that language.'

'I specifically told you not to upload anything to YouTube.' He glared at the boy.

'Actually, it was you who put the idea into my head.'

Kirby blew out his cheeks, trying hard to keep his temper pinned down and air in his lungs. 'I saw the time of the upload. You did it before I arrived on the scene.' He sighed. Their tech team were now trying to get the video removed. But he knew it would already have been copied and viewed thousands, if not millions of times, all over the world. The whole team had seen it. Lynch had thrown up on the spot. Something about the display of a snuffed-out human life on film was almost harder to accept than witnessing it first-hand.

'Detective, we are here voluntarily so my son can make a statement, so either get on with it or we're going home.' Mrs Ahern grabbed her son's hand.

'Right so,' Kirby said. 'What time did you arrive at the clubhouse?'

Fonzie appeared serious now, all bravado sucked out of him by his mother's hand on his.

'During the holidays there's not much to do, with no school, you know. It must've been around two o'clock. Chan got some cans from his dad's restaurant and we just hung out behind the clubhouse. Drinking. Watching videos and listening to music on our phones. That kind of thing. Causing no trouble to no one.'

'Minding your own business?'

'Exactly.' Fonzie smiled up at him. 'Then, around half three, Chan said he had to go to work. He helps out in his dad's restaurant. We gathered up the cans and put them in a bag, and rather than bringing them home, Kylie went to throw them in the bin.'

'That was good of you.'

'My son learns all about recycling and saving the earth at school. He's a good lad.'

'I'm sure he is,' Kirby said sincerely. But he didn't say anything about the underage drinking. It wasn't the time for that lecture.

'And then ...' Fonzie continued, 'Kylie screamed.'

*

In Interview Room 2, Lynch was sitting across from Kylie and her mum.

'So you approached the bin with the cans,' Lynch said. 'Then what happened?'

Kylie sniffed and wrung her hands into a knot. Her mother squeezed her shoulder.

'I ... I was about to lift the lid, to throw in the bag, when I saw ...'

'Go on, Kylie,' Lynch said. 'You're doing great.'

The girl nodded. 'I dropped the lid because something caught my eye. I nearly puked right there. Thought it was a dead cat or something. I should have just turned away without looking ...'

'Did you approach or touch the body?'

Kylie raised her head, her eyes wide with astonishment. 'What? No way. I couldn't ... I couldn't move. I screamed, and then Fonzie came running around the corner and grabbed me before I fainted.'

'Is Fonzie your boyfriend?'

'Are you joking me? We're just friends.'

'Did you recognise the deceased?'

'The what?'

'The dead boy.'

Kylie shook her head violently. 'I hardly looked at him.' She crumpled into her mother's chest like a little girl who'd been told a horror story and might never sleep again.

'Is that all?' her mum asked. 'I really need to get my daughter home.'

'Are you sure there's nothing else you want to tell me?'

Kylie sniffed. 'I'm not sure, but I think I recognised his hair.'

*

'And after Kylie screamed, what did you do?' Kirby said.

'Ran around to see what was wrong,' Fonzie replied. 'Caught her just as she was about to faint.'

'And it was you who called 999?'

'Yeah.'

'Not before you filmed the scene, though.' Kirby would never understand teenagers' obsession for snapping everything and anything.

The boy didn't answer. Hung his head. Bit his lip, his goatee looking like a disguise that had gone wrong.

'Can we leave now?' his mother asked.

'Did you know him?'

'Who?' Fonzie raised his head, eyes wide and still.

'The dead boy.'

A loud gulp. A nod.

Kirby leaned across the table, adrenaline pumping a red flush up his face. 'You knew him? You recognised him?'

'I never realised people could look so different when they're dead.'

'Go on.'

'I think … Mikey got his hair dyed blonde at the tips. Said it was cool.'

'Mikey who?'

'Jesus, Fonzie!' Mrs Ahern turned to look at her son. 'Not Mikey Driscoll?'

Fonzie nodded. The hard boy, now broken, tears flowing down his cheeks.

'Who is he?' Kirby asked the mother.

She blessed herself. 'The Driscolls live at the back of ours, in Munbally Grove. I can't remember the number. You can find out, can't you? Oh God, his poor mother. This will kill her.'

'What's the mother's name?'

'Jennifer Driscoll. We call her Jen. At the bingo. She goes every night. Wouldn't miss it. Never wins much. I don't either,' she added quickly. 'Poor Mikey. I heard he scored the winning goal yesterday too. Oh, this is just too awful for words.'

Kirby ended the interview and escorted mother and son out of the station with a caution not to say anything to anyone until the victim's relatives had been informed.

Now that they had the dead boy's name, there was a poor mother's heart ready to be broken. He was glad he wouldn't be tasked with that job. That was one for Lottie Parker.

And then he realised the boy was from the same estate as Hope Cotter.

CHAPTER FIFTEEN

The trees along the roadside blurred, making her feel dizzy. The radio was blaring unintelligible music and her uncle was banging the steering wheel in time to some rhythm only he was aware of.

'Where are we going?' Hope said. She felt so sick, she wondered how she hadn't already thrown up in his car.

'Somewhere safer than Ragmullin,' Robbie said. 'Don't you be worrying. You just need to get your memory back. I still find it hard to believe you can't remember what happened to your baby.'

'I'm telling you the truth. Not knowing, it's driving me insane.'

When she'd arrived home, feet oozing sores and clothes covered in blood, her uncle had grilled her about the baby and how her pregnancy had ended. She couldn't give him any answers. She knew he didn't believe her, but he'd said the guards had been around, and told her to wash quickly, change and pack a bag for herself and Lexie.

By the time she was ready, dressed in clean jeans and an old hoodie, and had Lexie sorted, the car engine was spluttering and his own bag was in the boot. He'd locked the front door and bundled them all into the car.

Now she was on the road with no idea whether she had successfully escaped the veil of evil that had shrouded her life, or if she was being catapulted head-first into a new horror show. Lexie cuddled into her chest, her thumb in her mouth, asleep.

Hope knew she had no choice.

She had to trust her uncle.

CHAPTER SIXTEEN

Jennifer Driscoll was tall and slim, dressed in black and yellow gym gear. Her smile was wide as she opened the door, though her green eyes were tinged with something Lottie couldn't quite put her finger on. She estimated the woman was aged about thirty.

'Come in, come in,' Jennifer said, as she walked into a small kitchen by the front door. 'Sit down. I'm sure you're here to ask about Hope Cotter. Poor girl. Heard she'd done a runner. And little Lexie. Cutest child you'd ever see. Even cuter than my Mikey when he was a baby.' She glanced at the clock on the wall as she filled the kettle. 'Mmm, he should be home by now.'

Lottie raised an eyebrow in Boyd's direction. 'Where has Mikey been, Jennifer?' she said.

'Call me Jen. He stayed at his friend Toby's last night. Getting a bit old for sleepovers now, I told him. He said he'd be home in time for tea today. They had a soccer final and I knew I'd be going to the bingo, so that's why I let him stay over. I heard today that he scored the winning goal. He's a good kid.'

Lottie thought she saw a hint of sadness in the woman's eyes. Was she regretting putting her bingo before her son's triumph? She'd have a lot more regret in a couple of minutes.

'What's Toby's surname?' Boyd said.

'Collins.' Jen pulled out a chair and sat down. Lottie watched the woman's eyes travel from Boyd's face to her own. Reality dawning. 'You're not here about Hope, are you?'

'No, I'm afraid not,' Lottie said.

Jen stared hard before her hand flew to her mouth.

'Not Mikey,' she cried. 'Please, dear God in heaven, don't let anything have happened to my boy.'

This was going to be hard.

'Jen?' Lottie reached out and placed her hand on the woman's shoulder. 'Is there anyone I can get to come and sit with you?'

'Don't tell me.' Hysteria had replaced the smile. 'Oh, Holy Mother of Jesus in heaven! Tell me.'

Lottie gestured for Boyd to say the dreaded words no parent ever wanted to hear.

'I'm so sorry, Mrs Driscoll,' he said. 'Earlier this afternoon, the body of a young boy was found at the rear of the soccer clubhouse.'

'You're wrong. It's not my Mikey.' She jumped up. Sat down again. 'Wait a minute. I'll ring him.' She stabbed her finger at her phone. After a few moments, her face paled even further. 'He … he's not answering. I'll call Toby.' More thumbing of the phone pad before she held it to her ear. 'Hi, Toby, don't want to worry you, but is Mikey with you?'

Lottie watched intently. She knew the answer as the animation faded from Jen's face and the phone dropped to the table.

'He … he says Mikey didn't stay with him last night. Doesn't know where he is. Jesus Christ. Fuck.' She picked up the phone again.

Lottie put out her hand to quell the woman's movement.

'I know this is hard to take in. Please listen to me.' She waited until Jen raised her head. 'There's no easy way to say this. We believe the body might be that of Mikey. But we need to make a formal identification. Do you have a recent photograph?' She knew this wouldn't be much use, but it would give Jen something to focus on while Lottie gathered her thoughts on what to do next.

The phone was in Jen's hand again. She sniffed away tears, flicked through photos and showed Lottie the screen.

'That's my Mikey. He's a good boy, a beautiful boy. My baby.'

'Can I send this to my phone? When was it taken?'

'Yesterday lunchtime.'

Lottie stared at the image of the boy with his hand raised over his head making rabbit ears. A broad grin on his face. Shoulder-length dark hair dyed blonde at the ends.

'What age is he?'

'Eleven. Almost twelve. It's his birthday next month. He doesn't want a party. Knows it's too expensive to organise. A pair of football boots, that's all he wants. Cost me as much as a party.' She laughed; then, as if she realised there would be no birthday and no one to wear the boots that were wrapped in gift paper under her bed, she crumpled to the table, her shoulders convulsing as sobs broke from her mouth. 'It's not Mikey. Not my Mikey.' Her voice rose a maniacal octave. 'You've made a mistake.'

Lottie turned the phone to Boyd. He nodded. Confirmed it was Mikey Driscoll who was now on his way to a cutting table in Jane Dore's morgue.

'Jen? Give me the number of someone to come over to you. Please,' Lottie said. Her inquiries before they had left the station had confirmed that Mikey's father was no longer on the scene.

'Next door. Dolores will come in.'

Boyd got up to fetch the neighbour. 'What number?'

'Twenty-four.'

Alone with the distraught woman, Lottie went round the table and put her arm around Jen's trembling shoulders. She knew how she herself had felt when Sean had been abducted; if anything happened to any of her children, she would be insane with grief. Could she even go on living?

Thinking of Jen's mental state, she said, 'Who is your doctor? You need a sedative.'

'I want to see him.'

'Tell me his name and I'll call him.'

'Not the doctor. Mikey. I want to see my son.'

'I'm afraid that's not possible. Not at the moment. We'll take his toothbrush and maybe something else that will provide us with DNA, for comparison purposes.'

Jen raised her head from the table, her eyelids drooping with the weight of her tears. 'I never asked. About this … this body you have. How did he die?'

Lottie wasn't sure, though the state pathologist at the scene had suspected strangulation. There was no way she could tell Jen, not yet anyway. She said, 'The death is being classed as suspicious.'

'He didn't … you know … kill himself?' Jen collapsed in a heap again, her head banging against the table.

'No, Jen, he didn't kill himself.'

Boyd arrived with the harried-looking neighbour. She was about Jen's age, but there the resemblance ended. Dolores was flabby and her tracksuit was straining against the ripples of fat at her waist. Boyd had briefed her outside, and she immediately rushed over to her friend and folded her in her arms.

'Phone her doctor,' Lottie said. 'There's a family liaison officer on the way.'

And she knew they hadn't enough FLOs for all that had happened today.

CHAPTER SEVENTEEN

Toby Collins looked out of his bedroom window as the car drew up outside. A man and a woman got out and approached the front door of the house. He was one hundred per cent sure they were guards. He racked his brains wondering why they were at his house. Why had Mikey's mother sounded so odd on the phone, asking where Mikey was? Had Mikey told lies about him? Probably.

But then his thoughts shifted. It had to be something to do with his brother. He slid off the bed and turned around to see Max standing in the doorway.

'There's two bastard guards downstairs. Da says they want to talk to you. You keep your big trap shut. Do you hear me?'

Toby nodded. He knew better than to blab about anything. Max wouldn't hesitate to throttle him. He'd tried once before, when Toby had told Ma about the little bag of weed he'd found under Max's pillow. He'd only been looking for cash. Learned his lesson that day.

Downstairs, he entered the living room. His dad was standing with his back to the unlit fireplace. The man and woman were by the window. Toby gulped and shoved his hands into the pockets of his tracksuit bottoms. The woman turned towards him. She was tall, dressed in skinny jeans and leather boots. Her white T-shirt looked grubby, and she had a jacket tucked under her arm and a raggedy leather bag slung over her shoulder.

'Toby? We want to talk about your friend Mikey Driscoll.'

What were they on about? Why would they be asking about Mikey? He thought of the phone call from Mikey's mum. Something weird was going on.

'What about him?'

'Sit down,' his dad said. 'All of you. You detectives are making him nervous.'

Toby sat on the nearest armchair and his dad sat opposite. The detectives remained standing. Now that he was sitting down, Toby felt like the two were giants in his small world. He was so nervous. He hoped he wouldn't cry, but he had done nothing wrong. At least he didn't think so.

'Toby, my name is Lottie,' the woman said. 'We just want to know when you last saw Mikey.'

'Has something happened to him?' Toby said.

'Answer the damn question,' his dad snapped.

'Mr Collins, please let us handle this,' the detective said.

Toby felt his heart beat a little faster. He was going to start stuttering, and if he did that, he knew his father would lash out at him. He wished his mother was home. He glanced at the digital display on the television. She'd still be at work. Her shift at the hotel didn't finish for another two hours.

'Toby?' The woman was looking at him.

He bit his lip and lowered his eyes. 'M-Mikey played in the match yesterday. He … he scored a b-brilliant goal. We … we all went to McDonald's afterwards. A treat from Mr B-Butler.' He looked up.

'He's the team coach,' his father explained.

'Mikey went with you?'

'Everyone was there. It was p-packed.'

'Did Mikey come home with you?'

Toby eyed his dad before shaking his head. 'No.'

'Why not?'

'He wanted to … to stay over. S-said he'd told his ma. But I hadn't asked mine because she was at work. I told him I'd have to check with her first.'

'And when did you tell him this?'

Toby shrugged, feeling a little more confident. He had to stop stammering or he would get a clout from his dad. 'Sometime after the match. I can't remember when.'

'Did you and Mikey leave McDonald's together?'

Toby gulped, tried to think back to the previous night. 'No. I'd changed my mind. I was going to tell Mikey he *could* come to mine for the night. But then I couldn't find him anywhere.'

'Where had he gone?'

Toby wrenched his hands into fists, kneading his knuckles. 'I thought he must have gone home.'

The two detectives looked at each other. Toby watched them. The man had been scribbling in his notebook. Now he put it away and hunkered down.

'Toby, you're not in any trouble, but you need to tell us the truth.'

'I … I am … I did.'

'The whole truth?'

Toby didn't trust his own voice any more. He nodded.

'Leave the lad alone. He told you what he knows. Will that be all?' Toby's dad stood up.

Breathing a sigh of relief, Toby sank back into the rough armchair. The detective rose to his feet, towering over his dad.

'If you remember anything else, tell your dad to call us,' he said.

Toby nodded. 'That's all. I swear. Is M-Mikey in trouble?'

'I'm afraid I can't tell you that,' the woman detective said.

*

Once the detectives had left, his dad closed the front door behind them and returned to the living room.

Toby hadn't moved. He felt his dad's hand on his shoulder. He looked up into the hard, glassy eyes.

'Are you telling the truth?'

'Y-yes, Dad.'

'If your friends want to stay over, you have to ask first. Didn't I tell you that?' He waited a beat. 'Answer me!'

'Yes, you did. And I told him he couldn't come.'

'But you told those two detectives that you'd changed your mind.'

'I felt sorry for Mikey. He'd scored the winning goal and his ma wasn't even there. He has no one else. I'm his best friend.'

'That's enough of this shite. Go to your room.'

Toby escaped and ran up the stairs. In his room, he climbed over the bed and leaned on the sill, looking out of the window. There were kids playing ball on the green, screeching and roaring. There was no sign of the detectives.

He returned to his PlayStation. The only luxury he was allowed. He eyed his phone. It was an old Samsung his ma had given him when she'd got an upgrade. It didn't even have Wi-Fi. He picked it up and checked to make sure he hadn't missed a message from Mikey. Nothing. Just the call from Mikey's mother earlier.

He booted up *Call of Duty*. Mikey wasn't online. He was always online during the holidays. Earlier, Toby had thought his friend had been pissed off with him about last night and that was why he wasn't playing. Now, he wondered: where was Mikey?

As he took command of a gun and began sneaking around the side of a virtual building, it struck him that his own family hadn't been at the match to see him either.

The door opened. Toby turned his head. Eighteen-year-old Max stood there.

'Well, what did the pigs want?'

CHAPTER EIGHTEEN

'That young fellow, Toby, is scared shitless of his dad,' Boyd said as he started the car.

Lottie thought about the encounter. 'He's definitely scared of something.'

'We will need to talk to him again.'

'Yeah, but let the dust settle first. Let's drive down to number fifty-three before we head back to the station,' Lottie said. 'See if Hope has returned home.'

'I doubt it very much,' Boyd said, but he swung along the narrow road around the back of the estate and into the horseshoe of houses where the Cotters lived, an exact replica of the one they'd just left. 'Didn't Mrs Driscoll say she heard she'd done a runner?'

'Yeah, well, I'm hoping she meant from the hospital.' She thought about Mikey Driscoll's body. 'At this moment in time, we have to class Hope Cotter as a suspect in the boy's death.'

'I thought she killed the baby?' Boyd said, as a piebald horse with a boy on its back made its way up the road.

'She said, "I think I killed him." She could have meant Mikey.'

They got out of the car and Lottie hammered the door. No answer. 'Where the hell are they?'

'Did you really expect her to run home and then hang around waiting for you?'

'She has a little girl,' Lottie said. 'I'm worried for Lexie's welfare. I should have reported them.'

'Too late now.'

'You can be so reassuring when you want, you know that, Boyd?' she said sarcastically, before jumping over the rickety fence and banging on the door of number 54. Boyd knocked at 52 with its barred and shuttered windows.

Lottie stood back as the door eased open a crack. Two brown eyes gleamed out from the darkness, blinking in the sudden sunlight.

'What you want?'

'We're looking for Robbie and Hope Cotter. Your neighbours. Have you seen them today?'

'I saw no one.'

'Please, Miss ...?

'Who are you, anyway?'

Lottie placed her foot in the doorway, just in case, then showed her ID.

'Pigs. What do you want with next door? They cause no trouble.' The woman edged the door closed.

Putting her hand on the jamb, Lottie conjured up a smile. 'I just need to speak with them. It's very urgent.'

A cry from inside caused the woman to turn round. 'Shh. I'll be there in a minute.'

'Miss?'

'I honestly haven't seen them today. So, if you take your foot away, I'd like to go back to watching my kids.'

When the door had closed, Lottie looked over at Boyd. He shrugged his shoulders. The Cotters were gone.

'Back to the office and we'll see if anyone else has found them.' She slammed the car door. 'And we need to get someone to drop Mikey's toothbrush to the lab. It's a pity we can't talk to Toby Collins alone. I want to know what he's afraid of.'

'He'll have to wait. We have a whole football team to interview now. Spectators and anyone else associated with it. And then there's the crowd who were in McDonald's last night.'

'We'll get CCTV footage from there.'

'Send Kirby. He always fancies a Happy Meal.'

'Boyd, this is serious.'

'I *am* serious.'

'So what happened to Mikey Driscoll last night?'

'Some lunatic grabbed him from outside the restaurant and murdered him?'

'Boyd, just drive. I need to think.'

CHAPTER NINETEEN

Pulling his hood up to shield his face from passers-by, Max Collins headed out of the estate, along the canal and into town. He crossed the road and entered Fallon's pub. He had a five-euro note and some loose change in his pocket. Time to do some thieving. It had never come naturally to him, but he had to do it if he wanted to survive. If he wanted to escape. There was a time when Jim Fallon, the landlord, would have let him drink for free even when he was underage, but not any more. That said, Max was going to chance it.

As his eyes adjusted to the darkness, he slid his long tobacco-stained fingers, nails bitten to the quick, under the rim of the hood, and smoothed down his hair. Letting the hood down, he undid the zipper, noticed the state of his T-shirt and zipped it up again.

'Hi, Jim,' he said, sitting onto a stool.

'I thought I barred you,' Jim said, his face a mirror of his grumpy voice.

'That was my twin brother.'

'I'm not serving you, and you don't have a twin brother.'

'I could have, you never know.' Catching sight of his reflection in the mirror behind the optics, Max thought he wouldn't serve him either.

'Come on, Birdy. Don't make me throw you out.' Fallon rubbed the glass in his hand furiously with a threadbare cloth before adding it to the selection on the counter behind him.

Max hated his nickname. It had started in school. Something to do with the fact that his nose looked like a crow's beak. But he let it go for now.

'A pint. Just need to gear myself up for … you know what.' Max noticed Fallon flushing bright red and smiled to himself.

'I don't know what, and I don't like your insinuation.'

'A pint.' Max put the money on the counter.

With a sigh, Fallon retrieved the glass he'd dried, pulled a pint of lager and slammed it on the counter, splashing it over Max's hand. 'Keep your dirty money, Birdman. Drink up, then leave me alone.'

Raising the glass in mock salute, Max watched as Fallon headed to the other end of the bar. He just about tolerated being called Birdy, but he hated Birdman.

His reflection continued to haunt him. A scar through his eyebrow he'd got from a bottle when he was ten, an indent in his cheek the result of another bottle, broken this time, when he was twelve. His teeth, yellow and chipped, self-inflicted, from three years of crack cocaine usage. He drew his finger along them as if the action could negate the effects. He'd tried; God, but he had tried. Last year, aged seventeen, he'd stopped, cold turkey, in an attempt to save himself. But he knew, being on the ladder below the lowest rung of human existence, there wasn't much hope of redemption. Still, he had planned to make something of his life. Something he could achieve while lying in the gutter looking up at the elusive stars. He remembered that some famous guy had once said that, but he couldn't recall who it was. Sometimes it was hard even to know who *he* was.

The hum of chatter seemed to disappear as the door to the bar opened. Max quelled the urge to turn around. He'd wait until he could see who it was in the mirror. But he felt the hand on his shoulder before he raised his head, fingers digging into the cotton of his jacket. He knew those fingers.

Birds sang in the tree on the footpath outside the pub.

But Birdy would not sing tonight.

He only hoped he would live to see another day.

CHAPTER TWENTY

Hope settled Lexie into the single bed, nestled her comforter under her chin and watched as the little girl rubbed the label up and down. Smoothing her hair, she kissed the child's forehead and went down to the kitchen. Every footstep she took was utter agony.

'You're not staying here long,' Jacinta Barnes said, buttoning up her purple velour cardigan.

'Can I make a cup of coffee?' Hope asked, ignoring Robbie's ex-girlfriend's sour face.

'Sit and I'll do it. You won't know where anything is.' Jacinta lit a cigarette and busied herself with the kettle and mugs. As she moved around, her arse wobbled in the tight tracksuit that Hope figured was at least two sizes too small.

Hope stared at Robbie. 'Why did we have to come here to Athlone?' she whispered. 'I did nothing wrong.'

'When detectives knock on my door asking questions, I know you've done something wrong.'

'What happened to innocent until proven guilty?' She sat at the table and pulled Jacinta's cigarettes towards her. 'Mind if I have one?'

'I do, but go on.' Jacinta slammed three mugs on the table. 'What did you do?'

Lighting up the cigarette, Hope took a drag. It made her feel even dizzier than she was already. The pain in her abdomen was unrelenting, and she knew she was losing too much blood.

'I did nothing.' But what had happened to the baby that had been growing in her belly? She scrunched her eyes shut and beat her forehead. 'At least I don't think I did. I can't remember.'

She felt Robbie take her hand away. She looked at him.

'What?'

'Where's your baby, Hope?'

Gulping down a sob, she stood up and shook her head. Her eyes were tearless, her heart heavy and her womb empty. 'I don't know.' She put the cigarette in the ashtray and took the mug of coffee from Jacinta. 'I'm going to sit with Lexie.'

Fear crawled up her spine as she climbed the stairs with their worn carpet and squeaky boards. The door creaked as she pushed it open, and Lexie sat up in bed and held out her hands.

'Mummy, I'm scared.'

Putting down the mug, Hope took her child in her arms. 'Don't be frightened, sweetheart. I won't let anything happen to you.'

'Where are we?'

'We're safe, Lexie.'

As her daughter fell asleep in her arms and her coffee turned cold, Hope prayed that she could rid herself of the noxious influences that stalked her life.

He had told her she was evil. She had believed him. But the priest with the sad blue eyes had said she was good. Who was right?

She lay down on the hard bed and held her daughter tight. Lexie was the most important person in her world. They could do what they liked, but she would fight to the death to protect her little girl.

She needed to get out of here. Somehow she had to snatch the car keys and sneak out past Robbie and his ex-girlfriend.

Once it was dark.

CHAPTER TWENTY-ONE

With everyone mobilised to search for Hope Cotter, and scores of interviews ongoing in the Mikey Driscoll case, there was nothing for Lottie to do except type up her notes about Hope's appearance at the station that morning.

Nothing showed up on the PULSE database for her. A few traffic misdemeanours for her uncle, Robbie Cotter. Nothing for Mikey Driscoll or Toby Collins either, or for their parents, though there was a warning against Toby's brother, Max, for possession of Class C drugs. For his own use. Let off with a warning.

As she tried to concentrate, her eye was drawn through the open doorway to the outer office. Voices carried to her ear as Boyd slipped an envelope from his post pile and opened it. He extracted the pages and began to read them.

'What's that?' Kirby asked, tapping the top of his computer monitor.

'You're the nosiest bastard around,' Boyd said.

'That's why I'm a detective.'

Holding the papers aloft, Boyd said, 'I'm a free man.'

'At last.' Kirby jumped up. 'This means drinks, a celebration.'

'What are we celebrating?' Lottie called from her office.

'Boyd got his divorce,' Kirby said. 'At last.'

Lottie feigned disinterest by lowering her head to her work. Why hadn't Boyd told her this was going on? For years he had resisted divorcing his estranged wife, Jackie, who now resided somewhere in the south of Spain. What would this cost him? Financially he wasn't wealthy, she knew that. But emotionally, what would it do to him? Now that he was finally free, would he once again direct his attention to her? Or would he seek out a new soulmate? She wasn't sure she wanted to find out.

'You've gone very quiet.' Boyd was standing in the doorway.

She roused herself from her musings. 'Nothing for me to say. Have you that report written up?'

'What report?'

'See, you're slacking. Get back to work, Boyd, and don't be annoying me.'

As he moved away she was sure she heard him say, 'Thick arse.'

She decided to escape the office to fetch something to eat. She needed her strength if she was to investigate the case of the unidentified baby and the suspected murder of Mikey Driscoll. She decided on Danny's Bar rather than Cafferty's. Most of the squad frequented Cafferty's, and she needed a quiet few minutes alone in the company of a cool white wine. No, she decided, too early for that. A coffee would have to suffice.

The interior of the pub was dark, and she squinted, refocusing her eyes after the outside light. A few men sat on bar stools drinking pints, and a couple of women with handbags at their feet were ensconced in a corner, near the door.

She walked through to the lounge. It was quiet. She beckoned to the young woman behind the bar and ordered coffee and a sandwich. As she turned towards a comfortable seat, the couple at the end of the bar caught her eye.

No, it couldn't be, she thought. She lowered her head and made for the corner. Once she was seated and her coffee arrived, she chanced another look. It *was* him. Boyd. In deep conversation with a dark-haired woman. The cut of the hair was familiar, and when the woman threw back her head in a laugh, Lottie felt her heart sink all the way down to the soles of her feet. She had to get out. Unnoticed.

Throwing a few coins on the table, she got up quickly and fled the pub.

As she walked back to the station, she kept wondering why Boyd was having a drink with the journalist Cynthia Rhodes. The scene had looked nice and cosy. Too cosy for comfort. What the hell was that all about?

Shit!

And she was still hungry.

*

Boyd eyed Cynthia Rhodes with unveiled suspicion. Had she followed him into the pub? Or was it, as she claimed, a happy coincidence? Whatever the truth was, he wasn't going to let his guard down. He had been on the point of ordering food when she took charge of the stool next to him.

'Detective Sergeant Boyd, isn't it?' she said, flicking up her spectacles with a short black-varnished nail. The rest of her grooming was shabby, he noted, as she pulled down the zipper of her leather jacket. An AC-DC T-shirt and black jeans gave her the full biker look. But Boyd felt she was trying a little too hard, and in doing so, she was failing.

'Yes, it is,' he said, and beckoned to the woman behind the bar. He hoped his sandwich would arrive as quickly as the tea he now ordered.

'I'll have the same,' Cynthia said to the girl.

'Haven't seen you in Danny's before.'

'You come here a lot, then?'

'That sounds like a corny pick-up line.'

'Maybe it is.' She laughed, even white teeth gleaming in the half-light. 'Or maybe I'm just asking a simple question.'

'I come in from time to time.'

'So, I could be here more than the odd time.' She grinned, but it slipped away instantaneously. 'I heard you found a body.'

'No, I didn't.' He wasn't falling into her trap. Cynthia had almost ruined Lottie's career on their last case by interviewing her at an inopportune moment, catching the inspector unawares and then broadcasting it to the nation. Only Lottie's diligence in solving the crime had saved her.

'Oh, come on, the whole town is talking about it.'

'Why are you asking me, then?' Boyd sipped his tea.

'I see you went to the Lottie Parker school of no comment. Let's just drop the job descriptions and have a normal chat.'

'About what?'

'Anything you like. Football. The weather. Ragmullin. I'm not picky.'

'Thought you were back working in Dublin.'

'I follow the stories. And Ragmullin's returned to the news. So here I am.'

'You won't get any news out of me, Cynthia. Wait for the press conference.' As he turned slightly towards her, he thought he saw Lottie rushing out of the pub. Surely not? But if it had been her, what would she have made of him chatting with her nemesis? Not good.

'When will that be?'

'What?'

'The press conference about the body?'

'What body?'

'The one that was found at the clubhouse. Gosh, you're hard work.'

Boyd's sandwich was placed in front of him. He no longer had any appetite. As he took out his wallet to pay, he said to the reporter,

'You can have that. I know it's not news, but you seem hungry for something.'

He didn't wait for his change.

'Hey, Boyd?'

He turned around.

'I only wanted to chat. Really.'

'Why don't you call your friend Superintendent McMahon, then?' And he kept on going.

*

That hadn't gone quite to plan, Cynthia thought as she munched Boyd's abandoned sandwich. With her other hand she swiped through the contacts on her phone, her finger hovering over David McMahon's name. Should she? No, he'd want her to dig up more dirt on Lottie Parker in exchange for information. She'd tried that a few months ago with an interview that should have seen Parker consigned to the early-retirement heap, but it hadn't turned out that way. Parker had dodged the bullet.

Maybe she could follow her again and catch her making a mistake. The best chance she had of that was by making friends with someone in the force besides David McMahon. She'd liked the look of Boyd, with his clean-cut looks and his nice suit. His ears did stick out a bit too much, but she could forgive him that. Yes, she would get him on side and then she'd find out Parker's real weakness.

With her mind made up, she drained her tea and left with the crust of the sandwich in her hand.

CHAPTER TWENTY-TWO

Lottie slammed the office door and shoved her fist into her mouth so that she wouldn't bite her nails. What was Boyd doing meeting Cynthia Rhodes? Was he beginning a relationship with her now that he had been granted his divorce? No, surely not.

A few minutes later, Boyd himself sauntered into the main office. She could see him through the glass in her door. He was wearing that smug grin, the one she normally loved, but now she found it galled her. Without thought for her actions, she jumped up and went out to the general office.

'Where were you?'

'Having something to eat,' Boyd said, the smile slipping down his face like a child caught with his hand in the cookie jar.

'Really?'

'Jesus, Lottie.' Boyd raised an eyebrow. 'What's got into you?'

'What's got into *you*, more like,' she snapped. 'The name Cynthia mean anything to you?' She mentally kicked herself. Why had she gone and said that? Too late to take it back now.

'If you want to know, Ms Rhodes sat herself down beside me while I was waiting for my sandwich and tried to start up a conversation. Anything else you'd like me to report?'

Sucking in her breath, Lottie turned on her heel and marched out of the office. She leaned against the wall in the corridor and exhaled long and hard.

When she looked up, Boyd was standing beside her. 'What was that about in there?'

'Nothing. Feck off, Boyd.'

He disappeared and she berated herself for her childishness. Damn it, Parker. It had been a long day. Too long. She had to get home. But first there was work to do.

Then she was having a drink. Fuck it.

With SOCOs still processing the scene where Mikey Driscoll's body had been found, Lottie would have to wait for the post-mortem to take place, probably in the morning, to know what she was dealing with. She'd forwarded the boy's toothbrush for analysis so they could get a positive ID. But there was no doubt it was Mikey.

With no reported sightings of Hope Cotter, she returned her attention to the baby. There was still no word on that PM. She thought of the teenagers who had found him. Her son and Barry Duffy. She knew Sean was fine, because she had checked in on him, but she had to be sure Barry was okay.

She left the office and headed to the Duffy home, which was built on an acre of ground on the outskirts of Ragmullin, by the old Dublin road. She parked the car on the shingle drive in front of the two-storey house, which sported a dormer window to one side of a whitewashed wall. The door was solid timber, painted bottle green. There was no bell. She lifted the brass knocker and let it fall loudly, thinking that there was plenty of money behind the glossy door.

She was about to knock again when the door opened.

'I'm Inspector Lottie Parker, Ragmullin gardaí. Can I have a word, please?'

As the tall woman stood back to allow her to enter, Lottie took in the thin, worried face, skin so white it was almost transparent, the dark hair tied into a loose ponytail hanging over one shoulder, and the pristine white jeans with a matching long shirt. Bare feet. Mid thirties, she estimated.

'Julia Duffy,' the woman said, and Lottie took her hand and found it damp. The diamond on the ring finger was bigger than any she had ever seen. 'Are you here about this morning? About Barry discovering that baby's body?'

'Yes.' Lottie seated herself on a leather armchair in a large room, minimalist in design and wanting in colour. A pale painting in a large frame hung on the wall. Otherwise there were no ornaments, books or clutter.

'Barry is fine. A bit shaken, if I'm to be honest. Paul – that's his dad, my husband – gave him a mild sedative. He's a doctor. Barry's in bed now. Resting. Don't think he's been in bed this early since he was a toddler. Is there something wrong?'

'No, nothing's wrong. He was fishing down by the canal with my son Sean when they discovered the body. A traumatic experience for them both. I just wondered how he was doing.'

'Your son? Sean is your son? Is he okay?'

'He's fine,' Lottie said. She felt her cheeks flush. *Was* Sean okay? It was a few hours since she had called her mother. He'd been fine then. But now? Shit, here she was checking up on someone else's son when she should have gone to her own first. Par for the course.

'Good.' Julia wrestled her hands together, her brow creased in a worry line. 'Was there anything else?' Her eyes kept darting to the door. Wide brown pools flickering around, like a frightened puppy.

Lottie said, 'I'd like Barry to come to the station tomorrow to make a formal statement. Either you or your husband will have to accompany him.'

Julia nodded, then looked up at Lottie from beneath long dark lashes. 'Someone mentioned to Barry at the station that you're assigning a family liaison officer to us. We don't need one.'

'It's advisable but it's also up to you. I'm concerned for your son's welfare. It must have been an awful shock for him.'

Julia shrugged. 'I suppose so. Any word on who the baby belongs to? Or do you know what happened?'

'No, not yet.' Why had she come here? She'd have been better served heading straight home to her own family.

The door opened and a man entered, also in his bare feet, dressed in blue jeans and an open-necked white shirt. His black hair was peppered with grey and his face was long and creviced. He appeared to be quite a bit older than his wife.

Lottie shook his proffered hand.

'Hello,' she said. 'Dr Duffy?'

'Paul,' he said. 'You're here about Barry? He's resting. Terrible thing to happen to him.'

'And to the baby,' Lottie said before she could stop herself.

'Yes, of course. Tragic. Any progress on your investigation?'

'Not yet. We're working flat out.'

'I'm sure you are.'

Was there an insinuation there? She wasn't at all sure. I'm tired, she thought. Seeing things that weren't there.

'Can we do anything to help?' Duffy asked, sitting on the arm of his wife's chair and taking her hand in his. To stop her fidgeting, or genuine concern? Stop, Parker.

'No, not at all. I'm just checking that Barry is okay and whether he remembered anything else.'

'He barely spoke about it. Quite spooked, actually.'

'I can imagine. Not a nice situation to find yourself in, especially for a young boy.' Lottie stood up. 'Well, if he recalls anything else, tell him to ring me, and please bring him to the station to make that statement.' She handed over her card.

Paul stood and took it before his wife's outstretched hand made contact. 'Of course. I'll see you out. Julia, are you going to finish off that painting any time soon? The kitchen is in a state and we have dinner to prepare.'

'Sure,' Julia said. 'Nice to meet you, Inspector.' She scuttled out before Lottie could reply.

She felt her elbow being gripped lightly, and Duffy led her to the front door. Her boots clattered on the marble floor and she wondered if perhaps she should have taken them off when she arrived. Too late now.

She turned to Duffy as he opened the door. Lottie was tall, but he must be over six feet, she estimated. 'Tell Barry he can talk to me any time. About anything. You have my number.'

'Of course. Thank you for your concern. Goodnight now.'

The door shut the second she was outside it. There had been an uneasy atmosphere in the house, and she wondered why Julia Duffy had looked so tentative and anxious when her husband entered the room. And how did she put up with being talked to like that?

By the time Lottie pulled up outside her mother's house, she was still none the wiser.

CHAPTER TWENTY-THREE

The house was warm, the smell of freshly baked bread permeating the air. Rose was fussing at the oven, so Lottie went in search of Sean.

She found him sitting up in bed wearing new earphones, which he pulled down to his neck when she entered.

'Hi, Mam. Any news on the baby?'

'You're pale,' she said, and sat on the side of his bed. 'Did Granny look after you all right today?'

He rolled his eyes. 'Save me from her. I can't take much more fussing.'

Lottie laughed. 'The house should be ready soon. Then we can relax a little.'

'I can't wait.'

'Did you eat?'

'Granny insists on force-feeding me. Afraid I'm going to faint or something. Tell her to stop. Please.'

'You'll have to make a formal statement. I'll bring you in with me in the morning. That okay?'

'Do I have to?'

'Yes.' She stood up and leaned over him, feathering his hair with a kiss. 'Want to tell me anything I don't already know?'

'It was only one can, Mam.'

'Sure it was. But tell me about this Barry. Is he a new friend of yours?'

'I know him from school. Met up a few times. Lives just down the road. Thought you'd be happy to see me getting out in the fresh air for a change.'

'I am. But—'

'But you didn't think I'd find a new case for you, did you?'

'No, I didn't.'

'Where's Dad's stuff? His fishing gear?'

'It's still at the station. You can pick it up in the morning. But no fishing for a little while, okay?'

'Whatever.' Lottie felt her son's eyes studying her. He said, 'You look stressed, Mam.'

'It was a hard day. Another body was found this afternoon.'

'What? That's terrible. Not another baby, I hope. That'd be too mental.'

'It was a young boy. And I had to break the bad news to his mother. Sometimes I hate my job.'

'Who was it?'

'Mikey Driscoll. Only eleven years old.' Looking at her son, she could see a line of worry creasing his brow. 'What is it, Sean? Did you know him?'

'Jeez, Mam. Mikey used to play under-eights hurling for a while, when I was playing under-twelves. He was the nicest, quietest kid ever. I only saw him yesterday, at the match. He scored a beauty of a goal.'

'And how did he seem last night?'

'He was flying. Buzzing, because he scored the winner. Oh Mam, I can't believe it.'

'I shouldn't have said anything. Don't you be worrying about it. Rest up. I'm going to find your sisters and Louis. The house is very quiet.'

'Oh, they went into town. To escape from Granny.'

Lottie checked the time on her phone. 'They should be back by now. It's getting late.'

'It's summer time. Let them have some fun.'

'Says the wise old man. Did they take Louis with them?' Lottie asked.

'I imagine so. Ask the Wicked Witch of the West.'

Lottie lightly swiped Sean away. 'Messer.' She was glad he appeared undamaged by his tragic discovery. Hopefully he would stay that way.

In the kitchen, the smell of a stew cooking caused her stomach to growl in anticipation. Her mother was reading a newspaper at the table.

'That boy needs minding,' Rose said without looking up.

'I know, and I'm eternally grateful to you for looking after him while I'm at work.'

'Don't be smart with me. I know you have to work and I know he is just gone fifteen; all the same, you should give your children more of your time.'

Lottie didn't rise to the bait. She was in no humour for a row. Today had been too traumatic already. 'Where are the girls? And Louis?'

'They went into town around three. Chloe has to work later. Should be home soon. I told them I was cooking a stew. They like that.'

Maybe they'd like it in the dead of winter, Lottie thought, but not in the heat of summer. She hoped the girls would at least attempt to turn up and eat something. Otherwise Rose would sulk. Caught between her elderly parent and three children, Lottie didn't know if she was coming or going at times.

A sweating Katie rushed in, dragging the stroller behind her.

'Hi, Mam,' she said, bumping by Lottie. 'I have to change Louis. He has a dirty nappy.' She took the boy into her arms and moved towards the bedroom. 'Can't go anywhere with him.'

'Where's Chloe?' Lottie said.

'Being a bore as usual,' Katie called, and Louis began to cry. 'I wanted to look at baby clothes and she wanted to buy a pair of jeans, so we had a row and she stormed off.'

'Drama queens,' Sean said, coming into the kitchen.

'Dinner's ready,' Rose proclaimed, standing up. 'She'd better be here soon.'

'You can always stick it in the microwave,' Lottie said, fetching plates from the cupboard.

The sharp look that Rose gave her was enough to staunch any further argument.

'Just saying,' Lottie muttered under her breath. And she couldn't stop wondering why Boyd had been sitting with Cynthia Rhodes in the pub.

CHAPTER TWENTY-FOUR

The vehicle shook from side to side. The back seat had been removed for this purpose alone.

When the man was finished, he kicked out at Max as if he were shit on his shoe.

Max felt for his jeans and tried to pull them up. The smell of cigarette smoke awoke a longing in him for nicotine and something stronger. Something to take away the pain.

'You're getting a bit old for me,' the man said.

'That's your problem.'

Another drag on the cigarette. 'Smart alec.'

'You're a bastard,' Max said.

'And so are you. Now get out. I've bingo ladies to pick up.'

Max jumped out. In the dimming evening light, there was no one around except a couple of joggers in the park, phones strapped to their arms and buds in their ears. Exhaust fumes belched from the departing vehicle, and the pint he'd downed in Fallon's bar earlier lurched from his stomach out onto the side of the road. Bent over, he thought he caught sight of someone behind a tree inside the park gates. Hallucinating now, he thought. He needed a joint. Badly.

He cleaned his mouth with the back of his hand and headed into town.

*

Toby couldn't believe what he'd just witnessed. He slid down the bark of the tree. Max? What had he been doing in that bus? Why had it made him sick?

Clutching his hand to his stomach, he felt ill. He didn't need to be asking himself these stupid questions. He knew right well what his brother had been up to. Making money, the only way Max Collins knew how. Mikey had told him about it. Mikey knew. Was that why Mikey was dead now?

Tears careened down his cheeks as he recalled Max telling him the news earlier. He plucked tufts of grass out of the ground. Dug his nails into the earth. Bit his lips. Quenched the scream that was waiting to escape his throat.

He'd only come into the park to escape his dad's bollocking about his stammering. Shouting and roaring ringing in his ears. Would it ever stop?

The cathedral bell chimed the hour.

His ma would be home soon. She worked long hours. Too long, slaving in the Joyce for a pittance. Maybe she wanted to escape his da too. Yeah, that was it. Or was it all to do with Max?

Toby wiped his nose with the back of his dirty hand and stood up. Everyone feared Max, but only Toby knew that Max was scared too. Though what – or who – his brother was afraid of, Toby had no idea.

CHAPTER TWENTY-FIVE

The house Lottie was renting was located on the opposite side of town from where she used to live. The estate had been a ghost development for years, and was currently in the throes of rejuvenation.

Detached, and with four bedrooms, the house was ideal, though it had been in need of serious redecorating after sitting empty for two years.

After scoffing down a few mouthfuls of stew that she didn't want, Lottie had taken a call from Ben Lynch, Maria's husband, who was phoning to say he needed her advice. She had escaped from her mother's house gratefully.

'Glad you could make it,' Ben said, swinging round on the top of a ladder, paintbrush in hand, as she walked through the front door.

'What's the problem?'

He climbed down and put the brush on top of a can of paint. Picking up a colour chart, he pointed to the aqua green Lottie had selected for the kitchen walls.

'This is out of stock. It'll be a week before it's in, so I need you to pick out something different. Otherwise there's no way you will be in here next week.'

'Damn, I liked the aqua.' She took the chart and sat on the arm of a chair covered with a sheet. The house came partially furnished, which was good, because the fire had destroyed all her possessions. She pointed to a similar colour. 'This one will do. I'm not fussy.'

'That's great. Sorry for dragging you out.'

'It's fine. I needed to dodge my mother anyway. Chicken stew in this warm weather? There's no talking to her.'

'Should have brought me a bowl.'

Lottie looked at Ben. He was a lot taller than Maria, which wasn't hard, and his face was more youthful than his wife's, though at nearly forty, he was the older of the two. His painting dungarees hung loosely over a white T-shirt.

'Won't be long now for you and Maria,' she said. 'Another baby. Wow.'

'Wow is right. I was more surprised than if I'd won the Lotto. There'll be big changes in Chez Lynch.'

'Your youngest is what? Five?'

'Five and seven, the two of them. And now a baby in the mix. Fun.'

Lottie stood up. 'At least you have your job in the uni to keep you occupied.'

'I can tell you, I'm glad of this extra work. College is closed for the summer and Maria is like a briar in this weather, so it's great to get out of the house in the evenings. Anyway, I love decorating.'

'Maybe you should take it up full-time,' Lottie said with a laugh.

Ben laughed too, his eyes sparkling under the light bulb. She felt a soft tingle in the pit of her stomach. If he wasn't married to Lynch, she just might be interested. Don't even think about it, she warned her inner self. Complications followed her around like a dark shadow.

'Don't be giving me ideas.' He turned back to his ladder and picked up the paintbrush. 'This should be finished by the weekend.'

'I'll have your money ready for you when you're done.'

'No need. Had an email from Mr Rickard. He's settled the bill. Money is in my account already.'

Lottie stood open-mouthed. 'What?'

'And with a bonus. Can't complain about that. I'll get that paint tomorrow and crack on.'

'Sure.'

'Lottie? Hope you don't mind me saying, but you look a little distracted. Anything you want to talk about?'

She hesitated. 'Just a hard day today. Two bodies. A baby and an eleven-year-old boy. Kind of hard to take in. And difficult to know where to start.'

'Such an evil world we live in, huh?' He started to climb the ladder. 'I'm a good listener, if you need to chat. Any time.'

'Thanks, Ben. I'll be fine.' No matter what, she knew she could count on Boyd, or talk to Father Joe. No point in bringing someone else into the equation.

As she headed back to Rose's, she phoned Boyd. No answer. Just when I need you, she thought.

*

Leo Belfield's room in the Joyce Hotel was comfortable enough, even if the furnishings were dated. And the bed linen was spotless and fresh.

He looked out of the window onto Ragmullin's Main Street and wondered at the series of events that had brought him here. He still hadn't decided what his course of action should be. But he knew he had to meet this Lottie Parker. He had only spoken to her once, on the phone, and she had brushed him off. He didn't like stuck-up bitches. She needed to apologise. Face to face. And she would have an opportunity to do that.

First, though, he wanted to find out everything he could about her. And being a half-decent cop, he would source a person whose job ensured they knew how to dig up the dirt. Another cop, or a journalist.

He did up the top button of his shirt and tightened his tie. Pulling on his leather jacket, he set off to quiz the residents of Ragmullin propping up the hotel bar. Then, armed with what he needed to know, he would embark on his mission.

CHAPTER TWENTY-SIX

The boy wandered around the units in the industrial estate. He was pissed off. Everyone was always rowing about something. His mother was worse now than his dad. She was a bitch, he thought, and then he felt sorry for even thinking that. She wasn't a bitch. Just a lost soul. So he'd heard his dad call her one night.

He felt his heart break a little for his mum. He loved her, really he did, but he didn't know how to help her. His dad was no good. Always going off about this and that. All he was concerned about was eating healthy food. Birdseed, his mum called it. Who can live on birdseed? she'd say. The boy smiled. Yeah. Whatever. He'd better go home. It was late. Very late.

Even though the sky twinkled with stars, it was dark in the industrial estate and he began to feel afraid. As he jumped over the stack of tyres that was piled up outside the old tyre recycling depot, he heard the soft purring of a car engine. He ducked back down and held his breath. He didn't dare lift his head.

At last, he heard the car leave with a whine of a turbo engine. He waited for a few minutes. Then waited some more, before taking off down the narrow road towards the dark underpass beneath the railway. Someone had smashed the lights. He didn't like the dark, even though he had witnessed enough darkness in his life that he should be used to it.

Tugging the belt on his jeans, he hooked it up another notch to keep them from falling down. He'd have to get new ones soon. But his mum wasn't about to buy him any if he kept acting the maggot, as she called it. He'd have a look online at ASOS when he got home. He quite liked the jogging bottoms that were tight from the ankles up to the knees and baggy at the crotch. Like the teenagers wore. Yeah. Black with a green stripe down the side. They'd be nice.

He was thinking about this when he heard a car pulling up beside him and the window sliding down.

'What are you doing around here so late? Bit dangerous for a young lad, don't you think?'

He kept walking but turned his head slightly to take a look. Phew. It wasn't some mass murderer out to nab him. He recognised the car first, then the driver.

'Hi,' he said shyly.

'Jump in and I'll give you a lift home.'

The boy opened the door and slid into the seat. He clipped on his seat belt and heard the door lock click. His trainer stood on something in the footwell. He looked down. It was a clear plastic bag. And inside it, a new pair of football shorts.

*

The boy's mother rubbed her eyes and stretched her arms in the air. What the hell? Looking around, she realised she'd fallen asleep on the couch. Again. She clicked the Sky button on the remote and saw it was almost two a.m. Oh God.

Dragging her legs out from beneath her, she heard the bottle rolling under the couch and hitting the radiator behind it. She paused with the remote still in her hand and listened. Her husband was a sound sleeper, especially after a few pints. At least she hoped he was in bed; she hadn't heard him come in. The second bottle of wine had been a mistake, she thought as she stood up and felt the room move with her. She got down on her knees and retrieved the bottle. Picking up the other one from the coffee table, she went to hide them in a kitchen cupboard. Tomorrow she'd bring the collection to the recycling depot.

And then she remembered her son and the row they'd had that afternoon. Was he even home? If he knew what was good for him, he'd be fast asleep in bed.

She turned off the television, then the lights, and crept up the stairs as quietly as she could manage. Her son's door was open. Strange. She pushed it inwards and gasped. His bed was empty. Flicking on the switch, she saw he hadn't been home at all.

A surge of panic rooted her to the floor. Her hands trembled and her knees almost buckled. Where could he be at this hour? She'd kill him. And then she thought, maybe it was better that he hadn't seen her so drunk, though it wouldn't be the first time. She backed out of the room, trying to decide what to do.

'What the hell are you at?' Her husband stood behind her.

'Jesus, you scared me half to death.'

'You're drunk again,' he said. 'Where's the boy?' He peered over her shoulder.

She shrugged, not trusting to get the words out of her mouth without slurring.

'I'll kill the little fecker when I get my hands on him. What time is it?' He walked into the bathroom and lifted the toilet seat.

She listened to her husband peeing and wished her life could go back to the way it had been. Before everything had gone wrong.

Another one gone, and I feel so good.

I slide the heavy bolt on the back door through the ring and twist round the double security lock. Turning out the light, I make my way through the house to the front door. Looking through the spy hole, I see only the dark of the night staring back at me before I check that all the locks are secure. To my right, at eye level, the alarm pad sits on the wall.

I punch in the four-digit code, listening to it arm, and turn on a red night light before switching out the remaining lights.

As I mount the stairs, I'm not sure if I am doing right. Am I keeping the evil securely locked outside, or are its venomous tendrils already pulsing in the walls of the house?

A tremor of unease rattles up my spine as my slippered feet glide on the carpet along the corridor to the bedroom. With my hand on the doorknob, I pause. Listening. All is silent, but as I push the door inwards, I'm sure I hear a laboured wheeze behind me, and feel it ruffling the hairs on my neck.

Rushing inside, I slam the door and turn the key. In the darkness, I lean against the heavy wood, knowing it is useless against the enemy I fear. Because it is already within me.

They had to die. It was the only way I could ever release the demons. I rub my hands together, to still the shaking, and dredge up the memory of the thin neck, flesh like that of a baby, soft and supple beneath my hands. The crunch of bone, or was it cartilage? The life easing out of the eyes. The silent mouth. The pinpricks of blood slipping down in lividity. And, at last, the white stillness of alabaster skin.

When my breath returns to normal, I flick on the light to prepare myself for a good night's sleep.

I have laid the demons to rest, for tonight at least.

DAY TWO

Tuesday

CHAPTER TWENTY-SEVEN

The morning light was too bright, the curtains too thin. Hope shifted onto her side and noticed Lexie wasn't beside her. She sat upright. She heard the child singing downstairs, vying with the strains of a cartoon character on the television. Thank God, she thought.

Swinging her legs over the edge of the bed, she felt dampness beneath her. The bedding was soaked in blood and the pain was festering like a boil in her abdomen. She needed a doctor. But she couldn't risk it. Because she had no idea what she had done with her baby, and the guards were looking for her.

*

Lottie hadn't slept well. The murders kept going round and round in her head. Then she'd spent long hours awake thinking about Chloe, who had come home late, looking like she had been in a boxing match. The girl shouldn't be working in a pub, even if it was only picking up glasses. Even if it was to give her independence. 'I'm fine, it's nothing for you to worry about' was all she had succeeded in extracting from her seventeen-year-old daughter. Sometimes Lottie felt like booking a one-way ticket to Outer Mongolia. Wasn't about to happen any time soon, was it?

And then there was Boyd. Don't go there.

She'd found a Xanax in a plastic vitamin bottle she kept hidden in her drawer. She'd swallowed it dry.

Now here she was, showered, looking fresher than she felt, in a pair of jeans belonging to Katie. She had no decent clothes. Her daughter and grandson had been in New York with the boy's grandfather at the time of the fire, and had come home with a suitcase weighing well above the twenty-three-kilo limit. Continuing to raid Katie's wardrobe was a short-term measure, Lottie concluded. As soon as the house was ready to move into, she would shop for new clothes. She was also wearing a long-sleeved white T-shirt. Her mother had suggested it. 'You're too thin to be going around displaying your scraggy arms,' she'd said. Lottie had looked at herself in the mirror and had to admit Rose was right. As usual. She had lost so much weight, she was verging on a scarecrow. She must remember to eat today.

She stared at the incident board. Two bodies. The unidentified baby and eleven-year-old Mikey Driscoll.

'The baby must belong to Hope Cotter,' Lynch said.

'We have no DNA confirmation on that as yet. Blood's being analysed at the moment. Let's not make assumptions.'

'It's fairly obvious it's her.' Lynch folded her arms defiantly. 'Why has she not been located?'

Her detective was in a ratty mood, Lottie thought.

'We have her billed as a person of interest. It's hard to hide with a four-year-old child in tow.'

'She has her uncle's help,' Lynch persisted.

'Anything show up for her on PULSE?' The garda database was a crucial source of information.

'The uncle has a few parking fines and driving with no motor tax on one occasion, but nothing worse than that,' Boyd said.

'Any sign of his car?'

'Nothing yet.' Boyd scanned the page in his hand. 'Hope's not listed on PULSE at all.'

Lottie said, 'Just means she hasn't been caught doing anything.'

'Or she hasn't done anything,' Boyd said, rolling up his shirt-sleeves, one crease at a time. Lining up the cuffs to ensure they were even.

'We need to contact Child and Family Services. She may be on their radar,' Lottie said.

'Wish you luck getting anything out of that lot.'

Were they all out to make her life hell this morning? She blew out her cheeks and decided she had to at least make it look like she was in charge.

'I'm waiting for PM results on the baby, so we'll have more information later.' She glanced up at the incident board and put her finger on the photograph of Mikey Driscoll. The one his mother had taken, not the death image caught by SOCOs. 'I'm hoping the state pathologist will get to Mikey this morning. Lynch, you spoke with his mother first thing. How is she doing?'

'Not great.'

Lottie grimaced but said nothing.

Lynch consulted her notes. 'The FLO stayed with her. We're trying to locate her ex-husband, Derek, but he's working in Dubai. We can cross him off our non-existent suspect list.' She flicked a page as if for effect. 'Here's the odd thing, though. Mikey didn't take his phone with him on Sunday. Jen found it in his room, buried under a pile of clothes in the bottom of his wardrobe. She claims he went nowhere without it. Even snuck it into school.'

'He probably didn't want to risk it being stolen at the match. Is it a new model?'

'No, it's an old one Jen gave him just so she could check up on him.'

'Anything from the messages or calls? Are our technical guys working on it?' Lottie wondered at the wisdom of an eleven-year-old having any kind of a phone, then recalled that she had bought one for Sean when he wasn't much older than Mikey.

'Doing it as we speak. They're looking through his social media accounts.'

'Social media? He was only eleven.'

'Just Snapchat. Not Facebook or any of the others. I'll let you know if anything turns up.' Lynch eyed Lottie with a death stare.

What the hell have I done to offend you? Lottie wondered.

'Were you able to construct a personality profile of the boy?'

'His mum talks glowingly of him. But she's in shock, plus you and I both know mothers don't always see the whole picture.'

Was that a veiled barb? Lottie parked the thought. 'Tell me what she had to say, and then we can see if friends and neighbours can corroborate it.'

'Hard-working boy,' Lynch said. 'Good at school, though his summer exams saw his grades slip somewhat. But it was his last year in primary and Jen says he was still adjusting to the idea of moving on to secondary school. Active in sports and on his PlayStation. Gaming and football seemed to be his interests.'

'That's normal for an eleven-year-old,' Lottie said. 'I should know.' And in a moment of whimsy, she wished she could go back to the time before Sean was eleven. When her family was secure and complete. When Adam was alive.

Lynch said, 'Thought it was hurling your boy's into?'

Lottie shook herself out of her memories. 'You know what I mean.' She heard Boyd snigger, and folded her arms. 'Mikey Driscoll is our concern. Anything stand out in recent weeks? Any trouble or fights at home?'

'All hunky-dory, according to Jen. She last saw Mikey on Sunday afternoon, before he headed out to meet up with his teammates for his match. She went to bingo and says she won twenty euros. Came home, shared a bottle of Merlot with Dolores, her neighbour. She believed Mikey was at Toby's house like he'd told her, and went to work the next morning. She's an instructor at Sweat-It-Out gym. Says she didn't normally contact Mikey when he was at a friend's house. He needed his space away from her every so often. That's what she said.'

'He was only eleven,' Boyd said.

'Welcome to the new world,' Lottie told him. 'Any bullying?'

'Jen doesn't think so. Just said that he was adjusting to the idea of leaving primary school. Might be something between the lines there. I'll dig a little deeper today.'

'Do that,' Lottie said. 'I'll have another word with Toby Collins. We need every member of the football team questioned, plus the spectators who were at the match and anyone associated with the team. How are those inquiries coming along?'

'Nothing to report so far,' Boyd said.

Kirby coughed. 'I've been wondering about something.'

'Sounds dangerous,' Boyd said.

'Go on,' Lottie said, ignoring him.

Kirby shuffled his bulk up to the incident board, running a hand through his bushy hair. He studied the photograph of the boy's body by the clubhouse wall. Then he pointed to another photo of the body, this one taken from a few steps back.

'There are three industrial-sized bins here,' he said. 'Two for rubbish and one for recycling. Why not just put the body in a bin? There'd be less chance of discovery if he had been pushed down beneath the refuse sacks.'

Lottie walked up and down in front of the boards. 'The killer wanted the boy found. I think he's sending a message. If so, what is it?'

Her words echoed off the walls as the room descended into thoughtful silence.

Lynch broke it. 'You're assuming the killer is a man. I think we need to take a long, hard look at Mikey's mother.'

'We'll be looking at everyone associated with Mikey,' Lottie said, her voice steely. 'Lynch, make sure the father, Derek Driscoll, really is in Dubai. We need to trace Mikey's steps from when he left his home on Sunday afternoon. Kirby, go over the official statements from the teenagers who found the body.' She thought for a moment. 'When were those bins last used?'

Kirby said, 'The clubhouse was open on Sunday night. Apparently, there was a twenty-first birthday party held there a few hours after the boys' match. Empties from the bar and rubbish were put in the bins. The next event is this coming Saturday night and the clubhouse is closed until then. No matches or training scheduled for this week, therefore the only people using the grounds are youngsters like Fonzie and company.'

'Once the post-mortem on Mikey is finished, we'll have a clearer timeline to work with.' Lottie paused. 'But we need to interview everyone who was at that party Sunday night. We know Mikey was still alive around nine p.m., because he was seen in McDonald's. Check the clubhouse security footage and see if the cameras captured anything suspicious. Surely one of them picked up the body being dumped. Can you drive a car up to the clubhouse?'

'Yes.' Kirby consulted his notes. 'The refuse truck has to get in there to empty the bins.'

'Check in with SOCOs and see if they've found anything. And grab the footage from McDonald's and anything else you can get from the businesses along the street.'

'Will do,' Kirby said.

'I'm heading to Tullamore for the post-mortem.'

'Will I go with you?' Boyd said.

'You need to see if there's any progress on the search for Hope Cotter and—'

Her words were cut off by the shrill ringing of one of the incident room phones. She waited while Boyd answered it.

Not liking the look on his face as he hung up, she said, 'What is it?'

'We have another body.'

CHAPTER TWENTY-EIGHT

Ladystown Lake was about seven kilometres from Ragmullin. A fisherman had found the body there at 7.45 a.m. There'd been no attempt to hide it. The boy had been left lying on a flat stone by the lake shore, in a private mooring area that was only accessible if you had a code to the gate.

Lottie made her way through a group of uniformed gardaí as Kirby and Lynch started interviewing the fishermen. Suited up in her protective gear, she felt perspiration bubble between her breasts, the underwired bra eating into her flesh. The sun was hardly awake yet, and already the temperature was nudging towards twenty degrees. A flock of birds in the trees above her head competed in a cacophony of song with the hum of voices beneath them.

A couple of SOCOs arrived, but there was no sign of their team leader, Jim McGlynn. Lottie hadn't the patience to hang around while they got the equipment sorted to erect a tent, so she breached the crime-scene tape and approached the body. Boyd walked in tandem with her.

'McGlynn would expect you to wait for him,' he said.

'What are you now, my mother?'

'I'll keep my mouth shut, so.'

'That'd be nice for a change.' She paused two feet from the stone slab and scrutinised the body. 'Jesus, Boyd. It's similar to the boy yesterday.'

I'm not sure I can handle much more of this, she thought as her heart lurched in her chest. One, two, three, she counted. Inhale.

Exhale. Inhale. When she felt the palpitations simmer down, she made her way forward.

The boy was lying on his back, and she could see he was young. Maybe eleven or twelve. Naked except for a pair of football shorts. His tightly cropped ginger hair glinted like sharp spikes under the rising sunshine. Wild flowers circled his head. Similar to the flowers where Mikey Driscoll had been found.

She shivered as if a shard of ice had pierced her heart. This boy reminded her of her brother. Eddie had been that age when she'd last seen him, over forty years ago. An imp. Cheeky and carefree. That was until their father had taken his own life. Or had he been murdered too? She had yet to get to the truth of that story. If her father hadn't died, how would Eddie have turned out? What would his life have been like if he hadn't been consigned to that institution of horror and murdered at the hands of a paedophile priest? She knew the blame did not all rest with her father's suicide. One day she would discover the full truth.

'Are you okay?' Boyd said.

She quickly shrugged off the shadow of the past, which was closing over her like an advancing avalanche, and concentrated on the boy in front of her.

'His neck is broken,' Boyd said, circling the stone.

'Thanks, Sherlock.' She moved anticlockwise and met him at the boy's head. 'He's so clean … almost as if he's been washed. I doubt we'll find any DNA worth talking about.' She pointed. 'Look there. Bruising on his upper arms.'

She heard a commotion behind her.

'Get out of my crime scene.'

Jim McGlynn appeared, panting and suited up, mask in place, sharp green eyes dancing with fire.

'Just having a cursory look,' Lottie said. 'The boy's mouth is hanging slack. Check inside for any foreign fluids.'

'I know my job without you having to tell me how to do it.' McGlynn opened his forensic case. 'Out of my way.'

'Wait a minute,' Lottie said. 'What's that in his hand?' She edged closer to the body.

'Don't touch it,' McGlynn said.

'I wasn't going to.'

'You could be walking on footprints, destroying evidence. Move away.'

'The ground is rock hard.' But she relented and took a step back. 'Can you open up his fist?'

With a sigh, McGlynn lifted the boy's arm with his gloved hand and prised open the fingers. With a pair of tweezers, he extracted a trio of buttercups, petals crushed and veined. He dropped them into an evidence bag and made a note on the outside.

'What's that about?' Lottie turned to Boyd.

'Maybe he grabbed them while he was lying on the ground?'

Lottie glanced around at the hard, gritted lake shore. 'Not from here. And those flowers around his head aren't from here either. Any idea how long he's been dead?' She waited as McGlynn shifted the boy onto his side and inserted a thermometer. 'And I don't need any technical mumbo-jumbo.'

After half a minute, McGlynn said, 'Five hours give or take, but the state pathologist will provide a more accurate timeline when she carries out the post-mortem. I can tell you that he was moved to this stone after death. No knowing where he was before that, is there?'

Lottie shook her head. 'Thanks. I'll call in Jane.'

McGlynn continued. 'I suspect a hyoid bone fracture, but the pathologist can confirm that when she opens him up.' He traced a gloved finger in the air over the neck area. 'Evidence of fingernail scratches. Could be the lad's own as he struggled, or if you're lucky, the assailant's.'

'Knowing my luck …' Lottie began.

'Knowing your luck …' Boyd said.

'I'll put bags on his hands,' McGlynn said.

The protective suit was sticking to her like glue. She needed to get out of it quickly. 'Anything else of note before we leave?'

'I can't see any other external injuries except for the bruising. The soles of his feet are scratched, though. Maybe someone walked him to his death over that hard ground you mentioned.'

Lottie opened her mouth to speak.

McGlynn got in first. 'Don't worry. I'll bag them.'

'Thanks,' Lottie said.

She couldn't help a feeling of motherliness as she took a last look at the dead youngster. She had an insane urge to fetch a soft blanket and wrap it round him. She walked away before she could contaminate the scene further.

*

Toby Collins woke to the sound of a scream. He sat up straight in his bed and looked all around. Had the sound come from his own mouth? Maybe he'd had a nightmare. He shook his head. If he had been dreaming, he couldn't remember it.

A thin line of light shone through the slit between the hard cotton curtains and sliced the room in two. He sidled up against the wall, trying to get as far away from his brother's bed as he could manage.

Only a bedside cabinet and a strip of threadbare carpet separated the two single beds. Max was lying on his back, fully clothed and snoring. As Toby watched, he shifted onto his side and his loud breaths eased to a quiet wheeze. Loose change lay on the bed, and Toby could see a roll of notes sticking out of his brother's back pocket. He squinted. The outer one looked like a fifty. He could buy the latest version of *Call of Duty* or *FIFA* with that. His fingers tingled. Reached out. But he snatched his hand back. Max would kill him.

He wanted to pee, but he was afraid of waking his brother if he opened the door. When he'd heard Mikey was dead, he had thought he might never sleep again. But he had slept all night.

He got up on his knees and put his head under the curtain. Leaning on the sanded windowsill that his dad had never got around to varnishing, he stared out at the calm morning. Was it his fault Mikey was dead?

The pain in his groin increased. He'd have to go. He slid off the bed and went to the door. Max let out another snore. Toby opened the door, clenching his teeth as it creaked, and eased out onto the narrow carpeted landing. His parents' bedroom door was closed, as was the door to his little sisters' room. The toilet door was open. He rushed in and relieved himself, then sat on the stained linoleum and cried for Mikey.

Who was he going to play with now?

CHAPTER TWENTY-NINE

Sitting behind the reception desk, Garda Gilly O'Donoghue scratched the side of her face, careful not to nick the spot that had sprouted during the night. She really needed to watch her diet. Kirby was a devil for late-night takeaways. Her constant moaning about his eating habits had little effect. She didn't think he would change a lifetime's habits for her or anyone else. Kirby would always be just … Kirby. And she loved him just the way he was.

But now she felt the morning going from bad to worse as a woman rushed through the door clutching a crumpled photograph.

'You have to find him. This is his photo. Take it. I know it's not great. I printed it off from my phone. It's black and white – we don't have a colour printer – but he's a colourful lad. Always laughing and joking. Most of the time. Please, do something …' Her voice rose with each word.

'Wait a minute,' Gilly said in a soft tone, hoping to calm the hysterical woman as a man came up and put his arm around the woman's shoulders.

'Our son is missing,' he said.

'What's your name?'

'Victor Shanley. This is my wife, Sheila. Kevin never came home last night.'

'Right.' Gilly picked up her pen and put her hand out for the photograph. The ink came away on her fingertips. 'What's your son's full name?'

'Kevin Joseph Shanley,' Sheila said. 'He's only eleven. He went out yesterday afternoon to play football with his friends but he never came home. I assumed he was at a friend's house and we spent all night ringing around, but no one remembers seeing him and he didn't stay with any of his friends and ... oh God, I don't know what to think.'

'Did you ring in earlier? To report him missing?' Even with the glass partition, Gilly could smell stale alcohol. She wasn't sure if it was from both of them or from Sheila Shanley alone.

'Yes, around three this morning. A squad car with two guards arrived and said they'd drive around looking for him. Said he was probably at a cider party down by the canal.' Sheila collapsed against her husband. 'Kev's not that kind of boy. He's only eleven.'

'Did they report back in about it?' Victor said. 'We need to find him.'

'Give me a second.' Gilly keyed the boy's name into the computer. It was there all right. Entered at 3.15 a.m. But there was no action noted. Shit. 'Have a seat in the waiting room. I'll get someone to take over reception and then I'll come and talk to you.'

'You'd do better to get out there and look for my boy,' Victor said.

'He's a good boy. Never causes us any trouble,' Sheila was saying as Gilly opened the waiting-room door for them. 'Music. He loves music. Always streaming it on his computer. When he's not out playing football ...'

'Take a seat and I'll be back with you in two minutes. Do you want some tea?'

'I want my son.'

Gilly closed over the door. She hoped the lad would turn up alive and well, but then she thought of the body that had sent half the force scurrying out to the lake earlier. Shit.

*

As Lottie made her way back through the cordoned-off area to the car, she spotted the fisherman who had found the body standing with Kirby and a group of uniforms.

'Daryl Cross?'

'That's me.' He twisted a canvas hat in his hands.

He was aged about forty, clean-shaven, and kitted out in all the regalia required for fishing. He reminded Lottie of her Adam.

'Those boats out on the lake.' She pointed. 'Were they there when you arrived this morning?'

'I was here at seven thirty. Took me ten minutes to unload the car and make my way to the mooring. I have the key to this particular dock. I locked it up at eleven last night. I can't say for sure there were boats already out, but I'd bet there were.'

'So why didn't one of those men find the body?' She was wondering if any of them had been on the lake during the night, and if they might have seen something.

Cross creased his brow and gave her a look.

'This isn't the only dock, you know. There are others all around the lake shore. There must be twenty miles of shoreline jutting in and out all over the place. Those boats could have set off from anywhere. This time of year, boats are out on the water all the time.'

Lottie scanned the area with steely eyes. 'All the time?'

'Most of the time. From early until late.'

She turned to Kirby. 'We need to speak to everyone who's out on the lake and try to find out who was fishing last night.'

'How the hell are we going to do that? Look around you. There are nooks and crannies everywhere.'

Cross said, 'You need a map with all the mooring areas marked out.'

Kirby's answer was to put a cigar into his mouth. Beads of perspiration were travelling at speed down his red face. 'And I suppose you have such a thing?'

Bending down to his fishing bag, Cross unzipped the front pocket and extracted a folded, tattered map. 'You could probably find it on Google, but I think this is clearer.' He handed it over.

'Get uniforms to each mooring dock and we'll organise it more comprehensively back at the station,' Lottie ordered.

Cross was scratching his head.

'What?'

'I should have said. The map shows only the public access points. I've no idea how you would find the dozens of private moorings.'

'Boyd?' Lottie called. He moved beside her. 'How can we find out all the access points to the lake shore?'

'No idea.'

Another, older fisherman stepped forward. 'There's the lord. He might know.'

Lottie squinted at him, the rising sun glinting in her eyes. 'The lord?'

'You know, the old guy at Swift House. Though I think he might be dead now. Heard his grandson lives there, but that might be fiction. Swift Dock is five hundred metres that way, but you can only access it via the private road.'

Lottie looked over at McGlynn and his team as they entered and exited the tent. The young boy was screened from prying eyes, but it would be a long time before she would get the image of a sacrificial lamb out of her head.

'Have you taken Mr Cross's statement and details? And those of the other men?'

Kirby said, 'I have.'

She turned to the fishermen. 'You can all go home. There'll be no fishing today, not from here anyway. And I would appreciate it if you didn't talk to the media on your way out. We have yet to identify the boy and inform his next of kin.'

Daryl Cross shook his head as he gathered his belongings and set off with his friends, flanked by uniformed officers.

Lottie tore off her protective clothing and dumped it in a paper bag held ready for her by a SOCO. Skirting the edge of the cordon, she walked to the water's edge. Soft foam frothed over pebbles as a warm breeze carried the scent of summer towards her. Swans were swimming around the boats.

Picking up a stone, she skimmed it out on the lake and watched the ripples extend. The boats were circling as men continued to fish. Was there someone out there who knew exactly what was going on? She had no idea, but she couldn't shake off the feeling that if they were dealing with the same killer, then he would strike again.

She looked over her shoulder. For a second she thought she could feel someone watching her.

I came back to the lake. Waited and watched.

He looked so beautiful lying there with his fair skin and red hair, like an angel waiting for a cloud to carry him to the heavens.

And then the fisherman with his arms full of equipment and jangling his keys made his way to open up the dock. What a shock he must have received when he saw what I had left out on display.

I hopped silently from foot to foot, watching and savouring his horror and panic. But I didn't feel any empathy or sorrow for him. My thoughts were already on my next target.

The horrors that were visited on me and mine must not go on. The demons that convulsed my soul are being sated.

I gripped one hand with the other and made a prayer temple with my fingers. But I didn't pray to any God in the heavens.

I prayed to the fires of hell to save me from my suffering.

I turned away, the long, dry grass crunching under my feet. I had no fear that anyone would hear or see me. They were all otherwise engaged.

CHAPTER THIRTY

Toby brushed his teeth. He knew they stuck out, and he wondered how he'd never been branded with a nickname. Something like Bugs Bunny. His brother was called Birdy because he had a nose like a beak. His granny had once had a dog called Toby, so his ma had told him. It had died the day he was born. His gran was so upset over the dog that his ma had called her new baby Toby in its memory. That was what he felt like now. A dead dog. Only he wasn't dead. His best friend was.

He put his mouth under the flowing water and rinsed his teeth. He turned off the tap and wiped his face with a towel, then went back to his bedroom. Max was still snoring. Hearing horses neighing up behind the houses, he went to the window. He wished someone would rescue them.

He smiled as he remembered the day he and Mikey had skipped school, robbed a bag of carrots from Supervalue and sneaked down by the canal where the horses were usually tethered. They'd fed a scabby piebald the whole bag. He'd love to do that again. And then he remembered. There would never be any more days like that.

'Toby? Are you getting up today?'

His ma.

He tried to answer. Opened his mouth and all. But nothing came out. He tried again, forcing sound from the back of his throat. A strangled groan began, then died. His eyes were spilling tears, his nose dripping snot, and his whole body was clogged with loneliness and sorrow.

He couldn't utter a word.

Not even a curse.

*

Acting Superintendent David McMahon was parading around the incident room as Lottie entered with her detectives. What the hell, she thought. He was in full dress uniform with his cap under his arm.

'What's the occasion?' She dumped her bag on the floor beside the top table.

'Some of us have a press conference to attend, and I don't want to be an ass turning up with no information. Tell me, what have you got for me?'

'It would help if I knew what the press conference was for.'

'Canal. Baby. Body. Soccer clubhouse. Another body.' He marched into her personal space, spittle landing on her cheek. 'Ring any bells in that empty skull of yours?'

Taking a deep breath, Lottie counted to three before exhaling. She wouldn't give him the satisfaction of seeing her retaliate, or step away.

'I've been at the scene of another suspicious death. If you give me five minutes, I'll gather the information for—'

'Five minutes? I haven't got five seconds. I'm supposed to be down there by now.' He made to walk away but turned back. 'What suspicious death?'

If you hadn't been dousing yourself with deodorant, she was going to say, you'd know. But she stopped herself just in time.

'The body of a young boy was found this morning at seven forty-five. A local fisherman made the discovery at a private mooring area on a remote corner of Ladystown Lake.'

'That's all we need.'

'I don't think the lad asked to be murdered.'

'Murdered? You sure?'

'Not confirmed yet. But he had marks on his neck and arms, and he is dead.' She couldn't keep the sarcasm out of her tone. 'Hopefully the state pathologist will conduct a post-mortem soon. I'll know more then. But first I need to find out who he is.'

McMahon said, 'Get to it. I'll try to deflect the questions.'

'Hope your suit is made of Teflon, then.'

'What?'

'You're good at handling questions, sir.' Lottie recovered in time.

He paused. 'Any news on the girl who fled the hospital?'

'It's been a busy morning and I've yet to check on that.'

'I want her found and arrested immediately. She is our number one suspect for the baby's death, and maybe the boy's. In my press statement I'm going to mention that we have a suspect and we'll be making an arrest later today.'

'I don't think that's wise,' Lottie said, squaring her shoulders. 'We don't know where she is and we have nothing to link her to the dead baby, let alone to the Driscoll boy.'

'She walks in here covered in blood. Tells all and sundry that she killed someone, and doctors say she had recently given birth. How many years have you been a detective, Parker? Don't make me laugh. Find the evidence. I want her in a cell on my return. And don't forget, she could have killed those boys too.'

'I think you're being a bit hasty, but leave it with me and—'

Lottie couldn't let him get away with it, but she had no choice. He had left the room.

She pinned up a photo of the boy lying on the stone slab. Next to the body of the baby. Next to the body of Mikey Driscoll. Jane had planned to do both post-mortems this morning, but she'd had to leave the morgue to attend their most recent victim. More delays.

'Right, everyone. We have three suspicious deaths. Kirby, you go to the clubhouse as we discussed earlier, and then McDonald's, because that's the last known sighting of Mikey Driscoll. Boyd and I will find out what we can about the victim at the lake.'

'The two boys' deaths must be related,' Boyd said.

'I agree. We'll meet here later this afternoon to discuss our findings.'

'Fine,' Boyd said. But he didn't sound happy.

Lottie squared her shoulders. 'First off, we need to identify the baby. The lab will run the girl's DNA against the baby's once we have it. As usual they've got a backlog, so God only knows when we'll have their results.'

Lynch came in, her huge bump slowing her, and sat down.

'Lynch, will you liaise with the Duffys? Make sure Barry turns up for his interview, with one of his parents.'

'What about your Sean?' Lynch said.

'He's coming in later.' Lottie didn't want her son being interviewed formally, but she'd have to go by the book. Especially with Cynthia Rhodes sniffing around Boyd. She glanced over at him. He had his head studiously bowed. She continued.

'This latest victim. Has he been reported missing? Check the database on missing persons, local and national. We need to identify him. I want a decent photo circulated, one that doesn't look like a death mask.' She eyed the picture she had put on the board. No, that wouldn't work out in the public domain. 'Have we any witnesses who saw him at the lake? According to Jim McGlynn, he was possibly alive up to two a.m. Where was he? How did he get to the lake? Check CCTV, taxi drivers. And find anyone who might have been at the lake or on the lake road last night. Kirby, any luck with the fishermen?'

'I have uniforms waiting at all mooring points. Those we could find. Still have to locate Lord Muck and interview him.'

'What about all our other work?' Boyd said.

Making a nuisance of himself again, Lottie thought. 'Reassign it.'

'Sure,' he said, without confidence.

Lottie sighed. She needed him on side. Now more than ever. Shit, she needed a drink.

'And,' he added, 'we have to think seriously that this girl Hope killed the two boys.'

'Don't think it hasn't crossed my mind,' she said. She just hoped McMahon didn't spit it out in his press conference.

Just as Lottie was leaving the incident room, Garda Gilly O'Donoghue rushed in.

'I think I've found him.'

'Found who?'

'The boy at the lake.' Gilly paused to catch her breath. She walked to the incident board. Studied the death-mask photograph of the boy lying on the stone with his face to the sun. 'Kevin Shanley.' She shoved a photocopied image into Lottie's hand.

Lottie studied the monochrome photograph of the bright-eyed, smirking lad. Her hand trembled. It was their victim. Gilly handed over another page.

'The parents came in earlier this morning to declare him missing.' She filled Lottie in on the Shanleys' visit.

Lottie looked at her. 'Are you busy?'

'I'm on desk duty.'

'Okay. I'll see if I can get you relieved. I need extra bodies.' Seeing the look on Gilly's face, she added, 'I have enough dead bodies. I need ones that can help. You up for it?'

'Sure am.' Gilly smiled.

'Where are the parents?'

'Gone home. Will I send a family liaison officer?'

'We'll need to get someone from another district. Lynch has the training but she's conducting interviews. I'll head over with Boyd. You see if you can resurrect an active FLO.'

'The desk duty?' Gilly said.

'Leave it with me. First I'd better go and see the Shanleys.'

CHAPTER THIRTY-ONE

Detective Maria Lynch was as sick as the proverbial dog. She hoped she didn't look as green as she felt. Julia Duffy sat beside her son Barry in Interview Room 1. She was dressed in a tailored button-through red dress, with long red earrings and her hair groomed in an upstyle that Lynch coveted but could never manage with her own.

Barry looked more relaxed than when she'd seen him yesterday, which wasn't hard. He slouched in the chair, his hair combed to the side, but his eyes were like sharp stones, boring through her. What's your problem? she wondered. A young garda set up the recording equipment and Lynch began the interview.

'Mrs Duffy, do you consent to your son being interviewed in relation to the finding of the body of an infant yesterday morning at the canal?'

'We don't have any choice, do we?' Barry said.

'Barry!' Julia looked horrified. 'That's no way to speak to Detective Lynch. Please be polite.'

The room felt stifling. Lynch ran a finger around the neck of her shirt. She needed air. But she had to do this job first.

'You were with Sean Parker, fishing along the canal, halfway between the harbour bridge and the Dublin bridge. Is that right?'

'Right.'

'How did you come to find the body?'

'I didn't find it. Sean did. We were messing with cans, getting ready to go home, when a can hit something in the water. Something … caught in the reeds. Sean put out his rod and dragged it towards us. That's when we saw it was a … a baby.' His voice broke and the hard act cracked.

'It's okay. Take your time,' Lynch coaxed.

'That's all he knows,' Julia said.

'After you found the body, what did you do?' Lynch kept staring at the boy.

He shrugged, burying his chin into his chest. 'Sean called 999. And that's it.'

'Did you notice anyone else around?'

'No. Why?'

'Had you been there before? At that exact location?'

'I fish there sometimes. Trout come up the river from the fisheries nursery and swim into the canal. You can be lucky, but mainly it's just bream.'

'When were you last there?'

'Dunno. A few days ago. Saturday, maybe.' Barry looked up. 'Why are you asking me this? Loads of people know about that fishing spot.'

'But it was you and Sean who found the baby.' Lynch felt dizzy. She held the edge of the table to ensure she didn't topple to the floor. Damn Lottie Parker assigning her this case when she knew it would affect her. So insensitive.

'I don't know anything else.' Barry folded his arms. His mother fussed with a button on her dress and gathered her handbag to her chest, ready for flight.

'Can we go now?'

'Do you think you were meant to find the body?' Lynch said.

'What a stupid question!' Julia stood up. Lynch noticed how she was careful not to touch the chair or table. 'My son just happened to be fishing and his friend just happened to find the body. End of.'

End of? Lynch didn't think so. It was only beginning. 'You can go, for now. Will you consent to giving a sample for DNA testing? Just because we need to rule you out of any forensics we may uncover.'

Barry shrugged, but his mother said, 'I think you need a warrant for that, don't you?'

'It makes things easier for us if you consent.'

'He is not consenting.' Julia huffed towards the door.

'I don't mind. I'll do the DNA thing,' Barry said mildly.

Lynch sighed with relief. The uniformed garda got the kit and swabbed the inside of the boy's cheek.

'If you think of anything that might help this investigation, please contact me.' Lynch handed her card to the boy. 'Someone put that baby in the water. Either killed it or left it there to drown.' She slipped a photo of the dead infant from the file and turned it face up.

Had she gone too far? Barry paled and his mother's cheeks burned red.

'How dare you!' Julia said through clenched teeth. 'I'm getting my husband to file an official complaint against you.'

After Julia had dragged her son out the door, Lynch couldn't help thinking about the fact that she had said she'd get her husband to make the complaint. Why couldn't she do it herself if she was that annoyed? She left the young garda to complete the paperwork and rushed outside to get some air.

It was her final trimester and her morning sickness had returned with a vengeance. She couldn't wait for the baby to be born. And then she thought of the death picture of the canal baby, and promptly threw up her breakfast on the back steps of the station.

CHAPTER THIRTY-TWO

Toby sat at the table with a fork in his hand, moving the fried egg around and around on the plate.

'Eat up,' his mother said.

He couldn't tell her he wasn't hungry. Couldn't tell her he couldn't talk. All he could think of was that it was his fault that his best and only friend was dead.

Fuckity-fuck. He looked up quickly in case the words had actually come out of his mouth. But she had her back to him, stuffing her work apron into her bag.

'I'm finishing early today, so I'll be back by six,' she said. 'I'm sorry I can't stay at home with you. You'll be okay?'

He nodded.

She slid her arm around his shoulders and kissed his hair. 'Toby. I know it's going to be hard without Mikey. Just remember that he's with the angels and has no more worries.'

But I'm still here, Toby thought. And now I have all the worries.

'Max, pick up your sisters from the crèche later, and keep an eye on your brother. Don't be skiving off to town. The grass out the back needs mowing and your father will be home around three. Okay?'

Toby thought there was nothing worse than being put in the care of Max for the day. The door banged as his mother left. He knew she worked hard for them all. Especially since his dad had returned from peacekeeping duties in Syria and now spent most of his days at the bookie's and in the pub. He couldn't wait until he went back

to school. Then he remembered he'd be starting at the big school in
September. And he wouldn't have Mikey with him.

'Here's a fiver, Tobes,' Max said. 'Run down to the corner shop
and get me a chicken fillet roll. Don't be long. This hangover isn't
going to cure itself. Go on, move your arse.'

Toby grabbed the money, glad to have a reason to flee the increasingly confined atmosphere of the house. He knew there was a word
to describe that feeling. Something-phobia. He couldn't think of it.

But Mikey would have known.

Mikey knew everything.

*

Lottie wasn't sure how much longer she could do this kind of work.
Breaking bad news to distraught families.

The Shanleys lived in a four-bed house on Greenway Road. All
the houses were individual in style but similar in status. They exuded
their worth. The Shanleys' lawn was so neatly trimmed she thought
it might be AstroTurf. Two silver-coloured saloon cars stood in the
driveway. Sensible yet cool.

Inside, the easy feel continued until Lottie, followed by Boyd,
entered the crowded living room. Everyone froze before she even
opened her mouth. Instantly, she knew which of them was the boy's
mother. With a wail, Sheila Shanley crumpled into an armchair.

'Can we have a word with Mr and Mrs Shanley, please?' Lottie said.

A silent procession of visitors exited the room and out the front
door. Victor Shanley stood, hands thrust deep into his trouser
pockets, steeling himself for what was ahead. His chest strained
beneath the buttons of his short-sleeved blue shirt. Gym freak,
Lottie concluded.

'We're trying to organise searches. You know. In the fields, by the
canal. Anywhere really …' Victor stood awkwardly by his wife's chair.

Good God, Lottie thought. I hate this. She was about to shatter the tenuous hope of this family.

'I'm afraid—' she began, but before she could finish her sentence, Sheila sobbed loudly into the arm of the chair.

Boyd made to go and comfort her, but Victor instantly folded his body over hers. She was like a bird with an injured wing in his arms.

He stared up at Lottie, eyes deep and dark.

'Spit it out,' he said. 'Don't prolong our agony.'

'I'm so sorry to have to tell you this, but a short while ago we found the body of a young boy by the shore of Ladystown Lake.'

'It can't be our Kev.' Sheila raised her head, wild mane of hair flying outwards, eyes lined with day-old mascara. 'He can't swim. He wouldn't go near the lake. How would he get out there? This is bullshit. He's off playing football somewhere. You have it wrong. All wrong.'

Boyd stepped forward. 'I'm afraid the photograph you provided Garda O'Donoghue with matches the description of the body.'

'Get out.' Victor stood up and took a step forward. 'I don't want to hear any more shite out of you.'

Lottie noticed Boyd moving towards the door, but she sat down on the chair nearest to her. She wasn't budging.

'I know this is painful for you both, but I have to ask some questions.'

'Another time. Not now.' Victor's hard-man act instantly disintegrated. 'Please, can you just leave us alone?'

'We can't. Not yet. You see, the body of another boy was discovered yesterday and we need to find out if there is anything connecting the two deaths.'

'What are you talking about?' Sheila raised her head. 'I thought you said this boy … the one you think is my Kevin … that he drowned.'

'He was found at the lake all right. But we don't think he drowned. We have reason to believe his death is suspicious.'

'That other boy ... I heard about him on the news. He was murdered, wasn't he?' Victor said.

'We believe so,' Boyd replied.

'It's not confirmed as yet,' Lottie said, looking at him with a dagger stare.

'But how ... I don't understand.' Victor slumped down beside his wife. They clung to each other in disbelief.

Lottie leaned forward. 'When you reported Kevin missing, where did you think he had been?'

'He was out playing football. He never came home.'

'I know you called the station during the night, but you only reported him officially missing this morning. Why wait?'

'I thought he'd come home.'

'Did you have an argument?' Lottie caught the look passing between husband and wife. 'You had a row with Kevin and he ran off? Is that it?'

Sheila nodded.

'Has this happened before?'

Victor spoke up. 'A few times. Kevin's changed. Over the last year.'

'His mood has deteriorated since the school holidays began,' Sheila said. 'He's more withdrawn. In his room a lot. Not playing sports. I suppose I nagged him, the way a mother does, you know. The weather's been too nice to be stuck inside all the time.'

Lottie thought of Sean and his gaming. His only outlet had been hurling, and when he did go out to fish, he found a body. Life was too shit at times.

'Did you speak to his teachers about his behaviour?'

'I was called up to the school on a few occasions. Kev had been in a couple of rows. So unlike him.'

'I need a list of his friends,' Lottie said. 'Had he any new friends? Someone you might not have approved of, maybe?'

Sheila thought for a moment. 'No. If anything, he lost the few he had. He didn't even go to the soccer final on Sunday. I hope he still gets a medal. It might cheer him up.'

Lottie winced at the continued denial in Sheila's voice.

'Was Kevin on the same team as Mikey Driscoll?'

'He used to go to all the training sessions but over the last number of months he stopped, and on Sunday he refused to go to the match to support the team.'

'Did you ask why?'

'He was belligerent. Said it was none of my business. Can you believe that? From an eleven-year-old?'

'Did you punish him?' Maybe this was the reason for the boy being out at night.

'No, we did not,' Victor butted in. 'Sport is recreation, not compulsory. If my boy didn't want to play, he had a very good reason.'

'What reason?' Lottie persisted.

'I don't know. But what has that to do with the boy you found dead at the clubhouse?'

'Probably nothing. Just that Kev and Mikey played for the same team.' She caught another look passing between the Shanleys. 'Did you know Mikey Driscoll or his mum?'

Sheila dropped her head and began to sob again. Victor shook his quickly. 'I can't see what this has to do with anything. Can I see my boy?'

Lottie decided to let her question hang in the air. She would ask the difficult ones later. But she had a feeling there was a connection between the Shanleys and the Driscolls, apart from school and the soccer team. Whatever it might be, she would find out soon enough.

'Can I have a look in Kevin's room?'

'Why? What are you looking for?' Victor said. 'Kev wasn't into drugs if that's what you're thinking. He's just a kid.'

'I need to have a look,' Lottie said softly but firmly.

'You'd better not touch anything.'

'Does he have a phone? I might need to check his contacts.'

'I confiscated it a month ago,' Sheila said. 'Punishment for … Well, he stayed out half the night then too. But that time he came home.'

'He's only eleven. Were you concerned at his actions?'

'Like we told you,' Victor said, 'he had become difficult to manage.'

Lottie let it go. They were too upset. 'I would like to see his phone, though.'

Sheila said, 'He only used it for streaming music.'

'I'd like to check it all the same. And his computer.'

'His computer is up in his room,' Victor said.

'I'll head up there, then.'

'My son is gone.' Sheila buried her face in a tissue.

Lottie stood.

'I'll show you up.' Victor headed for the door.

'Stay with your wife. She needs you.'

He relented, his muscular arms hanging uselessly by his sides, his short fair hair damp with perspiration. 'Second on the left, beside the bathroom.'

Sheila's voice followed Lottie as she took off after Boyd.

'All I have left of my Kev is up in that room.'

A Liverpool FC duvet on the boy's single bed and a poster of the team on the wall told Lottie of his love of the sport. A bag was flung in the bottom of the wardrobe. She went through it and found football boots, an empty water bottle, a towel and a green kit which she had learned was the colour of the Munbally team.

Boyd was looking through the contents of the desk in the far corner.

'Big room,' Lottie said. 'Find anything?'

His long fingers nudged the mouse and an action game, paused in motion, filled the screen.

She looked over his shoulder. 'Sean has that game. It's online. We might be able to find out who Kevin interacted with.'

'I'll get our tech crew to have a look,' Boyd said.

'Remind me to ask Sheila for his phone again.'

'Eleven-year-olds with phones.' Boyd shook his head.

Lottie got down on her knees and scanned under the bed. One sock curled up in a ball, inside out, and plenty of dust. She flicked back the duvet and found the other sock. She smiled sadly and opened a drawer in the chest beside the bed.

'He was neat and tidy. For a boy. My Sean has his stuff littered from one end of the room to the other.' The three drawers held the boy's underwear, T-shirts and jogging pants. No white football shorts to be seen.

She went back to the wardrobe. Kevin's old school uniform hung beside his brand-new one. For the school he would never get to attend. She feathered her gloved fingers over it and tried to distance herself from the human side of what she was dealing with.

'You found nothing incriminating then?' Victor stood at the door.

'We are only trying to get a sense of your son,' Lottie said, unable to hide the defensiveness in her voice. 'Where is his school bag?'

Victor shrugged. 'Might be in the utility room. Haven't seen it since the holidays started. Sheila was going to buy his new books this week.'

'Can I have a look?' Lottie sidestepped past the boy's father and walked down the stairs.

In the utility room, she noticed the stack of bottles lined up along the wall. She had counted fourteen before Victor bulldozed in front of her.

'This is his bag.' He took down a red rucksack from a hook on the wall. 'Here, have a look. You won't find any drugs.'

'Mr Shanley,' Lottie sighed. 'I'm not looking for drugs. I'm trying to find a reason why someone would want to harm your son. And I want to discover who that might have been.'

'I know, I know.' He rubbed his face and pinched the bridge of his nose with his thumb and finger. 'His mother … Sheila … she didn't *get* Kevin. They were always rowing. But she loves him. Loved him.'

Lottie saw that he was staring at the line of bottles. 'Did you have a party recently?'

'I've been meaning to go to the bottle bank. Busy at work.'

He hadn't answered the question.

'Where do you work?'

He must have misheard her, Lottie thought, when he answered, 'Sweat-It-Out gym.'

'No, I wasn't asking where you work *out*. I meant where do you work?'

'That's where I work. I'm a personal trainer.'

Lottie raised an eyebrow towards Boyd standing at the door. Victor worked at the same gym as Mikey's mum. 'So you *do* know Jen Driscoll?'

'What's that got to do with anything?' The broad shoulders appeared to shrink in contradiction to his defiant question.

'I asked you earlier if you knew Mikey and his mum, and you denied it.'

'I didn't deny it. I just didn't say anything.'

True. 'Have you been round to the Driscolls' since yesterday?'

'No.'

'Why not?'

'I didn't hear about Mikey until this morning.'

'Right.' Lottie didn't believe that for a second.

'Do you think they could be connected?'

'What?'

'Their ... deaths. Mikey and Kevin?'

'I don't know. But I know this, Mr Shanley. I will be back to take a formal statement from you and your wife.'

'What for?'

'I believe you're withholding something. Think long and hard about this. I *will* find out who killed Kevin, so you better decide to ditch the lies and half-truths.'

Without another word, Lottie grabbed Kevin's school bag and walked out with Boyd, leaving Victor mouthing like a goldfish.

On her way to the front door, she glanced in at Sheila, huddled like a lost child in the armchair. Hair shrouding her face, shoulders heaving with her weeping.

'Our scene-of-crime officers will be here soon. They'll need to check the house. And I'm sending round a family liaison officer to stay with you for a few days. Get some rest. You'll need it.'

Victor opened the front door. Lottie stepped out into the welcome fresh air and blinding sunlight. She hadn't realised how dark it was inside the house.

'You'll need this,' Victor said. She took the small black iPhone from him. 'It's Kevin's. But he hasn't had it for the last month.'

'Why was it confiscated? What did he do to warrant that?'

'Like we told you already, he stayed out half the night.'

'What happened?'

'I can't rightly remember. And it doesn't matter now, does it? He's never coming back. Our Kev is gone forever.'

Lottie made her way to the car. Boyd opened the boot for her. She put Kevin's phone into an evidence bag and the rucksack into a larger paper bag. She placed both in the boot and slammed it shut. SOCOs could take the computer. Sooner rather than later.

With one last look at the smart lawn and Victor standing at the door, she shook her head and sat into the car, a hundred more questions for the Shanleys running through her head. What the hell was she missing here?

CHAPTER THIRTY-THREE

Sean Parker leaned back in Barry's leather gaming chair while his friend sat on a cushion on the floor. He had to admit, it felt a bit weird after all that had happened yesterday. They had a controller each and were playing *FIFA*. He'd rather be in his own room, but there was no space for the two of them at his gran's. The sooner they moved into the new house the better. Before he was done for murdering one or both of his sisters.

'It's unbearable,' he said.

'I'd like a sister,' Barry said.

'No you would not. Not like mine, anyway. They're always fighting. If it's not over make-up, it's over jeans or shoes. They never stop. Even baby Louis is getting fed up with it.'

'How do you know how a baby feels?' Barry said. 'Goal!'

'Shite, I wasn't watching my defender.' Sean gritted his teeth and tried to concentrate on the game. The screen must be sixty inches. It took up most of the wall. Lucky prick, he thought, envying all the luxury that Barry had. When they moved house, he was bagging the biggest room.

'Goal!' Barry screamed again.

'Ah, shit. Can we start again?'

The door opened.

'Hi, Mrs Duffy,' Sean said.

'You know you can call me Julia,' she said. 'What's all the noise about?'

'Sorry, Mrs Duffy ... I mean Julia. We're playing *FIFA*.'

'And I'm beating ten shades of shite out of him.'

'Barry! Language, please.'

'Sorry, Mum.'

'I have lemonade and biscuits for you in the sun room. Whenever you're ready.'

She left silently.

Lemonade? Sun room? Sean wondered if they would have a sun room in the new house. Somehow he doubted it.

'Feck the lemonade,' Barry said. 'Let's find somewhere to kick a real ball around.'

*

Bertie Harris was small and overweight, his appearance belying the fact that he was the under-twelves' assistant coach, as well as being caretaker, bar manager and jack-of-all-trades.

'Hard to get anyone to volunteer nowadays,' he said, unlocking the door.

Kirby followed him into the clubhouse. 'But you're paid, aren't you?' He reckoned Harris was aged anything from thirty to fifty years old. He cast a downward glance at his own rotund waist and wondered if Gilly saw him in the same way. He realised the other man was talking.

'Minimum wage. Better than nothing, I suppose.'

'What was on here, on Sunday night?'

'The boys' match finished around seven thirty, quarter to eight at the latest. It was nearly eight thirty by the time the last of the stragglers left. Then it was party time. Twenty-first birthday. Local girl. Natalie or Naomi or something fancy like that. Big crowd. Cheap booze. You know the score.'

'Did you go to McDonald's for the after-match grub?'

'I did. Went down to show my face but was back here by nine.'

'What time did the birthday party finish up?'

'One. Got everyone cleared out by one thirty.'

'And what time did you leave?'

'Locked the door at quarter to two and was home in my bed by two.'

'Can that be verified by anyone?'

Two beady eyes scrutinised Kirby. He didn't flinch. Bertie looked away first.

'Nah. Not really. Unless one of the nosy neighbours heard my car pull up. I live on my own.'

'Have you cleaned up the place yet?' Kirby found his feet sticking to the floor as he walked.

'Of course I have. I was in at eight yesterday morning and wasn't home till one. Just need to do the floors.'

'And you didn't notice anything unusual outside?'

Harris turned his head slightly. 'Like the boy's body? No, I did not see that. I was in here all the time. Parked out front, just like you.'

'You hadn't to use the bins? The recycling?' Surely he would at least have had to put the empties out, Kirby thought.

'All stacked up in the storeroom behind the bar. Was going to do it first thing this morning. But … well, you know why I couldn't.' Harris shook his head, flesh rolling at the back of his neck.

Kirby made up his mind to lose weight. He didn't want to end up looking like Harris in a few years.

He followed the man across an open-plan area with a bar on one side and tables and chairs lined up along the wall. Harris went through a door at the end of the room and switched on a light. The office was tiny. A single shelf bulged with ring folders and another shelf acted as a desk, holding an old-fashioned computer modem and bulky screen. The chair was small and swivelled on its wheels as Bertie sat down.

'So how can I help you?'

'I was hoping to get your CCTV footage,' Kirby said. 'From the cameras outside.'

'Why didn't you say so?' Bertie shuffled upwards and shoved Kirby back out the door. He opened a cupboard in the wall, revealing an array of high-tech equipment.

'Wow!' Kirby was impressed.

'Bells and whistles,' Bert said, flicking buttons on the screen. A DVD slid out of the side of the machine. 'The last week is on that. Take it.'

'Have you checked it?'

'No need. Only reason I'd have looked is if we had been broken into.'

'And this includes the coverage from the camera at the rear of the clubhouse?' Kirby couldn't believe his luck.

'It should do.'

When everything was locked up, Kirby said, 'Why not keep the CCTV equipment in the office?'

'Anyone wanting to break in would see the cameras, and the office is the obvious place to search for recordings. But I'm smarter than them.' A grin spread across Harris's flabby cheeks.

'You'll need to come in and give a formal statement.'

'Why? I'm after telling you everything.'

'Mikey Driscoll is dead. You were with the boys in McDonald's that evening. Can you remember anything about Mikey there?'

'No. The place was packed tight. I'm no help to your inquiries.'

'Let me be the judge of that. It's the last known sighting of the boy.'

'I can't remember seeing anything or anyone suspicious.'

'Our interview questions will determine what you did or did not see. Come in tomorrow morning. Won't take long. About an hour or so.'

'An hour?'

'Just turn up. Don't make me come looking for you.'

Outside, Kirby took another look at the area where Mikey's body had been found. The crime-scene tape hung limply and a scraggy cat stood looking at him, tail arched in warning.

'Shoo,' Kirby said, and headed for his car.

CHAPTER THIRTY-FOUR

After their visit to Kevin Shanley's parents, Lottie dropped Boyd at the station then headed for Tullamore.

The air in the morgue was the same as always. Pungent disinfectant masking the stench of death. Bright lights, clean tiles and sterile stainless-steel tables. It gave her the shivers. She hoped the post-mortem on the baby had finished, because she did not relish viewing it.

After robing up, she followed Jane Dore into the room. There, she was able to decipher the outline of the bodies lying on two steel tables. No sign of the baby. Good, she thought, and exhaled the breath that she'd taken on entering the room.

'Have you finished the baby's PM?'

'Yes,' Jane said.

'And?'

'Death by strangulation.'

'He didn't drown?'

'Already dead when he was put in the water.'

'Was he born alive?'

'Yes, but he only lived a few minutes. It's likely that a hand was clamped around his throat.'

'A hand?'

'Yes. The indents of the fingers go around the face and behind the ears.'

'Sweet Jesus. Some guy in a rage?'

'Or a mother who didn't want the burden of a child?'

Lottie was surprised. She knew the pathologist rarely made assumptions, and it was even rarer to hear emotion in her professional timbre.

'Anything to help us identify the mother?'

'I took blood for DNA comparison,' Jane said. 'You just need to find her.'

'The hospital will have a sample.' Lottie thought of Hope. 'No other foreign substances? Can you get fingerprints from the marks?' She knew she was grasping for a little light to shine on her investigation.

'No other substances, and I wouldn't bank on getting fingerprints. Plus, it's hard to say how long he had been in the water. It could be up to two days.' Jane turned away and moved towards the body on the nearest steel table.

'Have you started examining either of the boys?'

'The second one has only just arrived.' She pulled back the sheet on the nearer table. 'This is the body of Mikey Driscoll.'

Lottie felt the familiar gush of nausea, and her kidneys contracted. She didn't know if she wanted to vomit or pee.

'He was a good boy, according to his mother.'

Jane raised a perfectly plucked brow and leaned her head to one side.

'What?' Lottie said.

'I'm not sure you're going to like this.'

'Go ahead. After the last couple of days, I don't think anything could shock me.'

Jane consulted her notes. 'First, the cause of death. Damage to the thyroid cartilage. He was strangled.'

'Like the baby,' Lottie said.

Jane nodded. 'The lividity patterns suggest he was murdered elsewhere.' She pointed these out to Lottie.

'Any forensic material recovered?'

'It's likely that his body was sponge-washed. I found a particle of yellow foam in one ear.'

'Shit.' What kind of sick bastard was she dealing with? Lottie shook her head.

Jane glanced over. 'Now, the thing that makes me wonder ...'

Lottie held her breath as the pathologist turned the body on its side. She caught Jane's eye above the mouth mask, staring at her, pleading. For what? That whatever she was about to announce might not be true? She exhaled. 'Go on.'

'Significant tissue damage. Internal and external.'

'He was eleven, for fuck's sake.' Lottie felt the hairs on her arms rise in protest, and a prickle knotted the hairs on the back of her neck, as though a thorn bush had taken hold of her. Her internal organs were fighting to release fluids. She held her gloved hand to her masked mouth. She had to get out of the room.

'I know,' Jane said.

'Recent or historical?'

'Both. But nothing in the hours prior to death. There are no bodily fluids present to check for DNA.'

'Oh God. His poor mother. Jesus, Jane, give me something. These crimes must be related.'

The pathologist walked over to the other table.

'I have yet to start on the second boy, but I did a quick visual check on the body. I am not one to suspect or assume, you know that.'

'Just this once,' Lottie said. 'Might give me an idea of what I'm dealing with.'

'Okay. I believe he was also strangled, and he has similar internal injuries.' Jane pulled down the sheet and turned the body on its side. 'That's just from an initial examination. And, he was not murdered where he was found. This is similar to the first body. I'm going to start the full post-mortem once I finish the paperwork for the other victims. I'll know more after that.'

Turning around, Lottie sought out a bin, pulled down her mask and vomited bile into the receptacle.

'He had flowers in his hand,' she said, wiping her mouth, 'and laid out around his head.'

'Sent to the lab.'

'Any signs of a struggle?'

'None on either boy.'

'So, they went willingly with their killer. Someone they trusted? Someone known to both boys?'

'That's your job, Lottie. Do you want to remain here while I do mine?'

'No. I need to have a word with Jen Driscoll,' Lottie said. And after that, she would visit the Shanleys again.

She escaped out of the cold room into the blazing sunshine.

CHAPTER THIRTY-FIVE

Toby kicked the ball against the wall.

'Hey, you! Get away with that ball or I'll burst it.'

He looked up at the window where the neighbour had stuck her head out, curtains flying with her hair. He picked up the ball and turned away, walking across the green with his head down. Someone had cut the grass and bits stuck to his fake Converses. He missed having Mikey around.

He came to a stop at the edge of the green. Max was lounging against the wall smoking a roll-up. Probably weed, Toby thought.

'Come here!' Max shouted.

Shit.

'I said come here.'

No way out. Toby went over and stood in front of his brother.

'You never gave me back my change.'

Toby opened his mouth to say there was no change. The chicken roll cost five fifty. He'd had to put in fifty cents of his own. But he couldn't get the words out.

'You a dummy now? Where's me change?'

Toby started to walk away, but Max caught the neck of his T-shirt and hauled him up to his sour-smelling face. A pony clip-clopped down the footpath and Toby jumped out of the way, landing on top of Max. They both fell into the small rectangle of a front garden.

'You pair of shitheads. Get out of the way.' The rider dug his heels into the poor pony and trotted off down the path.

Max jumped up, hurdled the wall and gave chase.

Toby smiled to himself. It wasn't often he saw someone get the better of Max, but when they did, it gave him a good feeling. For a moment, he forgot that he was starving but couldn't eat. Forgot that he couldn't talk. Forgot that his best friend had been killed. And then he saw Barry Duffy and another lad walking towards him.

'How's it going?' Barry said.

Toby shrugged.

'We're going to the field. Kick-around. You want to come?'

Toby felt Barry's arm around his shoulders, fingers creasing into the back of his neck. Kneading.

He tried to say no, he didn't want to go. But nothing came out of his mouth and his feet belied his hesitancy. Barry often hung around their training sessions with his dad. He liked to give the impression he was helping out, but Toby knew he was a bully. Kicking and tripping when he thought none of the adults were watching.

Toby kept walking with Barry and his friend, down the footpath and around the back of the estate towards the field. Even though, more than anything, he wanted to turn and run away.

*

Lottie picked up Gilly O'Donoghue at the station and headed to Munbally Grove. Boyd was organising a team to contact the dead boys' teachers and classmates. It was proving difficult, as many of them were away on holiday.

Her stomach churned with the thoughts that someone had abused Mikey and Kevin. They were only little children. Jesus Christ!

Dolores opened Jen's door. Lottie followed her into the small living room.

She hardly recognised Mikey's mother. The woman had faded to a shrivelled, broken skeleton. She sat on a narrow, frayed armchair, a football hoodie around her shoulders, her fingers wrapped in a school sweater, her body rocking to some soundless tune. A mug of tea sat untouched on the coffee table in front of her.

Dolores stood in the doorway, pale-faced and helpless. 'She just sits there. Won't eat or drink. Says nothing. Only cries and sobs. It's heartbreaking.'

Lottie nodded to Dolores, gestured for Gilly to sit, then approached Jen. The woman's pain emanated from her and Lottie felt it piercing her skin.

'Jen? I need to have a word with you. This is my colleague, Garda Gilly O'Donoghue. If you need anything, Gilly can get it for you.'

The rocking continued. Tears fell. 'He was all I had. Who took my baby?'

'Can we talk? About Mikey.'

'He was a brilliant child. He was my boy. Why would someone do this to him? I don't want to live any more.' She leaned her head to one side and stared up at Lottie. Eyes red-rimmed from crying, full of sorrow and death. 'How can I live?'

'It's hard, I know. Just take each minute as it comes. I can't tell you it'll get easier, because the pain of loss will be with you forever. But it will become bearable. Sometime. In the future. Now? Now you have to grieve.' Lottie took Jen's cold hand in her own and gave it a warm squeeze.

'Thank you,' Jen said. 'For being honest with me.'

'I have to ask you questions, though. I know it seems heartless, but it's the only way I can find out why this happened to Mikey and discover the identity of the person who … who took him from you.'

Jen sat up a little straighter. The hoodie slipped from her shoulders. Lottie rearranged it, then sat on the coffee table as she waited for a response.

'Okay. Go ahead. Ask away.' Jen offered a weak smile. 'I want to talk about Mikey. I have to.'

Lottie blew out her cheeks. Took a deep breath. 'I have a list of people involved with the soccer club, but I'd like you to tell me the names of anyone who would have been in close contact with Mikey.'

Jen scrunched her eyebrows and squinted. 'Close contact? What do you mean?'

'People who would have, say, taught him in school, run after-school groups. That kind of thing.' Lottie indicated to Gilly to take notes.

Jen's hands were trembling. Her eyes were wild and round. 'You think someone I know killed my boy?'

'We have to start somewhere.'

She sniffed back a sob. 'You have the names of those at the soccer club?'

'Yes, I got the official list. But you tell me.'

'I hardly ever went down there. I should have, I know. But I didn't.'

'Just tell me the names you remember Mikey mentioning.'

Another sniff. 'Rory Butler. He's the coach.'

'Has he been round here at all?'

'Rory?' Jen looked up, her tear-filled eyes incredulous. 'He's posh. No way would he call here.'

'Posh? How do you mean?'

'He's supposed to be well off and he has an English accent. Mikey tried to copy it one day.' She smiled sadly at the memory.

'Why would he be involved in the club?' Lottie wondered. The team were a group of misfits from what she'd heard. From the lower end of the social scale. She supposed that was why it was a big deal when they'd won the under-twelves final on Sunday. And Mikey had been instrumental in that success.

Jen shrugged and the hoodie slipped down again. 'You'd best ask him that, hadn't you?' She was silent, and Lottie waited her out. 'Maybe he felt he was contributing something to the community. What's that word millionaires use to describe themselves? The guys like Richard Branson?'

'Philanthropists. I'll be talking to Mr Butler. Who else?'

'Bertie Harris. Assistant coach, caretaker, bus driver. No, that's not right. Wes Finnegan is the bus driver.'

'Wes Finnegan? His name's not on the list.'

'He's a bit of a leech. Drives the bingo bus too. Gives me goose bumps. But I'd say he's harmless.'

Lottie shook her head. 'Leech' and 'harmless' didn't belong together in her vocabulary. Finnegan was definitely a man to be interviewed. 'Who else?'

'I'm not sure. Maybe Paul Duffy. He helps out at the matches. His son used to play but gave it up, I think. Dr Duffy stayed on to help the other teams.'

'Right,' Lottie said. She would pay the Duffys another visit. They might have seen someone acting suspiciously. Her mind was drawn back to the baby found in the canal by her son and Barry. Two tragedies in one day. 'Did Mikey say much about Barry Duffy?'

Jen tried to think, eyes closed. Shook her head. 'I don't recall. Sorry.'

'Was he close to any of the team staff? Did any of them pay him particular attention?'

Jen shook her head. 'I didn't go to his training sessions or matches. I had to work and … and then I had bingo. The pitch is only over the wall. I was sure he was safe. How wrong could I be?'

'Don't blame yourself. We're not sure his death had anything to do with the club. He was last seen in McDonald's, so it could be someone who saw him there or someone passing by in a car. We don't know yet.' Lottie made a mental note to check in with Kirby about the CCTV.

Jen said, 'I can't think of any other adults involved with the team. Have you interviewed all the parents and families?'

'We're conducting those interviews at the moment and speaking to supporters of the away team who travelled to Ragmullin.'

'And? Any leads?'

'Not yet, I'm afraid.' Lottie sighed. They had nothing so far, only another body. 'And school? How were things there? Were there any teachers or assistants Mikey was close to?'

'He had the same teacher for the last two years. Miss Conway. She's sixty if she's a day. He loved her.'

Lottie reminded herself to check with Boyd that he had contacted Miss Conway. He was working on the school list and more than likely was already on the phone to the teacher. 'Did Mikey brighten up much when the school holidays started?'

Jen thought for a moment. 'Actually, he seemed more distracted than usual. Spent a lot of time in his room. Gaming, he told me. I know it's not good for a young lad, but I had to work and he seemed contented enough to be doing that.'

'Who supervised him while you were at work?'

A deep flush crept up Jen's pale face and she shook her head. 'He was fine. Dolores kept an eye on him and I always had plenty of food prepared. I'm not a bad mother.'

'I'm not saying that, Jen. Just trying to establish if someone could have called in here while you were out.'

Dolores straightened her shoulders. 'I would have noticed if anyone called. My kitchen is to the front of my house. I can see the gate.'

'And you didn't notice anyone calling during the day while Jen was at work, or in the evenings when she was at bingo?'

The neighbour shrugged. 'Not that I can recall.'

'You go to bingo too, don't you? How many nights a week?'

A short silence ensued. Dolores was staring at Jen for advice. Jen spoke first. 'We go most nights. Nothing else to do here apart from the pub, and I don't like the pub scene.'

'So Mikey was alone a lot, is that correct?'

Jen nodded slowly. 'But he spent a lot of time with Toby Collins.'

'And did he know Kevin Shanley?'

Jen sat up straight, her eyes wary for the first time. 'Why are you asking about Kev?'

'I'm afraid we found his body this morning.'

'Oh my God!' Jen gasped. 'Poor Victor and Sheila!'

Dolores rushed to her friend's side. 'Shush, Jen, it's okay.'

The chime of the clock on the mantel pierced the air and Lottie jumped, knocking the cup of tea to the floor. 'I'm so sorry.'

'Leave it,' Jen said.

'I'll get a cloth.' Dolores rushed to the kitchen. Gilly stood up and followed her.

Jen curled into a ball on the chair and sobbed. 'Kevin and Mikey. Why?'

Lottie said, 'I'm doing my best to find out.'

'You'd better do more.'

'You mentioned the Shanleys by name. Do you know them?'

Jen clamped her lips together. Tears gathered at the corners of her mouth and dripped down her chin. 'I thought you were asking me about Mikey.'

'I'm trying to gain as much information as possible.'

'Kevin and Mikey are … were in the same class in school.'

'Was Kevin on the soccer team?'

'I think he left it.'

'Why?'

'I don't know. Ask them.'

Lottie felt her workload was getting more complicated by the minute. 'Can you tell me anything at all about the Shanleys?'

Jen turned her head away. 'Not really. We didn't know each other very well. Kevin and Mikey, they weren't that close. Sorry, I haven't any more to tell you.'

Dolores returned with a roll of kitchen paper and began to mop up the spilled tea. The room felt too small for them all.

Lottie moved towards the door. 'Ring me if you think of anything that might help us find who killed Mikey.'

She left to the sound of Jen's sobs. And realised she hadn't broached the subject of Mikey's abuse. The poor woman had enough to be concerned with at the moment.

CHAPTER THIRTY-SIX

Kirby was pacing around the incident room with a phone to his ear when Lottie arrived back at the station. After the encounter with Jen Driscoll, she hadn't the energy to face the Shanleys for a similar conversation. Later. Or tomorrow morning, maybe. Or she could send Kirby and Lynch.

Kirby hung up and filled Lottie in on his earlier conversation with Bertie Harris.

'A twenty-first party?' she said. 'How many people were at it?'

'That was Naomi Jones on the phone. It was her party. She reckons there were about sixty people there.'

'They'll all have to be identified and interviewed.' Lottie pulled at her straggly hair, feeling in dire need of a shower. 'We have dead bodies, a mountain of interviews to conduct and not one viable lead. Going around in circles, as usual.'

'I got the security recordings.' Kirby held up a disc.

Lottie rushed over to him. 'Well?'

'I'm not long back so I haven't had time to scroll through it. Next on my to-do list. Along with the McDonald's footage.'

'You got that?'

'And a complimentary Happy Meal.' Kirby smiled.

'Bump the CCTV job to the top of your list. Let me know if you find anything. Where did you get the clubhouse footage from?'

'Bertie Harris gave it to me, but I have to say, I found him to be a bit shifty.'

'Shifty? But he handed it over willingly, didn't he?'

'Might be his way of keeping below our radar. Especially as he had time to tamper with the footage.'

'Or he was just being helpful,' Lottie said.

'Or he knows there's nothing on it,' Boyd chipped in, rolling up his sleeves.

'I was just saying,' Kirby said.

'Check him out thoroughly,' Lottie said. 'After you've looked at the tape.'

'It's a DVD,' Boyd said.

Lottie walked off without answering him. Her entire body was screaming for rest. But there were too many dead bodies for her to take a break.

She returned after a moment.

'The two boys were sexually abused,' she said.

Her words were greeted with pin-dropping silence.

'Fuck,' Kirby said at last.

'And neither of the boys were murdered where they were found,' Lottie said, letting the matter of the abuse rest uneasily in the minds of the team.

'So we have to find a crime scene,' Boyd said.

'Any news from the school?'

'I spoke on the phone with Miss Conway, the boys' teacher,' Boyd said, shuffling papers on the desk. 'She retired in June, but she was very helpful. No mention of privacy or warrants for information, thank God. She's going into the school to get the records. I've sent Lynch to pick them up. And then we can organise interviews with kids, parents and teachers.'

'Come with me,' Lottie said.

'Where to?'

'We need to have a chat with Rory Butler, the team coach.' She fetched her bag. 'Wait till you hear where he lives.'

'I was going to grab some food,' Boyd said. 'I'm starving.'

'That can wait. And you're driving.'

*

Barry kept asking Toby questions about Mikey. Toby kept shrugging his shoulders. He couldn't talk about it. Couldn't talk at all.

'Do you play online?' Sean asked.

Toby nodded.

'*FIFA*?'

Toby nodded again.

'What else?'

A shrug.

'Jesus, you don't say much, do you?'

An incline of his head to one side. Even if he could talk, he didn't want to.

'I play *Call of Duty*,' Sean said.

'Me too,' Barry said. 'When we're not fishing babies out of the canal.' He laughed.

Toby didn't think there was anything funny about that.

'Shut up, Barry,' Sean said, and turned to Toby. 'Are you okay?'

Toby kicked the ball and ran after it. He wanted to get as far away from Barry as he could. He heard feet running behind him and looked over his shoulder as Barry slide-tackled him, knocking him to the ground. He twisted around on the freshly mown grass and tried to push the older boy off.

'Scaredy-cat.' Barry thumped him on the shoulder.

Sean tried to pull Barry away. 'Will you stop acting like a dick? You're scaring him.'

'Watch yourself or you might be next,' Barry whispered into Toby's ear before standing up and brushing grass off his clothes.

'What are you on about, Barry?' Sean asked, putting out a hand to drag Toby to his feet.

Yeah, what *are* you on about? Toby thought. He caught Barry looking around before leaning in.

'First it was Mikey Driscoll, then Kevin Shanley. Two friends of yours, weren't they, Toby boy?'

'Another boy's been murdered? Is that what you're saying?' Sean said.

'Yeah, last night. He was found out at Ladystown Lake. Heard it on the car radio with my mother this morning.'

'Was his name mentioned on the radio?' Sean said.

Barry touched his finger to his nose. 'For me to know and you to find out.' He grabbed the ball and kicked it down the field.

Sean took off after him. 'You're cheating. I wasn't ready.'

Toby slumped down on the ground and tugged a dandelion out of the grass. His breath caught somewhere in his throat and he couldn't breathe. He tried not to freak out, but it was hard.

Was it true? Was Kev dead too? Was it because of what had happened? And would he be next?

He didn't see the ball coming at him hard and fast, until it hit him smack in the face.

'Next goal wins,' Barry shouted.

*

Hope pushed Lexie on the swing in the overgrown garden. Houses on either side and to the rear. As much as she hated Munbally Grove, she wished she was back there. Away from Jacinta and her weed and booze. Home in her own bed and Lexie in hers. What had Robbie been thinking when he'd brought her here? He was afraid of the guards, he'd said. But why? She had done nothing wrong. Or had she? She'd run out of the hospital in a state of panic because she had no memory of what happened to her baby. But what had brought her to the garda station in the first place?

'Mummy, please slow down. I'll fall off.'

At the sound of Lexie's high-pitched squeal, Hope pulled the swing to her chest. She scooped up her daughter in her arms to return inside. Robbie stood blocking the door.

'What?' she said.

'You're on the news. Come inside, quick.'

'On the news?' She let Lexie slide to the ground and rushed in past her uncle. 'What are they saying?'

'You're a murderer now,' Jacinta drawled, smoke escaping from her lips like the tendrils of an evil spirit.

Hope stood on the threshold, mouth open, ears pinned, listening as the reporter streamed live news feed from outside Ragmullin garda station. A press conference had been held earlier that morning.

When the reporter had completed her ninety-second slot, Hope looked at Robbie, who was holding Lexie by the hand.

She said, 'I have to go home.'

CHAPTER THIRTY-SEVEN

Swift House was situated in an area that looked like something out of a Constable painting. Lottie surveyed her surroundings. Could someone have accessed the lake shore this way? She was certain this was close to where Kevin Shanley's body had been found.

Roses in full bloom threaded the hedges and the air throbbed with a floral scent. The house was three storeys high and a series of indents along the eaves gave it the appearance of a castle, with a turret on both ends. The brickwork on the outer walls looked ancient, but the windows were modern.

'I've lived in Ragmullin most of my life, and I've never seen this place,' she said.

'That's because it was almost a ruin up to a few years ago. I reconstructed it.'

Lottie turned on her heel. The voice had come from behind her. A head of dark brown hair had appeared over the top of a rose bush, followed by a face ringed with a trim beard. What Boyd called designer stubble. The man stood up, pulled off gardening gloves and made his way towards her, clad in a dirty white T-shirt and cargo shorts. Lottie thought he looked quite fit.

'Rory Butler.'

His hand was like a garden fork, with long, slender fingers, neatly clipped nails. All clean.

Lottie introduced herself and Boyd. Butler was in his thirties, and where there was no beard, his skin was clear. He had glittering blue eyes.

'You're a bit younger than I was expecting,' she said without thinking.

'And what *were* you expecting?'

'I don't know … An old man in a tweed suit with a rifle slung over his shoulder ready to go pheasant shooting?'

He laughed, and she felt like smiling, despite the horrors she was dealing with.

'You'd be thinking of my grandfather, then. My mother's father. Called Rory too. Rory Swift.' His eyes lit up when he smiled.

'And does your mother live here?'

'No. My father never took to the land. Pair of them hightailed it off to London first chance they got. I returned when my grandfather died three years ago and put my money into the place.'

'It looks great,' Lottie said, and wondered how she had been drawn into chit-chat. 'Is there somewhere we can talk? Out of the sun, maybe?'

'Forgive me, I forgot my manners. Come this way.'

He led them around the side of the house. A paved courtyard spread out before them, and Lottie marvelled at the expanse of modern equipment and furnishings.

He must have caught the expression in her eye. 'I like entertaining. Top-of-the-range barbecue. Good weather for it at the moment.'

'Gosh, you could fit a hundred people out here,' Boyd said.

'Slight exaggeration, but forty is comfortable.'

Rory directed them to a table with a parasol overhead, and Lottie flopped down on a cushioned chair. Her bones ached, and when Butler offered coffee, she hoped he'd bring out a sandwich or a few biscuits with it. But instead of going into the house, he sat himself down beside them and pressed a gold buzzer on the table. Boyd raised an eyebrow and she hoped he wouldn't blurt out a smart comment.

A young woman in jeans and white apron appeared and Butler asked her to make a pot of coffee. 'And see if you can find some cake.'

He turned back to Lottie. 'Now, what do you want with me?'

She decided to get straight to the point. 'You're the coach of the under-twelves soccer team, is that right?'

'Yes. Terrible about poor Mikey.'

'We have yet to interview you about Sunday night.'

'I had a phone call from one of your detectives to come in to make a statement. I was planning on doing it later today. Is that why you're here?'

'That and another matter.' Lottie dived in. 'This morning we found the body of a boy on the lake shore at the area known as Tudenham Point. Hadn't you heard?'

'Oh God, no. Who is it? What happened?' His face paled and he sat forward on the chair. 'Tudenham Point is only a few hundred metres from here via the shoreline. Further if you take the road.' He paused as if realisation had dawned. 'Surely you don't think I had anything to do with it?'

'I'm not saying that at all.' Lottie hoped the coffee would arrive soon. She was beginning to feel weak from hunger. 'How did you become involved with the team?'

'I volunteered. Needed something to do with my spare time. I play five-a-side soccer, and about a year and a half ago, someone mentioned that there was this team of youngsters from Munbally that needed a coach. I decided to give it a go.'

'What did you get out of it?'

'The satisfaction of seeing young lads out in the fresh air, playing as a team, competing and winning. It gave them purpose in their otherwise miserable lives.'

'You coached Mikey Driscoll?'

'I did. Great young footballer. And before you ask, I only knew him on the training ground.'

'What about Kevin Shanley?'

'Kevin? Is he the boy you found today?'

'Did you train him?'

'I did. But not recently. He only turned up now and again.'

'When did you last see them?'

'I saw Mikey on Sunday night. Haven't seen Kevin in weeks. He might have been at the match, but I don't know. It's awful. Do you have any leads?'

'We will have to conduct a formal interview with you.' Lottie wasn't about to give him any information. 'We were wondering if you know of any private access points around here.'

'Access points?'

'You know. To the lake. The area where we found the body is locked up at night, with no access unless someone either uses a boat or has the gate code. Therefore, we're looking for other routes that may have been used.'

He leaned back, as if his body was a spring uncoiling. The coffee arrived. He waited until cups were filled and cake was cut and they were settled again.

'You think someone used a boat?'

'That's one theory. The other is that they used your private road.'

'There are numerous mooring places around here. I have an old map inside somewhere. I'll root it out if you like?'

'That would be great.' Lottie sipped the coffee and savoured the aroma and taste. It was strong, just what she needed. 'Have you noticed any unusual activity over the last few nights?'

'Look around you,' he said. 'This place gives definition to solitude.'

'And still you build a patio to cater for forty people.' Lottie didn't intend to be sarcastic, but that was how it must have sounded. Butler put his cup on the table with a clatter. Was that a slight tremor in his hand?

'Inspector Parker, I am thirty-four years old. I left London but London didn't leave me. I like the peace here but I also like to party now and again.'

Defensive? Hmm. 'Forgive me if I was rude,' she said, wondering why she was suddenly mirroring his mode of speech. 'I was just making an observation. When was the last time you had people round?'

He shrugged his broad shoulders. 'A week ago, maybe ten days.'

'Do you have a partner? Girlfriend? Boyfriend?'

'I'm single. For the time being,' he said, a disarming glint in his eye.

Lottie felt herself blush. 'Is there anyone who can verify your whereabouts the last two nights?'

'I doubt it. As you can see, I live alone. Except for Helen, who comes in during the day.'

She would have to delve deeper on his alibi, but for now she needed to see how close he lived to the lake.

'We accessed your property via a local road off the main one. Does it continue to the shore?'

'The local road ends at the entrance to this estate. Then it's private. Doesn't stop people using it, though.'

Here was a man with connections to both dead boys and access to the lake. Lottie wondered why she hadn't got him in the station already.

'Did you hear a car or any other sounds last night?'

'I can't say that I did. You might have noticed I've had triple glazing installed throughout the house.'

No, she hadn't. After another sip of coffee, she glanced at Boyd, who was scoffing the last slice of cake.

'Can I have a walk down to the lake shore?' she asked Butler.

'Of course. Give me a moment to change and I'll go with you.'

When he had disappeared into the house, Boyd said, 'Charming young man.'

'Jesus, Boyd, you're as transparent as the glass on that table. Why don't you like him?'

'He's full of bullshit. Triple glazing? Where does he work? Where does his income come from? I'd like to know that.'

Lottie wasn't quick enough to warn him that Butler had returned.

'I've managed my own online insurance business since I was twenty-one. Quite successful. I'm sure you can read all about me on Wikipedia.' He was now wearing a crisp white shirt. He picked up his cup and drained it. 'Follow me.'

'This is a lovely time of the evening,' Butler said.

Lottie had to agree with him there. The water was like a mirror, its sheen reflecting the blue of the sky. A slight haze lingered over the centre of the lake, and she saw a few boats circling for fish. Two swans dipped their heads at the water's edge, flipped their black legs and glided away through the bank of reeds to her right.

She walked down to the rocky shore and gazed over to the left. Less than five hundred metres away she could see the area where they had found Kevin's body. It was still cordoned off, with a uniformed officer standing beside the tent. The air was eerily silent.

'So where is the mooring area for the boats that use this access to the lake?'

'Over there.' Butler pointed behind him, to the right. She followed the direction of his finger to where two boats were sheltered under a Perspex awning. There was space for two more.

'Are they yours?'

'They were my grandfather's. I haven't taken them out. The motors need to be serviced.'

'And those two spaces. Who uses them?'

'No one. I suppose most people keep their boats at home and tow them here for the day.'

'I don't see any cars here, so does that mean there's no one on the lake today who used this mooring?'

'Come with me.' Butler took off between two hedgerows.

Boyd fell into step before Lottie. 'He's a bit stuck-up, isn't he?' he whispered.

'Shut up, Boyd.'

'What's that you're saying?' Butler asked.

'Very cut up. The ground, I mean,' Lottie said, noticing the furrowed grass underfoot. 'We've had a week of mainly dry weather, so that's a bit unusual, isn't it?'

'Don't forget the three weeks of rain prior to that. And a couple of showers over the weekend.'

A clearing opened up in front of them. Three jeeps were parked end to end along the edge of a narrow roadway with grass growing up the centre.

'Do you know who these belong to?'

'No.'

'I thought this was a private area.'

'I have no way to stop people using it. They can drive right down to the shore, unhook their boat, then come back up here to park and head out fishing.'

Lottie looked around. The area was shaded with overhanging trees, but she could see that the shingle ground had numerous tyre tracks criss-crossing it. She photographed the registration numbers with her phone.

'Can you get us that map now?' she asked.

'It's up at the house.'

She tried to keep her eyes off his long, tanned legs as he walked ahead.

Lottie stood in awe. Boyd's jaw had dropped, so she clamped her own mouth shut. The inside of Rory Butler's house blinded her with brightness. The contemporary fittings were like something she had only seen in magazines. White, sterile and new.

'Gosh,' she said.

'The usual exclamation is "wow",' Butler laughed.

'Wow,' she said. 'It's so different from the outside. You'd never expect it to look like this.'

'An IKEA catalogue,' Boyd said, and Lottie glared at him.

'This is far from IKEA,' Rory said. 'Clean lines, pure white and very expensive.'

'And you did it all?'

'No,' he said. 'I just paid for it.'

He pressed a button on a remote control and a drawer slid outwards from what Lottie had thought was a wall. Everything was integrated. Butler nimbly feathered through the documents inside.

She gazed at the painting above the unit. Pale and abstract, it was framed in thick white timber with non-reflective glass. It was unsigned. Where had she seen something similar recently? She turned to ask him about it just as he stood up holding a map aloft.

'This is it. All marked out by my grandfather. Be careful with it. It's quite old. It details every point along the shore. I'm sure there are locations on it that you won't find online.'

Boyd took it. 'I'll make a copy at the station and get it back to you. You're sure there's no one to verify your whereabouts last night?'

Lottie saw Butler's eyes shift slowly from Boyd to her. A furrow deepened between his eyebrows.

'No. Why?' The worry was replaced by a crooked smile.

'You have access to the lake shore. We need to establish where you were last night and this morning.'

The smile left his face as quickly as if someone had slapped him.

'I was here, alone. Helen came in at nine. Do I need an alibi?'

'You knew both dead boys, Mikey Driscoll and Kevin Shanley. We need to ascertain where you were on Sunday night too.' Lottie folded her arms and leaned against one of the white units.

'If I'd known I'd need an alibi, I'd have ensured I had someone here with me.' His voice was guarded.

'I'm not accusing you of anything,' she said. 'You do understand that?'

'Look, I live by myself. I can't offer any alibi. Sorry.' He walked towards the door. 'Will you please send that map back in one piece. It is a family heirloom.'

'I'll bring it back,' Boyd said, 'personally.'

'When might you come in to the station to make a formal statement?' Lottie asked.

'Is tomorrow morning okay with you?'

'I'll see you at nine, then.'

They stepped outside. 'The roses are lovely,' Lottie said. 'Did you plant them all yourself?'

'Now you really are asking inane questions. Good day.'

Back at the car, she said, 'Why did you have to antagonise him?'

'Me? That arrogant son of a bitch is so far up his own hole, he—'

'That's enough. It's been a long day. I need to get home.'

Boyd drove in silence. Lottie drummed her fingers against the seat.

'Why spend all that money on renovating an old house out in the middle of nowhere?' she asked.

'I was thinking that,' Boyd said. 'He must have ploughed millions into it.'

'Could his business have been that profitable?'

'I'll run a check on him.'

'I think we have enough to be doing without concerning ourselves with Mr Butler's motives for redecorating his house.' Lottie gazed out at the waning sun. 'We have to find a murderer.'

'And Hope Cotter.'

*

Rory Butler watched from the window as the detectives drove away. Then, shoving his hands into his pockets, he sighed and went to his well-stocked bar. He poured a double measure of vodka and drank it neat before refilling the glass. The evening light cast a V of illumination, and dust rose like fireflies as he replaced the bottle on the shelf.

'Are you going to stand there like an idiot for the rest of the evening?'

He heard the voice behind him. He didn't turn around. He couldn't face anyone. Not with his eyes bulging with tears. Not now.

'Jesus, Rory. Don't be such a jerk.'

'Go away. Leave me alone. I can't deal with anything just now,' Rory said.

He heard the glass splintering before he realised he had flung it at the wall.

CHAPTER THIRTY-EIGHT

Garda Gilly O'Donoghue yawned. She'd been stuck back on the desk, but her shift was almost over.

'You believe the money was taken from your bus?'

'Yes, I'm sure it was.' His reply was more like a grunt than speech.

With her pen poised, Gilly eyed Mr Wesley Finnegan. Even though she was sitting behind the counter, she found herself looking at the top of his head. Five foot nothing, give or take an inch, she thought. His head was bald, sunburned and freckled. Stubble riddled his chin, and the collar of his checked shirt lay flat on the shoulders of his padded gilet. Bubbles of perspiration dotted his upper lip and he appeared nervous. She had seen or heard his name somewhere during the day. Was it in relation to the murder of the two boys? She needed to be sharper if she wanted to make detective.

'Why did you leave cash in your bus?' she said, trying to instil a modicum of enthusiasm into her jaded voice.

'That's where I always leave it.' Each word was accompanied by a breathless puff. A lifetime smoker, Gilly concluded.

'Not very clever.'

'Why do you say that?' His eyes scrunched together in indignation. 'I'm not stupid. It was in a cash box under my seat.'

'And you have regular customers. Any one of them would know where you keep your money. Did you think of that?'

'The bingo ladies?' He laughed. 'They're more concerned with their Sharpie markers and clipboards.'

'Right.' Gilly wrote on the incident report.

'You needn't be writing the bingo ladies down there. I know who took it.' This time Finnegan broke into a fit of coughing.

'You do?' Sighing, Gilly put down her pen, leaned back in her chair and crossed her arms.

'Sure I do.'

'If you know who it is, why don't you ask for the money back yourself?' It really had been one of those days.

'I want you to arrest him. That way I'll get my money back and he'll get a fright.'

'Are you going to tell me who this mysterious thief is?'

She watched as Finnegan ran a tobacco-stained finger under his nose, wiping away a non-existent drip. He chewed gum vigorously on one side of his mouth, glancing over his shoulder before leaning into the glass partition. Gilly instinctively recoiled.

'Max Collins. Goes by the name of Birdy sometimes.'

'And where does this Mr Collins live?' She blew out her cheeks and picked up her pen again.

'You'll have to find him yourselves, because I don't know. He's scum and probably has no fixed abode, as you call it.'

'Age?'

'Forty-six.'

'And what does he look like?'

'Wait a minute,' Finnegan said. 'Thought you were asking for *my* age. Birdy's around eighteen. Scar through his eyebrow and another on his cheek.' He drew his finger along his own jaw. 'Tall and stringy, but always clean, however he manages that.'

Gilly had had enough of this verbal sparring.

'I'll check him out.' She pushed the form out under the glass. This was just hearsay, with no evidence, but she wanted to get rid of Finnegan, finish her shift and go home to a nice cool shower. 'Sign your name there and fill in your phone number and address. I'll let you know if we find out anything.'

'I need that money. Motor tax is due on the bus. Don't want you lot fining me.' His laugh was short and stiff.

'We'll be in contact. And if you happen to bump into Mr Collins before we do, let us know.'

'Will do.'

Wesley Finnegan turned and headed for the door, and Gilly couldn't help feeling as if a slug had trekked slowly down her arm, leaving a trail of slime in its wake. She shivered. One of those days.

*

The incident room was winding down for the day. As she waited for the skeleton night shift, Lottie was taking school books out of Kevin Shanley's rucksack, flicking through the pages, searching for one little clue. But her mind was racing, reeling around like a roller coaster.

'I want a background check run on Rory Butler,' she said as she took another book out and opened it. 'I want to know who he is, where he's been and how he made his money.'

'I'll do that,' Boyd said eagerly.

'Victor Shanley worked with Jen Driscoll at the gym. That angle needs to be investigated. See if anything turns up in their private lives that would warrant the murder of their sons.' She turned to Kirby. 'Do you have anything for me?'

'I've gone through the clubhouse CCTV. Nothing. But there's a blip on the DVD. Every hour or so, it loses around ten minutes. Might be something. Might be nothing. I'm itemising the times and will go back to Bertie Harris.'

'Lynch. You met with the teacher?'

'Got the list of students and teachers. I've spoken with most of the staff. Some are abroad on holiday, so that rules them out for the murders.'

'Follow them up in any case. What about the boy's classmates and their parents?'

'I've organised a team of uniforms to do the interviews. A good few cross over with the soccer team and have already been spoken to.'

'Reduces your workload a little.' Lottie studied her pregnant detective. 'Are you feeling okay? You don't look the best.'

'Tired, that's all.'

'Maybe we've done enough for today. That work will still be here in the morning.'

'And we'll still have two dead boys and a dead baby,' Lynch said.

'Speaking of which, any sign of Hope Cotter or her uncle?'

Kirby spoke up. 'Robbie used to have a girlfriend. Lives in Athlone.'

'You need to go there and check.'

'But I still have the McDonald's CCTV to look at.'

'Priorities, Kirby,' Lottie said and picked up another book from the stack of Kevin's school things.

'Jesus Christ,' Lynch said, her face animated.

Kirby stood up. 'Is it the baby?'

'No, no. Bugger off, Kirby.' She held up a page. 'Boss, look at this. The list of staff at the school. Look who was a part-time cleaner.'

Lottie focused on the line that Lynch was pointing out.

'Hope Cotter. What the hell? This gives her another link to the boys.'

'What's the first one?' Kirby asked, shuffling an unlit cigar between his thick fingers.

'She lives in Munbally Grove.'

'But the Shanleys live in Greenway,' Boyd said.

'Yeah, but they can't have been there longer than a year. Before that, they lived in Munbally.'

'When did you find that out?'

She held up the school book. 'Kevin scribbled out his old address.' She showed them the inside cover. 'Munbally Grove.'

'Maybe that's why he dropped away from the football team. Moved to the other end of town. Didn't want to associate with them any more,' Boyd suggested.

'Or his parents were trying to get away from something. An affair, maybe?' Lottie said, thinking of her conversation with Victor Shanley and her suspicion that he had more than a working relationship with Jen Driscoll.

'You lot are going around in circles here.' McMahon was standing at the door. 'I thought Hope Cotter was your prime suspect?'

'Maybe, for the baby,' Lottie said.

Boyd said, 'I'm thinking more along the lines of Rory Butler, the football coach, for the boys' murders.'

'We're still in the process of gathering evidence,' Lottie said quickly.

'Gathering fucking moss, as far as I can see. Get the ball moving. I don't want to come in tomorrow morning to hear of another young lad lying dead somewhere. I have the media baying at me. You hear that? Baying. They want answers and I want a suspect in the cells. Those granite cells – which, I may add, cost a fortune – are bare. Budget's through the roof in this place. Through the fucking roof.' He caught his breath. 'I want a suspect and I want them charged and shining that granite with their arse.'

He glared at the incident board, which held photos of the dead but had yet to be adorned with images of any suspects, then strode out. He didn't even bang the door behind him.

'Well, you heard the man,' Lottie said. 'Before I finish for the day, I want to have a chat with Mikey's friend Toby Collins. Let's see if he knows anything about Kevin.'

*

As Julia Duffy waited for Paul to come home, she thought about how her life was shrivelling into a mouse-hole existence.

A dog was barking somewhere. Had been for the last hour. Children were bouncing on a trampoline at a house down the road. She fetched her noise-reduction headphones and slapped them on her head. That was better.

Dinner was prepared and on a low heat in the oven. She hoped Barry was in his room. On his computer playing some game, his fishing expeditions on hold for the foreseeable future. She didn't mind that he had been fishing, because it was better than roaming the streets. Wasn't it? No good would come of that carry-on. But it was just as well he was somewhere she could keep her eyes firmly on him. And she would hear if he left the house.

That thought prompted her to take off the headphones. She went up the stairs. Opened his door. Empty.

Where had he got to? She flew back downstairs, picked up her phone from the breakfast bar and called. No answer. He'd better be home before his father got here.

Paul would be back soon. She had to shower and make herself presentable.

She had to keep him happy.

Otherwise things might return to the way they were before.

CHAPTER THIRTY-NINE

Lottie pulled at her hair and ran a finger over her teeth. She was tired and frustrated with everything. Boyd parked the car and they went to the door.

A crowd of noisy kids were kicking a plastic Coke bottle around on the footpath. Others were screeching and screaming as they chased each other across the green. She would have smiled at their carefree abandon if she hadn't been weighted down with guilt over the lack of progress on her investigations.

But the kids were not alone. Most doorsteps held anxious mothers. Hunched, watchful, some with infants in their arms or rocking buggies with their feet. Eyes full of suspicion.

Lottie rang the doorbell.

She heard the clang of a chain being freed from a lock, and the door opened.

'Hello, Toby. Can we come in for a few minutes?'

She noticed the boy's face turn pale with wariness.

'It's okay. Nothing to be afraid of. I only want to talk about your friend Mikey. Is that all right with you?'

He bit his lip and opened the door wider.

The distinct odour of weed lingered in the hall, but the boy's eyes appeared clear, despite the dirt on his face, the state of his T-shirt and the rip in his jeans. His black Converse trainers, one without any laces, slapped against the floor tiles as he led her into the kitchen.

'Are your parents around?' she said as Boyd loitered beside the door.

Toby shook his head. Despite his height, he looked younger than eleven. A child, unable to halt the growth spurt. She instantly felt a deep sorrow for him. She pulled out a chair.

'Sit down, Toby.'

He slid onto it. Obedient. Lottie sat down opposite him.

'I just want to have a little chat with you. You know I'm trying to find whoever did that horrible thing to your friend?' She shouldn't be talking to him without a parent present, but she knew she could put up with the consequences if she got something from him.

He nodded. Fidgeted with his hands under the table. She noticed his shoulders quivering.

'Were you friends with Kevin, too?'

A nod.

'The three of you. You, Mikey and Kev. Were you all best friends?'

A shrug of the shoulders. What did that mean?

'Do you know why Kev's family moved out of Munbally?'

A head shake.

'Toby, why can't you talk to me?'

The boy's shoulders shrugged again and he looked up at her and then at Boyd. His mouth hung loose and his eyes swelled with terror. He was afraid to talk, Lottie realised. Shock? Or something else?

She chanced one final question. 'Do you know Hope Cotter?'

Toby jumped up and ran from the room, his face as white as a sheet.

Kirby had checked the McDonald's CCTV footage by the time Lottie and Boyd returned.

'Just had a quick look,' he said. 'I've scribbled down the times relevant to people who may be of interest.'

Lottie looked at the list. 'So, Mikey leaves the restaurant at nine ten p.m. Followed by Wes Finnegan a minute later. He's the bus driver?'

'Correct.'

'Then Rory Butler at nine sixteen.'

'Right. And the Duffys at nine eighteen.'

'Any sign of Bertie Harris?'

'I've footage from another camera to look at yet. This info is just from the side door.'

'Anything look suspicious to you?'

'I've checked from the time the crowd started to enter, right up to nine thirty, when most had left. The atmosphere seemed jolly and happy. Mikey was sitting on his own most of the time. Odd, seeing as he was the match-winner. But it is a bit blurry and I'm only seeing what went on at one side of the restaurant.'

'Okay. Have a full report in the morning. Any word from Athlone?'

'I got a phone number for this Jacinta Barnes. Was going to give her a call, see what she has to say and maybe drive over.'

'If she seems to be economical with the truth, head on over, but don't waste valuable time that you could be spending on important CCTV.'

'Righto, boss.'

CHAPTER FORTY

At seven o'clock, Gilly O'Donoghue handed over to Garda Thornton. At last her day was done. She headed downstairs to the locker room to pick up her bag and jacket. She was looking forward to having a cool drink with Kirby later. That put a smile on her face.

Outside, she walked straight into the bus driver who had reported the theft. What was his name? Des or Wes or something.

'Did you pick him up yet? The thieving bastard?'

'I'm off duty now, sir.'

'I just want to know if you got him.'

Gilly turned around as the man tugged on the strap of her bag. He dropped his hand immediately. She recalled his name then.

'Mr Finnegan, you need to understand that we're dealing with the deaths of two young boys, and things are quite hectic. I will look into your stolen cash tomorrow. But now I have to go.'

Marching off towards her car she had a quick look over her shoulder. He was still standing there holding a cigarette, sweating buckets, his mouth hanging open.

She drove out of the station and made her way down Main Street. She pulled up at the traffic lights, urging the red to turn green.

It was the scar that made her look twice. Exactly the same as the one that Wes had described. The teenager was walking along the footpath, hood up. As he crossed the road to head down Gaol Street, she saw his face. She was still in uniform. She could stop him. And then what?

When the lights changed, she took a right and drove slowly. At the courthouse, a giant crane hung precariously across the road. She parked up on the footpath and watched the boy in her rear-view mirror, hood pulled up despite the warmth of the evening. Maybe she should follow him. That might get Finnegan off her back.

She watched him meander down Gaol Street, and when she was sure of the direction he was taking, she took off after him.

At the greyhound stadium, she parked on double yellow lines. It was race evening and the area was buzzing with people and dogs.

She kept watch in her mirror. He had to walk this way. There was no other option. Unless he had spotted her. But suddenly, there he was. Strolling along as if he hadn't a care in the world. Well, Birdy, I know all about you, she thought. All that they had on PULSE, in any case.

She followed his route with her eyes. He passed her and turned into the industrial estate. Not much there, she thought. A few retail outlets and empty units, along with the road that circled the town, its tributaries criss-crossing back up to Main Street. Gilly's inquisitive nose had helped save an abducted young woman a few months ago, and it was once again itching with curiosity.

Putting the car in gear, she pulled out onto the road. By the time she'd negotiated the roundabout and driven into the industrial estate, Max Collins had disappeared.

'Where did you go?' she muttered in frustration.

After driving up and down twice, she gave up. He could be anywhere, and she was hungry. Kirby was calling round and she was cooking. Slimline tonight, my friend, she thought.

*

The events of the day lay heavy on Lottie's shoulders as she opened the front door of her mother's house. She heard the sound of voices coming from the living room. She couldn't face them yet. She needed to wash away the stench of death and the tears of broken families.

Rushing into her bedroom, she was immediately assaulted by its onslaught of nostalgic claustrophobia. Too many years she'd spent lying on that bed staring at the flowered wallpaper, which was still adorned with her posters of pop stars who were no longer stars and definitely not popping. Stripping off her clothes, she pulled on her mother's dressing gown and ran to the bathroom. At least in the new house she'd have an en suite. That's if she got to claim the largest room before either of the girls did.

Stepping out of the robe, she set the shower to full power and stood under the trickle of water. She needed to check that out in the new house too. Maybe she'd go for a run later and pop round. Anything to escape the constant chatter and rows. She closed her eyes and let the water slowly wash away the day.

Not that easy. She saw the baby. Defenceless. Dead. Why? By whose hand had he died? Who had slipped him in among the reeds hoping his little body might never be found? She'd have to speak to Father Joe again, about the girl he'd mentioned, the girl that she was sure was Hope Cotter. And why had Toby baulked the minute she'd mentioned Hope's name? Poor boy, he was in a state of trauma. He needed help. She'd speak with his parents. Tomorrow.

She stepped out onto the cold tiled floor and realised she'd forgotten to bring in a towel. Pulling on the robe, she ran back to the bedroom, leaving a trail of wet footprints behind her. Something else for her mother to give out about.

*

The shower was strong, and Toby closed his eyes and stood there letting the water pound down. The detective woman had scared him. Why was she asking about Hope?

'To-by. To-beee … Come out. We want to pee-pee.'

He switched off the water.

His little sisters, Meggy and Kim, were outside the door. They were two lovable nuisances. He dried himself and pulled on clean underwear and the grass-smudged jeans and T-shirt he'd been wearing all day. Didn't want his ma complaining about the amount of washing he generated.

Tugging a comb, thick with Max's hair, through his mop, he ran his fingers along the shaved edges above his ears. He'd have to use his dad's razor to tidy it up. He'd ask Max to do it. If he could catch him in a good mood.

He unlocked the bathroom door. The landing was empty. The little witches. He could hear someone moving around in the kitchen. His ma must be home. At least he wouldn't have to mind his sisters.

In his room, he sat on his bed and thought of Mikey and Kev. Then he thought of Rory. He'd be devastated, wouldn't he? Rory had looked out for them. But was that all there was to it? Coach caring for his players? Or was there something else? No. Rory was good. Wasn't he? He stopped the older lads picking on them, not that it happened much to Toby. Mikey had stood up for him too. He smiled, thinking how it would have been different today if Mikey had been with him. Barry shitface Duffy wouldn't have got away with pushing him around like that.

A shudder rattled Toby's shoulders and suddenly his skin froze. Inside, it was like he'd eaten beans and his belly was filled with curling wind so that he wanted to belch or fart or maybe just scream.

It was like a bird pecking at the back of his brain.

Telling him …

Telling him what?

To tell?

No.

Toby knew he could never do that.

He switched on his PlayStation. Well, it was really Max's because he'd paid for it, last Christmas. Probably killed him to spend the money, but Toby was grateful.

He brought up YouTube. Kev had loved YouTube. He was so into music. Toby noticed the trending video and clicked on it.

He blinked his eyes. It looked like a blurry copy of an original and it was only thirty seconds long. He hit the replay button. Oh God, he thought. That's Mikey. Dead. Jesus, Jesus, Jesus.

He had to get out.

*

The old tyre recycling depot, which had closed down two years ago, acted as Max's unofficial hideout. He sometimes stayed in the hostel on Kennedy Street, on the occasions when his dad kicked him out, but this was his secret go-to location. He was thin enough to ease between the doors held with a linked chain and lock. Once inside, he blinked to focus his eyes in the darkness and made his way to what had once been a partitioned office.

The floor safe was still intact and he'd had keys made. He opened it up and took out his earnings. Counted it all. He added the money he'd stolen from Wes Finnegan's bus. Soon he would have enough. But he wanted to have more than enough. It wasn't greed. It was survival. To ensure his escape forever. For the two of them.

The old corrugated doors screeched and the chain lock strained. Hurriedly he secured his money, locked the safe and hid the keys.

Looking out through the broken glass partition of the office, he saw the man enter. Max stood tall and his heart hardened. This was a job; he was no longer lost and vulnerable like he used to be. Only a select few knew where to find him. Slowly he left his hiding place.

'Over here, you scum of the earth. Quickly. No slacking. Run.'

Max stood unmoving. You can wait, shithead, he thought.

'I said run, you lazy tart.'

A fifty-euro note was held out.

Max moved forward.

'I hear you have a younger brother.'

'Fuck off,' Max said, watching as the note was waved in front of him.

'That's no way to speak to your elders. You need to learn some respect.'

Max stuck his hands into his jeans pockets. There was no way anyone was getting their slimy paws on Toby.

The face before him smirked. 'Toby. That's his name, isn't it? I know you've been thieving. I know you need money. There's plenty more where this came from.'

Max said nothing.

The money was pocketed. 'I want Toby. I'll be back tomorrow night. And you'd better bring him to me. If you don't, I might start looking at one of your little sisters.'

'You keep your filthy paws off my sisters.'

'Do what I say, then.'

'How much?' Max heard himself ask.

CHAPTER FORTY-ONE

'Are you working tonight?' Lottie asked as Chloe walked into the kitchen dressed in tight jeans and a white shirt with the top three buttons undone. She could see the red lace of her bra peeking out.

'Yeah, I am.' Chloe munched on a raw carrot.

'But it's Tuesday.'

'Gosh, I'm so lucky to have a detective mother.'

'Leave her alone,' Rose piped up. She was combing her short silver hair at the mirror out in the hall.

'She's my daughter,' Lottie said. 'I didn't think they'd be busy midweek.'

'I was asked to come in, and I'll get paid, busy or not.' Chloe dumped the end of the carrot into the bin.

'Put that in the compost,' Rose said.

'Has she eyes in the back of her head?' Chloe whispered to Lottie.

Lottie smiled at her daughter. 'Don't be late. Here. I'll give you money for a taxi.'

'Have my own money, thanks.' Chloe pulled on a denim jacket and swaggered out of the kitchen.

'Don't be late.'

'You said that already. Bye, Gran.' The door banged.

'You need to give your kids more leeway. They're growing up.'

Lottie bit back her retort. She wasn't in the mood for a row with her mother. She'd pulled on running bottoms and a Nike top after her shower. She'd only just eaten dry lasagne that had spent the better part of the day in the oven, but she needed to get out.

'I'm going for a run.'

'You've just eaten.'

Tell me something I don't know, Mother. She hoped she hadn't said that out loud as she made for the front door.

She paused. 'Where's Sean?'

'He's over at his friend's house.'

'What friend?' Lottie felt the hair on the back of her neck stand to attention.

'Barry. The lad he went fishing with yesterday. Any news on that unfortunate baby?'

'No news.' She pulled the door closed behind her and walked slowly down the path. Once she was out on the road, she started to jog. She wasn't at all sure about Sean's friendship with Barry. Jen Driscoll had said that Dr Duffy was involved with the under-twelves soccer team. Another interview to add to the list. She would ask the good doctor about his motives then. And Rory Butler had better turn up tomorrow, or she'd be issuing him with an arrest warrant.

She rang Boyd to see if he would run with her. He answered but said he was out. She hung up without asking what 'out' meant. An aching loneliness replaced the fatigue in her bones.

She inhaled the scent of cut grass. Eyeing the sun dipping behind the fields to the rear of her mother's house, she remembered that she'd been planning to run down to the new house to see how Ben was getting on. That was an idea. She began a slow jog, and with each step she found a renewed energy, her steps becoming fluid and strong.

She passed the old tobacco factory, noting signs of recent construction. Maybe at last the town was picking up. At the Dublin

Bridge, she could see the crane standing tall at the courthouse, like gallows hanging over the townscape. Before she realised where she was going, she found herself at the entrance to Munbally Grove. And in the evening air, she smelled something she couldn't identify.

She slowed down slightly but continued to jog. Down through the maze of houses, built so close she imagined you could hear your next-door neighbour boiling a kettle or snoring during the night. Children were playing football in one of the small green areas in front of a semicircle of houses. Parents standing guard at their front doors. That was what she could smell. Fear.

Her heart tightened and she had to count her breaths to keep moving. A baby and two boys had been murdered, and it was her responsibility to find the killer or killers. The burden of that task was more evident as she felt the pull of scared eyes tracking her movement.

She had to get out of here.

Turning right, she found herself on an identical close. She made another right. Up towards the football pitch and clubhouse. Where they'd found Mikey Driscoll. It was dusk, with the yellow hue of the street lights casting long shadows over the pitch. She paused at the gate, peered over at the crime-scene tape her officers had erected, swinging lightly in the soft breeze.

Tugging the gate, she saw it was locked. Pity it hadn't been locked on Sunday night. She climbed the small wall and vaulted down into the grounds. At the rear of the clubhouse she looked around. Tried to see the scene through the eyes of the killer.

What made you bring the boy here? You didn't kill him here, we know that, she thought. Jane Dore had told her that Mikey's and Kevin's bodies had evidence they had been murdered elsewhere. She looked up at the cameras. Why take the risk of moving a body?

Unless you knew they couldn't capture your image from there. Hopefully Kirby would have something for her in the morning.

Dipping under the garda tape, she stood where she imagined the killer had stood after laying Mikey Driscoll on the grassy bank. Among the waste bins. Was there a subliminal message there? Detritus beside growth. The body laid out among the flowers, ready to be found. Not hidden. Not dumped in one of the bins. She pressed her fingers into her temples. And then thought of Kevin Shanley. Out on a rock at the lake. Also surrounded by a halo of flowers. She shook her head. There was something in that thought but she couldn't figure it out. Maybe in the morning, when her brain was fresher. Yes, Mikey Driscoll, I will find who did this to you, and to Kevin Shanley. And then she remembered the baby dumped in the canal.

With a sigh, she turned back, over the wall and out onto the road. She jogged into town. As she moved down through Friars Street, she noticed a man standing, lips moving as if he was interrogating the twin brass monks with their hollow eyes watching over the town.

It takes all sorts, her mother would say.

Now she had to be the eyes of the town. She had to stop this killer before another young resident was murdered. And with that thought, the weight in her legs returned and she slowed to a walk as she headed towards her new home.

A light was on, and through the window she could see Ben Lynch on a stepladder, painting the sitting-room ceiling.

She paused. Should she call in and see how he was getting on? Maria had been so difficult recently, more so than usual. It was late, and maybe this was not a good idea. But she needed to talk to someone.

She knocked on the window.

*

Leo Belfield wasn't at all sure he liked the small-town feel of Rag-mullin. A million miles away from the towering architecture he was used to.

He had walked around all day, sourcing information. Hired a car. Driven for miles. Finally got used to driving on the left-hand side of the road, steering from the opposite side of the car than at home in the States.

Papers hidden by his mother, Alexis, had led him here and he needed to find out what they meant. From what he'd discovered, this was Alexis's home town, and it was possible he had a half-sister. Was it Lottie Parker? He had to talk to her, but with no idea how he was going to approach her, he'd decided to don his detective's hat and do some digging.

And his first source was someone who was good at digging too. A journalist.

*

Sean hadn't wanted to stay at Barry's for dinner.

'It's okay, Mrs Duffy. My gran cooks every day. She'll be put out if I don't eat there.'

'I have enough for everyone. Please stay. I like it when Barry has friends round, which is not very often.'

Sean caught Julia giving Barry a sideways look, but he couldn't read what the unspoken message was. He glanced at his phone, wondering why his mum hadn't rung him to check up on him.

'All right so,' he said, and reluctantly took his seat at the table.

'Did you wash your hands?' Paul said.

He hadn't, but he didn't want to have to get up again, so he nodded. He was still thinking about the way Barry had treated that young lad, Toby, earlier. It wasn't nice and he didn't like being part of bullying. Maybe he should have stood up for him. But then Toby had run off. He'd check up on him tomorrow. See if he was okay. He must live somewhere near the field.

'Sean?'

He realised Julia was speaking to him. 'Sorry. I was miles away.'

'We always say grace. Bow your head.'

Sean didn't like being told what to do, but he was in someone else's house and he'd been brought up to respect other people's beliefs.

Paul Duffy clasped his hand. Julia said a prayer he had never heard before. And then his hand was released and he realised he was expected to bless himself and hoped he was doing it properly.

'What did you boys do this afternoon?' Julia said. 'I thought you were in your room, Barry. I was surprised to realise you'd gone out.'

'It's too warm to be cooped up all day,' Barry said.

'You didn't answer your mother's question,' Paul said.

Sean butted in, 'We were playing football.'

'Yeah,' Barry said. 'Down near where the boy was found dead.'

'I don't know what this town is coming to,' Julia said, putting down her fork. 'First a baby, and then that boy.'

'And another one was found today,' Paul said.

'That's just awful.'

Sean didn't like the food. It tasted of … nothing. Some health-food junk. Bits of stuff that looked like breadcrumbs and tasted how he thought sawdust might taste. And a plate of green stuff. Yuck. His gran's lasagne would have been a whole lot nicer. He tuned out the conversation and concentrated on moving the food around the plate to make it look like he was eating.

'Are you not hungry?' Julia said.

Caught out. 'Not really.'

'I have Greek yoghurt and wild berries for desert. Would you like that?'

Laying down his cutlery, Sean said, 'I really ought to get home. My mum will be wondering where I've got to.'

'Give her a call. Put her mind at ease.'

'No, really.' He stood up. 'I have to go.'

'We don't leave the table until everyone is finished,' Barry whispered.

Sean sat down again. The stark whiteness of the walls was beginning to make him dizzy. He suddenly missed his gran's cluttered house.

*

Boyd sat in the lounge bar of the Joyce Hotel in the centre of Ragmullin. It was semi-dark, with a man crooning to the strum of his guitar in a corner. About ten people were dotted around the bar and a few in the nooks.

Nursing a pint of lager, he eyed his phone on the table. Maybe he should have gone for a run with Lottie. But he didn't want to be too available. He had made his position clear and she had rebuffed him. Tough on you, Lottie.

He took another sip, his heart not really in it, when over the rim of his glass he saw the short black curls of someone he knew, sitting at the bar.

The head turned slightly and he recognised her profile, even though she wasn't wearing her spectacles. He picked up his glass and stood to go and join her.

She laughed and dipped her head.

Boyd stopped.

Cynthia Rhodes was with a man he didn't recognise. But even in the dim, orangey-red hue of the bar lights, he thought he looked familiar. How could that be? He was sure he'd never seen him before in his life.

He sat back down, sipped his pint and studied the pair.

After all, he had nothing else to do.

CHAPTER FORTY-TWO

Maria Lynch combed out her hair, disgusted at how her pregnancy hormones were playing havoc with it. She flapped some air up under her floral cotton shirt and pulled on a loose pair of pyjama bottoms.

She needed Ben. Right now. The kids were in the living room watching some loud cartoon. She wanted to talk to an adult. The image of the dead baby refused to fade. Running her hand over her protruding belly, she held her breath. Waiting. At last she felt the little one kick. And again. Thank God.

She went and sat with her children, but a dark shadow of foreboding hung over her. Why? The sound of the television? The voices and laughter of her children? She didn't know, but she knew she wanted Ben here. They were a family. He should be with them. Not off decorating Lottie fucking Parker's house.

Making up her mind, she switched off the television, to groans from her children.

'Ah, Mam, it's not bedtime yet.'

'I know. We're going to see if Daddy's finished painting. And we might get chips on the way home.'

'Yeah!' came the chorused reply.

They pulled on their hoodies and she hustled them into the car.

After all that had happened the last two days, she wanted her husband by her side.

*

'You're almost finished, Ben.' Lottie spun around in the middle of the living room. 'Love the colour.'

'Better than your aqua?'

'I have to agree, it is.' She slumped on to the sheet-covered armchair.

'You look bushed.' He came to stand in front of her. 'Hard day?'

'Very hard.'

'Want to talk about it? Maria says I'm a great listener.'

Lottie smiled up at him. 'I hope she's okay. Can't have been easy on her seeing that dead baby.'

Ben sat down on the arm of the chair. 'She never told me about that.'

'Probably didn't want to worry you.' Lottie stifled a yawn and jumped up. She was tired, and she still had to run the few kilometres back to her mother's. And now she'd put her foot in her mouth. Typical.

Ben said, 'I'll have a chat with her tonight. Bottling things up is bad for her blood pressure.'

Lottie put her hand on his. 'Maria's a tough cookie. You've nothing to worry about.'

She felt him squeeze back and suddenly it felt all wrong. Not just two people having a conversation. Tension filled the air around her. And suddenly she started to cry.

'Oh God, Lottie what's the matter?'

She turned her back. 'I'm such a wuss. I don't usually cry over nothing.' She felt his hand on her shoulder. 'It's just those two dead boys. I can't stop thinking about them, and about whatever it is I'm not seeing.'

He turned her round to face him, then put his paint-smeared hand under her chin, forcing her to look at him.

'You are one of the best detectives I know, Lottie Parker – along with my wife, of course. Don't go beating yourself up. Have a good night's sleep and you'll be ready to get stuck in tomorrow. Doctor's orders.'

She smiled. 'You're not a doctor.'

'I could've been,' he laughed. 'That smile suits you so much better. Now go home and let me finish this work before Maria comes looking for me.'

He gave her a tight hug before picking up his paint tin and brush.

'Thanks, Ben.'

'For what?'

'For listening.'

As she went to leave, she saw the headlights of a car on the road outside. It swerved and sped off.

*

'The lying, cheating bastard,' Maria Lynch muttered under her breath as she gunned the engine and sped down the road.

'Mummy! You said a bad word.'

'Sorry, honey. We'll be home in a minute.'

'I want chips. You said we could get chips.'

'Tomorrow. Please, let me drive in peace.'

As her children lapsed into silence, Lynch wondered how she was going to handle this. Her suspicions were correct. Lottie Parker would pay for this.

She'd let her off with it before. Not this time.

She felt the baby kick hard.

Tears streaming down her face, she gripped the steering wheel, oblivious to her children shouting at her to slow down.

'Ben,' she whispered. 'How could you?'

CHAPTER FORTY-THREE

It was almost dark when the car pulled up at Robbie's house. Hope stepped out as Robbie took the sleeping Lexie in his arms.

Once she was inside, she moved in the darkness up the stairs and put Lexie into her own bed, then slid in silently beside her. The sound of her daughter sleeping lifted her heart. She thought of the baby that had grown in her womb. Her baby. What had happened to it? She wished she could remember.

Back downstairs, she cornered Robbie as he flicked through channels on the television.

'I need to take the car.'

'Why?'

'It's just for an hour or so.'

'Jesus, Hope, I thought you wanted to lie low. Half the guards in Ireland are probably looking for you at this stage. Where do you want to go?'

'Don't ask and I won't have to tell you any lies.'

She caught the keys as he threw them to her.

'Thanks, Robbie.'

He had turned his attention back to scrolling through Sky and she eased the door shut and crept out to the car.

*

Toby knew he really should go home. But he didn't feel like sitting in the silence that had consumed him all day. The fact that he knew

Max would be out half the night still didn't entice him back. He walked through the tunnel and up the canal bank. He should be afraid, he told himself. But he felt unnaturally calm.

The lights from the town and the round moon in the sky lit up the high path along the canal. He stopped now and then to pick up a handful of stones and threw them into the water as he walked. Mikey would love this, he thought. Skiving off at night. Under the moon. And then he remembered the image of Mikey's face and started to run.

It had rained a bit earlier but it had stopped now. He hoped it didn't start again. He had come out without a jacket. He was wearing his Chelsea T-shirt. The one that made Mikey go red in the face. Ha, he thought. Mikey and Kev loved Liverpool.

He felt his smile slip away in the night when he remembered that he'd never get to share anything with Mikey again. Never get to outscore him on the soccer pitch. It had been a good goal, though, he had to admit. The one that had won them the final. Mikey's goal. And then he'd been a shithead not letting Mikey stay at his house.

He had reached the harbour bridge without realising he'd come so far. The cathedral bell clanged. He'd be dead if he didn't get home before his dad missed him.

He crossed the bridge and headed towards town. He'd circle around by the shopping centre and run through the tunnel. Quickest way home now.

Then he remembered. That was the way Mikey might have walked on Sunday night. If he'd even got that far.

He pursed his lips and tried to whistle, even though he knew he couldn't. Mikey could, though. But Mikey wouldn't, ever again.

He saw a group of lads coming out of Fallon's pub on the corner, so he stepped into the road to let them pass him by. As they disappeared, a car drove up beside him. It slowed, and he glanced at it, feeling his heart thump like mad. He jumped back onto the footpath, put his head down and started to run. Straight into a girl coming out of the pub.

'You little pup. Watch where you're going.' She grabbed his arm.

Toby twisted out of her grasp. The car sped off.

'S-sorry,' he said, his voice miraculously returning after a day of silence.

She stood there unwrapping her long blonde hair, then began rolling it back up in a knot on top of her head.

'It must be way past your bedtime,' she said, with a hair grip between her teeth. 'You look scared to death. Can I ring someone to come and pick you up?' She finished doing her hair. Her eyes were bright and kind. 'You shouldn't be out on your own. You know little boys have been murdered.'

And Toby burst out crying.

I knew then that I couldn't help myself.

After I'd done it, I wanted to do it again. My objective filtered into the darkest corners of my mind and was replaced by a blaze of euphoria. The moment of death, the squashing of life – that second before the last breath exhaled, never to be inhaled again. The widening of the eyes and the falling of the long lashes, shutting down on baby flesh.

Yes. I had more work to do. I would show my power in more ways than one. A whisper of a spider web brushed my face as I kneeled beside the tree. Looking up at the black arachnid weaving its way around and up and down, I was mesmerised. I put up my hand and grasped its work, then squeezed it. When I opened my palm, the spider was a nugget of black mush and its web was no more.

Above me, birds chirped before nesting down. I ran my hand along the clean stem of a buttercup and plucked it, root and all, from the parched earth. Looking up at the sky, I felt the first drops of welcome rain pitter-patter on my face.

Earlier tonight, I had failed.

He'd got away.

But I knew I would have another chance to succeed.

Tomorrow night?

I stood up, dropped the flower and walked away.

DAY THREE

Wednesday

I'd kept an eye on the detectives as they travelled around Ragmullin with their heads a mile up their backsides. Not a clue. Asking all the wrong questions of all the wrong people. Well, almost.

The crow looked up at me with its black eyes and yellow beak. I clapped my hands and it flew off into the trees.

Looking up at the boy's window, I noticed the cotton curtains twitch. He was in there. Hiding. From me?

'I am coming for you, little boy,' I whispered, and walked back to my car. Hiding in plain sight. No one bothered to look at me. No one knew who walked among them. I was invisible to everyone. But no more.

I am coming for you.

CHAPTER FORTY-FOUR

The steps of the station were crowded with reporters, cameras, phones and microphones. Vans with satellites were parked up along the narrow road.

She should have entered through the back door. But she was here now. Nothing for it but to brave her way through the crowd.

'Inspector Parker.' Cynthia Rhodes was first to approach and stuck a microphone under Lottie's chin. 'What are you doing to protect the children of Ragmullin from this serial killer?'

She had been about to storm up the steps, ignoring any queries. It was Acting Superintendent McMahon's job to give press statements. But Cynthia had slithered under her skin like a slug. Have you not learned your lesson, Parker? Lottie chided herself. But having seen Boyd in deep conversation with the reporter in Danny's on Monday, she couldn't help herself. She cleared her throat and turned to face the journalists.

'We in An Garda Síochána are working tirelessly to bring the perpetrators of these murders to justice. If you will allow us to continue with our work, I'm sure there'll be no more of these terrible deaths. I'd like to personally offer my condolences to the families of the deceased, and if anyone has any information, no matter how insignificant it may seem, please ring our hotline. Now if you will excuse me ...' She began to walk up the steps.

'Was the baby murdered by the same person who killed the two boys?' Cynthia asked.

Without turning around, Lottie said, 'We are investigating all leads.'

'You're not denying that there is a serial killer in Ragmullin?'

'Jesus Christ.' Lottie swivelled round on the step. 'If you lot kept out of my hair and stopped whipping up hysteria, we might be able to do our jobs.'

'Is Rory Butler, the boys' football coach, a suspect?'

Lottie stared at the reporter. What the hell? 'Where did you get that from?'

'I have my sources, who shall remain anonymous.'

The smug smirk irked Lottie more than the statement. Boyd, she thought. Goddamn him. She didn't trust herself to speak, so instead she pushed through the door and into the relative safety of the reception area.

A man seated inside on the wooden bench stood up.

'Shit,' Lottie said.

*

Toby curled up in bed and refused to go downstairs for his breakfast. His mum had given up calling him about five minutes ago. Max's bed was empty; he hadn't been home all night by the looks of it.

He crawled over to his PlayStation. Switched on his game. It was no use, he missed playing with Mikey, so he slunk back to bed. He heard the ping of a message on the machine. He supposed it was another like the one he'd got last night. Before he'd gone off walking in the dark. Luckily he'd bumped into that nice girl, Chloe. She'd insisted on walking him to the tunnel. She'd told him she had a brother always playing *Call of Duty*. Toby told her he liked *FIFA* better. And she said that was good and that she'd ask Sean about it. Sean? Not the same Sean who'd been with Barry Duffy yesterday, surely?

Toby realised that he had actually been able to talk to this girl. That was strange.

The PlayStation pinged again. He went over to the desk, clicked the control and zoomed into the message box to read what was written there. He dropped the controller and opened his mouth to shout for his mother, but nothing came out.

Jumping back into bed, he burrowed deep beneath the duvet and pulled the pillow over his head.

He wasn't going outside the door today.

Max could swing for his chicken roll if he came home with a hangover.

*

Hope decided she needed to get out of the house. She didn't know what else to do. She brought Lexie with her. She used the streets at the back of the town, but as she exited Burke Road, she felt someone watching her. She picked Lexie up and ran, down the street, right to the end. Only then did she glance over her shoulder. There was no one following her. She stopped. Caught her breath. Noticed Lexie crying.

'I'm so sorry, baby,' she said. 'Mummy got scared.' She was truly spooked and knew she couldn't go on living like this. She had to find out the truth about what had happened to her baby.

'Swings?' Lexie said.

Hope placed her daughter on the ground and held her hand tightly.

'Okay, sweetheart, we'll go to the park.'

She pulled up the hood of her sweatshirt to shield her face and walked as fast as Lexie could manage, her eyes darting around in fear that the guards were watching her. Or maybe it was someone else.

*

Chloe stood at the door to Sean's room. It was closed, but she turned the knob anyway and entered.

Her brother was sitting on their gran's old rocking chair with a controller in his hand. She put her hands on her hips, then dropped them as she caught sight of herself in the mirror. Image of her mother! Oh God, no, she thought.

'Is there ever a time of the day when you're not playing those games, Sean Parker?'

'Let me think,' Sean said. 'Er ... nope.'

'I was wondering, do you play *FIFA* with a boy called Toby Collins?'

'How would I know? Everyone uses an alias online. Shit. Now I'm dead.' Sean closed his eyes and smacked his forehead with one hand.

'Why are you dead?' Chloe peered over his shoulder at the screen.

'It's the game.' Sean put the controller on his lap and turned towards her. 'How do you know this Toby Collins?'

'He literally bumped into me as I was coming out of work last night. He was terrified. I walked him home a bit.'

'What age is he?'

'Dunno. Ten or eleven.'

'And he was in town on his own and a murderer on the loose?'

'Don't be so melodramatic. I'm glad I only have the one brother. You are such a dick.'

'Are you finished? Can I get back to my game?'

'I told Toby that you play *Call of Duty*. Keep an eye out for him. Make sure he's okay.'

'Right, Mother Teresa.'

'You don't even know who she is,' Chloe snapped.

'Gran told me. So there.'

'Please look out for this Toby, won't you?'

'If I knew his alias, I might do, but seeing as I don't, I can't.'

'You know what, Sean? You're worse than Mam, talking in riddles all the time.'

He didn't grace her with an answer, so she went in search of Katie. Maybe her sister would talk to her. She heard Louis crying in the kitchen. Then again …

*

When Chloe had closed the door, Sean stared at the screen, unseeing.

Toby Collins. The same boy Barry had been an ass to yesterday. He lived somewhere down in Munbally Grove. And he was Mikey's friend. Sean remembered the sheer joy on Mikey's face after the match on Sunday night. Maybe he should look out for Toby.

He stood up and pulled off his pyjamas and got dressed. He'd see if he could find Toby. It seemed like he needed a friend. He gulped down tea and toast and told his gran he was going to meet Barry. He had no intention of meeting Barry Duffy. He might want him to say the rosary or go to Mass or something religious like that. And then Sean thought there was nothing Christian about the way Barry had treated Toby yesterday.

He zipped up his black hoodie as he left the house. The ground was damp. Must have rained during the night, he thought. He could smell the soil, that fresh smell you got after days of sunshine followed by a night of rain. It was good, and he smiled.

But the smile dropped off his face when he saw who was leaning over his gran's front gate.

CHAPTER FORTY-FIVE

'Presenting myself as requested,' Rory Butler said with a mock salute.

'Oh, right. To give a statement.'

'Spot on,' he said. 'But it looks like you're in need of a coffee after your encounter with that mob out there.'

'Come with me.' With a nod to Gilly behind the glass screen, Lottie keyed in the code and directed Butler to the interview room.

'I'll be with you shortly. Take a seat. I need someone to sit in with us, and a DNA testing kit.'

'Wait a minute,' he said, divesting himself of his grey suede jacket. 'I'm not sure I have to provide a sample. I just want to give the formal statement. That's what you said yesterday.'

Lottie sighed. 'Mr Butler, I've a very busy day ahead of me. You're either here to help with our inquiries into the deaths of two young boys or you're not. Which is it?'

He answered by pulling out a chair and draping his jacket over the back. He'd swapped yesterday's cargos for navy chinos, pink shirt and brown loafers, no socks. He sat down.

'Seeing as I took the time to come in, you might as well start,' he said with a shy grin.

'Give me a second.'

She found Boyd in the office and returned with him to the interview room. When they were ready, she began.

'State your name and address for the tape.'

'Rory Butler, Swift House, Ragmullin.'

'How long have you lived at that address?'

'Three years.'

'And prior to that?'

'London. Though I was born in Swift House. My family moved to the UK when I was eleven.'

'Why the move?'

'Didn't I tell you all this yesterday?'

Lottie gave him her best withering look.

He relented. 'My dad got a better job.'

'Why did you come back to Ragmullin?'

'My grandfather died and left the property to me. I decided to renovate it, and now I call it home.' He shifted in the chair. 'I can't see what these questions have to do with anything.'

Lottie ignored him and continued.

'You live there alone?'

'Most of the time,' he said.

'What does that mean?'

'Sometimes, if I'm lucky, I might have someone stay over. But currently I'm alone. Helen, my housekeeper, is there from nine to five each day.'

'What persuaded you to become the under-twelves soccer coach?'

'I told you this yesterday. I wanted to do something to help the community. I know it's hard to get volunteers. I can play a bit of soccer. So I volunteered.'

'How long have you been their coach?'

'Year and a half, I'd say.'

'Tell me about Sunday night.'

'Sunday night?'

'There was a final, I hear.'

'Yes. It was great. All square with five minutes to go. Then up pops little Mikey ...' He paused, lowered his eyes, fidgeted with his hands. 'Mikey scored and we won.'

'Mikey Driscoll?'

'Correct.'

'Where were you at that time?'

'On the sideline, roaring myself hoarse.'

'And after the match?'

'I gave a team talk and invited all the lads to McDonald's, where I bought them a meal.'

'Did you go to McDonald's with them?'

'I drove myself there, alone. Some of the boys went on the minibus, others with their parents.'

'What time was that?'

He shrugged. 'Maybe eight. Eight thirty? I'm not sure. Can't you check the CCTV footage?'

She ignored his comment.

'You joined the boys and their families? You paid for their victory meal?'

'I did.'

'What time did you leave?'

'I'm sure you already know this, so why are you wasting my time? And yours.' He raised an eyebrow.

He was uneasy, Lottie noted. Why? She knew he'd walked out of the restaurant at 9.16 p.m. 'I'm waiting, Mr Butler.'

'I don't know. Probably sometime around nine fifteen.'

'And did you speak with Mikey Driscoll at all?'

'When?'

'In the restaurant?'

'I probably congratulated him. Maybe I asked if he wanted more fries. But I have absolutely no recollection of it.'

'And outside. Did you see him then?'

'Outside? No. I fetched my car from the car park and drove home.'

'Did you see anyone hanging around outside the restaurant or in the car park?'

'I can't recall. Wait a minute. I saw Wes. He drives the team bus. Brings the lads to away matches.'

'That'd be Wesley Finnegan?'

'Yeah.'

Lottie had yet to interview Mr Finnegan. 'Did you see Mikey on the street or making his way home?'

'I can't recall.' He ran a hand through his carefully constructed hair.

'And you drove straight home?'

'That's what I said.'

'Is there anyone who can verify this?'

'No.'

'Did you like Mikey?'

'What kind of question is that?'

'Answer it, please.'

'I liked him no more and no less than the other boys. He was a good little soccer player.'

'Do you know his mother, Jen Driscoll?'

'I don't think so.'

Lottie thought she saw a flicker of unrest flit through his eyes. But his mouth remained firm. 'You sure?'

'That's what I said.'

She'd find out in her own way. 'What did you do on Monday?'

He leaned his head to one side as if he was thinking for a moment and his face visibly relaxed. 'Worked in my garden. All day long. It was nice and sunny. Good day for gardening.'

Rather you than me, Lottie thought. 'And in the evening? Later that night? Where were you then?'

'At home, I think. What is this about?'

'Kevin Shanley. You know he was found dead just over half a kilometre from your home?'

'You told me that yesterday.' He folded his arms. Getting fed up, Lottie thought.

'Kevin used to play on your soccer team. Do you remember him?'

'Ginger-haired lad? Yes, of course.'

'Why did he stop playing for the team?'

'You should ask his parents that, not me.'

'I will. When did you last see him?'

'Inspector, I really don't know where this conversation is leading. I had nothing to do with the death of either boy. If you're going to continue in this vein, I'll have to get a solicitor.'

'And what vein might that be?' Lottie stuck her pen behind her ear and leaned over the desk. Eyeballing him.

'Your tone is accusatory. I did nothing to either of those boys. If that is all? Then I'm leaving.' He shoved back the chair and stood. Picked up his jacket.

Lottie smiled. She had him rattled. But had he murdered two boys? What would his motive be? She really hadn't a notion.

As he went to the door, she said, 'We'll take that DNA sample now.'

'You know what? I've changed my mind about that. If you want it, you can either arrest me or get a warrant. I'm not giving my consent at this time.'

She let him go.

Boyd hadn't uttered a word during the interview. Turning to him, she said, 'What do you think?'

'He's just a lonely sod doing his bit for the young lads, and then he finds himself in the middle of a murder investigation.'

'You're being sarcastic?'

'Probably.'

'You feel sorry for him?'

'Doesn't matter what I feel.'

Lottie stared open-mouthed as he gathered his paperwork and left the room.

CHAPTER FORTY-SIX

Max picked up his dole and rolled the cash into his jeans pocket.

He had a dilemma. A big one. He could handle the low-life, arse-sniffing, pig-shit-eating Wes Finnegan. But now there were serious euros on the table. He could smell it.

Once he got home, he ran up the stairs to have a quick lie-down before seeing what the day would bring him.

Toby was standing by the window.

'What are you staring at, Tobes?'

The boy shook his head. Jesus, he hadn't spoken two words since he'd heard about Mikey. Thinking of Mikey, Max remembered the clip he'd seen on YouTube and hoped Toby hadn't spotted it. Fonzie was due a visit from him. He intended to rip every bit of bristle out of his excuse for a beard. Little fucker.

'I'm going to die,' Toby whispered.

'What did you say?' Max leapt off the bed and went over to his little brother.

Their father's voice bellowed from the room next door. 'Stop jumping around. I'm trying to sleep.'

'Now you've woken Da up,' Toby said.

'Tell me what's bothering you.'

Toby turned around and Max gasped. His usual bright smile had been replaced by white lips, an even whiter face and eyes circled with deep black rings.

'Did you sleep at all?' Max said.

Toby shook his head.

'Jeez, little bro, this is seriously fucked up. You have to talk to me. Tell me what's got you in such a state.'

Toby stared, and Max felt as if it went right through him. It was seriously freaking him out.

'Mikey,' whispered the boy.

'It's bad luck what happened to Mikey. That's all,' Max said.

'And Kev.'

'Double bad luck.'

'I'm next.'

'What the …? You know what, Tobes? You need to chill out. Hey, I got my dole. Fancy a feed in McDonald's?'

'That's where I last saw him.'

'Who?'

'Mikey. He wanted to sleep over. And I wouldn't let him. It's your fault really, not mine.'

'What the hell are you on about?'

Max studied his younger brother. Saw the tears at the corners of his eyes. The quiver of his lip. And he knew. He knew then that Toby was right. It *was* all his fault.

He pulled the boy to his chest and slapped him on the back. Then he hunkered down and looked into those sad eyes. Held him at arm's length.

'I'm going to fix this.'

Toby shook his head. 'You said that the last time.' He wriggled out of Max's grasp and flew out the door.

Max heard him thump down the stairs and the door slam. Standing by the window, he watched as Toby took off across the green, running as if the devil himself was on his heels. His black Converses flapping, with a lace in just one of them.

He slumped down on the bed, shook his head and tried to think about what he was going to do next.

'What's all that racket about?' his da shouted. 'Can a man not get a sleep in his own home now? Pair of fuckers.'

*

The first thing Lottie needed after the interview with Rory Butler was a strong coffee. The canteen was on the other side of the building. She thought about asking Kirby to fetch her a steaming Americano but decided the walk would help ease the tightness in her muscles after last night's jog. And Kirby was busy with the security footage and the interviews that had been conducted with the soccer teams' supporters. Lots of legwork and paperwork and not one definite clue. Coffee was surely needed.

As she rounded the corner in the corridor, she walked straight into Maria Lynch. Immediately she sensed the frost in the air, hanging around her detective like a shroud.

'What's up?' she said. 'I'm going for a coffee. You want to tag along?' She felt her arm being tugged and looked down to see Lynch holding her wrist in a vicelike grip. 'Hey, what the hell?'

'You stay away from my Ben,' Lynch said, her tone venomous though her voice was low.

Lottie dipped her chin towards the smaller woman, freed her arm and widened her eyes. 'I've no idea what you're talking about.'

'Course you do. You and Ben. Behind my back. Bitch.' Lynch's voice was so sharp, Lottie felt it cut her in two.

Holding her hands up in surrender, she said, 'You'd better explain, because honestly, I have absolutely no idea what you mean.'

With her ponytail swishing, Lynch turned on her heel. 'I'll be watching you.'

'Ah, for shite's sake, Maria, come back.'

Lottie followed Lynch down the corridor. Grabbed her arm. Lynch swiped her hand away.

'Don't you dare touch me. And if I see you with a hand near my Ben again, I'll cut it clean off. So help me God, I will.'

Lottie stared open-mouthed as Lynch walked away, the weight of her baby bump labouring her steps.

What the hell was that all about?

*

Hope pushed her daughter slowly on the swing, looking around as she did so. She noticed a boy sitting at the back of the playground. He had his head down, minding his own business.

She felt a few drops on her bare arm. It was starting to rain. She lifted Lexie off the swing.

'Time to go home,' she said.

As she turned to go, her daughter's hand in her own, she looked over at the boy. He raised his head. And she recognised him.

'Toby?'

*

Lottie sat in the canteen, nursing a mug of coffee. Boyd sat down opposite her.

'What's up?' he said.

'Having a bad day. Wish I could go for a drink.'

He laughed.

'It's not funny. Lynch thinks I'm having an affair with her husband.'

Boyd laughed even louder.

'I'm serious.'

'It's pregnancy hormones.'

'What would you know about that?'

'Not a lot.'

'What am I going to do?'

'Kick some ass?'

'Be serious for a minute,' she said.

He was staring at her, eyes filled with compassion. 'It's the boys, isn't it? And that prick Butler. Nothing to do with Lynch's fantastical imagination.'

'As usual, Boyd, you're right. I have this awful feeling in my bones that the killer isn't finished yet.'

'We need to concentrate on what links Mikey and Kev. What caused some maniac to strangle two young boys?'

'The way he left their bodies as if they were on display. I can't figure that out.'

Gilly O'Donoghue came into the canteen and walked quickly over to them.

'What's up?' Boyd said.

'It's probably nothing, but that bus driver, Wesley Finnegan, was in yesterday reporting a theft from his vehicle.'

'So?'

'Well, Kirby told me he's one of the guys of interest in the boys' murder cases. And the lad he's pointing the finger at for the robbery is Max Collins. The brother of Toby Collins. The lad who—'

'Was friends with the two murder victims,' Lottie said. 'Boyd, we need to have a talk with Finnegan.'

CHAPTER FORTY-SEVEN

Lottie poured her coffee into a takeaway cup. Boyd brought the car to the front of the station.

Wesley Finnegan lived seven kilometres outside Ragmullin. A dirt lane led to his cottage. You couldn't miss it. Two minibuses parked up on the road made passing virtually impossible.

Lottie jumped out of the car and, without waiting for Boyd, marched through the front garden up to the door. There was no visible footpath. Rain was falling steadily, beating into her face and churning up mud beneath her boots.

She pressed the doorbell. The house appeared to have been left to rot. She found it hard to believe anyone lived within the crumbling walls. Ivy was stippled along the ledge above the door and clung in long tendrils to the cracks in the faded pebble-dash.

'No one here.' She walked around the side of the house to the rear.

Someone had made an attempt to build a shed, but it had ended up looking more like a badly constructed barn. Three sides of corrugated steel, with sheets of galvanised tin sitting precariously on top as a roof. No door. Open to the elements. A man was leaning into the open bonnet of a bus. He was standing on a cement block. Gilly was right, Lottie thought. Five foot nothing.

'Mr Finnegan?' She noted his soaked appearance. His shirtsleeves were rolled up, displaying oil-soaked arms. A cigarette hung from dry, scabby lips.

'Who's asking?' he said.

She made the introductions. 'Can we talk inside? It's a bit damp out here.'

'I've work to be doing.' He spat out the cigarette and ground it under his boot.

Lottie moved into the relative shelter of the shed. It was long enough to house the bus but not wide enough to hold anything else. She walked slowly down the side of the vehicle, feeling damp and cold. A bird flapped its wings and cawed from a corner above her head. I hate damn birds, she thought, and moved back to Finnegan.

'Are you here about my stolen cash?' he said.

'We're investigating the murders of Mikey Driscoll and Kevin Shanley.'

'Awful business.' He picked up a greasy towel from the ground and rubbed his hands on it. Then, as if something alarming had registered in his brain, he said, 'What's that got to do with me?'

The rain ping-pinged on the roof, giving Lottie a headache. 'Can we go into the house?'

'It's a bit of a mess. I'd prefer to stay out here. I can work while you talk.' He picked up a wrench and turned back to the engine.

Lottie stood into his space. The smell of body odour made her gag. 'We can either talk inside or at the station. The choice is yours.'

Finnegan stopped working and looked at Boyd as if imploring some kind of male solidarity. Finding none, he threw down the wrench. He walked across the yard, muttering to himself. Lottie thought she caught the words, 'bitch' and 'arsehole'.

The interior of the cottage was even more dilapidated than the outside, though Lottie would have thought that was impossible. Wesley Finnegan was evidently more at home in his makeshift garage than in his kitchen.

He lifted a stack of magazines from a chair and indicated for Lottie to sit. She remained standing, but Boyd sat down.

The room was cold. The stove had a pile of pots stacked on top, and a basket of turf stood on the ground. She wondered when a fire had last been lit. A plastic clothes line ran the length of the kitchen, an array of clothing hanging haphazardly from it. She lowered her eyes. She didn't need to see Finnegan's underwear.

He was fussing with a kettle. How had he known where to find it?

'No tea for us,' Boyd said.

'Sit down, please,' Lottie said.

Finnegan grunted, moved a plastic basket of rolled-up socks from a chair to the table and sat down. Lottie walked around the crowded space and stood beside the small fat man. She leaned down towards him and almost recoiled. When had he last washed?

'Mr Finnegan, we—'

'Call me Wes. Everyone else does.'

Lottie straightened her back, unzipped her jacket and folded her arms.

'We want to talk to you about the two boys who were murdered.'

'You think I could do that to those poor defenceless creatures? You're barking up the wrong tree there, missus.'

'I'm not barking, I'm asking questions.'

'You haven't asked one yet.'

So, he was a smart-mouth. She walked over and stood beside the silent Boyd.

'Where were you from seven thirty Sunday evening until Tuesday morning?'

Finnegan's eyes narrowed. Wary now. Greasy fingers worried away at stumpy broken nails. The silence was broken by a cuckoo clock chiming out the hour. Lottie jumped. Jesus, it was like being in a time warp.

'Sunday, I did the bingo run. Ask anyone.'

'I'm asking you.'

'I know nothing about them poor boys.'

'For Christ's sake, answer the questions.' Boyd slammed his hand on the table. At last, Lottie thought. Support.

Finnegan sat up straighter and tapped his fingers against the side of his forehead. As the rain drummed down outside, more persistent now, the kitchen darkened.

'I went to the match. I drive the lads to the away games and I wanted to support them in the final. They'd been so good all season.'

'I thought you said you were on a bingo run?' Lottie said.

'Sunday-night bingo is in Gaddstown, just up the road. I dropped off the ladies and the few auld fellas that go, and came back to see the match. It was near over by then. But it was a great win. The whole place was full of excitement. The lads got their medals and headed into town for a feed.'

'Did you go with them?'

'I took a few in the minibus. Lads that had no lift from their parents.'

'Who did you bring?'

'I don't know all their names.'

'I'll give you a hint. Mikey Driscoll? Kevin Shanley?'

'Young Shanley didn't train much in recent times. His family moved out of Munbally.'

Lottie looked at Boyd. 'Do you know why they moved, or why Kevin stopped playing for the team?'

'You'd better ask his parents that.'

Same answer as Butler had given her.

'Who did you drive to McDonald's on Sunday evening after the match?'

'I told you, I don't know. I think maybe young Driscoll and his friend came. Not sure of his name.'

'Toby Collins?'

'Could be.' Finnegan's eyes were shrouded by thin lids. 'And a few others. A couple of the parents too.'

Lottie sighed. There had been adults on the bus. 'You arrived at McDonald's, then what?'

'I let them out at the side door and drove round the back and parked. I joined the gang inside. I had a double cheeseburger with fries and a large Coke, if you want to know.'

'At nine eleven p.m. you exited the restaurant. What did you do then?'

'Drove back out to Gaddstown and waited for the bingo to end. Then I brought them home. Dropped them off at their houses and came home. To bed. My own bed. On my own.'

She'd have to find holes in his story if he was the killer. Now all those who'd taken the bus to bingo would have to be interviewed. The lists kept getting longer.

'On to Monday night then,' she said. 'Tell me about that.'

She pulled out a chair. She hadn't noticed the black cat lying on it. Now it stood up, stretched and jumped to the ground, where it curled around her legs. She shuddered, shooed it away and sat down.

'Bingo is in Tullamore Monday nights.'

'Did you collect and deliver?'

'I need the fifty-four-seater for that run, but mine was out of action. Had to call in a replacement. Pat Kinnity in Kilbeggan has one, and he did the run for me.'

'Mmm,' Lottie murmured.

'What does that mean?' Finnegan looked over at her, beads of sweat gathering on his bald head.

'You didn't do the bingo on Monday night, so what did you do?'

'Worked on the fifty-four. That's it out there in the shed. Carburettor is fecked.'

'Why don't you buy a new one?' Boyd said.

'My cash was robbed, wasn't it? And what are you lot doing to find that bad bastard who stole it?' He slapped his hand on the table.

'That's nothing to do with us,' Boyd said.

Lottie butted in. 'When you made the report, you said you believed Max Collins might have taken your cash.'

'I did.'

'Was he one of your bingo fares?'

'No.'

'How do you know him, then?'

Finnegan's finger picked at a dried bean on the table. 'I just know of him. From the pub,' he added.

'What pub?'

'Fallon's.'

Where Chloe worked, Lottie thought. Maybe it was time her daughter found a different part-time job.

'And you don't know him in any other capacity?'

'I have no idea what you mean.'

Lottie decided she needed to have a chat with this Max Collins. She leaned her arms on the table but lifted them quickly when she felt them sticking to the surface. 'Monday night into Tuesday morning. Is there anyone who can vouch that you were here?'

'No. I live alone.'

'I gathered that.'

'I was working on that heap of shite out there all night.'

'I think you need to come to the station.'

'I want my solicitor.'

'Oh, for Jaysus' sake. Why do you need a solicitor?' Lottie couldn't keep the exasperation out of her voice.

'Because you see a poor bus driver with no alibi and you want to fit me up for a murder I didn't do. Leeches. Sucking the life out of me. That's why I need a solicitor.'

'You had access to the boys. You drove them to matches and—'

'Wait a minute. Any time I carried them to games, there were always adults. The team coach, sometimes Dr Duffy, and always the assistant coach. He's like a ferret where the young lads are concerned. Goes everywhere, so he does.'

'Are you talking about Bertie Harris or Rory Butler?'

'Harris. I'm never alone with any of the team. I'd like it if you two would shove off now.'

'And *I'd* like it if you would come to the station to provide a DNA sample.' Lottie had had enough of his shite talk. 'I'd also like your permission for our forensic team to examine your buses.'

Finnegan's transformation was instantaneous. His face turned puce and his button-like eyes darkened. He shot out of his chair, frightening the cat, which was coiled around his feet.

'You can fuck off, that's what you can do.'

'I want to have a look around your house while I'm here.'

'Out, get out. And don't come back without a warrant.' He opened his belt, slid it up a notch and tightened it around his waist. Lottie noticed it had missed a loop and his grimy waistband fell below his sagging belly. She had no desire to stay in his presence any longer. She moved around the table and towered over him.

'Mr Finnegan, it is in your interest to help us with our inquiries. Otherwise I might think you have something to hide.'

'A warrant. That's the only way you'll get through my front door again. Now I'm asking you one last time to leave.'

Sighing, Lottie found her eyes drawn to the clothes dangling from the line over the range. A startlingly white piece of material was sticking out from behind a faded blue shirt. She put up her hand and tentatively drew the shirt to one side. She found herself staring at a small pair of white football shorts.

Slowly she turned around and faced Finnegan. The puce of anger slid down his face, leaving pale mottled skin behind.

'I can explain,' he said.

'I hope you can,' Lottie replied.

CHAPTER FORTY-EIGHT

Hope peeled a sticker from the book and handed it to Lexie. The child found a place on the wall that satisfied her and slapped on Peppa Pig.

'Hope, are you cooking lunch today or what?' Robbie shouted up the stairs.

'Or what?' she replied.

'I'll go for a takeaway. Do you want anything?'

'Do you want anything?' she asked Lexie.

'Chicken nuggets,' the little girl said, her eyes sparkling with delight.

'Chicken nuggets, Big Mac and fries,' Hope shouted down to her uncle.

When she heard the front door slam, she peeled off another sticker and Lexie took it from her finger. Her skin prickled with fear. After Toby had fled the playground without a word, she'd hurried home. What was up with him? He was like a frightened rabbit.

Her hand rubbed the sagging flesh where her baby had grown for nine months. She couldn't even mourn the child she had never wanted. She thought of the baby's father, and shuddered. She squeezed her eyes shut. Tried to recall anything about that night. But it was dark and blank. The guards wanted her for questioning in connection with the baby found dead in the canal. Robbie had quizzed her relentlessly, but she could only remember waking up in a pool of blood and wandering around blindly until she reached the garda station. Why had she gone in there? Had she actually killed her baby? Or had someone else done it? She struggled to breathe as she realised that that would make her life all the more perilous.

Alone with her daughter, she felt naked and exposed to the danger that was out there. Danger she could touch with her hand, as real and tangible as the soft pads of Lexie's fingers.

She knew that fear. She had lived with it for the last nine months. And now she waited in a different kind of fear for the guards to arrive at her door.

She banged her fist against her forehead. Why couldn't she remember what had happened?

'Why're you angry, Mummy?'

When Hope opened her eyes, she saw her little girl staring at her, terror streaking across her face.

'Mummy's not angry, sweetie. Let's get some ice cream from the freezer.' She picked up her daughter and let her cling to her neck as she made her way down the stairs.

She was on the bottom step when the shadow appeared behind the glass of the front door.

CHAPTER FORTY-NINE

Lottie called in Jim McGlynn and the SOCO team with instructions to search every inch of Wes Finnegan's property. She then called a squad car to haul the bus driver's arse down to the station.

She sat in silence as Boyd drove her back to town. Mulled over Finnegan's excuses. He'd found the shorts in a plastic bag on his bus one day after returning from an away match, he'd said. And then he'd told her something very unusual, a revelation that directed them to Dr Paul Duffy's house.

Both the Duffys were at home. Lottie had no idea if Barry was there or not, but he wasn't her concern at the moment.

'You're lucky to find me here. I work a half-day on Wednesdays,' Paul Duffy said, leading the two detectives into the pallid-looking living room.

Lottie welcomed the sparseness and breathed in the clean air. Stark contrast to the odour of Wesley Finnegan's hovel. Duffy was dressed in a tailored cream shirt, no tie, blue jeans and flip-flops. Flip-flops? She could hear the rain thundering against the window.

Julia rushed in behind them, long black hair flowing loosely around her face. 'Tea, anyone?' she said.

'No thanks,' Boyd said.

'If you don't mind, I'll have a cup,' Lottie said. They needed to speak to Paul without interruption.

When Julia left to rustle up the tea in some distant corner of the house, Lottie took a seat opposite the doctor as he eased himself into an armchair. Boyd pulled up a high-backed chair and sat erect, his legs crossed at the ankles, mirroring Duffy's posture.

'Barry is coping fine now, so how can I help you? Any nearer to catching whoever dumped the baby in the canal?'

Lottie sat back in her chair. Why did she feel as if he was reprimanding her?

'The baby wasn't just dumped. He was murdered. And we're not here about the baby or your son.'

'What then?' Duffy uncrossed his ankles and leaned forward, feet planted firmly on the floor.

'Two young boys have been found murdered, and—'

'I know. It's terrible.'

'You're the team physio, is that right?'

'Oh, not in any official capacity. I just help out. Carrying water most of the time.'

'Dr Duffy, we are interviewing everyone who was in contact with the dead boys. We are trying to establish who last saw them and—'

'Stop right there.' He held up his hand. 'I only helped the team on a voluntary basis. Not a board member or anything like that. I became involved when Barry used to play, and I stayed on when he gave up. He helps out too.'

Lottie kicked her bag under her chair and leaned forward. 'I'd like to ask you a few questions. In an official capacity,' she added, using his own words. 'We can talk here or at the station. The choice is yours.'

He folded his arms, his crisp shirt wrinkling with the movement. 'Go ahead.'

Before Lottie could utter another word, the door opened and Julia bustled in with a trolley holding teapot and china cups. She looked from one to the other. 'Am I interrupting?'

Parking the trolley between the chairs, she began to pour. Once they all had their cups filled, she dispensed milk from a jug and sat down.

'Mrs Duffy,' Lottie said, 'we are interviewing your husband. Would you mind if we talked to him in private?'

'But we keep nothing from each—' Julia began.

'Just go,' Paul commanded. 'I'll call you when we're done.'

His wife stood up and slammed her cup back down on the trolley, spilling the tea, then turned and walked silently out of the room.

'Sorry about that,' Paul said. 'Julia can be a little intense at times. I'm sure you're almost finished here anyway.'

'We haven't even started,' Boyd mumbled.

Lottie shot him a look to keep quiet. She knew from experience that this interview could go belly-up in an instant.

'We were talking about the soccer team. When did Barry give up?' She was trying to put Duffy at ease before she embarked on the difficult questions.

'Barry has nothing to do with this,' he said.

Lottie held his stare, and won out.

He said, 'My son played each age division up to under-sixteens. But last year, he decided to quit the game. He stayed on to help out a bit with the younger teams and that's why I maintained my involvement.'

'Why did he quit?' Boyd said.

'Outgrew it, I'd say. Didn't give a reason.' Duffy turned to Lottie. 'You have a son, Inspector. I'm sure you know what teenagers are like. A new interest every five minutes.'

She nodded, and thought of Sean being here for dinner last night. She'd have to ask him what he thought of the family. 'What role do you currently hold with the younger teams?'

'Rory asked me to help out whenever I'm available.'

'Rory Butler?'

'Yes.'

'Are you two good friends?'

'Acquaintances.'

'And you've been involved in youth soccer for a few years?'

'Is that a question?'

'It is.'

'I've just told you I was involved up through the ranks with Barry.'

Lottie put down her cup but remained leaning forward. She decided to get to her point.

'Tell me about the football shorts.'

Duffy didn't blink. His hand was steady. Just a slight bite of his lower lip.

'I don't know what you're talking about.'

'Wes told us.' Feck, she thought. She shouldn't have said his name.

'Finnegan? The bus driver? That man – well, he's just the lowest equation in humankind.'

Lottie glanced at Boyd. He shook his head. He was leaving it up to her.

'I take it you don't like him?' she said.

'What's to like? I wouldn't trust him an inch. What did he say about me?'

'He said nothing *about* you. Just mentioned that you encouraged the boys to wear matching white football shorts, even while training. Said it demonstrated their commitment to the team. Which to me doesn't make sense at all.'

'So what? I don't understand what it has to do with the boys' deaths.'

Lottie ignored the question. 'You don't deny supplying the team with football shorts?'

'Most of those boys are from poor backgrounds. Little or no money coming into their homes, and what there is, the parents drink or shoot up their arms. I donated money to the club for new training kit, but with Bertie Harris running things, I never saw much improvement in their gear.'

'You admit you bought the boys new football shorts?'

'I can't recall exactly, but I probably did, among other items of kit. That doesn't make me a murderer.'

'Why would Wes Finnegan have some of that kit in his possession?'

Duffy leaned back, opened his mouth wide and laughed. 'I have no idea. You're the detective. You will have to find that out for yourself.'

'Where were you on Sunday night, Mr Duffy?' Lottie said. He was really getting up her nose now.

'I went to the match, joined the team in McDonald's. Then I went home. Julia can corroborate that.'

'And Monday night?'

'I was here. With Julia.'

'And Barry. Where was he?'

'My son has nothing to do with this. He was unfortunate to find that baby's body. Please don't think you're going to drag him into anything else. I think you should leave.' He pointed to the door.

'I'd like to speak with Julia.'

'What for?'

'To verify that she can corroborate your alibis.'

He rose swiftly for a man of his size. Lottie was not about to be wrong-footed. She stood also, but in her haste, caught her foot in the strap of her handbag and almost toppled over. Boyd caught the back of her jacket and hauled her upright.

'Sorry about that.' She slung her bag over her shoulder. 'I'll just have that word with Julia.' She moved to the door, but Duffy reached it before her.

'Leave Julia out of this. She's under a lot of pressure, what with Barry and all that business with the baby. He's been through enough. We all have.'

'Mr Duffy, you are a person of interest in the investigation into the deaths of two young boys. Your cooperation would be appreciated, if you wish to be eliminated from the inquiry.'

Duffy sighed, opened the door and shouted, 'Julia? Come here, please.'

She appeared almost instantaneously, rubbing her hands in a white fluffy towel.

'The detectives would like you to confirm that you were with me on Sunday and Monday nights.'

'I was.' Julia gulped. 'With him, I mean.'

'And do you wash the team kit?' Lottie asked.

'I take turns with some of the parents.' Julia's eyes slid to her husband, who was standing behind Lottie's shoulder.

'Did you collect the kit on Sunday?'

Paul Duffy moved out past Lottie and stood beside his wife, putting his arm around her shoulder. Protective or possessive?

'The boys kept their jerseys on after the match. They were so pumped up to have won,' Paul said. 'Now, we have things to be doing.'

Walking to the front door, Boyd said, 'Do you buy the kit yourself, Paul, or does Julia do it?'

'I don't know what you mean,' Julia said.

'We mainly purchase online,' Paul said.

'What?' Julia pulled away from her husband. 'What are you talking about?'

Lottie smiled. 'The two murdered boys were wearing similar new football shorts. It's odd, because Kevin Shanley no longer played for the team. We have reason to believe your husband purchased the shorts. Did you not know that?'

'Paul?' Julia said, her mouth drooping along with her eyes.

Duffy squeezed her shoulder and turned to Lottie. 'Good day.'

As they walked out onto the porch, two lads came riding bikes up the drive in the rain. Lottie's stomach lurched when she recognised Sean with Barry, and she had no idea why she suddenly wanted to get her son out of here and home.

'Sean,' she said as the boys drew close. 'I think your granny had plans for today. Maybe you should head back.'

Sean appeared to look relieved. 'See you later, Barry,' he said, and pedalled furiously back down the drive.

In the car, Boyd turned to her. 'What was that all about?'

'When I figure it out, I'll let you know.'

CHAPTER FIFTY

Rory Butler sat on the large stone and looked out at the calm waters of the lake. The activity to his left had ceased, but he could see the crime-scene tape hanging unattended around the slab where Kevin's body had been discovered. He thought of Mikey. Poor Mikey.

He shook his head and looked to his right. Beyond the trees and wild bushes. His grandfather had told him it had been an ice house. Used before the time of refrigerators. Covered in ivy and vegetation, its door was invisible to the naked eye, unless you were right up beside it. Only a handful of people knew of its existence. His grandfather had done some work extending it, but Rory had no use for the place. He was glad the guards hadn't investigated further, because it had nothing to do with them. And he had learned the hard way that some things were best left secret. That was what he'd been told anyway. A long time ago. He had enough problems without bringing the guards back to his doorstep.

He put down the mug of cold coffee and stood, breathed in the fresh air. He listened to the chirp of the birds in the branches all around him. The sound should have been soothing. But it wasn't.

He wondered if he had done the right thing in coming back to Swift House, returning to Ragmullin with the weight of the past awaiting him.

He picked up the mug as a soft sheen of drizzle began to fall and headed back up the track to the house he now called home.

*

Barry opened the refrigerator and scoured the contents for something edible. Something that wasn't pulped into juice.

'Go to your room, Barry,' his mother said.

'But I want to go back out. It's so fucking boring in here.' Barry shut the fridge door empty-handed and discovered his error when the slap caught him on the side of the head, propelling him into the wall.

'Barry! Language!'

His father stood framed in the doorway. 'Do what your mother says. Go to your room.'

'Why?' Barry demanded.

'Listen to me,' his mother said. 'I don't want you hanging around with that detective's son any more. He's not the right kind of friend for you. Okay?'

He caught his father staring at him and knew that now wasn't the time to begin another argument. But they could piss off, the both of them. They were not going to dictate who he should have as friends. They had done that all his life. Now it was his time to choose.

Tramping up the stairs, he made as much noise as was possible in his soft-soled trainers, and made sure to give his bedroom door a good loud bang.

CHAPTER FIFTY-ONE

'We might as well call to the Shanleys now,' Lottie said.

Boyd headed for Greenway. 'Did I imagine the atmosphere in the Duffy house?'

'Well if you did, that makes two of us. He seems to be a very domineering character. I feel sorry for Julia. She appears to be terrified of him.'

'You think so?'

'Do you not?'

Boyd stretched and yawned. 'I can't put my finger on it. But something is definitely off.'

'Tired?' Lottie asked.

'Julia?'

'No, smart-arse. Are *you* tired?'

'A bit. This case is draining.'

'I know. I seem to be spending my life talking to grieving people and obstructive witnesses.' She glanced at him. 'What did you do last night?'

'Went out for a pint.'

'Where?'

'Jesus, Lottie, does it matter?'

'Just making conversation.'

'If you must know, I went to the Joyce.'

'You don't normally drink there.' She couldn't let it go.

'Felt like a change of scenery. Somewhere I wasn't likely to bump into anyone who knew me.'

'Like me?'

'Doesn't always have to be about you, Lottie.'

Suitably chastened, she slammed both feet into the footwell and turned to stare out of the side window. The town melded into a kaleidoscope of colour as Boyd sped through.

'Sorry,' he said.

'It's okay. I was just being nosy. Thought maybe you were out celebrating your divorce.'

'I wasn't.' He seemed to soften. 'What did you do?'

'Went for a run. I'm so unfit. Might go for another one tonight. Care to join me?' She stole a look at him. His strong profile unwavering as he drove.

'Not sure what I'm at tonight. I'll let you know,' he said, and turned into Greenway.

All the curtains were drawn at the Shanley house. A black net twisted into a bow with a white card pinned to the door proclaimed their loss.

Victor led them into the living room. Relatives and friends, seemingly from every corner of Ireland, were gathered in mourning.

'When can we have our Kevin home? We need to organise his funeral,' Victor said.

'Is there somewhere quiet we can talk?' Lottie said.

He guided them through the throng to the kitchen, which was similarly crowded. He opened the back door. The garden had a small concrete patio with table and chairs, a barbecue in a corner. Everything was dripping from the earlier rain. The sun nudged a cloud, and a stream of light caused the wet to steam.

'Nice area,' Boyd said.

'Low-maintenance,' Victor said. 'Can I have my son home soon?'

'I'm afraid we have no news of when his body can be released,' Lottie said. 'As soon as I know, I'll inform you.'

Victor got a towel and wiped down the chairs. They sat, and he said, 'Mind if I smoke?'

Boyd lit a cigarette too, but much as she yearned for a hit of nicotine, Lottie declined and satisfied herself with the secondary smoke.

'Victor,' she said, 'we had some disturbing news from the state pathologist regarding Kevin.'

'Disturbing? What do you mean?'

She blew out her cheeks and gathered her thoughts. How best to approach this? Straight out with it, she decided.

'During the post-mortem, the pathologist discovered that Kevin had been the victim of abuse. Not recent,' she added, 'historical.'

Victor's mouth hung open, the cigarette dangling precariously from his lips. He reached up with both hands and clutched his head. Then he slumped back on the chair.

'I knew there was something. But never, not in my worst nightmares, did I think it was anything like that. My poor boy.'

'When did his misbehaving start?' Lottie said.

'Before we moved from Munbally. We thought it was the estate. There's a lot of drugs and stuff going on. Bad for a young lad. So we decided to move. But Kev didn't change. If anything, he became more withdrawn, and at the same time disruptive.'

'In what way?'

'Nothing was right for him. Sheila said it was part of growing up. But I felt it was more than that. Now I know.' His hand stilled, cigarette halfway to his mouth. 'That's when his mother started drinking in earnest. Jesus Christ. Did she know?'

'I have to speak to your wife,' Lottie said.

'But abuse? Who? Why? I don't understand. This will kill Sheila.'

'Can I get you a glass of water?' Lottie asked. She needed to calm him down, otherwise she would get nothing from him.

'No, no.'

'Do you feel able to talk about it?'

'I have to, haven't I?'

'Who do you think might have been close to your son? Can you give me a list of names?'

'No one. Not that I can think of straight off. His mother might know, but Jesus, you can't go in there asking her those kind of questions.'

'I'm asking *you*.'

Victor closed his eyes, tears squeezing out beneath short lashes. 'Poor Kev. What must he have gone through? And we were punishing him. Taking his phone off him. Locking ...'

'Locking him in his room?' Lottie nudged.

'Yeah. After the time he stayed out most of the night. What must he have thought of us? Why didn't he tell me?'

'Do you think maybe he told Mikey Driscoll?'

'Mikey? Why would he tell him?'

'Weren't they friends?'

'They were, I suppose. I don't know.'

'Had he any other friends?'

Victor shrugged. 'Let me think.'

Lottie breathed in a sigh and noticed Boyd light another cigarette. He offered it to Victor, who took it and nodded his appreciation.

'There is one lad that he used to hang around with a lot when we lived on the estate. But I think he was more Mikey's friend than Kev's. Toby something. What the hell is he called? Collins. That's it. Toby Collins.'

'We know of him,' Boyd said.

'He has a brother. Big lad. Must be seventeen or eighteen. Tough-looking git.' Victor looked up. Wide eyes, disbelieving. 'You don't think this brother could have abused my son? I'll kill the bastard myself. Maybe *he* killed Kev and Mikey. My own son, and I didn't know ...' Victor crumpled up on the chair.

Lottie said, 'Were there any other adults who took an interest in Kevin? Teachers, or people associated with the football team, for instance?' She knew she was leading him, but she had nothing else.

'I thought they were all good men to volunteer their time to help a team that was going nowhere ...'

She wondered if the abuser was also the murderer. Most likely. Though she had no evidence to suggest or deny it, she didn't think Victor had abused his own son. Or Mikey Driscoll, for that matter. But he'd have to be investigated all the same.

'Your son, Mr Shanley, when his body was found he was wearing brand-new football shorts. When we looked in his room, we didn't notice anything similar. I can show you a photo to see if you recognise them.'

'You'd have to ask Sheila that, and I don't think she's in any fit state for questions. Where are the clothes he was wearing?'

'They haven't been located.'

'Okay. I'll ask Sheila later, and let you know.'

'I'd appreciate that. Thank you. One other thing. Do you know Hope Cotter?'

'No, but I heard her name on the news. Something to do with that dead baby.'

'What's your relationship to Jen Driscoll?' Quickfire. Catch him off guard.

He raised his head and glared through his tears. 'Are you insinuating something other than a working relationship?'

'Just asking.'

'What went on between me and Jen, it's ancient history and has nothing to do with the death of my son or hers.'

'What did go on?'

'Just a fling. A few years ago. We work together. It's all over. Don't say anything to Sheila. She doesn't know about it.'

'Did you know Jen's husband?'

'He's been out of the country for the last ten years. I don't think caring for a child was ever on his horizon.' He stood up and walked inside.

'Where were you going with that?' Boyd asked.

'Maybe his relationship with Jen sparked a murderous streak in someone else.' Lottie gathered her bag and jacket. The clouds were beginning to congregate into one black mass above her head. It was time to talk to Sheila Shanley.

*

Victor cleared the house of people in three minutes flat. Lottie watched him as he hustled and bustled everyone out, taut muscles beneath his shirt quivering with pent-up anger.

Sheila took a sip from a tumbler. Lottie smelled the brandy. Inhaled its aroma. Beat back the urge to ask for one. This was going to be a tough interview.

'Out with it,' Sheila said, her words slurring.

As Lottie was about to begin, Victor butted in.

'Sheila, they've discovered something very upsetting. It's to do with Kev.'

'He's dead. Is that not upsetting enough?' Her eyes glazed over.

'Perhaps we should have this conversation later,' Lottie said, recognising the signs of too much alcohol in the distraught mother. She tried to catch Victor's eye.

'You've cleared out my house for a reason, so ask your questions.' Sheila held out her glass. Victor picked up the bottle from the floor beside the armchair and poured a hefty measure.

'I'm sorry to be blunt, Sheila, but we suspect that Kevin was the victim of abuse.'

'I never laid a hand on him.'

'Not that kind of abuse,' Lottie said, hoping Sheila would understand what she meant. She did.

'No way. My son was never ... No! I would've known.'

'The post-mortem confirms it. And I hate to have to ask these questions, but it may be relevant to why he was murdered.' She paused and watched as the woman's anger gave way to horror.

'I didn't know. Oh my God, my poor boy.'

'Sheila, can you think of anyone who might have done this? Someone Kevin tried to avoid, maybe? Anyone?'

'I don't know.' Sheila turned to Victor. 'You were off screwing your skinny bitch. Sweating it out in that kip of a gym. And now I hear that some bastard was abusing our son.'

As if the exertion of her words had acted as a catalyst, Sheila visibly deflated. Lottie could see it as surely as if the woman's body was a balloon with the air whistling out.

Her voice nothing more than a fluttering of words, she went on, 'You never knew where Kev was or what was going on. I tried my best. I really did.'

Victor was burning the carpet with a circle of disbelieving footsteps. 'I'm sorry. I should have been home more often. If I'd known something like this was going on ... But you and your drinking ... you weren't watching out for him either.'

Lottie knew she had to take control of the situation. She glanced at Boyd, then leaned her head to one side, nodding to the door. 'Take Victor to the kitchen.'

Alone with Sheila, she said, 'You knew about Victor's affair?'

'Yes. I knew. But I swear to God, I never knew about anyone doing anything to Kev. I can't think straight. Who would do that to a defenceless child?'

'That's what I'm trying to find out.'

'Can you get me a drink?' Pleading eyes from behind her wild ginger hair.

'I will. But first I need some answers. When did you first notice a change in Kevin's behaviour?'

Sheila ran the back of her hand over her nose, sniffed, picked up her son's photo and stared at it.

'He became more withdrawn maybe about a year ago. It was a running battle to get him to school. I could count on one hand the number of times he had his friends over.'

'Did you do anything about his behaviour? Besides moving out of Munbally?'

'I thought maybe he was depressed. I know he was only ten at the time, but I was so worried. I even brought him to the doctor.'

'And what did the doctor say?'

Sheila straightened up in the chair. 'Kevin just cried and cried. The doctor said perhaps some counselling would help, but Kev refused to go to anyone else. I just put it down to his age.'

'Do you think it could be someone from your old estate?'

Sheila wrung her hands. 'He never said anything. Why didn't he tell me?'

Victor came back in with Boyd. He said, 'I'm so sorry, Sheila. I should have realised there was something seriously wrong with Kev.'

'You were always at work. All those late sessions. Well, that's what you told me. But I know different now.' Her voice was flat, no emotion.

'You were drinking a lot,' Victor said.

'That was your fault. You and Jen Driscoll.'

Lottie said, 'You mentioned earlier that Kev disappeared one night. Tell me about that.'

Sheila struggled to catch her breath. 'It was about a month ago. He came home in the middle of the night. Wouldn't say where he'd been. I confiscated his phone. I checked it. There was nothing on it. You have it now. Maybe you'll find something.'

Lottie had one last question.

'Sheila, this might sound odd, but do you recall how many pairs of football shorts Kevin had?'

Sheila looked up from beneath her reddened eyelids. 'I'm not sure. They should be in his kit bag. Why? Is it important?'

'There was just one green Munbally kit in his bag. But don't worry about it for now.' Lottie couldn't bring herself to show the devastated mother the photograph of the last item of clothing her son had worn. She looked at Boyd. He shook his head. No more questions. 'We're leaving now. I think you and Victor need to have a chat. And if you can think of anything, contact me immediately.'

Lottie was at the door when she heard a soft whisper come from the broken woman. She turned back and crouched down beside her.

'Do you think … Oh, God in heaven,' Sheila whispered. 'Could Victor have done this to our boy?'

'Don't worry, Sheila,' Lottie said. 'I will find out who did it.'

CHAPTER FIFTY-TWO

Toby sat on the floor beneath his window and gripped his knees to his chest. He was sure someone had been calling his name. He wished Max would come home. He'd even go to the shop and get him a chicken fillet roll if he wanted it.

He wasn't sure what time his ma had said she'd be home from work today. And his dad was out. He thought of Hope and Lexie. Playing in the town park like nothing had happened. The way she'd stared at him. The sound of her voice when she'd said his name. It gave him goose bumps. He'd been right to run, hadn't he?

Mikey, what would you do?

The smell of the burned toast that he'd eaten for his lunch rose up the stairs. The taste of it lingered on his tongue and at the back of his throat. He rubbed the floorboards with his finger until the skin reddened and started to bleed. He stuck it in his mouth and sucked the blood.

Outside. The screech of car brakes.

He knelt up and peered over the sill. A car turned the corner at full speed. Gone. But someone called his name again. Not from downstairs. It was from outside.

He slid to the floor. Gripped his legs tighter together, bit the top of his knee through his tracksuit.

It was a woman's voice, maybe a girl's. A high whisper, but still he heard it, above the rumble of the cars on the main road and the bark of a dog and the sounds of kids playing carelessly on the green.

He listened. Got back up on his knees. Grabbed the windowsill. Waited. He heard the voice again. This time it called, 'Max!'

Slowly he peeked over the ledge. Through the grimy glass into his garden. She stood there at the gate, looking up at him.

And then she beckoned. Hurried and frantic.

He shook his head.

No way was he going down there. No way. Not down to her, anyway.

He sat on the floor, dragged his shoes across and put them on. Didn't even bother to tie the one with the laces.

Slowly he looked out of the window again. No one there. She was gone.

He had to do something before he ended up like Mikey and Kev.

He had to go out.

He had to find out.

*

Sean cycled like the devil himself was behind him. He'd nearly died, seeing his mother standing on the Duffys' doorstep with Boyd. What was that all about? The dead baby?

As he headed up the road to his gran's house, his phone vibrated in his pocket. He stopped and checked it. Barry.

We need to talk, the text said.

'No we don't,' Sean said to the rain that had started once again.

He was still thinking of how Barry had treated Toby. It hadn't been nice at all. And then the incident outside the pub that Chloe had told him about. Making up his mind there and then, he decided to go over to Munbally and find Toby and tell him he was sorry. His mam would be proud of that.

Turning the bicycle around, he headed back into town. This would be his good deed for the day. Maybe for the whole year.

Yeah!

CHAPTER FIFTY-THREE

There was no one home at Jen Driscoll's house, so Lottie and Boyd drove round to Robbie Cotter's. Kirby had rung to say that his talk with Jacinta Barnes had yielded the news that Hope and her family had returned to Ragmullin.

Lottie knocked on the door, transferring her anger to her knuckles. No answer. Banged louder. Shouted through the letter box.

'Come on, Lottie, there's no one there.'

As she turned, a car drew up by the footpath. Robbie Cotter got out, loaded with paper bags. She could smell fried food.

'Mr Cotter,' she said.

'Er … Detectives. Hello.'

'Can we come inside?'

'No. I don't think so.' He fidgeted with the bags, locked the car and tried to edge past Lottie. She blocked his movement.

'Your niece is wanted for questioning in connection with the death of a baby boy found in the canal on Monday morning. Now, we can either do this the hard way, or you can let me in to speak with Hope.'

'Don't you need a warrant or something?' he said.

Boyd moved into Robbie's space. 'Open the door.'

'Okay, okay.' Robbie placed the bags of food on the step and opened the door. 'Hope?'

'No need to warn her,' Lottie said, and stepped by him into the hall. Silence.

'They might be up in Lexie's room,' Robbie offered.

Taking the stairs two at a time, Boyd ran up.

'No one here.'

A draught of air whistled into the hallway. Lottie moved into the kitchen.

'Boyd! Down here, now.'

The kitchen door was wide open. She ran into the overgrown shoebox-sized garden. She couldn't see a gate.

'Can you get out this way?' she said to Robbie.

'Over the wall. There's a laneway.'

She ran through the long grass and heaved herself up on the wall. Looked up and down. The lane was empty. She returned to Robbie.

'Where are Hope and Lexie?'

'They were here when I went for food.'

'How long ago did you leave?'

He glanced at his phone. 'Maybe half an hour. But I went into the bookie's, so it could have been longer. God, I don't know.'

'Mr Cotter, you've been aiding a person of interest in a murder investigation. I should take you to the station for questioning.'

'But you won't, because you need me here in case Hope comes back.'

'And when I find them, Lexie is being taken into care. I'm calling Child and Family Services. This is no way to raise a four-year-old.'

'Hey, hold on a minute. Lexie is well taken care of. And no matter what you think, Hope didn't kill her baby. I've had a good chat with her. I know her. She didn't do it.'

'She told me herself that she killed someone.' She spied Boyd walking back up the garden, a small pink bicycle in his hand. She rounded on him.

'When you've finished tidying the garden, radio for someone to get over here immediately. And they are not to let Mr Cotter out of their sight.'

She marched back through the house.

There was nothing here to help her.

Hope was in the wind. Again.

*

Hope was standing at the bus stop outside Supervalue. She had no money. She watched a homeless man wrapped in a blue sleeping bag with a little dog by his feet. A hat with coins in it too.

No, she couldn't steal from this poor guy.

She had run out the back door with Lexie in her arms, the weight of her daughter bearing down on her already painful abdomen. They had no coats. Nothing. Only the clothes they stood up in.

'Mummy, I'm hungry. I want chicken nuggets.'

Hope felt her heart constrict. What was she to do? Who could she go to for help?

She waited as the bus for Dublin drew in to the kerb and the commuters loaded themselves on. A blast of heat from inside the vehicle hit her in the face as she peered in.

'Are you getting on?' the driver shouted down from his seat.

Hope shook her head, tightened her hand on Lexie's and walked away.

There was only one person she knew of who might be able to help her. Much as she didn't want to talk to him, ever again, she knew she had to.

'Come on, Lexie,' she said.

She trudged past the Joyce Hotel and on down Gaol Street, carrying way too much pain in her heart and in her body. No one turned to stare. No one knew who she was, even though her photo had been on the news. She was anonymous in her own town. And that was a good thing. She continued under the crane at the courthouse but her steps slowed as her breathing became laboured. The exertion of the last few days was catching up with her.

'Are you sick, Mummy?' Lexie asked.

'Not really. Don't worry, sweetheart, I'll be fine.'

'I'm hungry.'

'I know, but it's only another little bit. You're a brilliant girl, and I love you so much.'

He hadn't been at home when she'd called over earlier, so there was only one other place she knew where she might find him.

Past the greyhound stadium, she took a right and headed up towards the old tyre recycling depot.

Max Collins was her last hope.

*

Sean had almost given up when a lad on a pony pointed out the Collins house. He leaned his bike against the wall and walked up to the door. Why was he here? To apologise? But he hadn't done anything wrong. That had been Barry. Then he remembered the terror in Toby's eyes. He had to do something.

No one answered the door. Ah well, I tried, he thought. As he returned to his bike and got ready to cycle away, a hand grabbed the handlebars.

'Not so fast, shithead.'

Sean looked up into the face of a teenager with sunken eyes and drooping lids. He gulped. 'Sorry, I was just looking for Toby.'

'Toby? What you want with him?'

'Nothing.'

The teenager bared his teeth. 'Tell me what you want with my brother or I'll wrap the wheels of your fancy bike around your neck.'

'He ... he was upset, yesterday. I just called round to see if he was okay.'

'Everyone is upset. Did you know there's a killer going around looking for young boys? Fellas just like you.'

Sean felt his guts rumble and slide down to the bottom of his stomach. Toby's brother was now eyeing up the bike.

'How much did that cost you?'

'Don't know. My mother bought it for me for my birthday.'

'I like the sound of your mam. Rich, is she?'

'No, she's a detective.'

The change was instant. Sean watched as the teenager stepped back from the bike and stuck his hands in his tracksuit pockets as if they'd been burned.

'Get out of here. Don't want no pup out of a guard sniffing around. Go on. Fuck off.'

Sean threw his leg over the crossbar, but in his haste to escape, he rode the bike off the kerb and fell face-first onto the road. Blood was pouring from his nose and down his white T-shirt. He untangled his legs from the bike and felt himself being hauled to his feet.

'The state of you. I think you broke your nose. You'd better come inside. I don't want your pig mother blaming me for this. Hurry up. I won't bite.'

The teenager threw the bike into the overgrown garden and dragged Sean towards the door. Maybe he should make a run for it, Sean thought. No, his ankle was killing him, as well as his nose.

The door was opened and he was dragged inside.

'Welcome to our humble abode, as my da says. I'm Max. What's your name?'

CHAPTER FIFTY-FOUR

Lottie stuffed a crust of bread into her mouth and watched Boyd eating a house-special sandwich. Cafferty's was quiet. The television hummed out a rolling news channel. They had half the district out looking for Hope and Lexie, and Jen Driscoll hadn't been at home or at the gym, so Boyd had insisted on food before they returned to the station.

'Can I ask you something?' Lottie said, pushing away her own sandwich.

'You can, if it's not about the job.'

'Okay.'

'And only if you eat first,' Boyd said. 'You're fading away, Mrs Parker.'

'Do you feel any different?' She watched as Boyd studied her, trying to figure out what she was talking about, she supposed.

'Different?'

'Since you got your divorce?' Why did she have to ask stupid questions? Shit, now that it was out there, she had to follow through. 'I know you and Jackie had been separated, like forever, but now it's official, how does that make you feel?'

'Where is this coming from, Lottie?'

'It's just a question.' Shut up, she told herself.

He was curling his lip, biting it, squinting at her. Trying to figure her out. Best of luck there, Boyd, she thought. If she couldn't figure herself out, well, he hadn't a chance.

'I'm the same as always. No different. A bit of paper doesn't change things. Not for me.'

Lottie reached out and touched his hand.

'I'm sorry,' she said.

'For what?' He looked stunned.

'Oh, I don't know. Jesus, Boyd, you make conversations like this very difficult.'

He picked up his sandwich and took a bite out of it. 'Conversation? I have no idea what it is with you.'

'Don't talk with your mouth full. You're worse than a child.'

'You sound like your mother.'

'My mother?'

'Yeah. How is she?' He gulped down a mouthful of tea.

He was changing the subject, but she let it go. She didn't know what she wanted from him so there was no point tying both of them up in knots.

'Rose is being Rose,' she said, thinking that her mother was actually being very accommodating of late.

'Have you told her yet about the phone call?'

'What phone call?'

'The day after your house burned down. From that Leo guy in America.'

Lottie had thought very little about it. She had enough on her plate without some long-lost relative turning up on her doorstep. Or her mother's doorstep, for that matter. 'No, I haven't.'

'I think you should. What if he rings again? Maybe even turns up here?'

'Can you read my mind?'

'Just saying.'

'He's not going to turn up. And anyway, I've enough on my mind at the moment.'

'Then why are you worrying about my divorce?'

'I only asked you a question, which you refused to answer. Are you finished eating? We'd better get back to work.'

'Just so you know, I'm no different from before I got the piece of paper confirming what was already dead years ago. Okay?'

It was on the tip of her tongue to mention his liaison with Cynthia Rhodes, but common sense intervened. They split the bill, though she left most of her sandwich behind. She just couldn't eat.

*

Gilly cornered Kirby as he exited the team meeting.

'Hi, can I have a word?' she said, blushing slightly as Maria Lynch passed them in the corridor.

'I'm up to my lugs,' Kirby said. 'Later.'

'This is work-related.'

'Two minutes.' He walked towards the office, but she pulled him back.

'In private.' She started walking down the stairs. On the turn, she stopped and faced him.

'What's so important?' he said.

'I need to have a word with Wes Finnegan, the bus driver. Can you arrange it?'

'Why? You're not involved in the murder investigations.'

Pushing defiance into her demeanour, Gilly folded her arms. 'I was following this Max Collins yesterday. The guy who Finnegan reported for stealing cash from his bus. And he disappeared into the industrial estate. I was thinking that maybe Finnegan might know where Collins's bolthole is.'

'And why would you think that?'

'I tried Collins's home earlier and he wasn't there. And if he knew where the money was kept on the bus, that suggests he was a little more familiar with Finnegan than he reported.'

She watched Kirby closely as he stuck a file under one arm and tapped his shirt pocket for a cigar. He found his e-cig instead, and jammed it in his mouth.

'Seems plausible enough,' he said. 'Do you want a formal interview or—'

'Just a quick word in the cell. Before he's released.' She unfolded her arms and grabbed the e-cig from his mouth. 'These things are as bad as cigars.'

'Hasn't been scientifically proven,' he said. 'Come on. We have to let him go soon, nothing to hold him on.'

Wes Finnegan was marching around the cell when the duty sergeant opened the door. The blue light caused a ghostly shadow to spread over his face.

Gilly closed the door behind her. 'Sit down for a minute, Mr Finnegan.' She had to act quickly. The bus driver was about to be released. Without forensic evidence, they had nothing, and the football shorts could have been bought anywhere.

'You've no right to be keeping me here. I didn't do nothing to those boys. I'll be complaining to my solicitor when he gets here – if he ever gets here, the useless bastard.'

'This isn't about the boys. You reported money stolen from your bus and pointed me in the direction of Max Collins. Is that correct?'

Finnegan sat down on the cold seat and stared at his laceless shoes.

'I want to withdraw that report.'

'Why?' Gilly was confused. 'You were adamant yesterday that you wanted him arrested and your money returned.'

'That was yesterday. Before all this shite. I need to get out. I've a business to run. I'll deal with Collins myself. Just let me out of here.'

He sounded like a petulant child who'd had his toys confiscated. The smell of his body odour was overwhelming, and Gilly wondered how anyone travelled on his bus without passing out.

'You've reported a theft. It's my duty to follow that up. You've also made an allegation against a young man who has the right to defend himself. My question to you, Mr Finnegan, is do you know whereabouts in the industrial estate I might find Max Collins?'

'The industrial estate? I don't know what you mean.'

But his face told her he did. The colour swept up from his neck and settled in a red blush beneath his sagging eyes.

'If you want to get out of here today, you should tell me,' she bluffed.

A loud sigh flew from his bulbous lips. 'Tyre depot. The one up the first right-hand road after the dog track. It's closed down, but I think he hangs out there. Smoking dope, if you ask me.'

Gilly pressed the buzzer and the door opened. She stepped out into the fresh air and inhaled deeply. As the duty sergeant swung the door shut, she could hear Finnegan cursing and swearing to be released.

She went to find Kirby.

*

Kirby was huffing down the corridor when Lottie and Boyd returned.

'Any luck at Munbally?' he said.

'No. Hope wasn't there.' Lottie squeezed past him into the office. He traipsed in after her.

'I followed up with Miss Conway,' he said.

'Miss Conway?'

'The boys' primary school teacher.'

'What did she have to say?' Suddenly Lottie felt hungry. She should have brought the sandwich back with her.

'She says Hope hadn't worked at the school for six months. Said she shouldn't really have been on the list of staff.'

'Why did she give up work?'

'Miss Conway wasn't sure. Apparently she just stopped coming in. No explanation.'

'Dead end there.'

'But it still gives her a connection to the boys,' Kirby said.

'She also lived in the same estate,' Boyd added. 'Plenty of opportunity for contact.'

'Yeah. She had to have known both boys. We really need to find her. Closure is needed on the death of the baby as well.'

'She's run away twice now,' Boyd said. 'Why run if you're not guilty of something?'

'Maybe she ran because she was terrified.'

'Is Wes Finnegan still in the cells?' Boyd asked.

'I hope so,' Lottie said, 'or McMahon won't be happy. He said he wanted someone's arse shining the granite.'

'More like greasing it,' Kirby said, turning up his wide nose. 'Yeah, he's there. Waiting to be released. Our time for holding him is almost up.'

'Finnegan says he found a plastic bag containing the football shorts on the floor of the bus. Brand new, he says.' Lottie mulled over the bus driver's explanation.

'But why were they on his clothes line in the kitchen?' Boyd said. 'He didn't answer *that* question.'

'Too busy pointing the finger at Dr Duffy.' Lottie threw her bag under her desk and went back to the main office.

'Diversionary tactics,' Kirby said.

'Have you finished your trawl of the security footage from McDonald's and the clubhouse?' Lottie asked.

'Tech guys have it now.'

'And have you interviewed those you could identify?'

'Most of them. All appear sound so far.'

'What about the car park CCTV?'

'I cross-referenced it with the times of people leaving McDonald's. Anyone who said they had a car there drove off within a few minutes of leaving the restaurant.'

'Go over it again.'

Kirby said, 'There is something you might be interested in.'

Lottie leaned against the wall and folded her arms, still thinking about what could have made Hope run away. Again. Could she really have murdered her own baby and the two boys?

'Sorry, what did you say?'

'I was running background checks on the people associated with the boys' team. And I think I found something.'

'Spit it out.' Lottie straightened up and stood at Kirby's shoulder as his thick fingers punched keys on his computer.

'Rory Butler,' he said.

'What about him?' Boyd moved to Kirby's other shoulder.

Another punch of the return key and Kirby scrolled down through a charge sheet. Lottie scanned it.

'Mr Butler left London in a quite a hurry.'

'There was a warrant for his arrest,' Boyd said, reading the words on the screen. 'Insurance fraud.'

'Yeah,' Kirby said. 'But look down here. All charges were dropped.'

'How was he able to pour so much money into renovating his grandfather's house?' Lottie looked over Kirby's head at Boyd. 'If it wasn't his own cash, whose was it? We need to bring him in again. He has no alibi for either night and he had access to both boys.'

'And another thing …' Kirby said.

'Go on.'

'I followed up with Gaddstown bingo group. Spoke with one very inquisitive lady there. Mrs Courtney. Runs the community centre where the bingo takes place. She seems to know everyone by name. And she told me Jen Driscoll was not at the bingo on Sunday night.'

'So where was she when Mikey was taken?'

Acting Superintendent McMahon stuck his head around the door. 'Inspector, I've been looking for you everywhere. My office, now.' He disappeared again.

Kirby looked up at Lottie and Boyd. 'Is it my imagination, or is he sounding more like Superintendent Corrigan with each passing day?'

'I think you're right,' Boyd said. 'What are you going to do now, Lottie?'

She was already following McMahon down the corridor.

'I've had a call from Cynthia Rhodes.'

Lottie remained standing even though McMahon had indicated for her to sit down.

'Interesting conversation,' he continued, walking to the window and looking out. He turned around. 'She's been talking to a relative of yours.'

'My mother?' What had Rose done now? Just when Lottie thought things had calmed down.

'No, not your mother. Do you know a Leo Belfield?'

What the ...? Where had that come from? A hundred scenarios whirled around in her brain. She sat down.

'No. Why?' Play dumb, she thought.

'He's asking questions about you.'

'Really. Can't say I recognise the name.'

'Your face tells a completely different story.'

'I might have heard it. Not sure where, though.'

'You're not a great liar.' He moved back to his desk and sat down. 'Will I tell you what I've heard?'

'That would be a help.'

'This Leo Belfield is a NYPD detective. And he is in Ragmullin and—'

'What?'

'Let me finish.'

When Lottie closed her mouth, she nodded for him to continue.

'He's asking around about you. Sourced Cynthia and quizzed her. But she, not being that long in Ragmullin, didn't know a whole lot, so she referred him to me.'

Clamping her mouth shut, Lottie waited him out.

'I had a coffee with him this morning. Nice chap. Very American.'

'Well, he *is* an American,' she said.

'Ha! You do know him.'

'You said he was NYPD.'

He opened a notebook on his desk. She craned to see if she could read it upside down. He slapped his hand over it. 'He's trying to trace family from the Ragmullin area. Said he might be your half-brother. Know anything about that?'

'No.'

'He mentioned that his mother is Alexis Belfield. From Farranstown. And then I recalled the case that initially brought me to Ragmullin. The murder of Marian Russell.'

'So?' Still playing dumb, but she knew McMahon wasn't buying it.

'If I find out you did not declare an interest in an active investigation, you will be out on your ear.'

'How could I declare an interest in something I knew nothing about? Come on, give me a break here. What does this Leo guy want with me?'

'I don't know. But I'm warning you, if you've been untruthful, it will spell trouble for you.'

She could feel the blood boil in her veins. She repeated, 'What does he want with me?'

'Digging for dirt. Some half-brother that is, though it doesn't surprise me.'

She bit down a retort. No point in giving McMahon more ammunition. He appeared to have amassed quite enough as it was. And no matter which way she analysed it, she knew he was keeping something from her.

'Is that all?'

'I want an update on the murders on my desk in the next ten minutes.'

'Consider it done.' She stood up and left the office.

In the corridor, she leaned against the wall, trying to catch her breath. This Leo had sought out Cynthia Rhodes for information. And she'd seen the reporter with Boyd in Danny's Bar. Had she been pumping him for information? What had McMahon got written in his notebook? And who the hell was Leo Belfield?

She slapped the heel of her hand against her forehead. She could do without this shite right now.

CHAPTER FIFTY-FIVE

Lottie walked back to her office and sat at her desk, wondering about Leo Belfield and the fact that this stranger had been asking questions behind her back. One thing was certain, she would have to confront Boyd about his chat with Cynthia. First, though, they had a job to do.

'Boss?' Maria Lynch walked in, a file open in her hand, perched on her baby bump. 'Have you got a minute?'

Lottie wanted to hightail it out of the station before anyone else landed bad news in her lap, but she directed the detective into her office, conscious that they'd hardly spoken two words since Lynch's accusation about Ben.

'What is it?'

'I was helping Kirby with the background checks for the persons of interest in the boys' murder, and—'

'Wait a minute. Didn't I tell you to concentrate on the death of the baby?'

'You did, but the only lead in that investigation so far is Hope Cotter, and she's gone to ground. Everyone in the district is on alert for her. Unless you want me to twiddle my thumbs …'

'There's follow-up on the lab work. The post-mortem report. I can't do it all. I need you to concentrate.'

Lynch stood in silence.

'Okay, what?' Lottie said.

'Jen Driscoll, Mikey's mum. She lived in London for a few years.'

'Go on.'

'She worked at Butler and Associates.'

'Rory Butler's business?'

'His father's.'

Lottie put out her hand and took the sheet of paper. 'Good work, Lynch. I'm sorry for snapping.' Lynch walked out in silence.

Lottie checked her emails. There was one from the state pathologist, Jane Dore. Post-mortem information. She read through it quickly.

'Boyd?' she yelled. 'Where the hell is he when I want him?'

*

Max wasn't there. Hope searched the office part of the old unit. No, definitely no sign of him.

'Mummy, I'm so hungry,' Lexie complained.

'Shh. We're going home in a minute. I'm just looking for my friend.'

She lifted Lexie into her arms, wincing with the stab of pain caused by the weight of the child. She really needed to see a doctor. She was still losing a lot of blood, and the pain shouldn't be this bad.

Maybe she should go to the guards. Hand herself in. But wasn't that what she'd done on Monday morning? Why had she done that if she hadn't committed a crime? Why couldn't she remember? Was it so horrific that she had blocked it from her consciousness? She wished she knew.

'Let's go, hunny bunny.'

She eased Lexie down from her hip. Gripping the child's hand, she walked around the old tractor tyres and over towards the door. The space in front of her darkened. A shadow? A rattle of iron and the door slid open.

Her breath stuck in her throat and her hand tightened on Lexie's.

'Hello, Hope. Do you realise that everyone is looking for you?'

*

Lottie gathered the team in the incident room. If McMahon wanted a report, she needed to have something concrete for him.

'We've been running rings around ourselves looking at family members, those who were associated with the boys, neighbours and bingo ladies. We need to concentrate on the victims for a few minutes.'

She walked up to the board. Stared at the photos there.

'First question. Why were these two boys, Mikey Driscoll and Kevin Shanley, targeted? What or who had they in common?'

Kirby said, 'They were in the same class in school. They played on the same soccer team. Mikey's mum, Jennifer, worked as an instructor in the same gym as Kevin Shanley's dad, Victor.'

Lottie said, 'And Victor admitted that something had gone on between him and Jen, though he did say that it was long over. Jennifer Driscoll needs to be formally interviewed.'

'Because she had an affair with the other victim's father?' Boyd again.

'That, and she said she was at bingo the night Mikey was murdered, which we now believe to be untrue. And because Lynch has discovered that Jen lived in London twelve years ago.'

'So?'

Shut up, Boyd, Lottie silently prayed. 'She worked for Butler and Associates.'

Boyd remained silent. Good.

'Jen Driscoll has a link to both Victor Shanley and Rory Butler. And she lied about her whereabouts Sunday night. What does that tell us?'

'I thought we were looking at the victims,' Boyd said.

'Will you concentrate on what I'm saying and quit the sniping.'

'Right. Go ahead, boss,' he said, and began to roll up his shirt-sleeves, slowly and neatly.

'Jen Driscoll has to be brought in for a formal interview and Rory Butler needs to be interviewed again. On top of what I've just said, he also lives a few hundred metres from the site where Kevin's body was found. Kirby? Are you noting this down?'

'I am.'

'Okay. Mikey Driscoll was strangled, which is one of the less messy forms of murder and somewhat personal. And Kevin Shanley was murdered in a similar manner.'

'What's the motive?' Lynch said softly.

'Good question. And why these two boys? What else have we got, Kirby?'

'The school,' Kirby said. 'The teachers all check out. The only anomaly is Hope Cotter. She worked there as a cleaner but quit six months ago.'

'She lives in the Munbally estate too. And she's wanted in connection with the murder of the baby boy found in the canal. Any update on where she might be?'

'Nothing yet,' Lynch said.

Lottie turned to look at the crime-scene photos. 'Why leave the boys' bodies in these particular locations? The grounds of the football club and the lake shore. Do they mean something to the killer?'

'They were out in the open,' Boyd said. 'The killer wanted them found.'

'I also believe the killer was sending a message.'

'To who?' Kirby said.

'To *whom*,' Boyd corrected.

Lottie glared. 'We need to figure that out too. Was it a warning to someone else? See what I've done to these two boys? If you don't do what I say, you'll be next?' She stood up straight. She had surprised herself with this conjecture.

'If it was, that means someone else may be in danger,' Lynch said. She stood up suddenly. 'Sorry. Baby pushing down on my bladder. Be back in a minute.'

Lottie sat on the edge of the desk nearest the incident boards and waved the email she had printed off. 'The state pathologist has sent me the results of the toxicology screens. Both boys had diazepam in their systems. High doses, if I'm reading it correctly.'

'Valium?' Kirby said.

'Yup. Used to subdue them, no doubt.' Lottie wrinkled her nose in distaste.

'Jesus, they were just children,' Boyd said.

'Apparently it was more than enough to put them straight to sleep,' Lottie said. 'However, Jane says that on conclusion of her examinations, she can confirm that neither boy was abused immediately before death.'

'What kind of sicko are we looking for?' Kirby said.

'We need to go back to the beginning. Where were they abducted from? Where were they taken to and where were they killed? The state pathologist confirms they were not murdered where they were found, so we need to trace back to last-known sightings. And keep in mind there may be someone else out there who is in danger.'

Kirby said, 'I read through all the door-to-door reports. Kevin wasn't seen at all on Monday evening.'

'He went out earlier that afternoon to play football with his friends, according to his mother,' Boyd said.

'Did he, though?' Lottie said. 'His home needs a further search by SOCOs. It's possible he was killed there.'

'And if Jen Driscoll wasn't where she said she was ...' Boyd said.

'Then we need to do the same forensic analysis of Mikey's home. Get on to Jim McGlynn immediately.'

'We need a warrant,' Boyd said.

'Do you always have to come up with the problems? Prepare the documents and I want them signed by a judge before the day is out.'

'I'll do my best.'

'Do better than your best,' she said.

'I'll get to it then.' He slapped his chair against the wall.

Lynch returned as Boyd left the incident room.

Lottie turned to her. 'Keep on with the search for Hope. That's one case we can more or less wrap up, once we get her into custody.'

Lynch rolled her eyes, but Lottie kept her thoughts to herself. Enough damage done for one day.

CHAPTER FIFTY-SIX

Gilly had to wait until the team meeting was over and then she sweet-talked Kirby into accompanying her.

'It will only be a few minutes,' she said, driving the squad car out of the yard.

'A few minutes I don't have. I'm tasked with the boys' murder investigations. You should see the mountain of paper—'

'Kirby! I know what's involved. I only need a witness with me, and I trust you. This could be nothing, but if this Max lad is there and junked up on drugs, I don't want to face him on my own. Okay?'

She swerved the car around the corner by the greyhound stadium and drove into the industrial estate. Cutting across the roundabout painted on the road, she sped up the narrow laneway and applied the brakes. Dust rose from the gravel forecourt.

'You were driving so fast you could have used the flashers,' Kirby said, clutching the dashboard.

Gilly leaned over and pecked him on the cheek, then fetched her cap from the back seat, slapped it on her head, checked the mirror and jumped out.

'Come on, slowcoach.' She walked towards the galvanised door.

'Wait up,' Kirby said, and huffed up beside her. He checked his weapon was ready and stepped in front of Gilly. She watched as he cocked his ear to the door and carefully slid it to one side.

Sticking his head around it he said, 'I'm Detective Larry Kirby. Is anyone there?'

Gilly peered in around him. 'I heard something.'

'Like what?'

'It might just be a cat. Come on, I thought you were in a hurry.'

She followed Kirby as he stepped inside. The air was stifling hot. A cone of light fell from a split in the roofing. Dust danced in its glow. Tyres were stacked along the walls and in the middle of the floor space. She thought she saw a flash of colour behind a pile of tractor tyres.

'Kirby. Over there.' She started to run. He pulled her back.

'Wait. Let me take a look first.'

'You have the gun. Cover me.' She broke free of his hold and dashed around the tyres. 'Oh my God. Kirby, quick. Here.'

Curled in a ball on the oily ground lay a child. Her leggings were dirty and her hair was plastered to her head. Gilly couldn't see any visible wounds.

'Is she alive?' Kirby said.

*

Max had stuck a plaster on Sean's damaged nose.

'That should do until you see a doctor,' he said, and sat down at the table. He took out a pouch of tobacco and began to roll a cigarette. 'You want one?'

'Don't smoke,' Sean said. 'Is it just you and Toby? In the family, I mean?'

'Nah, we have two little sisters. They go to the community crèche. Toby should be here, though. Do you have any idea where he might be?'

'I don't know him,' Sean explained, 'but I met him yesterday and he seemed very frightened of something.'

'Yeah, two of his friends were murdered. That kind of thing would strike terror into anyone.'

'I know. But … Oh, it doesn't matter.'

'Tell me,' Max lit the taper and inhaled. The sweet smell reminded Sean of the weed he'd once tried with Jason, Katie's boyfriend. That memory conjured up a whole new heartache.

'Well, he wouldn't talk. At all. And when Barry said—'

'Barry Duffy? What the shite was he doing near my brother?'

The vehemence of Max's tone caused Sean to shrink a little into himself. He really had to get out of here.

'Come on, young pup of a guard, tell me what that dick was doing.'

'He was with me, actually. We were just kicking a ball around the field up the back of the estate. When Barry mentioned that Kevin was dead, Toby looked so scared, I thought he was going to be sick.'

'What else?'

'My sister, Chloe, works in Fallon's bar. She said she met this young boy last night who was scared witless. She thought he'd been about to be picked up by someone in a car, and he was terrified. She walked him part of the way home.'

Max inhaled and closed his eyes. When he opened them, Sean knew he had to leave soon. Max was getting high.

'What's a nice girl like your sister doing working in Fallon's?'

'You know my sister?' Sean asked, horrified.

'I know Fallon's, and take it from me, you don't want to be hanging around with the likes of Barry Fuckwit Duffy. He's bad news. Him and his dysfunctional family.'

Sean thought it was more likely that Max and his family were the dysfunctional ones. He said, 'Can I go now?'

'I haven't kidnapped you or anything. Go on. Get out.'

Sean moved to the door. 'Can I ask you something?'

'What?'

'Do you know Toby's username on PlayStation?'

'I bought him that, you know,' Max said. 'Had a bit of extra work at Christmas. Never played it myself. Used to be a bit hooked on the crack. Having a good time, so I thought.'

Sean wondered if Max was referring to crack cocaine. He looked at the scars on his face and decided not to ask.

'You have no idea what his username is, do you?' he said again.

'Why do you want to know?'

'Because I think Toby needs a friend, and if he hasn't got one in the real world, maybe I can be one in the virtual world.'

'You're a nice kid,' Max said, 'but you're still a pig's son, sniffing into things that don't concern you.'

Sean put his hand on the door, ready for a quick escape.

'Wait a minute.' Max left the spliff in the ashtray and stood up. 'If you take a look at the PlayStation, would you find this username you're talking about?'

Sean's instinct was to get the hell out of this house. But he remembered Toby's terror-stricken face.

'Yeah, sure.'

Max pushed out past him. 'It's upstairs. In the bedroom.'

*

Kirby put his hand on Gilly's shoulder.

'Is she alive?' he repeated.

'I ... I'm not sure.'

She held two fingers to the child's neck, and the little girl's eyes flashed open.

'Mummy?' The voice was faint. Gilly moved slightly to block out the light falling behind her. It was blinding the child.

'What's your name, sweetheart?' She lifted the little girl into her arms.

'Lexie,' the child said weakly. 'I want my mummy.'

'What's your mummy's name?'

'Hope.'

Gilly looked back at Kirby. 'This must be Hope Cotter's daughter.'

'Does she need a doctor?' he said.

'I think she might be dehydrated. I need to take her to the hospital.'

'She'll get lost in the system,' Kirby said, locking his gun into his shoulder holster. 'We'll take her to the station. Might be a way to entice her mother out of hiding. First, I want to give this place a quick scout.'

'We need to get her out of this heat.'

But Kirby was directing his bulky frame towards the portioned area to the rear of the unit. 'Looks like an old office. And someone's been using it as a place to kip down. Sleeping bag and cans here.'

Gilly stood up with Lexie in her arms, the child's head on her shoulder. She could feel the little body trembling.

'Come back later. Hope isn't here.'

'Nor your Max. I wonder if the two of them know each other. Maybe they're connected in some way.'

Outside in the blazing sunlight, Kirby opened the door for Gilly and she slipped into the back seat.

'Where is your mummy, darling?' Gilly asked as Kirby drove them to the station.

Lexie looked at her directly, eyes like saucers. 'The bad person took her.'

CHAPTER FIFTY-SEVEN

The room was tiny. Two single beds. An unvarnished hand-made table with nails sticking out held the console. Sean reckoned Toby had to sit on one of the beds to play his games. There was no wardrobe or dresser. Clothes were stacked on a chair in the corner.

A small locker stood between the beds. It was overflowing with plastic bottles, and the floor around one bed was littered with food wrappers. He suspected this was Max's, while the neat one with the Chelsea duvet cover was Toby's. He suddenly felt sorry for the way he'd been complaining to his mam about needing to have his own space. God, he didn't know how lucky he was.

Max picked up a scratched controller from the floor. 'Here. See if you can find anything.'

Sean started clicking and the screen filled with a paused game. He recognised it as *FIFA 2012*. Way out of date. He clicked on Toby's profile.

'You find it?'

Glancing over his shoulder, Sean saw that Max was lying on his bed, arms behind his head, eyes shut.

He snapped a photograph of the profile with his phone camera. Then he opened the chat on the PlayStation and photographed the messages without reading them. He clicked back to the game and snoozed the screen. As he turned to leave, Max jumped off the bed and tugged his arm.

'Let me go,' Sean said, his whole body still hurting from the fall.

Max's crooked and broken teeth were up against his face.

'I'm warning you, don't get Toby in any trouble.' He let Sean's arm fall away. 'And if you know what's good for you, run a million miles from Barry Duffy.'

*

Gilly carried the child to the family room. That was a misnomer. It was just the least intimidating interview room.

Kirby went to phone the duty doctor to have Lexie checked over. They'd already dispatched a squad car to the Cotter address. But Gilly didn't think Hope would be there. Something had happened in that old depot. Something to terrify a four-year-old girl.

Entering with a small juice carton, Kirby poked the straw into it before crouching down and holding it out for Lexie. Gilly was surprised to see the child reaching for the drink.

'Doctor is on his way. I've sent a team to carry out a full search of the unit and to take away the bedding for analysis purposes,' he said.

'Right,' Gilly said, stroking the child's hair from her eyes as she drank greedily. 'Poor thing is parched.'

'Hungry.' Two frightened eyes looked up at her.

'Will you get her something to eat?'

'Nuggets,' the little girl said.

'I'll send out one of the lads,' Kirby said. 'I'd say you'd love a Happy Meal. Would I be right?'

A series of nods provided his answer. He stood up and moved to the door.

Gilly said, 'Did anyone working near the depot see or hear anything?'

'I've dispatched a crew to ask questions. But we're so stretched with the other investigations, it will take some time.'

'She's been abducted. Lexie said so.'

'Gilly, the child is only four. Maybe her mother had had enough of—'

'Shh. Will you stop talking like that in front of her.' Gilly cradled the little girl to her chest, resting her chin on her head.

'Suits you,' Kirby said, and exited before Gilly could retort.

'Mummy loves me,' Lexie said.

'I know, sweetheart.'

Gilly was sure someone had taken Hope. She just wished Lottie would return quickly. She would understand. After all, hadn't she been through the same thing last year? Then she remembered how that had turned out, and she pulled the child even closer to her.

'Where's my mummy?'

I wish I knew, Gilly thought. Aloud she said, 'She'll be back for you soon, petal.'

*

As Toby rounded the corner, the first thing he saw, lying inside the front wall of his house, was a bicycle with a buckled wheel. Barry Duffy's? No, he wouldn't have the neck to turn up here, he thought.

A youngster was screaming in hysterics from a house to his left. Bouncing up and down on an old couch in the front garden. Toby shook his head. He'd love to escape Munbally. His teachers at school were always telling him that if he studied hard in secondary school, he could make something of himself. But Toby didn't agree. He'd seen too much in his short life. He knew it would take a lot more than studying hard. He needed something else. Something he'd never had. Luck.

He stubbed his Converse on a crack in the footpath and almost fell head over heels. As he steadied himself, he caught sight of his front door opening and a boy running out. Toby leaned in against the low wall, hoping to make himself invisible, but failing. The boy picked up the bike and began walking it towards him. Toby sighed with relief. It wasn't Barry.

'Hi, Toby. I remember you from yesterday. I'm Sean.'

'Why were you in my house?' Toby found his voice. From somewhere deep within him, the fear had released his vocal cords.

'Looking for you, bud,' Sean said. 'Met your brother.'

Toby groaned. Max. Again. 'Wh-what did he say?'

'Nothing much. Scared the shit out of me. He's a bit of a monster, isn't he?'

Toby smiled. 'Yeah.'

'I'd better get this bike fixed before my mother sees it. Might bring it to Kenny's Cycles. Do you want to walk with me?'

Toby was going to say yes, but then remembered he had to speak to Max. And he didn't want to chance running into Barry Duffy.

'No, I have to get home.'

'Look me up on *FIFA*. We can have a chat. Okay?'

'Sure,' Toby said, and watched until Sean and his bike had disappeared around the corner.

He turned towards his house. Max was standing on the doorstep.

'Little prick, I want a chat with you,' Max yelled.

Toby dropped his head but didn't move. He didn't like it when Max was angry. It only meant one thing. A slap or a thump. He turned and looked at the youngsters bouncing on the couch in their garden. He eyed the corner around which Sean had walked. At the end of the terrace of houses that curved around the green, he noticed a lad on a bicycle pedalling like mad towards him.

Barry Duffy.

Oh no.

Toby Collins made his decision.

CHAPTER FIFTY-EIGHT

With the hood of his windcheater pulled up, Rory Butler speared the spade into the ground. Despite the drizzle, the soil was still hard. He applied more pressure, his work boot slipping off the edge of the tool onto the ground.

'Ouch!' He felt the ligament in his ankle tighten, but it was only a niggle. He jammed the spade in again.

'This is a long way from your shiny London office,' came a voice from behind him.

He swung round.

'What are you doing here?' he said, dropping the spade.

'I had to get out of the house. I can't work. I can't do anything. Oh Rory.'

He looked at her, no jacket and her hair stuck to her face. Pitiful. He folded her into his arms and patted her head as if she were a child.

'Come inside,' he said. Before anyone sees you, he thought.

*

There was still no one at the Driscoll house. Lottie posted two uniforms on the street outside and headed for Rory Butler's.

Outside his house she stood on the step with Boyd. No answer.

'Let's go around the back,' she said.

She followed in Boyd's footsteps, taking the route Rory had brought them yesterday.

The air was fresh from the fall of rain and the garden furniture was damp. There was no one sitting under the canopy. Lottie peered in through the large glass doors. 'Appears deserted.'

'But there are two cars out front,' Boyd said.

She tried the handle, pulled then pushed. The glass door opened. Stepping inside, she shouted, 'Hello? Anyone home?'

'We'd better go,' Boyd said. 'No point in aggravating a suspect.'

'We need to speak with him.' She ventured towards the open-plan living area, ran her fingers along the automated integrated units. Nothing sprang forth. She moved to the hallway. Looked up the mahogany spiral staircase.

'Anyone up there?' No reply. 'Wonder where the housekeeper is?'

A door banged somewhere in the house. Then she heard the engine of a car burst into life.

She looked at Boyd. He turned and ran through the living room and out the back. Lottie opened the front door in time to see a car speeding away.

'How the hell …?' Boyd came running around the side of the house.

'Must be another exit,' Lottie said.

'What are you doing in my house?'

She twirled round to find Rory Butler standing behind her.

'Mr Butler, the very man. We were looking to speak with you.'

He walked out barefoot onto the damp step, shirt swinging open above tight jeans, hair unruly. Lottie could see the lines around his eyes creasing in annoyance, and she had a feeling he had been angry long before she trampled muddy footprints through his house.

'I have nothing further to say to you, Detective Inspector. You are trespassing in my home. If you don't mind, I'd like you to leave.' He turned back into the house.

'I do mind.' She followed him inside, with Boyd close behind. 'Who was that who left in such a hurry?'

Butler rounded on her. 'None of your business.'

But he didn't tell her to get out.

'Where's Helen today?' Lottie trailed after him into the kitchen. Stainless steel top to bottom and snow-white tiles beneath her feet. She felt a little guilty about her damp boots, but only for a moment.

'I gave her the day off.' He filled a mug from a coffee pot. Didn't offer her any.

Lottie dragged a chair from the breakfast bar and sat down. Boyd lounged against a wall beside the door. She wondered about the guest who had made such a quick getaway. Someone who was aware they'd arrived and wanted to avoid them? Or someone Rory wanted to keep secret? Curiosity was running furiously through her blood.

'Rory, please sit down for a moment.' She was trying her best to be pleasant.

'I'm fine here.' He stood in front of the glittering refrigerator.

'You left London under something of a cloud,' she continued.

'Is that a question?'

'It's a statement. You embezzled money from your own company.'

'The charges were dropped.'

'Because your father paid off your debts.'

'Nothing to do with you.'

'And Jennifer Driscoll?'

For the first time since they'd entered the kitchen, Lottie noticed a flicker of unrest in his demeanour. His eyes were suddenly wary.

'What about her?'

'She worked for you for three years.'

'If you know all this, why are you here?'

'What was your relationship with Jennifer?'

'You are barking up the wrong tree.'

'Answer the question.'

'It has absolutely nothing to do with Mikey.'

'I never said it did. I'm wondering if she's the reason you came back to Ragmullin.'

'I told you. I returned because I wanted to renovate my grandfather's house.'

'And you ended up coaching a boys' soccer team.'

'I explained all that to you this morning.'

'A team that included Mikey Driscoll, Jennifer's son. Who, tragically, is then murdered.'

'Tell me something I don't know.' He put the mug, still full, into the sink.

'You tell me, Mr Butler. What was your real interest in Mikey Driscoll?'

Butler began buttoning up his shirt, as if only just realising it had been open. Lottie averted her eyes from his well-toned chest.

He paused, one button from the bottom, and appeared to be thinking up the best way to reply.

'Mikey was Jen's son. He was a great footballer. Small for his age but he could mesmerise a team with his footwork. I had no interest in him other than coaching him. I'm so sorry this awful thing has happened, but …' His voice faltered before he continued. 'I had nothing to do with his death.'

'Do you know where Jennifer Driscoll is now?'

The look of surprise was evident on his face as he widened his eyes. 'Jen? I presume she's at home, preparing for her son's funeral.'

'When did you last see her?'

'Inspector, I have no idea why you're asking me about Jen.'

Boyd stepped forward. 'Was that her car we saw leaving just now?'

'Car?'

Boyd sighed. 'Your innocent act doesn't do anything for me, Mr Butler. It might work with young lads on the football pitch or ladies in nightclubs, but not with detectives investigating the murders of two young boys, both of whom were known to you. In fact, if you want to know, it makes you look damn guilty.'

'Guilty of what?' Butler squared up to Boyd. 'Are you accusing me of murder?'

'Not accusing you of anything,' Boyd said. 'Yet.'

Lottie watched the exchange, noted Butler's body language when confronted by Boyd. She was surprised when the younger man appeared to suddenly wilt before her eyes. He sat down, ran his hands through his hair, clutching the ends of it like he wanted to tear it out from its roots.

'You don't understand,' he said, his voice breaking.

'Help us understand,' she said.

He looked up at her then, eyes filled with unshed tears.

'What is it you need to tell us, Rory?'

He shook his head. 'I couldn't kill anyone, least of all Mikey. You see, no one knew. No one.'

'No one knew what?'

'Mikey … he was my son.'

CHAPTER FIFTY-NINE

Boyd made fresh coffee for the three of them, and they sat at the breakfast bar, Rory facing the two detectives.

'Start at the beginning,' Lottie said.

'We were just kids, Jen and I. Not long finished school. We'd known each other before I left for the UK with my parents. But when she completed her Leaving Certificate, she followed me. We'd been writing, and ringing each other. Just good friends, you know. I'd got a job in my father's insurance company and she needed work, so I persuaded Dad to give her a job in the office. Billing and filing. That type of thing.' He sipped his coffee.

'And?' Lottie said.

'And we were the best of friends. Went drinking and clubbing in Kensington. Jen, well, she was astounded at the glamour and glitz of city life. We used to … we dabbled in cocaine. It was in all the clubs and I had money. Or so I thought until the drugs became a habit.' He held up a hand. 'Not any more, Inspector, I learned my lesson. Eventually.'

'What lesson might that be?'

'I stole from my father's company to fund my drug habit. That wasn't the wisest thing to do. He didn't know it was me, so he went to the police. But when I owned up, he bailed me out, dropped the charge and sent me here. Gave me the job of restoring Grandad's old house. And I actually love the country life. This, all here, is mine if I want it. So Dad says.'

'What has any of this got to do with Jen Driscoll?' Boyd said, seemingly impatient to get to the crux of the tale. But Lottie found herself interested in Rory and his London story.

'Go on. Tell it in your own time,' she said, and smiled at him, hoping Boyd got the message to keep his mouth shut.

'Jen and I, we weren't an item back then. Not now either, I hasten to add. We were friends. But one night, we were so high we ended up sleeping together. The next day, we were mortified by what we'd done, but never for a second did I suspect she might be pregnant.'

'What happened then?'

'She upped and left. Said she missed Ireland. Wanted to go home, and that's what she did. She broke off all contact. After the incident with the money, my dad signed me into a rehab unit. I stayed clean until three years ago. When my grandfather died, I lapsed again. That was when I stole the money from the company. And now, here I am.'

'And Jen? How did you make contact again after all those years?'

He was silent so long, with his head bent over his mug, that Lottie wondered if he had fallen asleep. At last he raised his head.

'There was another reason why I lapsed three years ago, besides the death of my grandfather. You see, Jen emailed me. Said she was in dire straits. She had no money. Her marriage had failed and she had a son.'

'And she told you that you were the father?'

'That's what she said. The timeline added up. I had no reason to doubt her.'

'And you do now?'

'No. Not at all. I believe Mikey was my son.'

'You've known this for the last three years. How did you handle it?'

'I came home and gave Jen some money, but she didn't want Mikey to know anything about me. Mikey believed Derek, her ex-husband, was his dad and she didn't want to upset him. Mikey was going through a troublesome time. I realised the only way I'd have contact with him was through the coaching. Jen wasn't happy, but there was nothing she could do.'

'Why did she tell you at all?'

'Because she needed the money. She told me about the difficulties of living on a council estate, and said she was trying to make a better life for our son. Emotional blackmail, you'd call it.'

'And you never told Mikey?'

Butler shook his head. His shoulders were heaving and Lottie felt like putting her arm around him.

Boyd said, 'I find it hard to believe that you just accepted Jen's word for it. I know I'd have got a paternity test.'

'How could you say such a thing? The boy is dead. I never got to be his dad and now you're insinuating that Jen was lying. You are low.'

'I was only saying—'

'Boyd! That's enough,' Lottie snapped.

But Butler had already lunged across the table and grabbed Boyd by the collar of his suit jacket. As he drew his arm back, Lottie caught it, wrenching it up behind his back. Boyd was on his feet in seconds and pulled Butler close by his shirt, ripping the buttons.

'You have a temper,' he spat. 'Is that what happened with the boys? You only meant to comfort them but you couldn't help your hands going around their necks. Is that it? Is it?'

Lottie twisted away with Butler in her grasp. 'Get out, Boyd. Leave this to me.'

'He's liable to attack you too,' Boyd said.

'I can handle myself. Just go.'

When Boyd had marched away and banged the door, she relaxed her hold and Butler slumped to the floor. She stepped back and stood at the giant window, looking out at the calmness of the garden.

'Did you kill Mikey and Kevin, Rory?'

He didn't answer.

'Did Jen tell you something you didn't want to hear? Something that spurred you to violence?'

'Something?' he murmured. 'Like what?

She turned. He was sitting with his back to the bar, his knees up to his chin, arms wrapped around them. She knelt down in front of him.

'Maybe Boyd is right. Maybe Jen came here on Sunday night and told you that Mikey wasn't your son. That she was having an affair with Victor Shanley, Kev's dad. And maybe, just maybe, the veil of red anger we've just witnessed descended and you had nothing but murder on your mind.' Even as she said the words, Lottie felt they did not ring true. The boys had had no injuries. Their murders did not appear to have been committed in anger. She was sure they were the victims of someone who was slow and methodical.

Butler sobbed. 'I don't know.'

'She *was* here Sunday night, wasn't she?'

He nodded.

'And what had she come to tell you?' She kept her voice low and soothing, trying to get him to open up.

'I can't say.' He looked up at her, his eyes glassy, and shook his head. 'I can't tell you. I made a promise.'

'What can be so important that you can't reveal it to me? It might help clear your name.'

'My name doesn't need clearing, Inspector. No, not *my* name.'

'Who are you talking about?' This conversation was going around in circles and was beginning to make Lottie queasy.

He stood up so quickly she slipped backwards. He put out a hand and pulled her upright, his grip sweaty and slippery.

'Unless you have something concrete with which to charge me, I have no more to say to you.' The change in his demeanour was instantaneous. 'And I will be reporting your sergeant for assault.'

*

'That wasn't very helpful,' Lottie said, sitting into the car beside Boyd.

He was smoking a cigarette, with his arm leaning on the open window.

'The softly-softly approach wasn't working, so I thought maybe brute force might wake him up. It seems to me that there is something dark lurking beneath the false tan of Mr Butler. Don't you think?'

'Something's there all right, but I'm not sure it's murder.'

'You saw how angry he got.' Boyd pulled on his cigarette. Lottie took it from him and had a drag. The nicotine made her feel light-headed, so she took another drag to balance it out and handed it back.

'We know that minimal violence was used on the boys. That tells me it was a calculated assault. The killer knew what he was doing. And Rory Butler doesn't fit that bill. I agree he is hiding something. I just don't think it's murder.'

'He knew both boys. He had access to them via the football team. Some people I've interviewed mentioned that he took an unhealthy interest in Mikey—'

'He was the boy's father. He wanted to get to know him, but Jen wouldn't allow it. Maybe that's why it appeared unhealthy to outsiders.'

'Did you stop to think that maybe he was abusing the boys?' Boyd said, throwing the butt out of the window and starting the car.

'That possibility crossed my mind. But Jen was here on Sunday night. She told him something and made him promise not to tell anyone else. And I believe she was here just now, when we arrived.'

'Let's go interrogate Mrs Driscoll then,' Boyd said.

'If we can find her.'

CHAPTER SIXTY

The media pack was still hounding the footpath outside the Driscoll home as Boyd parked the car. Lottie jumped out and made straight for the house, dodging the noisy barking of questions.

Dolores, Jen's neighbour, opened the door and the two detectives stepped inside quickly.

'She's in the kitchen,' Dolores said. 'I'm just leaving.'

The smell of freshly brewed coffee hung in the air. Jen sat at the table, head down, a photo of Mikey clutched to her breast.

Without preamble, Lottie said, 'What's going on between you and Rory Butler?'

Jen didn't raise her head, a shrug of her shoulders the only indication that she'd heard the question.

'He tells me that Mikey was his son,' Lottie said, sitting down, getting on eye level with Jen. 'Is that true?'

Another shrug.

'You don't know if Rory was Mikey's father or not? You just wanted him for the money, is that right?'

Slowly Jennifer Driscoll raised her head. Her face wasn't tear-stained. It wasn't filled with grief. No, Lottie thought, it was a void. Blank. No emotion. Not even the flicker of an eyelid. The woman was zombie-like.

'Do you need a doctor?'

The laugh stunned Lottie, and she felt Boyd shudder beside her. Jen had thrust her head backwards, her mouth hanging open emitting loud, manic laughter. Lottie caught Boyd's eye and he shook his head. No, he had no idea what was going on either.

'Jen, I have some disturbing news and there's no easy way to tell you.' Lottie changed direction quickly. 'We believe your son was the victim of sexual abuse.'

That brought the laughter to a stop. The dead eyes blazed fire. 'What are you saying? You're making that up. It's not true.'

'I'm afraid it is true. My top priority is to find your son's killer. If you know anything about the abuse, it might help me find who took your son away from you.'

'Now it makes sense.'

'What does?' Lottie was confused.

'That must be the reason Mikey changed, about ten months ago.'

'Changed how?'

'He got so quiet and stopped eating properly. Sat in his room. Didn't want to go outside with his friends. I had a running battle to get him to keep up the soccer. His school work suffered and his grades dropped. I put it down to hormones. Jesus, I had no idea what was going on. What type of a mother am I?'

'Jen, don't blame yourself. How were you to know if Mikey never told you?'

'I *should* have known. He was my son.' Her face twisted in anguish. 'My boy was taken from me almost a year ago. Some bastard stole his childhood from him. You can't bring that back. You can't bring Mikey back. But I will make the fucker pay. Believe me, I will.'

Lottie knew something had changed since she first met Jen on Monday. Something had happened to cause this transformation. She knew grief well, and this was way above that. This was pure hatred.

'Was it Rory?' she said.

'Rory? No, that man can only hurt himself.'

'Why did you tell him that Mikey was his?'

'It was the only way I could support my son. I needed money and I knew Rory was loaded, especially after he inherited his grandfather's place.'

'A bit harsh on him, don't you think?'

'Harsh? I struggled for years raising that boy alone. On this dump of an estate. My job brings in next to nothing. I saw an opportunity and I took it.'

'Why didn't you let him have contact with Mikey?'

Jen sniffed and bit her knuckles. She shrugged. 'Maybe I should have done. I've made plenty of mistakes in my life, and that's probably another one.'

'You didn't think that maybe Rory would harm Mikey?'

'I can assure you, Rory Butler would never hurt a child.'

'Has he a partner?' Lottie wondered if there was someone else in Rory's life she needed to be looking at.

'Not that I know of.'

'What did you tell Rory on Sunday night?'

'Sunday night?'

'I know you were with him. He admitted it.'

'He promised me he wouldn't breathe a word.' Jen gazed vacantly at the photograph in her hand. 'Maybe if I hadn't gone out to his place, Mikey would be alive.'

'You can alibi Rory, you know. If you were with him Sunday night. Even though Dolores said she was drinking with you here after bingo.'

'Dolores is a good friend.'

'Did you stay with him?'

'I was there for a while. Went out there around nine. Didn't bother with the bingo. Can't stand the smell of that bus. Or the bastard that drives it. Waited at Rory's for him to get home after the match. Must have been well past nine thirty. Not sure, really.'

She stopped speaking and stared at a point above Lottie's head. Her mouth clamped shut.

Lottie looked at Boyd for help.

He said, 'Jen, what was so important that you had to go and visit Rory on Sunday night?'

'What?' She turned to stare at him as if she had just realised he was in the room.

'You had something you needed to talk to Rory about. Was it to do with Mikey?'

Jen sighed, kept her head bowed. 'It seems so inconsequential now but I just wanted to rekindle my affair with Rory. Of course, he rebuffed me. I made him promise not to mention it to anyone. I felt like a fool.' She looked up at Lottie. 'I'm stupid and I'm lonely, Inspector. I don't like to spending my nights at bingo. Can you understand how I was feeling?'

'You had Mikey.'

'My Mikey is gone. No one can bring him back.'

'You still called out to Rory again today, didn't you?'

'I told you, I'm stupid.'

They were losing her again. Lottie reached out and gripped the other woman's hand.

'Jen, I need your help. There may be other boys in danger. Maybe the killer is hunting down another boy as we speak. You need to help us. Tell us what you know.'

'Another boy? That could be Toby. You need to find him.'

'Toby Collins?' Lottie said. 'Mikey's friend?'

'Toby might be next.'

'Oh Jesus Christ,' Boyd was exasperated. 'Just tell us what you know.'

'I don't know anything. Mikey was so secretive. He wouldn't tell me what was going on, but now that I know about the abuse, I'm thinking maybe the killer thought he *had* told someone. Was that why he was murdered?'

First Butler sending her in circles, now Jen. Lottie didn't know which way to turn.

'Jen, please tell me more.'

'Just go and get Toby. Before someone else does.'

Lottie knew it was hopeless to pressurise the woman any further. She had to find Toby Collins.

The satellite dish hung from one hook on the front of the house. Wires twisted in the growing breeze.

'Summer didn't last long,' Boyd said.

'I noticed.' Lottie searched for the bell, but it swung precariously loose. She tapped the cracked glass panel on the door.

'For feck's sake,' Boyd said, and tried to wipe the dog shit off his shoe in the overgrown scrap of lawn.

The door opened and Toby's dad stood there, a khaki shirt unbuttoned with a white vest beneath. He was wearing army fatigues and black boots.

'Mr Collins, can we come in? We need to talk to Toby.'

'Toby? You've already talked to him. Terrified the lad so much he's hardly spoken a word since.'

'Is he here?' Boyd said. 'Just a quick word will do.'

Collins turned back to the stairs and shouted, 'Toby? You up there?' No answer. 'He's not here.'

'Where do you think he might be?' Lottie said.

'I've no idea. Out kicking a ball around, I suppose.'

She handed over her card. 'Ring me as soon as he gets home.'

'Did he do something? Because if he did, I'll kill the little fecker.'

'No, sir,' Boyd said. 'It's about Mikey Driscoll and Kevin Shanley. The boys who died. You need to protect your son.'

'What? He's in danger? Why didn't you say so? Max?' He shouted up the stairs again. Still no answer. 'I'll get Max to watch the girls and I'll go and look for Toby. Right. Thanks. I'll call you.'

The door was shut in their faces.

Lottie turned to Boyd. 'I hope to God he *is* only kicking a ball around somewhere.'

'Isn't that what Kevin Shanley was doing when he disappeared?' Boyd said.

*

Toby was still running when he came to the wall that separated the houses from the soccer pitch. He climbed up on top of the wall. He wasn't sure if he'd shaken Barry off, but he had run through back gardens and over fences – places Barry couldn't go on a bike. But he could have abandoned the bike. Couldn't he?

He jumped. Fell awkwardly and instantly knew he had damaged his ankle. He heard footsteps. Tried to drag himself backwards, came up against the wall. There was nowhere left to run.

The club caretaker, Bertie Harris, stood in front of him. Breathing like he was about to die if he didn't keep puffing in and out, Toby began to shake. His whole body trembled as he clutched his ankle.

'Please don't hurt me. I never said anything. I didn't tell anyone,' he cried.

'What the hell is up with you? Running like the devil is on your heels. You never ran like that on the pitch, so what has you so scared?'

Toby grabbed a handful of gravel in his fist and tried to stand up, but found his shoulder firmly held by the man. If only he could get up, then he could throw the stones in Bertie's eyes and run. Keep on running. That was what he had to do.

'He ... he's after me,' he stammered.

'Who are you talking about? I can't see anyone after you. You seeing ghosts now, are you?' Bertie laughed. 'Is it Mikey's ghost or Kev's that you see? Which one of them is the devil, do you think?'

Toby didn't know what to do. Terror clutched at the back of his throat and he thought his words might be swallowed and he would never be able to speak again.

'Are you hurt?' Bertie leaned down and ran his fingers over the swelling on Toby's ankle.

'I think I sprained it.'

'Come on,' Bertie said, dragging him upright. 'Let's go inside and I'll make a cup of tea.'

'I don't like tea,' Toby said.

'A bottle of Coke, then. I bet you'd like that.'

Toby was parched after all the running, and his ankle hurt so badly. A bottle of Coke sounded good. But he wasn't sure he should be going anywhere with Bertie Harris.

'Then I'll phone the doctor,' Bertie added, pushing him in through the door.

And Toby could feel the blood draining from his face, all the way down to his bruised and swollen ankle.

CHAPTER SIXTY-ONE

When they returned to the station, Lottie ordered a search for Toby Collins. Gilly rushed into the office.

'Inspector Parker, can I have a minute?'

'I'm busy. Later.' Lottie needed to go home. It was late, and Boyd was yawning. That was a sign the day had been way too long already.

'But it's about Max Collins.'

'Toby's brother?'

'Yes. I found out from Wes Finnegan where Max hides out when he's not at home. I went there, and you won't believe—'

'What, Gilly?'

'Hope's daughter, Lexie, was there. Alone. By herself. Crying.'

'What? Where?'

'The old tyre depot, on the industrial estate.'

'And where is she now?' Lottie couldn't help wondering why Hope would abandon her child in such a place.

'Kirby called Child and Family Services. A social worker is with her and Hope's uncle Robbie has arrived.'

'But where is Hope?'

'I don't know. She must have been there. Maybe something happened and she had to run. Robbie says she would never leave her daughter alone voluntarily.'

'Right. You deal with the little girl. I want Robbie Cotter in an interview room. Now.'

'Kirby interrogated him but he found out nothing we don't already know. And Lexie told us that a bad person took her mummy.'

'We still have a team searching for Hope?'

'Yes, boss.'

'Tell Kirby to keep me up to date.'

'I will.' Gilly ran out of the office.

Lottie's phone rang. Would she ever get home tonight? She saw the caller ID and answered.

'Hi, Jane. Good news, I hope, because I've had a bitch of a day.'

Jane got straight to the point. 'I re-examined the football shorts the victims were wearing. I found a minuscule hole near the waistband of both sets. Right where you would expect to find a plastic price tag.'

'Okay. What does that tell us?'

'Someone bit it off.'

'What do you mean?'

'Someone bit off the plastic holding the tag. I know that for a fact, because I swabbed the material around the area and found a minute trace of saliva.'

Lottie tried to stem the rising excitement in her chest. 'Maybe the boy bit it off himself.'

'I don't think so, as I found it on both pairs of shorts. I sent the samples for DNA profile. Initial report states it doesn't match either of the boys.'

'Really? You got a result already? Amazing work, Jane.' Lottie silently punched her fist in the air.

'I rushed it through. I got so excited, and you know me, I don't do excitement.'

'I know,' Lottie agreed.

Jane was still talking. 'It's just that we had nothing. Not a trace of anything until this.'

'You're brilliant, Jane. I can't thank you enough. We've taken DNA from some people of interest. I thought it was fruitless at the time because they all had reason to be with the victims at some stage. But if we can match someone's sample to the profile you've discovered, that would be a step in the right direction.'

'I've fast-tracked everything to the Dublin lab. They're cross-checking as we speak.'

'Fingers crossed.'

'You know I don't do that kind of thing,' Jane said.

'I know, but if I was with you right now, I'd kiss you.'

'And I definitely don't do that! Goodnight, Lottie.'

'Goodnight, Jane.' Lottie ended the call.

Night? Was it actually that late. Shit.

It was after eight o'clock by the time Lottie eventually arrived home. Everyone possible had been mobilised, including the garda helicopter, but so far, nothing to report. No Hope. No Toby. Robbie Cotter had left the station with Lexie and a social worker in tow. They still had no idea why the baby had been killed and dumped in the canal, or whether Hope had been responsible. And they were no closer to finding the killer of Mikey Driscoll and Kevin Shanley. The day had contained many revelations, but nothing pertinent to catching a murderer.

McMahon had hunted the team out of the office, telling them to get some rest and to be back at six in the morning. A replacement team was manning the investigations for the night. Boyd had disappeared before Lottie could ask him if he cared to have a drink to unwind before they headed home. Instead, she'd bought a bottle of wine in Tesco along with some groceries. When everyone was in bed, she'd relax.

She flung her handbag on the hall table, put down the plastic shopping bag and pulled off her boots. Her feet were sore, her head was thumping and all she could think of was a warm bath and a bite of food. She glanced into the living room, where Katie and Chloe had Louis on the floor, making him roll over.

'Looks like fun,' she said.

Katie glanced up. 'Trying to tire him out for bed.'

'All okay, Mam?' Chloe asked. 'You look wrecked.'

'I am. Are you working tonight?'

'Supposed to be.' She glanced at the clock. 'Oh sugar, I'll be late.' She ran past Lottie to the stairs.

'Where's Sean?'

'In his room, probably,' Katie said. 'Mam, there's something I want to talk to you about …'

'Later, okay? I need a wash.'

'Sure.' Katie picked up Louis, and Lottie brushed her grandson's forehead with a kiss.

In the kitchen, Rose was sitting at the range, her head lolling to one side, her eyes closed. She opened her eyes and straightened up in the chair when she heard Lottie come in.

Immediately, Lottie saw that her mother had been crying. And Rose rarely cried. She noticed, too, how old she looked. Rose was only seventy-six, an active woman, but now she appeared drained. Was it the strain of having the family lodging here? Probably. The sooner Ben Lynch finished up his work, the sooner Lottie could move out and set up her new home. 'What's up?' she asked warily, not at all sure she wanted to know.

'Sit down,' Rose said.

'I'm dying for a shower or a bath. Looking forward to it all evening, and—'

'Sit down. We need to talk.'

What was going on? This wasn't good. Lottie dragged out a chair and sat opposite the woman she had called mother for over forty years, but who she had recently discovered was not in fact her biological mother.

'What's wrong?'

'I had a visitor today,' Rose said.

'That's nice,' Lottie said hopefully, knowing instinctively that it had been anything but nice. 'Anyone I know?'

'You tell me.'

'What? Who was it?'

'An American man. A policeman, no less.'

Lottie held her breath. She knew what was coming.

Rose said, 'Does the name Leo Belfield mean anything to you?'

'I've heard of him,' Lottie said, and dug her nails into the palms of her hands. First he'd been to see McMahon, and now Rose. What was he up to? 'What did he want?'

Rose shrugged. 'Stirring up problems in my life. That's what.'

'What do you mean?'

'He knows about you, Lottie. About your father and what he did. But he doesn't know everything. That's why he was here. Thought I was going to fill in the gaps in his family tree.'

'And did you?'

'What do you take me for?' Rose stood up suddenly and flicked the kettle on. 'You might think I'm tottering towards my grave, Lottie, but I'm not doolally yet.'

'I don't think that. And I'm grateful for all you're doing for me and the kids. I don't know what I'd have done the last few months if you hadn't been there for us.'

'I'll always be here for you, Lottie.' She turned around as the kettle began to hiss. 'But I'm warning you, that Belfield man is trouble. I could smell it from the pores of his skin as he sat in that same chair you're sitting in now.'

'Trouble?' Lottie wondered what Belfield had said to cause Rose to be so rattled. 'What did he say to you?'

'He was raised by Alexis Belfield. She's the sister of your biological mother, who is also his mother. Which makes him your half-brother.'

'That's trouble all right,' Lottie said. She thought back to the family history she had unearthed while heading up a murder investigation last year. Her biological mother had had four children, including a set of twins. One daughter had died last October, and the other, who was likely Leo's twin sister, was now incarcerated in a state institution. As a baby, Lottie had been taken in by Peter and Rose Fitzpatrick and raised as their own child. Her birth certificate had been doctored, and Lottie had been unaware of the truth until that awful, violent case had laid her heritage bare.

And now Leo was here. Asking questions. What did he hope to gain? She scratched her head and tried to come up with a logical answer.

'You'll have to talk to him,' Rose said, putting a mug of coffee in front of her. 'It's the only way you'll get rid of him.'

'Talk to him about what?'

'You'll have to tell him about his twin sister.'

'I'm sure he could find that out on his own. No, he's after something else,' Lottie said. 'And I don't think it's a new family.'

*

Sean lay on his bed, controller in hand, scrolling through Toby's PlayStation profile. He took out his phone and looked at the photograph he'd snapped of the messages that had been on Toby's screen. He couldn't make out what they were about. But he could see that they might be something like a warning. A code?

Should he tell his mother? After all, Mikey had been Toby's friend, and she was investigating his murder. His thoughts swung to the body of the baby he and Barry had found. The poor little thing, he thought. Born into such a horrible world before his life had been snuffed out mercilessly. Why had Barry insisted they go to that exact spot? Did he know the baby was there? He had been acting funny all that morning, come to think of it. Nervy, Sean concluded. But why?

He sat up straight and scrutinised Toby's messages again.

No, that couldn't be it.

He clicked his controller, logged on to the game. Checked Barry's username. Looked at the messages again. Double shit. If Toby was in trouble, Sean knew he had to help. He also knew that this was something he couldn't tell his mother.

He pocketed his phone, pulled on a hoodie. Downstairs, he checked that no one was around, and sneaked out the front door. His bike was parked up under the front windowsill. He was delighted with the way Kenny's Cycles had mended the buckled wheel. It was better than new. Throwing his leg over the crossbar, he cycled out the gate and down the dark road. He glanced up at the full moon and hoped the werewolves were already asleep.

CHAPTER SIXTY-TWO

Lottie sat on the wall and looked in at the dark windows of what would soon be her new home. There was no sign of Ben doing any painting. Maria had probably warned her husband to stay away.

Holding the key in one hand, and her mobile phone in the other, she debated whether to go in. She'd love a smoke. A few quick drags. She could ring Boyd to come over. They could sit on the wall and smoke like a couple of teenagers. That would be nice. But Boyd wasn't answering his damn phone. She could go over to his apartment. But no. That was too intrusive. Feck it.

She walked up to the door, turned the key in the lock and stepped into the hallway. She flicked on the light and inhaled the smell of fresh paint.

The front door closed silently behind her and she walked through the house. Every room looked sparkling new. The floors had been sanded and varnished, the walls and ceilings painted. Ben had done a great job. And she didn't even have to pay for it. Tom Rickard was a blessing in disguise.

She was about to leave when the doorbell rang. The shape of a man was outlined beyond the frosted glass. Someone selling something? Not at this hour. Catching sight of the faint red glow of a cigarette, she opened the door.

'How did you know I was here, Boyd?'

'Your mother told me. Are you going to ask me in?'

'I am.' She opened the door wider, and he stamped out his cigarette on the doorstep.

His hair was damp and she could smell the citrus freshness of a recent shower coming from his skin. He wore a white T-shirt and jeans. He smiled as he passed her, and she felt her heart float around in her chest and a small tingle take root at the base of her abdomen.

'What brings you here?' she asked.

He stood in the hallway, the naked light bulb casting shadows on the grey peppering his hair.

'You,' he said. 'It's been a tough few days and I thought you could do with some company.'

'You could've answered your damn phone,' she said with a smile.

'I'm here, aren't I?'

'You are. I can't offer you tea or coffee; there isn't even a mug, let alone a kettle here yet.'

She felt his arm snake around her waist as he drew her towards him. She smelled the faint cigarette smoke on his breath. The best part of all was that she had not expected this reaction. None of it.

As his lips covered hers, she dropped her phone, keys and bag to the floor and allowed herself to drown in his presence. Even if it was only for a few seconds, Lottie Parker felt she had flown on the wings of an angel and arrived at the gates to heaven.

When they broke apart, she said, 'What brought that on?'

'Don't know. Perhaps you and your jealousy.'

'My what?'

'You thought I had something going with Cynthia Rhodes. Are you daft?' He leaned in and kissed her again.

'There's no bed here, Boyd.'

He laughed. 'Who said we need a bed?'

'No one. But there is a couch in the sitting room.'

'Hold on a minute.' He turned back to the front door and picked up a bag from the step. 'I have wine.'

She took the bottle from him. 'Screw top. Good.'

'The very best. Check the label.'

'Ah, shit, Boyd. This is zero per cent alcohol.'

'It's nice, though, and you won't have a hangover in the morning. Just the way to celebrate my divorce. Now, where's this couch you mentioned?'

He held out his hand, and she put hers into it and allowed him to lead her into the living room. While she opened the bottle, he strung the sheet from the couch over the window.

'Can't have you making a bad impression on your neighbours before you even move in,' he said.

Lottie settled on the couch and Boyd sat beside her. She looked up at the window, draped in paint-splattered cotton, and felt the happiest she'd been in months.

*

He sat in his hired car at the end of the road, and watched. He had seen the man arrive, light a cigarette in his car and smoke most of it before he approached the door. Dutch courage?

After the man had entered the house, he drove up behind the car. He could see their outlines behind the glass of the door. Embracing. Interesting, Leo thought. Lottie Parker was indeed a very complex person. Someone he wanted to get to know, now more than ever.

CHAPTER SIXTY-THREE

'Hello, Sean, what has you out so late, and all on your own?'

Jesus, thought Sean, I'm fifteen years old. He said, 'Dr Duffy, is Barry home?'

'It's almost midnight. He'll be fast asleep. I was just about to head to bed myself.'

Sean noticed that Barry's father did not look like he was on his way to bed. He was wearing a zipped-up sweater and had a waxed jacket under his arm. Just come home, or ready to go out? He could feel his mother's detective instincts taking hold in his brain.

'That's grand, Dr Duffy.' He turned back to his bike.

'Wait up. What did you want him for?'

Paul Duffy was standing right behind him, so close Sean could almost hear his heartbeat. He reached out and grabbed Sean's hand. His grip was sweaty and tight. Sean went to pull his hand away, but Duffy held on, dragging him towards him. Sean looked into the man's eyes, and something he saw there caused the hairs to stand up on the back of his neck.

'You're right, I'd better get going. Mam will have a search party out for me. Thanks again.' But still Duffy wouldn't let go. Sean tried to disentangle his fingers but the grip tightened further and Duffy was right in his face. He stepped back, hit against the bike at his feet. Duffy was still glued to him. What the hell?

'What do you want with Barry at this late hour?'

'Nothing. Honestly. I couldn't sleep. Just thought I'd see if he was up or out or whatever. I'd better go and—'

'I scared you. I'm sorry, Sean. Come in. Come in. I'll call Barry down. It must be something important to have you out this late.'

Dr Duffy's face had softened. Maybe they'd just scared each other, Sean thought as he moved into the hallway. The door shut soundlessly behind him, and he wondered at the complete silence inside the house. So unlike his granny's, with all of them living there cheek by jowl.

'This way.'

Duffy's voice propelled Sean to motion. He walked down the hall and entered the living room, all the while trying to shake off the voice in his head telling him to get the hell out.

The soft lap of the waves against the pebbles and rocks on the shore of the lake keeps me grounded. The ripples of silver twinkling in the moonlight are as calming as any Valium I've been ordered to take. I am almost near completion of my tasks. The studio is still secret, and I must keep it that way. There is no other option but to kill.

The evil spirits are all around me, hovering, whispering in my ear, and I know of only one way to still their mutterings.

The final one is awaiting.

I know what I must do.

So sorry, little one.

The end is nigh.

DAY FOUR

Thursday

CHAPTER SIXTY-FOUR

The first rays of sunshine spilled into the room. Lottie leaned up on one elbow and tilted her head towards the window. The curtain looked so dirty. Her mother was slipping. Shit, that wasn't a curtain. She turned over and saw him there, asleep on the floor beside her, more painting sheets for covers.

'Boyd! Wake up. What the hell time is it?'

He groaned and turned over. 'Good morning, gorgeous.'

She pulled on her clothes and waited impatiently while he dressed. When she dragged the sheet from the window, the glare of the rising sun almost blinded her.

'It's only five a.m. and it's—'

'It's a beautiful way to wake up,' he said, turning her around and kissing her.

She hadn't time for this. Good God, what had she been thinking?

'Let's go. I need to have a shower, and so do you.'

'Want to test the one upstairs?'

'Boyd. For Christ's sake. Come on. We have to go. McMahon told us to be in at six.'

'And when did you ever do what you were told?'

She smiled and made for the door. 'Never. But I don't want my kids putting out an SOS for me.'

Rose had a pot of tea ready when Lottie came into the kitchen, showered and dressed in fresh jeans and white shirt. She was going to miss being treated like a queen. That thought disappeared when she saw the scowl printed on her mother's face like a newspaper headline.

'You should marry him,' Rose said.

Lottie stilled her hand with the mug halfway to her mouth. 'What? Who?'

'The lad with the ears that stick out. Boyd. No point in sneaking around like teenagers. You're both adults.'

'Mother, we are not together.'

'You were last night, weren't you?'

'That may be so, but we're not a couple. We get on and we—'

'Sleep together from time to time. Yes, I know. But he loves you, you know that? What is it that you're waiting for?'

Lottie remained silent. She didn't know what she wanted any more. Now that Boyd had his divorce, something had shifted inside her. Was it because he was finally free of his ex-wife? Or because she had thought he was seeing Cynthia? Was that it? Jealousy? She couldn't put her finger on it. But for now, she had to go to work and solve three murders. Then and only then would she decide what she wanted to do with the rest of her life.

'I might be late again. Things are hectic with the murder investigations,' she said, shoving a slice of toast into her mouth.

'And what are you going to do about that Leo Belfield?'

She crunched the toast. 'Leave him to me. If he calls around here, don't answer the door.'

'Right so.' Rose poured a cup of tea for herself. 'Oh, and tell Sean that in future he's to let me know in advance when he's staying over at his friend's house for the night. I was awake worrying about him until I got his text this morning.'

'What friend?' Lottie picked up her bag and went to the kitchen door.

'Barry Duffy. The lad he went fishing with the other day.'

She opened her mouth, but closed it again. Hadn't she told Sean to stay away from Barry Duffy? At least she had meant to. Damn.

'I'll have a word with him later.'

In the hall, she pulled on her shoes – Katie's shoes really. Her children were all sound asleep. Little Louis was an angel of a child. Katie was so lucky. She wondered what would happen when Katie went back to college in September. They'd have to get a nanny. More money. Tom Rickard would probably stump up for that too. Good.

A long day beckoned, and Lottie had an uneasy feeling it was going to be horrendously busy. But she and Boyd were back on good terms. That was great. She jumped into her car and turned the key. Nothing. Just a click. Tried again. The same.

'Ah, shite!'

*

Boyd waltzed into the office. Kirby lifted his head and nodded, looking like he'd been at his desk all night, his hair wilder than usual and his nose dripping sweat.

'You get a bit of the old roll in the hay last night?' he asked.

'What's it to you?' Boyd began lining up his keyboard with the stack of files on his desk. He couldn't keep the smile from his lips.

'Boyd, can I have a quick word?' Lynch was standing at the door, beckoning him out to the corridor. He followed her.

'What's up?' he said, watching her march up and down, her hand on her bump. 'All okay with junior in there?' He leaned back with one foot against the wall, hands in pockets, trying to relax, to hear her out, but keen to get working.

'I have a problem and I need your help,' she said.

'Okay,' Boyd said warily. Lynch never asked him for anything. She was tight with Kirby. Well, she had been until he started dating

Gilly O'Donoghue. She seemed to have lost her confidant when that relationship sprouted up.

'This is a little delicate.' She stopped pacing and stood in front of him. 'I'll get straight to the point. You see, I caught my Ben in a compromising position with the DI. And I think I need to report her.'

Boyd let his foot drop slowly to the floor. He tightened his hands into fists inside his trouser pockets. 'What are you talking about?'

'The night before last, I drove round with the kids to her new place. Ben was doing a spot of decorating there. I could see in through the window. The light was on. I know what I saw.'

'What *did* you see?'

'Ben and Lottie Parker, if you want me to spell it out for you. In each other's arms.'

'You're having a laugh.'

'Do you see me laughing? No, I am not. This is serious.'

'Why are you telling me? Talk to your husband.'

'I did, and he denied it.'

'Talk to Lottie, then.'

'I tried. She stared at me the way you are now. All innocent and disbelieving. But this is not baby brain.' She tapped the side of her head. 'I know what I saw. And she needs to be brought up on it.'

Boyd swallowed hard. 'Lynch, listen up. If you saw what you think you saw, it's a personal matter. You'd better sort it out yourself. I honestly don't know what you think I can do for you.'

'I just want to warn you. She's a bitch. She'll trample over all of us to get what she wants. She's done it before. I know and you know. And this time, I'm going to make sure she pays for stamping all over my marriage.'

'Don't do anything stupid.'

'She's the stupid one, underestimating me.'

With an angry toss of her head, she turned and walked down the corridor. Boyd watched her go. If what he'd just heard was true, what did that mean for his relationship with Lottie? She'd already told him that Lynch suspected she was having an affair with Ben. Why would she do that? So that he wouldn't be shocked when Lynch revealed all? He didn't know what to think.

Bollocks!

CHAPTER SIXTY-FIVE

Lottie stood at the front of the incident room and watched as the team filed in. She felt refreshed this morning and hoped she could instil some of that energy into her detectives. She'd eventually got her car started with the help of a neighbour's jump leads, and had arrived at the station just before McMahon.

One glance at the incident boards and her mood deflated. Two young boys and a baby, and the only piece of evidence they had was a trace of saliva found on the waistbands of the boys' shorts.

Kirby ambled up to her. 'Can I have a word before you start?'

'You look like you slept in that suit,' she said. 'All okay?'

'I didn't sleep in it because I haven't been to bed, which is more than I can say for some people.' He winked, and she felt a blush creep up her cheeks.

'Go on.'

'I spent most of the night with the traffic-cam guys going over and over anything we could find for Sunday night. Looked at our own CCTV and that of the business owners who supplied us with discs for the relevant timeline.'

'And you found something?'

'Painstaking work.'

'Put it up on the board.'

He took a sheaf of papers from a file that he'd lodged under his arm. 'These are stills I printed from the pertinent footage. Rather than trying to trace the persons of interest from McDonald's on Sunday night, I tried to follow in the footsteps of Mikey Driscoll.'

'And you found where he was abducted from?'

'Not conclusively, but I think so.' He pinned a series of grainy black-and-white images on to a blank board. 'This first one is Mikey walking alone by the newsagent's. You just catch him as he passes under the camera.'

Lottie looked at the small boy, a kit bag on his back, shorts over bare legs. And was that the glint of his medal around his neck? Looked like it.

Kirby continued. 'This next one is from the pharmacy near the monks' statues. You can see he stopped and looked at them.'

'Right. It's definitely Mikey,' Lottie said, glancing at the colour photograph she'd got from Jen on Monday.

'I know he walked along Friars Street, because the next piece of footage was taken from the travel shop.' He pinned up another page.

Lottie noticed his hands were now empty. 'That's it?'

'Walsh's garage on the bridge has three cameras. And Mikey doesn't appear on any of them.'

'He was snatched from the main street?' Lottie said incredulously.

'No.' Kirby tapped his pocket for a cigar. A nervous tic, as Lottie knew he would never smoke inside the station. 'At four o'clock this morning, I walked the streets along the route I believe Mikey took, and I now have evidence that he made a left at the pub just before the garage forecourt. He could've been heading for the short cut to Munbally Grove. Through the tunnel under the canal. I found this in a drain just before the turn for the supermarket.'

He handed Lottie a plastic evidence bag.

'A football boot?'

'I'm sure we can confirm it's Mikey's.'

'Good work. Any security cameras down that way?' Lottie asked, though she knew it was unlikely.

'The ones on the apartment walls are smashed, so I put a call in to the supermarket, but they told me they have nothing trained on that road. Our only hope is that someone has a private security system. A team of uniforms are knocking on doors down that way as we speak. We're stretched at the moment. There's still a crew down at the tyre depot, and everyone else is searching for the boy Toby.'

'Tell me something I don't know,' Lottie said.

'Okay then. When I'd finished that, I went back to scan the footage for any of the persons of interest or their cars. And I found this.'

He opened the folder with more drama than Lottie thought necessary, but she was itching to see what he had discovered. She took the sheet of paper from him. Looked at the image of the car. Then at the fuzzy close-up of the number plate, and finally at the time captured by the camera.

'Where is this from?'

'The garage. As I said, I walked the route this morning, and the time fits. That car passed the garage on the way out of town just minutes after our last sighting of Mikey.'

'Can you get the tech crew to enhance the image of the driver?'

'They're working on it, but I wouldn't hold my breath.'

'Really good work, Kirby. Thank you.'

Lottie felt her heart lurch upwards and miss a beat, because even without a positive ID on the driver, she knew who owned that car.

'Boyd. You're with me.' She noticed he had a sour look plastered on his face. What was wrong with him now?

'What about the rest of the meeting?' Lynch said.

'Later.'

She rushed out with Boyd trailing behind her, leaving Kirby to explain to the others what was going on.

*

As Lottie left, Kirby remembered the last sheet of paper in his folder.

'Boss!' he called.

But she and Boyd were gone.

'What is it?' Lynch asked.

'Come with me.'

'Where are we going?'

Kirby paused, and Lynch crashed into his bulk. He could feel the hardness of her baby bump against the small of his back. 'Sorry, are you okay?'

'I'm fine,' Lynch said. 'What has you in such a rush?'

'I need to find Bertie Harris. I scrutinised the club CCTV disc last night, and I think I know why he tampered with the footage.'

'Are you going to tell me, or what?'

Kirby glanced at the clock on the wall. 'Where do you think we'd get him at this time of the morning? At home or at the club?'

'I'd chance home.'

'Right. Let's see what Mr Harris has to say for himself.'

*

Boyd drove in silence. Lottie couldn't figure out what was up with him. She'd tried conversation, even put her hand on his as he held the steering wheel. But he'd swatted her away as if she was a fly on cow dung.

The house looked silent in the morning sunshine as she stepped out of the car.

She rang the bell. No answer. Tentatively she put her hand on the door to see if it was open.

'Hello?'

'You can't walk uninvited into another house. You tried that with Butler yesterday. You need a warrant.'

'Boyd, don't tell me how to do my job. And I'd love to know what's eating you this morning.'

'I'm fine,' he said, and made to move around the side of the house. 'There's someone back here. I hear a lawnmower.'

She cocked an ear. 'Come on.'

Passing Boyd, she rounded the house, her feet crunching on the white gravel. The lawn was circular and large. A man sat on a ride-on-lawnmower, headphones clamped to his ears.

She raised her voice to call above the din. 'Dr Duffy? We'd like a word, please.'

The noise stopped the instant the mower turned. The man pulled the headphones from his head.

It wasn't Paul Duffy.

'What's *he* doing here?' Lottie said.

CHAPTER SIXTY-SIX

Bertie Harris lived above the Chinese restaurant on Main Street. Third floor. No elevator. By the time Kirby was standing outside the door, his breath was coming in bursts, and his usually bushy hair was flattened to his scalp with sweat.

'Are you okay?' Lynch said. 'Don't have a heart attack, because I can't get you back down those stairs.'

Kirby saw that she was as stressed as he was. 'If I have a heart attack, you won't be carting me anywhere. Let the paramedics do that.' He pressed the doorbell.

Lynch leaned against the wall, trying to get her breathing back to normal. 'After this baby is born, I'm having my tubes tied.'

'Why don't you get Ben to have the snip?' Kirby jammed his thick finger on the bell again.

'It'll be more than the snip if he doesn't behave himself.'

'What? Is there trouble in chez Lynch?'

'Ben ... Well, he and the boss—'

The door opened. A sleepy-eyed Bertie Harris was standing there dressed in a pair of trousers, belt hanging loose and no shirt.

'Looks like we woke you up,' Kirby said. He stepped into the apartment. 'Sorry about that, but we need a little chat.'

'Come in, why don't you?'

The door closed behind them and Kirby took in the cramped surroundings. A conglomeration of sports gear cluttered every available surface. He stood with his back to the only window, glad that it was open an inch.

'What's with all the kit, Bertie?'

'I store the new stock here. It's not safe at the clubhouse.'

'Oh, I thought you had high-tech security installed there.'

'I do ... I mean, there is. But this is new kit, for next season, and I said I'd hold onto it. Can't be too careful, you know.'

'You mean, you're supposed to store it but you sell it on and make a tidy profit. For yourself.'

'I don't know what you mean.'

'I think you do.' Kirby watched as Lynch lifted up a pile of plastic bags containing football socks and placed them on the floor. Then she sat on the chair. Gosh, she was very red in the face. He hoped she wasn't going to go into labour. 'I know you doctored the CCTV footage you gave me.'

'I've no idea what you're talking about. Do you mind if I finish getting dressed?'

'Stay where you are.' Kirby lifted the sash window another few inches and welcomed the breeze that entered the room. 'Do you live here alone?'

'I do, but that's nothing to do with you.' Harris sat down on a chair, on top of a bundle of jerseys.

'The timeline on the disc you gave me has about ten minutes missing on Sunday night. Care to tell me why that is so?'

Harris shrugged.

'Come on,' Kirby said. 'We have two murdered boys and another is now feared missing. 'Fess up.'

'Missing? Who's missing?'

'Tell me about the CCTV from Sunday night. What did you cut out?'

Harris seemed too big for the small room, especially now that there were three people in it. His eyes kept darting to a door. Possibly a bathroom, or maybe his bedroom. Kirby intended to have a look as soon as he got the information he wanted.

'I didn't cut anything from those tapes.'

'If you didn't, who did?'

'No one.'

'If you want to have this conversation at the station, I'm happy to arrest you.'

'On what charge?'

'Tampering with evidence in a murder case, for one. Impeding an ongoing investigation. Perverting the course of justice. Shall I go on?'

Harris had a plastic bag in his hands. A pair of football shorts inside it. He was running his finger along the edge of the bag.

'I did nothing.'

'Who do you sell the kit to? Say, for instance, the piece in your hand. Who would be in the market for that?'

The bag dropped from Harris's hand, landing on the floor at his bare feet.

'I don't sell it.'

'Who do you give it to, then?' Kirby was getting fed up with the man's obstruction.

'I store it. End of. Can you go now?'

'Not leaving until you tell us.'

Harris bent down and picked up the bag he'd let fall. 'I store it here. I was asked to.'

'Who do you store it for?'

'Can't say.'

'Oh, but you will,' Kirby said. 'On Sunday night, what was going on that you had to cut ten minutes from the security footage?'

'I didn't think I was doing anything wrong. Not really. It's those rich feckers, Rory Butler and Dr Duffy, who buy the kit. I get paid a pittance. Barely more than a volunteer, I am. So you're right. I make a few quid off the books. Sell it on here and there. To young lads, mainly. I don't know what they do with it. Probably sell it on the streets of Dublin, making a neat little profit for themselves.'

'Who did you meet on Sunday night?' Kirby said.

'I didn't sell anything Sunday night. They usually come here to buy. Too risky at the club.'

'Why did you alter the CCTV footage then?'

'There's no cameras trained specifically on the area where the body was found, so why do you care?'

'Humour me.'

'He asked me to.'

'Who?'

'I told you already, I can't say. But I looked at the time he asked me to delete and I swear to God there was nothing on it. Not a thing.'

'You should have come forward with this before now.'

'I thought you'd find out about the kit and ... You said another boy is missing. Who?'

Kirby eyed the man thoughtfully. Harris had lied. He had stolen from the club. Tampered with CCTV. But had he killed? He made his decision.

'What do you know about Toby Collins?'

'Toby? No, he can't be missing.'

'What do you mean?'

'I saw him yesterday evening. He'd fallen over the wall. He'd been running like the hounds of the devil were on his trail. Damaged his ankle, I think.'

'Where was this?'

'At the soccer pitch. He was terrified. I brought him inside and got him a Coke. Called the doctor. I'd say if he's not in the hospital, he's at home.'

'He's not at home.' Kirby looked over at Lynch. She shrugged her shoulders. 'Which doctor did you call?'

And Bertie Harris told them what had transpired.

CHAPTER SIXTY-SEVEN

Max had a pain in his head. He didn't know if it was from exhaustion or withdrawal. He hadn't had a joint in hours. Not since his father had cornered him at the front gate and sent him out looking for Toby. He'd searched everywhere. Not a sign of his brother. He needed to put his head down. Away from here. An hour. Even ten minutes. It might stop the throbbing.

As he walked from the underpass down towards the tyre depot, he stopped. Two squad cars were parked across the road, blocking the traffic. No, not Toby. His brother couldn't have gone in there. Max started to run. As he reached the first squad car, he slowed down. Two uniforms were guarding the door to his hideout. His stash of weed and all his money was in there! No!

He was on top of the guards before he realised it. One of them put up her hand and stopped him.

'Where do you think you're going?'

'I'm looking for my brother. He's missing. What are you lot doing here?' Max laced his voice with arrogance. They had no right to be here. None whatsoever. But what if Toby was in there? Had they found him?

'And who is your brother?'

Max shrank into himself. The guard was looking at him intently. What was her problem?

'Toby,' he said. 'Toby Collins. Have you found him?'

'Not yet,' she said. 'You must be Max, the older brother.'

'What if I am?'

'I've been looking for you. Max Collins, you are under arrest for the theft of a sum of money from Wesley Finnegan. You have—'

Max wasn't hanging around for the remainder of the speech. He'd heard it before. He turned on his heel, ready to run. But his escape was blocked by another guard, who pulled his arms behind his back and snapped a set of handcuffs into place.

'You pair of bastards,' he spat. 'I'm just trying to find my little brother.' He felt a hand on his head as he was shoved into the back seat of the squad car. 'I did nothing to that old Finnegan fag. It's him you should be arresting. Going around molesting youngsters. That's what he's up to, you fuckers.'

The female guard climbed in beside him and smiled. Max opened his mouth and roared.

*

Lottie watched as Victor Shanley dismounted the ride-on lawnmower and walked towards her.

'What are you doing here?' she said.

Victor reached her, sweating through a vest top. 'I cut the lawn here regularly. Once a month. I couldn't just sit at home watching my wife disintegrate, so I decided to come and do some work here.'

'Do you know the Duffys well?'

'Just through the football team, you know.'

Lottie said, 'And you didn't think it appropriate to tell us?'

'My work here has nothing to do with Kev's death.' He paused, and Lottie could see he was trying to read her reaction. 'What have you found out?'

'Nothing I can tell you for now,' she said. 'Did Kevin ever accompany you here?'

He thought for a moment. 'Maybe a couple of times. He helped me empty the grass into the compost. I miss my boy so much. I have to be doing something, seeing as you lot won't release his body.'

'That should happen later today. I'll check with the pathologist.' Lottie wondered if Jane had had any success in matching the DNA found on the shorts. She'd have to follow that up on her return to the office. Now, though, she needed to find Paul Duffy.

'Do you know where Dr Duffy is? Or Julia or Barry?'

'There was no one here when I arrived. That was about half an hour ago. Paul may be at work. Did you try his surgery?'

'Next on my list. And his wife and son? Any sign of them?'

'I told you, there was no one here.'

'Okay. You can go back to your work.'

Lottie went in search of Boyd. She found him on the far side of the house, peering through a bay window. 'What did you find?'

'Nothing,' he said. 'No sign of life at all. What do we do now?'

'Did you look for their cars?'

'None in the garage. There are two registered to them. The one that showed up on the CCTV and another registered to Julia. Neither is here.'

'We already have an alert on Paul Duffy's vehicle, so organise one on the second car, and we need to process a warrant to have the house searched.'

'I don't think we have enough for a warrant,' Boyd said. 'Paul Duffy had a logical reason to be driving his car on Sunday night. We know he was with the team at McDonald's, so he had to get home somehow.'

'Why are you so negative all of a sudden?' Lottie stomped back to the car. 'Two boys are dead. I think we have enough for a warrant.'

'You're the boss.'

'Yes, I am. Now get driving.'

CHAPTER SIXTY-EIGHT

Gilly was glad when Kirby let her sit in on the interview with Max Collins. She had a feeling Max was into something other than stealing money from a bus driver.

'Max, the charges against you have been explained to you,' Kirby said. 'Have you anything to add?'

'You're wasting your time with me. You should be searching for Toby. He's in danger. I need to look for him. Let me out of here.'

'Do you deny you took cash from Wesley Finnegan?'

'I wouldn't believe a word out of his mouth. But he might have Toby. Did you check out his kip of a place?'

'Why would you think Mr Finnegan might have taken your brother?'

'To get back at me? I don't fucking know.' Max slouched down in the chair.

Gilly watched every tic and flinch, every breath the teenager was taking. He seemed genuinely worried for the safety of his brother. She scribbled a note and passed it to Kirby.

Kirby raised an eyebrow but read it. Good, Gilly thought.

'Max, why do you think Toby is in danger? Does he know who killed Mikey and Kevin?'

Max shook his head in silence.

'Why else would he be in danger?' Kirby asked.

'Someone killed his two best friends. It's logical to think that the same person might want to kill Toby.' His voice caught in his throat as he said the words.

Gilly could see the scar on Max's face pulsing. He was hiding something.

'Did *you* know those two boys were in danger?' Kirby asked.

'No. How would I have known?'

'We found a substantial amount of cash in the office at the tyre depot. Care to comment on that?'

'No.'

'Don't worry, it's being examined by Forensics. I'm sure your fingerprints are all over it.'

'That money's mine, you bastard. I earned it. I didn't steal it.'

'So you admit you had access to the unit. Were you there yesterday?'

Max looked confused. 'Yesterday? No, I don't think so.'

'You don't think so? Think a little harder, son,' Kirby said.

'What do you want from me?'

'A simple answer to my questions would help.' Kirby flicked through a folder.

Gilly was enjoying the exchange. She wanted to butt in and ask questions, but Kirby was managing the teenager skilfully. She could see Max thinking things over as he digested the questions. She believed he had a genuine concern for his brother, but he knew something. What was it?

'Hope Cotter.' Kirby threw the name into the mix. 'Do you know her?'

'She lives on the estate. Seen her around with her little girl.' Max looked relieved that the conversation had shifted slightly.

'Did you see her yesterday?'

'I don't know when I saw her last.'

'How about yesterday?' Kirby repeated.

'I told you, I didn't see her.'

'You arrived at the unit. Took Hope. Left her little girl there all by herself. Why did you do that, Max?'

Max straightened his back. 'What are you talking about? I never saw Hope or her daughter yesterday. What's happened to her?' Gilly noticed genuine fear creeping into the teenager's eyes.

Kirby said, 'I thought you could tell us that. Seeing as you use that place to kip down, to store your drugs and cash. I thought you could tell us what you did to Hope when she came snooping around.'

Max kept his mouth shut.

'Had she been there before? Is that why she went there? Looking for somewhere to hide out while the guards were searching for her?'

'Don't know what you're talking about.'

'We need to speak with her urgently. In connection with the death of a baby.'

Max jumped up. 'You're sick. You know that? A toxic bastard. Hope wouldn't hurt anyone. She's not like that. You don't know her.'

'Oh, and you do?' Kirby smiled.

'It's not funny.' Max slid back into the chair.

'You're right. I don't know her. But I think you do. Would Hope kill her own baby?'

Max shook his head. Gilly felt sorry for him. He was trembling and biting his lip, blood coming from a cut.

'No, she could never do something like that,' he said.

'If she didn't kill her baby, someone else did. Any idea who?'

'How would I know?'

'I'm asking the questions,' Kirby said, slapping the table. 'Look at me, Max. Do you know where Hope is?'

'No.'

'Do you know where Toby is?'

'No.'

'Did you take Wes Finnegan's cash?'

Two dark eyes looked up from beneath long lashes.

'Yes. I took his fucking filthy money.'

*

Jane phoned Lottie as she and Boyd were on their way back to base.

'Lottie, the lab has run the DNA from the waistband of the football shorts against samples taken from the people of interest in the case. Namely, Rory Butler, Paul Duffy, Bertie Harris, Wes Finnegan and Victor Shanley.'

'And?' Lottie held her breath, looked at Boyd as he drove, gaze fixed on the traffic.

'No match,' Jane said.

'What? It has to be one of them.'

'No match with any of those people. But there is a match with someone who is a witness in another case.'

'What other case? Who?' Lottie couldn't dampen the frantic beating of her heart.

'We took samples from the two boys who found the baby by the canal. The DNA profile of one of those boys matches the sample on the shorts.'

Lottie held her breath. Her Sean was one of those boys. Dear God, what was going on? She crossed her fingers. 'Who is it, Jane?'

'Barry Duffy.'

She blew out a gasp of relief. 'Thanks, Jane. We've got his father's car on CCTV near the scene where we believe Mikey Driscoll was abducted. Maybe Barry was driving, though he is only fifteen.' She took a long deep breath. She had no idea what this meant. 'Can you email the results across? I need them to get a warrant to search the Duffy property.'

'Will do. And another thing—'

But Lottie had already hung up.

Lottie gathered everyone in the incident room for an impromptu meeting and outlined what she'd just learned.

'Strange as it may seem, fifteen-year-old Barry Duffy is now our lead suspect in the murders of Mikey Driscoll and Kevin Shanley.'

'He could be their abuser too,' Boyd said.

'Along with the CCTV footage of his father's vehicle in the vicinity of where we believe Mikey Duffy was abducted from,' Lottie continued, 'Barry's DNA has been found on the new football shorts worn by the two victims. I've instigated a district-wide alert. Boyd and I were at the Duffy house earlier and the family were not there. We've put out an all-points bulletin for their cars.'

'They could be anywhere,' Lynch said.

Kirby said, 'I don't know what this can add, but Lynch and I went to Bertie Harris's apartment earlier.'

'What's he got to do with anything?' Lottie said.

'I discovered that there was ten minutes missing from the clubhouse security footage he supplied me with for Sunday night.'

'Go on.'

'Harris's apartment is full of boys' soccer kit. New stuff. Including football shorts.'

'Jesus,' Boyd said. 'Are we dealing with a group involvement?'

'I don't know yet. But Harris told me that one of the boys who buys the kit to sell on at a profit is Barry Duffy.'

'For feck's sake,' Lottie said. 'What is the little shite up to? He's only fifteen!'

'And,' Kirby went on, 'Toby Collins turned up at the club grounds last night.'

Lottie stood with her mouth open. Too much information hitting her at once. She sat down and nodded for Kirby to continue.

'Toby had been running. Wouldn't say from whom, but his ankle was twisted after he fell over a wall. Harris called a doctor for him. Paul Duffy.'

'What? Did Duffy take Toby? Are Barry and his father in this together?'

'I don't know, but apparently Dr Duffy said he'd take him to A&E.'

'Toby is at the hospital?'

'No. I've checked Ragmullin and Tullamore hospitals. No record of Toby having been brought in.'

'Where the hell did he take him?'

'No idea.'

'Did Harris say how Toby reacted to Duffy?'

'He said that when he mentioned calling the doctor, the boy appeared terrified. But once Duffy arrived, he seemed okay. Though that's to be taken with a grain of salt. I wouldn't believe a word out of Harris's mouth.' Kirby curled his lip in disgust.

Lottie studied the incident board. 'This is a mess. What is going on? Where did Paul take Toby?'

'Maybe he was able to fix up the damaged ankle himself.'

'That's the most likely scenario, but in that case, why isn't Toby at home in Munbally now? We need to find Paul and Barry Duffy immediately.'

Boyd stood up and looked at the photographs on the board. 'Mikey and Kevin had been sexually assaulted. Not at the time of their murders, but previously. We know Paul Duffy was the team doctor and had contact with the boys, so we now need to check with the victims' families whether the boys were his patients too. Sheila said she brought Kevin to the doctor. Was it Duffy? And had Mikey been in contact with him also? Is Paul Duffy the murderer?'

Lottie moved beside Boyd. 'Or Barry? He knew the boys through the club too. That scenario makes sense when you take into account what Harris said about who buys the kit from him, and the DNA found on the waistband of the shorts. It's entirely possible that Barry Duffy was the abuser. Maybe the boys were going to tell on him and he murdered them to shut them up. Toby could be an abuse victim too. And now he's missing.'

'Paul Duffy picked up Toby yesterday. Where did he bring the boy?' Boyd said.

'Maybe to his own house?'

'But there was no one there earlier. Just Victor Shanley.'

'Julia could be in danger too.' Lottie felt like her body was full of lead, and she had no idea which direction to take.

Boyd nodded. 'Another scenario is that the Duffy parents know about Barry and are trying to protect him.'

Lottie said, 'All I know is that we need to find them all, before it's too late for Toby.'

The room emptied, and as Lottie followed them out, she wasn't quick enough to escape.

'Have you caught up with the little murderer yet?' McMahon pushed himself away from the wall in the corridor outside the office.

'Who are you referring to?' She felt drained of all energy, her bag as heavy as a cement block on her shoulder. She'd been trying to come to terms with Kirby's revelations when Boyd had taken her aside and told her what Lynch had said about her.

'The Cotter girl,' McMahon prompted.

'Nothing yet.'

'And the missing boy, Toby Collins. Have you managed to find him?'

'Not yet.' She let her bag fall to her feet.

'What have you got?'

'A DNA match in the boys' murder investigation. Barry Duffy, aged fifteen, son of Dr Paul Duffy. It's a tenuous link, seeing as he had access to the kit, but I'm getting a warrant processed. We need to search the Duffy home. It's possible that Toby was brought there yesterday. The Duffys were not in earlier this morning when I called with Boyd. And Dr Duffy is not at his office. It's imperative that we find them as soon as possible.'

'What are you standing here for then? Get to it. I'll prepare a press briefing. Keep me up to date.'

He walked off full of his own importance. Lottie picked up her bag from the floor and went to her office.

Her phone rang. *Mother* flashed on the caller ID. She was about to reject the call when she decided to answer it. Might give her time to get her head in gear.

'What's up?'

'Sean hasn't come home yet. Have you been in contact with him?'

'No, I haven't had a minute all morning.' And then Lottie remembered where he was supposed to have been last night. 'Leave it with me.'

She hung up and rushed into the main office.

'Boyd? Kirby? Where is everyone?'

She ran back to the incident room. Neither Boyd nor Kirby was there. Shit, she had sent them looking for the Duffys.

Now, to add to the growing list of people she was unable to contact, her own son was missing. She put the back of her hand to her forehead and closed her eyes. Think, Lottie, think. Where could she turn next?

CHAPTER SIXTY-NINE

He heard the mower's engine shut down. Heard them talking. Voices. In the distance. But still close. He tried to move, to speak, but his throat was filled with blood.

It was no use anyway. No one would hear him. He was concealed by shrubs and bushes. He could feel thorns crushed beneath his body, pressing into his torso.

The pain. Oh God, the pain. His smashed legs. And his face, throbbing from ear to ear and from his forehead to his chin. The knife had been sharp. He'd fought hard, but in the end, he had succumbed, hoping that if he appeared dead, he would be left alone.

The surprise. That had been his downfall. Shock at the vehemence of the anger directed at him.

He knew he had to tell someone what he knew. Before it was too late. Before someone else died. Before *he* died.

'Help …'

The drone of the lawnmower's engine started up again.

And he knew he had no hope of being heard. No hope at all.

*

Victor Shanley couldn't get the image of his son out of his head. He had tried his best. Tried for Sheila and their relatives and neighbours. Tried to be strong. The mower turned at the end of the garden, but he couldn't see through his tears. The trees rustled around his head, drowning out his sobs. He switched off the ignition and got off the machine to empty the grass. As he moved towards the trees where the compost heap was, he thought he heard something. A sound like a whimper. He stopped. Stood still. Listened. Nothing.

He upended the box of grass, and had turned to pick up the garden fork when he caught sight of a flash of colour beneath a clump of bushes.

The sun blinded him. He took a step backwards. Probably a badger or a fox, he told himself, thinking of the fields of green beyond Duffy's garden.

There it was again. The whimper.

Fuck this, he thought, and crouched down, pushing the bushes away with the fork. A magpie shot out and up and settled in a tree above his head.

'Damn birds,' Victor said, and poked again, careful not to damage the animal he was sure was lying injured just beyond his reach.

But it was no animal. He yelled in horror and reached his hands into the bush.

'You're okay now. I've got you.'

He pulled the body towards him carefully. There was a lot of blood. He dug around in the pocket of his jeans for his phone and hit 999.

He turned the figure over, and when he saw who it was, he gasped.

*

Lottie was pacing the corridor, trying to figure out who to call, when Gilly ran up to her and started going on about Max Collins and Wes Finnegan's stolen cash. She wanted to tell the young garda to shut up and help search for her son, but she couldn't.

'Does Max know anything about where his brother might be?' Lottie asked.

'Says he was searching all night. Thought he might have been hiding out in the tyre depot; that's where we picked him up.'

'Did he know *why* Toby would be hiding?'

'Something to do with a message he got.'

'What message?'

'I don't know yet,' Gilly said. She paused and looked warily at Lottie. 'What's up?'

'It's Sean. I don't know where he is.'

'Oh shit.'

'He didn't come home last night and I believe he may have been at Barry Duffy's house. I'm heading back there. Warrant or no warrant. You see if you can find out anything further about Toby from Max.'

Lottie's phone rang and she paled.

'What is it?' Gilly said.

'Emergency services are on the way to Duffy's. A body has been found.'

*

Hope kept her eyes fixed on the shaft of light seeping through the jamb of the door. She was parched dry from thirst, but she didn't care about that. She just wanted to know that Lexie was okay.

Why had she been taken? She couldn't figure it out. The pain in her uterus was unrelenting, the bleeding uncontrollable. She should have gone back to the hospital. She should have done a lot of things. But everything she'd done so far in her life had been wrong. Everything, that is, except little Lexie.

She remembered the day Lexie was born, and wrapping the pink blanket around her little body. Telling no one who the dad was because that was her secret. She sat up straight. An image flashed in her memory. Something to do with the birth of her baby. No, not Lexie. The baby she'd given birth to a few nights ago. She scrunched her eyes. Trying to remember. But it vanished as quickly as it had appeared.

She was no wiser as to what had happened or why she had been taken to this place. The only thing she did know was the identity of her abductor.

CHAPTER SEVENTY

The ambulance arrived at the same time as the gardaí. Leaving Gilly to park the car, Lottie jumped out and ran as fast as she could through the gates and around the side of the house.

She pulled up short when she saw Victor Shanley walking in circles, a body on the ground at the edge of a clump of bushes. Slowly, she moved towards him.

Victor was crying, wringing his big hands together.

'I was too late,' he cried. 'He just died. In my arms. He died. Just like that.'

'Who ... who is it?' Lottie said.

Victor didn't answer. She held her breath, dropped to her knees beside the body. Thank God. It wasn't Sean. She exhaled in relief. But as she stared at the bloodstained face, she couldn't figure out what was going on.

Somewhere high above her head, a bird was cawing loudly. Too loud. She wanted to shout at it to get the hell away. Another breath and she inhaled a modicum of calm.

'You can take your time,' she told the first paramedic to reach her. 'He's dead. Get someone to call the state pathologist.'

Running her eyes over the body, she tried to spot the fatal wound. But it was difficult. She took a pair of nitrile gloves from her bag and pulled them on, then lightly traced her fingers over the hair and neck. McGlynn would go berserk. Let him. She didn't have time to wait.

The victim's hands bore evidence that he had fought back. Scrapes and bloody scratches criss-crossed the knuckles. The white shirt was saturated with blood, buttons torn from it. Why was he here? Lying dead in the Duffys' back garden.

'You know who he is, don't you?' Victor said.

She'd forgotten he was standing behind her. She needed to get him out of here. Standing up, she took him to one side. Steered him towards Gilly, who was standing with her mouth open and her face green.

'Garda O'Donoghue, take Mr Shanley to the station. He needs to make a statement.'

'I didn't do anything,' Shanley protested.

'You found the body. We need to eliminate you from our inquiries.'

'Okay, but I need to go home soon. Sheila … she needs me.'

'Of course. Garda O'Donoghue will look after you.'

He shook his head as if trying to make sense of everything. 'Why did this happen?'

'I don't know, but I will do my best to find out.' Lottie watched the man being led away and wondered if she was past her best at her job. Things were spiralling out of control and she had no idea how to reel it all back in.

As the area was being cordoned off, she phoned Boyd, then studied the body at her feet. Something was clutched in the man's hand. Still wearing her gloves, she reached down and opened the clenched fist. Two things lay there. A torn piece of white paper, and a key.

Boyd arrived at the same time as the advance SOCO team.

'Who is it?' he said.

'Rory Butler.'

'What the hell? Someone stabbed him, did they?' He stared at the body.

'What do you think, Sherlock?'

'Why? Who?'

'I don't know, and we can't waste any more time here. We need to find Sean and Toby.'

'Sean? What are you on about?'

Lottie shook her head and pressed her fists into her eye sockets, trying to squeeze back the tears. When she felt composed enough, she said, 'He never came home last night; as far as I know, he stayed here, with Barry. Any word on the Duffys' whereabouts?'

'Kirby and I liaised with all units. No sight of either of the cars.'

'Where is Rory Butler's car? He must have driven here.'

'I'll get the traffic lads to check.' Boyd turned to find someone.

'I'm going inside. Warrant or no warrant, we now have cause to suspect a murder has occurred on these grounds. Are you coming?'

'Sure. But let's suit up first. Just in case … Sorry.'

'Just in case there are more bodies inside? I know that's what you were about to say. If there are, let's just hope my Sean isn't one of them.'

Boyd organised a cordon around the house and an inner one around the body. With trembling hands, Lottie pulled on the protective clothing. She felt ill, bile rising up her throat and falling back down into her stomach, nestling there like stale alcohol. But she couldn't start thinking that something awful had happened to her son. No. She had to stay strong and search and find him. For all she knew, he was at home right now. She checked her phone. Nothing. She knew her mother would contact her if he had turned up. Where on earth was he?

'What do you think the key is for?' Boyd asked as they neared the back door.

'The one in Butler's hand? I don't know. Possibly his own house? We can head there after we've had a look around here.'

A uniformed officer ran up to them.

'We found Butler's car. Parked up a lane about a kilometre away. It's empty.'

'Why not park closer to the house?' Boyd said.

'No idea, sir.'

'Secure it for SOCOs.'

'Will do.'

Lottie watched the officer hurry away. 'Butler didn't want to be seen or heard driving up. This gets weirder.'

She tried the back door. It was locked. Boyd went to his car and returned carrying the enforcer.

'Stand back.' He braced his legs and swung. The door shattered.

Inside, Lottie stepped over the debris and listened. All was quiet. She was standing in a utility room bigger than the kitchen of the house she would soon be inhabiting.

'There's no one here, Boyd.'

'I've damaged my shoulder as well as that door, so it had better be worth it. Let's take a good look around.'

She agreed with his enthusiasm, but her heart was filled with dread.

When they had determined that the downstairs was clear of life, she took the lead and headed up the staircase. She pushed open the door nearest to her, the first of five, then ran from room to room.

'Will you slow down. What's the mad rush?'

She rounded on him. 'My son is missing. He could have been here … could still be here. You don't have children. You have no idea what it's like.' She knew she sounded irrational. Well, she was. Tough, Boyd.

'I do have some idea. Remember Grace.'

She did. Boyd's sister had disappeared a few months ago, only for a short period, but in that time, he had developed serious panic attacks. Maybe she was being a bit harsh on him. But she had no time for apologies.

'Stay with me,' she said.

*

Gilly had seen the mutilated body of Rory Butler and it screamed at her to do something. After she had Victor processed and a DNA sample secured, she drove him home.

Sitting in the squad car outside his house, she recounted in her head all that had happened over the last few days. One thing niggled at her. No one had yet determined where Kevin Shanley had been abducted from. She looked at the green area in front of the house. If it had been from here, someone would have seen him, surely. So where else would an eleven-year-old boy go? Who would he trust? His mates? Of course, but Mikey was already dead by then. He had to have gone somewhere. Somewhere he could be alone and mourn his friend.

She got out of the car and went back to the house. Knocked loudly. Victor opened the door.

'Mr Shanley, can I have a word?'

'Come in.'

She followed him into the kitchen, where Sheila was sitting at the table.

'I know you've been asked this over and over, but on the evening Kevin went missing, do you have any idea where he might have been taken from?'

'I don't know. I was out. Sheila was here all day.'

Sheila looked up. 'It's like I told the other guards. Kevin and I had had a row. He ran out the door with his football under his arm. I thought he'd come back later, but he never did.'

'You saw him, did you? Out on the green, playing football?'

Sheila shrugged. 'He had the ball with him. I assumed that was where he was. But he had to have gone off somewhere else. Otherwise he would've come home, wouldn't he?'

Gilly knew she had to ask the right questions, but she wasn't at all sure what they should be.

'You told detectives that he was friends with Toby Collins. Was there anywhere in particular Toby and Kevin liked to go? You know, a hideout, or a den?'

'They played on the green at the back of Munbally when we lived there. And sometimes they messed around at the old tyre depot on the industrial estate.'

'Okay.' Gilly knew Toby wasn't there. They'd had it cordoned off since she'd found Lexie.

Sheila said, 'I wouldn't trust that brother of Toby's, though.'

I wouldn't either, thought Gilly. 'Why do you say that?'

'Max was into hard drugs a few years ago. I can't prove it, but I heard rumours he sold his body for sex. To make money for his drug habit.'

'Where did you hear these rumours from?'

Sheila shrugged. 'Perhaps I heard it on the estate when I lived in Munbally. Everyone gossiped there. Much better living here.' Then, as if she realised the irony of her words, she began to sob.

Gilly noticed the glass in the woman's hand. Possibly the drink talking, she thought. 'I'll have another chat with Max Collins.'

Sheila took a mouthful from her glass. 'And that Hope one, the cleaner at the school, she was into him too.'

'Hope Cotter and Max Collins?'

'Yeah.'

Gilly was thinking hard and fast. Could Max Collins have abused the boys? Was he involved with the death of the baby at the canal?

Sheila started to cry.

'Thanks, Mrs Shanley.'

Gilly ran to the car. She had to talk to Max Collins, and quickly.

CHAPTER SEVENTY-ONE

Rose was wary about opening her front door, especially after her encounter with Leo Belfield yesterday. But she was worried about Sean. Maybe he'd forgotten his key. Chloe and Katie had gone into town and she was minding the baby. She hefted her nine-month-old great-grandson onto her hip and went into the hall.

She opened the door tentatively and sighed with relief.

'Sean! Where were you? You had me worried to death. Come in. Come in. And who is this?'

Sean was looking at her with a strained expression on his face. His voice was a higher pitch than usual. 'This is Barry. He's leaving right now.'

'I'm coming in. That game, Sean. The one you wanted to lend me. Can I get it now?'

Rose stood to one side as the teenager shoved Sean through the door in front of him then paused to tickle Louis under his chin.

'That's one cute baby you've got there, Granny. Anything to eat?' he said. 'I'm starving.'

'Where were you, Sean?' Rose said, ignoring the other boy.

'It's okay, Gran. I'm fine. Just put Louis in the buggy. Go for a walk.' Sean was giving her that funny look again.

'This is my house, Sean Parker. I'm not going anywhere. Speak up or I'm ringing your mother.'

'You're not going to ring anyone,' Barry said.

Rose looked on in horror as the boy produced a knife from his trouser pocket.

'Put that down now,' she said, in a voice she didn't recognise as her own. 'And get out of my house this instant.' Her phone was on the counter beside the refrigerator, where she'd left it before she went to answer the door. How could she get a message to Lottie? The teenager was approaching her. Why wasn't Sean doing something to stop him?

'Oh no, Granny,' Barry mocked, 'you're going to do things my way.' He walked over, picked up her phone. 'Unlock it.'

'Barry,' Sean said, 'leave my gran alone.'

'You shut your face and sit down. I told you what'd happen if you crossed me. One call and he's dead. Okay?' He pointed the knife towards Louis.

'Okay.' Sean sat down in the nearest chair.

Barry held the phone out to Rose. There wasn't much she could do with Louis in her arms, so she put in her code and handed it back.

'Now let's get the detective over here,' Barry said.

Rose watched as the teenager opened up her messages and started to tap out a text to Lottie.

'Can I put the baby down in his cot? He needs his nap.'

'Here, let me hold him,' Barry said.

Backing up against the wall, with a pain banging like a drum behind her eyes, Rose held on to Louis as tightly as she could. As Barry approached her with the knife, she felt the blood drain from her body and a lightness spread though her brain. Don't faint, she warned herself. But as the boy wrestled the baby from her arms, she sank to her knees and the world turned black.

CHAPTER SEVENTY-TWO

The Duffys' master bedroom was dark with the curtains drawn. The only brightness in the room came from a massive painting hanging above the bed, which was unmade.

'This picture is like the one they have in the living room, and both are similar to the one in Rory Butler's house.' Lottie walked closer, trying to see beyond the abstract lines and colour. 'I think it has a signature.' She leaned over the bed to get a closer look. 'I can't make it out, can you?'

Boyd drew back the heavy curtains and a stream of light highlighted dust swimming in the air. He joined her and they both squinted at the signature.

'Looks like a D,' he said. 'Could it be Duffy?'

Her phone vibrated in the back pocket of her jeans before she could reply. Her fingers were clumsy with the protective gloves as she tried to swipe upwards to unlock it.

'It's a text from my mother.' She read it quickly. 'Shit, Boyd, we'd better get over there. Something's not right.'

'Why? What does she say?'

'I don't think she's the one who sent it. I think someone's got her phone and is pretending to be her.'

She was already running past him, out of the door, and was almost at the bottom of the stairs when she realised he wasn't following. 'Come on, Boyd!'

'What did the text say?'

'I'll tell you in the car. Something about Sean being home and needing me. It's signed "Mum". Rose never refers to herself that way. I always call her Rose or Mother, even though she isn't—'

'All right, I'm coming,' Boyd said. 'No need to go over that old ground.'

*

With Maria Lynch sitting beside her, Gilly faced Max Collins in the interview room. The boy looked wired. Withdrawal symptoms, worry or just belligerence? She had no idea, but she needed answers.

She was glad Lynch had allowed her to take the lead, mainly because she hadn't had time to explain anything to the detective. She supposed subconsciously she looked on it as a chance to progress her career, but most importantly she knew Toby's life was at risk, and possibly Sean Parker's, and that she might be their only hope.

'What was in the message Toby got? The one you referred to.'

'I don't know. It was just something on his PlayStation chat.'

'Did it tell him to go to the tyre depot? Is that why you turned up there looking for him?'

Max was silent.

'Did you know your little brother was being abused?' Gilly didn't know if this was actually true, but she needed to rattle Max into giving her something.

'What? You're a stinking rotten bitch. He was not. That's a fucking lie.'

'Were you abused?'

'Fuck off.'

Gilly studied his bodily reactions. Eyelids flickering. Fingers drumming on his folded arms.

'How young were you when it first happened? Not much older than Toby, I'd guess. Then you got into it for money. For your drugs.

Now you're afraid the same person has Toby. That same person abused your little brother. Is that right?'

He shook his head. 'No one touched Toby. He'd have told me.'

'Do you think so? I imagine he might be terrified to tell you anything. I know I would be.'

Max's eyes filled up and he sniffed. 'The boys hung around the depot sometimes. I didn't think there was any harm. Gave them somewhere to go other than that kip of an estate.'

'And did they go there often?'

'A bit.'

'What did they do there?'

'Used it like a den, I imagine. They're only kids. They need their own space.'

'It's likely then that Kevin Shanley was there the night he was abducted and murdered?'

'Is that a question?' Some of the arrogance had returned, but Gilly could see his heart wasn't in it any more.

'Who else knew the kids hung out there?'

He shrugged.

'Any of your clients know?'

He uncoiled his body slowly and leaned across the table. His eyebrows were knitted together and she could smell an acrid staleness coming from his breath.

'What are you talking about?'

'Max. Please cut me some slack here. I'm trying to find your brother.'

He seemed to consider this; leaned back in the chair, ran a hand over his eyes, squeezing the bridge of his nose.

Eventually he said, 'Wes Finnegan knew about it.'

'He was here in the station most of yesterday, until he was released late last night. He couldn't have taken Toby.' She already knew Toby had been injured at the clubhouse and brought away by Paul Duffy. But Max didn't know that.

'Are you sure he was taken?' he said.

'The only thing we know at the moment is that we can't find him. Who else went to the depot?'

Max ran his hand under his nose, like a child. The man he was trying to be had all but disappeared.

'Duffy.' His voice was so low, Gilly wasn't sure she'd heard correctly. She glanced at Lynch, who appeared to be half asleep.

'Paul Duffy? The doctor?'

'Yeah, and Rory Butler.'

'The guy who coached the soccer team?' Lynch said, wide awake now.

'Duffy was all flash with his cash. And Butler appeared one day looking for him.'

'So you're saying Paul Duffy could have abused the boys?'

'Maybe.'

'And Rory Butler?' Lynch asked incredulously

'Butler? I don't know about him.'

CHAPTER SEVENTY-THREE

Boyd radioed for backup as Lottie sped from Duffy's house over to her mother's.

'That's Paul Duffy's car,' she said, parking up behind it. 'Radio the backup crews to approach without sirens. We need to assess the situation first.' She couldn't understand how she was so calm. Her whole family could be in danger, but her professionalism was overriding her fear. Good. 'Are you ready?'

'Ready for what? Jesus, Lottie, we need to wait,' Boyd said. 'You can't go in there all guns blazing. You might be putting your family at risk.'

She twisted round to face him. 'You saw what was done to Rory Butler. Either Paul or Barry or both of them did that, and you know what was done to the two boys. Let me tell you this, you can sit out here and wait if you like, but I'm going in.'

'Okay, okay. I'm coming.'

Outside the car she said, 'I'm sorry, Boyd. I'm wired. I'm terrified …'

'You're not wired. You're too calm. That's what I'm afraid of.' He tightened the Velcro on his stab vest. 'What's the plan?'

Lottie made sure her holster clip was unlocked, and nodded at him to do the same.

'We're going to wing it. Play it as if I believed the text was from Rose. Let's see what the good doctor has to say then.'

At the door, she took a deep breath and turned her key. Time for the final act.

'Hi, Mother. Got your text. Glad Sean is ...'

The remaining words died in her throat. Barry Duffy was sitting on a chair with her grandson in his arms and a knife in his hand.

He looked at her with bloodshot eyes. 'Stay where you are.'

'Barry? What's going on? Are you okay?' She tried to put on her mothering voice.

'Oh, I'm fine, Mrs Parker. Sean's granny, over there, I think she needs a doctor. Though I would strongly advise against phoning my bastard of a father.'

From the corner of her eye, Lottie saw Boyd drop to his knees next to Rose, who was lying in a heap on the ground. Shit, now Boyd was no use to her.

'Where's Sean?' She had to keep the boy talking.

'Here.' Barry kicked at something by his feet. Sean was sitting on the floor, his back to the table, his hands cable-tied to a chair leg, a cut on his forehead. The baby squirmed in Barry's arms.

'Can I take Louis?' Lottie tried.

Barry snorted. 'He's happy enough here. Not a squeak out of him.'

True, Lottie thought. She had never seen Louis so quiet. She hoped he hadn't been drugged. She had to act quickly.

'Can we have a chat, Barry? Tell me what this is all about and how I can help you.'

'No one can help me now.'

She kept her eye on the baby. She needed to get him to safety. She was glad Katie wasn't here. The girl would be hysterical. And Chloe. Where were they? A terrible thought crushed like a boulder down on her brain. Surely he hadn't hurt her girls? She stifled the terror-streaked gasp before it left her lips. One thing at a time.

'Barry, talk to me. I *can* help you.'

'I want you to arrest my father. He's ruined my life, and my mum's.'

'I need to know what he's done before I can arrest him. Tell me, Barry, what did he do to you?' She edged in closer. One step at a time. One breath at a time. But she knew she wasn't fooling him. She only hoped the backup team didn't storm the house. The first one to die would be Louis. She had to separate them. Her heart was beating so hard, she was sure he could hear it. 'What did he do, Barry? Did he abuse you?'

'Not me. But the boys. Mikey, Kevin and Toby. He abused them. All three of them. I tried to warn them off. But they were more afraid of me than of my father. Funny that, when you think of it.'

Lottie knew they had Barry's DNA on the football shorts. Would that turn out to be innocent transference from when he sold them on, or was he involved with his father?

'Why didn't you report this before now?'

'Because I've had enough of his rules and regulations. The fuss he created last night when Sean arrived at the house. It was something else. Isn't that right, Sean?'

Sean nodded his head frantically. 'That's right. He even—'

'Shut up!' Barry stopped him. He turned back to Lottie. 'Are you going to arrest my father now?'

'We have no evidence to connect him to the deaths. But Barry, can you tell me how we found your DNA on the waistband of the football shorts the victims were wearing?'

Barry paled, and the hand gripping the knife trembled. 'I don't know what you mean.'

'I think you do. You took soccer kit from Bertie Harris with the intention of selling it on. He told us, so there's no point in denying it.'

'That old fart would shop his granny if he thought it would get him out of trouble. No offence, Rosie,' he said with a smirk towards the floor, where Rose was now sitting up, breathing regularly.

Lottie watched him carefully. She had to get Louis away from him. She couldn't understand how her grandson wasn't screaming the house down. But no, he was fast asleep, his head resting on Barry's shoulder. From the corner of her eye, she could see Boyd slowly moving away from Rose. But he was still in Barry's line of vision.

'Are you saying that you didn't abuse or kill the boys?'

'Isn't that what I've been trying to tell you? You're supposed to be a detective. Why didn't you work it out? It was my dad.'

'Where is your father, Barry?'

She took another step forward. He inched the knife closer to the baby. The sound of the blood reverberating in her ears threatened to deafen her. Keep calm.

Barry was staring at a point above her head. As if he was in deep thought before he conjured up an answer.

'Is he dead?' she asked.

'No. Death would be too easy for him. He's in the boot of his car.'

'How ... I don't understand.'

'That jerk Rory Butler arrived at our house last night. Raving and shouting accusations. The next thing I knew, Dad was fighting him out in the garden. Thumping each other good and hard. I went to investigate. Sean here can testify to that, can't you, Seanie?'

Sean said, 'Yeah.'

Lottie focused on Barry. She didn't dare drop her eyes to look at her son. 'How did you overpower him? Your father's a big man.'

'And I'm stronger than him. He was bruised and battered. Easy for me.'

Noticing a shadow cross the glass of the back door, Lottie knew she had to get the knife away from Barry before the house was stormed. Louis stirred in the boy's arms. Opened his eyes and howled. Barry jerked, startled. Lottie raced forward. The back door opened.

'What's going on?' Chloe stood there with Katie beside her. Katie screamed.

Wrestling the baby from Barry, Lottie handed him to her daughter – she didn't know which one – and slammed her arm across Barry's throat. She knocked the chair flying and both of them crashed to the floor.

'It's okay, Lottie. I have him.'

Boyd wrenched Barry from her grasp and pulled him out from under her. Only then did she realise she had been about to smash her fist into the boy's face.

CHAPTER SEVENTY-FOUR

'Thanks for coming out to Swift House with me,' Gilly said. 'I can't locate Kirby. Everyone else is either out looking for the Duffys or over at the boss's house. Some drama going on there. I think they might have found Sean. It's a long shot but I thought if Rory Butler was involved in all this, maybe Toby could be here.'

Lynch wiped perspiration from the back of her neck. How did Kirby put up with Gilly O'Donoghue? The girl never shut her mouth.

They stood at the boot of the car and Lynch pulled on a vest. It was way too small.

'Bit tight for you?' Gilly said.

'It'll be grand.' Lynch fastened the straps loosely, knowing it wouldn't be much good if it came to a tussle with an enemy. But then again, she didn't think they were marching into trouble. The house looked deserted.

'Bulky old yokes, aren't they?'

Lynch nodded, and the baby kicked hard against her ribs. Dear God, she prayed, don't let me be putting my child in danger.

All around was quiet. No car. They approached the front door.

'How do you want to do this?' Gilly said.

'Carefully.'

Gilly knocked. 'No answer. Will we try around the back?'

'Sure.'

As she followed O'Donoghue around the side of the house, Lynch tried to block out the constant chatter. Unsuccessfully.

'I'd love to have loads of kids,' Gilly said, stepping onto the patio. 'This is your third, isn't that right? I'd like two. A boy and a girl. Don't know about Kirby, though. We haven't discussed it. We're in the early stages still, you know. But I do love him. Haven't said as much yet. Waiting for him to declare his undying love for me first.' She laughed.

Lynch smiled to herself. She could never imagine Kirby as a dad. Then again, it just might suit him.

Gilly knocked on the back door. 'This is some set-up. Rory Butler must be loaded. I find it hard to imagine he'd kill Mikey, his own kid. How could someone do that? And the poor baby found in the canal. Do you think he was murdered by his mother? Do you want me to fetch the enforcer to break down this door?'

'Garda O'Donoghue … Gilly. Stop chattering for a minute. We have no warrant. And no evidence that Rory Butler was involved in anything. Max Collins is in such a state that he'd say anything to give him a chance of keeping out of jail. Let me think for a minute. In silence.'

She sat down on one of the garden chairs to take the weight off her feet and to put distance between herself and the chatterbox.

'I'd love a house like this. My flat is so poky.' Gilly was peering through the windows. 'Here, look. I think something's happened in here.'

Lynch stood up and glanced over Gilly's shoulder. The reflection of the sun was making it hard to see. She went back to the door and tried the handle. It was open.

'Oh, sorry, I never checked. I thought we needed a warrant to enter the premises if we're not invited in,' Gilly said.

'You've seen broken crockery and upturned chairs through the window. We have reason to believe a life may be in danger. Let's do this.'

'You're the boss,' Gilly said.

'I wish.'

*

Kirby knew Gilly was impulsive, but this was taking the proverbial biscuit. Lynch should have had more sense, though. The state pathologist had just finished her preliminary examination of Rory Butler's body on site, and the team with the body bag was waiting patiently to take it to the morgue. He checked Gilly's text again.

'Okay if I leave you with uniforms?' he said.

McGlynn glared at him over his face mask. 'Get out of my sight. And when you see that inspector of yours, tell her if she ever invades a crime scene again, I'm reporting her to the chief superintendent and the commissioner and anyone else who can get rid of her.'

'Right so.'

Kirby shuffled off quickly. When he reached his car, he lit a cigar and set off to find Gilly and Maria Lynch. This whole case was a major fuck-up. As he drove towards Swift House he listened to the radio dispatch. It sounded like all had been resolved at the boss's house.

He tried to call Lottie, but the phone rang out.

*

Rose was adamant she was staying put.

'I'm not going in any ambulance to any hospital. I'm staying here in my own home and caring for these children.'

Lottie rolled her eyes and handed Louis back to a sobbing Katie. 'He's fine, pet. Not a mark. He won't remember a thing.'

Katie took the baby and rushed to her room. Chloe made to follow her sister. Lottie called her back.

'The night you saw Toby outside Fallon's, was it Barry Duffy who was in the car following him?'

Chloe shook her head. 'I think it was the same car as the one out on the road there. Looks a similar colour, but I'm not sure of the make. And I didn't see who was in it.'

Lottie sat down beside her son. 'Are you able to tell me what went on last night?'

'I shouldn't have gone there. But I'd been at Toby's earlier in the day and took screenshots of messages on his PlayStation. I was positive they were from Barry. Threatening or warning him, I'm not sure which. Telling Toby someone was coming for him. Now I think maybe Barry was warning him to be careful.'

'But why didn't you tell me? Why did you go over to the Duffys' on your own?'

'I wanted to tell Barry to stay away from Toby. He'd been mean to him the previous day and I didn't like it. And when Chloe told me about the boy being terrified by the car, I called to Toby's house to talk with him, but only Max was there. He's a scary guy and I felt that Barry needed to stay clear of the Collins family; that he had to end the tough act.'

'Okay. Tell me what happened when you got to Barry's house.'

'Dr Duffy opened the door and I thought he was a bit aggressive, standing up close to me, talking loud like. But he brought me inside. While I was in the hall waiting for Barry to come downstairs, someone began hammering on the door. The doctor opened it and Rory Butler stormed inside. He had some sort of painting in his hand and was shouting about an art studio and someone killing his son. He was mad, like really mad. I couldn't make out what he was saying most of the time. Dr Duffy tried to calm him down and they went outside to the garden.'

'And then?'

Sean shrugged. 'Barry came down the stairs. Told me to wait in the kitchen, then grabbed a knife and ran out.'

'Did you see what went on?'

'I saw nothing until Barry and his dad came back inside. They were both covered in blood. I was terrified. I wanted to leave, but they wouldn't let me, and then Barry started on at his dad. He hit him and the doctor fell against the corner of the bench. He was knocked out, I think.'

Lottie squeezed Sean's hand. 'You're doing great, son.'

'Barry made me help him drag his dad outside, and we heaved him into the boot of the car. I think Barry had gone stone mad at that stage. He still had the knife. He locked the car and made me sit in the kitchen until morning, and then he drove the car over here.'

'And Julia, Barry's mother. Where was she when all this was going on?'

'I have no idea.'

'Go and lie down for a bit. You're tired and in shock. I'll check in on you later.'

When Sean left the room, Lottie said to Boyd, 'At least we have Paul Duffy in custody now. If what I've heard is correct, he is the abuser, and possibly the killer. Now we just have to find Toby.'

Boyd said, 'But we have no idea where he might be.'

'None of this makes sense. I don't understand what Rory Butler has to do with it. But we need to get to the bottom of it.' She grabbed an apple out of the fruit bowl, realising she'd eaten nothing so far that day.

'Will we talk to Paul Duffy first?' Boyd said.

'Where is he now?'

'At the station with his son. In separate rooms.'

'Okay. Let's see what the bastard has to say for himself.' Lottie turned to Rose. 'I've posted uniforms at the door and detectives out on the road. You sure you're okay here?'

'Finish your work. And ... bring a takeaway for dinner when you're on your way back.'

Lottie smiled. Rose *never* did takeaway.

*

'This is some house,' Gilly said, leading the way up the stairs, careful not to touch anything.

'Shh,' Lynch said. 'Be quiet.'

'It doesn't look like there's anyone home and Rory is dead.'

'Will you ever shut up?'

'Okay so.' Why was Lynch such a moaner? If that was what pregnancy did to you, Gilly wasn't sure she wanted a baby after all.

All the doors on the landing were closed. She leaned against the first one. Put her ear to the white timber.

'I can hear something,' she whispered. 'Sounds like crying.'

'Open it,' Lynch said, 'and then stand back. I'll go in first.'

'No, I will.'

'I'm the detective, Garda O'Donoghue, and you will follow my orders. Agreed?'

'Agreed,' Gilly sighed. But she wasn't about to let a pregnant detective take a hit if there was someone dangerous inside. She turned the silver doorknob, then moved quickly into the room and stopped.

'Hope?' she said.

Lynch elbowed past her. 'Hope Cotter?'

Gilly moved to the bed. The girl was bound hand and foot, a piece of material tied around her mouth. As Gilly made to pull down the gag, she found herself drawn to the girl's eyes. They were dancing around, bulbous, her head nodding in a direction somewhere behind Gilly.

She turned to see what had the girl so agitated. 'What the ...? Lynch, watch out!' she yelled.

As if in slow motion, Gilly felt herself leap away from the bed and jump in front of Lynch, who was frozen to the spot, her mouth open in horror.

Someone dressed in white lunged again. Gilly held up her arm to shield her face as she dragged Lynch to the floor.

A cold sensation pierced her neck. She noticed a spurt of blood shoot into the air. Shit, Lynch! As she tried to see where the detective had been struck, a stabbing pain sliced through the back of her neck.

Someone was screaming. The girl on the bed? Lynch? Herself?

A door shut and then there was silence.

Gilly couldn't keep her eyes open. They felt so heavy. She could hear a voice in the distance. Lynch? So far away. Getting further. She tried to open her mouth but it was full of something liquid. Eyes. Tired. Her lids drooped shut, and she thought of Kirby.

CHAPTER SEVENTY-FIVE

Lottie asked Paul Duffy if he wanted to see the duty doctor, but he refused. From what she could see, he didn't appear to have any injuries other than dark-ringed eyes from being tied up in the boot of his car all night, and most probably a huge bump on the back of his head.

After they had the formalities concluded, she got the interview under way. She started with a few preliminary questions.

'Mr Duffy.' She did not give him his title. 'You have been arrested for the murders of Mikey Driscoll, Kevin Shanley and Rory Butler. Do you have anything to say?'

'I did not kill those boys.' The man appeared to have shrunk since she'd last seen him.

'I don't believe you. Admit it, you killed them.'

'I did not.'

'Was your son involved?'

'My son? Barry? What are you talking about?'

'He lured the boys for you and you abused them, isn't that correct?'

Duffy shook his head. 'Barry? No way. He just lost his head last night. I'm sure he didn't mean to hurt anyone.'

'Your wife, Julia, gave you alibis for the nights Mikey and Kevin were taken, but I'm confident that when we find her and she hears what you've done, she will change her statement.'

'You know nothing about my wife.'

'Where is she?'

'I don't know. I want to see my son.'

'Why?'

'Because he's got it all wrong.'

'Got what wrong?'

'I did not kill anyone.'

Lottie snorted her derision. 'Oh, so Rory Butler beat himself up and then stabbed himself, did he?'

Duffy shook his head. Sank his chin into his chest and clamped his mouth shut.

'Look, Mr Duffy, you can have your solicitor and speak to your son all in good time. My main concern at the moment is finding Toby Collins. Where is he?'

'Toby?' Duffy looked genuinely confused.

'Yes. Where have you put him?'

'I don't know what you're talking about.'

'I have a witness who claims that you picked him up yesterday evening from the clubhouse. Where did you bring him?'

Duffy swallowed hard, bit his lip and lowered his head. 'I brought him to my house. Fixed up his ankle. It was just a sprain. He was fine when he left.'

'He left of his own accord?'

'Yes.'

'Was he able to walk? It's quite a way from yours to Munbally Grove, isn't it?'

Duffy remained silent.

'Is Toby dead?' Lottie said.

'You're out of your mind.'

'Right now, I am in full control of my faculties, but if you don't answer my question, I can't be held responsible for my actions.' Shite talk, but she had to find Toby. He could be lying injured somewhere. Or dead. 'Where is the boy?'

'Julia said she'd bring him home. That's all I know.'

Lottie leaned back in the chair and shook her head. How many lies could she listen to?

The sound of running feet outside caused her to look at Boyd. Suddenly the door burst open. Acting Superintendent McMahon beckoned Lottie out of the interview room. He was flushed and wringing his hands.

'We have a report in of a stabbing out at Swift House. Rory Butler's place.'

'Oh no. It's Toby. We're too late. Duffy already killed him.'

'No, Inspector. This has just happened. Neither Paul nor Barry Duffy had anything to do with it. Get yourself and Boyd out there. Kirby called it in.'

There was something he wasn't telling her. She stood her ground. Eyeballed him. He looked away.

'It's one of our own.'

My plans have gone a little off kilter. I hurriedly wash the blood from my hands, but I have no time to wash my feet or change my bloodied clothing. I return to my easel. I cannot quell the thundering beat of my heart or the buzzing in my head.

I watch the boy. He should be a perfect specimen of virtue. Alas, he was violated like the other two. Touched by man. I must hurry to quash the evil from his soul, and in so doing I will absolve all sin.

I can hear water. It is so soothing. I feel myself sway in rhythm to the flow. But it must be my imagination. I'm not that close to water. Then again, maybe I am.

The drug is wearing off, because the boy says something. I cannot hear what it is. My ears are now deaf to the ways of this world. I am transported to a place where no one can touch me. No one can touch the boy. I was too late for the others. But this boy, Toby, I can save him. And save myself.

I eye the bloodstained knife lying on the palette of muddy colours. I really should wash it. The palette. I can hardly make out the blue any more.

And then I wonder, Why is the air around me so still? So quiet?

CHAPTER SEVENTY-SIX

Kirby radioed for help. Ambulances – the whole shebang. He had no thought for forensics as he crashed into the room.

His breath slid down his throat as he took in the scene before him. The girl on the bed, Hope Cotter, was tied to the headboard, her head hanging forward, shoulders heaving. The blood that spattered her body looked to him like arterial spray. But it had not come from her. He dragged his eyes downwards and gasped. Two bodies on the floor. Neither appeared to be moving.

Falling to his knees, he reached out to the first woman. Felt for a pulse. Blood, there was so much blood. A strong beat beneath his fingers. Her eyes opened.

Lynch whispered, 'Gilly …?'

Only then did Kirby allow his eyes to turn to the young garda. His Gilly. Lying face down on top of Lynch. Reaching out his hand, he wiped her short hair, matted with blood, from the back of her neck. Saw the gaping wound. He put his hand to her throat. Feeling for a pulse. Please, God, please let her be alive.

'Is she …?' Lynch said, her voice faint.

Kirby kept his fingers pressed to his girl's neck. Fat tears fell from his face. He turned her over and looked into her open green eyes. A trickle of blood had snaked from her mouth and dried. He pulled her lifeless body to his chest and wrapped his arms around her, resting his chin on her hair.

'Kirby?' Lynch again.

He shook his head. Again and again. He kept on shaking his head and he kept on crying.

*

Lottie stood in the doorway, Boyd crushed beside her. She moved to one side as the paramedics eased out with Lynch on a gurney. Hope Cotter was already downstairs, being comforted by a uniformed officer. She would get to her soon enough.

'I'm fine,' Lynch protested.

'You need to be checked over,' Lottie said. 'And the baby, to make sure it's okay.'

'It's kicking like mad. It's fine. But Gilly …'

Lottie nodded and moved towards Kirby as Lynch was wheeled out.

She knelt down beside him. She didn't care that they were in the middle of a crime scene. Nothing mattered now.

'Kirby?' She rested a hand on his trembling shoulder, his shirt damp beneath her fingers. Her big burly detective, the life and soul of the station. And she had no idea what to say to him as he held on to Gilly and wouldn't let go.

'She'll be fine, boss,' he said. 'She's so young and there won't be a bother on her in a few days. Just you wait and see.'

Lottie gulped a sob, tears blurring her eyes. 'Kirby, I think you need to put her down now. SOCOs have to get in. We need to find out who did this.'

'Leave her be,' Kirby said. 'Just a little while longer. Wait and see.'

Lottie glanced at Boyd, pleading silently for help. He crouched down beside them.

'Hey, bud,' he said. 'There's a doctor here. Needs to have a look at Gilly. Will you come outside for a smoke? I think you could do with one. I know I could.'

Kirby raised his head, sniffed back a sob and lifted a hand to Gilly's face. 'She's gone, isn't she?'

'I'm afraid so,' Boyd said.

Kirby gently closed the young woman's eyes. Their emerald green would never again light up Ragmullin station. The light that had been Garda Gilly O'Donoghue was now permanently extinguished, and something deep within Larry Kirby had broken into a million tiny pieces. Lottie knew it would be impossible for him to ever join them back together again.

'I loved her, you know.' With great care, he laid her back down on the floor, pooled with blood.

'I know.' Lottie put her hand under his arm, and together she and Boyd eased the big man to his feet. He walked like a wounded animal from the room, without a backward glance. Boyd went with him.

Alone in the scene of devastation, Lottie looked down at the young woman who had been so enthusiastic about her job. Who had yearned to be a detective. She knew Gilly O'Donoghue would have made a brilliant detective. She was one brave woman.

'I'll get the bastard, Gilly. Don't you worry.'

She stood back to allow McGlynn and his team to enter. For once, the forensic investigator's eyes did not challenge her. He nodded, and brought his hand to his head in salute. Lottie left the SOCO team to do their work.

Lottie snatched two pulls of Boyd's cigarette before returning to the kitchen to see what Hope Cotter had to say for herself. She could have done with a couple of Xanax, but she didn't have any with her. Maybe she could raid Butler's fancy bar for a drink. No, she needed her wits about her.

Hope was shivering, despite the heat of the room and the foil blanket placed around her shoulders by a paramedic.

Lottie wanted answers. The most urgent one was: who killed Gilly? The remainder of the inquisition could wait.

'Who killed my colleague?' she said.

The girl stared, eyes red-rimmed. She was no more than a child, her shoulders too thin for the weight she was carrying in her heart.

One sound came from her lips. 'Lexie?'

'She's fine. She's with your uncle Robbie, though social workers are now involved.' Lottie couldn't even begin to think of the trouble ahead for Hope. Now, though, it was imperative for the girl to be as cooperative as possible. 'Please tell me who murdered my friend and colleague.'

'What was her name?'

'Gilly.'

'Gilly was so brave. She saved the other woman. So brave ...' Hope's shoulders hunched further beneath the crinkling foil.

Leaning in towards her, Lottie put her finger under the girl's chin and raised her head. 'Look into my eyes, Hope. This is so important. There's a little boy missing. His name is Toby Collins. I think whoever attacked you and my colleagues took him.'

'Toby? Oh no.'

'I have to find him. His life is in danger. Who was it? Who else was in that room with you?'

Hope swallowed a gulp. 'The doctor's wife. Julia. It was her. She was wild. Like a madwoman. Swiping and stabbing. And then she ran out. I don't know where she went.'

Lottie blew out a sigh. 'Thanks, Hope. One last thing. How did you get here? Who took you from the industrial estate yesterday?'

'Rory. He ... he was looking for Max, I think. I don't know.'

'Why did he tie you up?'

'He said it was for my own safety. I was manic because he left Lexie alone in that place. Why did he do that?'

'I don't know.' Lottie wondered if they would ever find out. 'You're being brought to the hospital to be checked over, then you have to be interviewed. Promise me something.'

'Anything.'

'That you won't run away this time.'

'No. I won't. I just want to see my little girl.'

'I can arrange that.'

When Hope had been brought out to an ambulance, Lottie joined Kirby and Boyd outside.

'Who killed my Gilly?' Kirby said.

'Julia Duffy. Where the fuck is she?'

I sit back and look at the painting. I have to admit, it's not great. Not as good as the one Rory tore from my hands as he stormed from the house last night. I only wanted to gift it to him. To thank my own cousin for giving me the ice house to use as my studio. To tell him I forgave him for everything. For taking our grandfather's house while I inherited nothing. But he couldn't understand how I felt. He was like a soul demented as he swore at me and said Paul had taken his son from him. I had no idea who he meant. Surely Rory had no son? But then I realised it had to be one of the two boys. Mikey? Or Kevin? Doesn't matter to me now; they have been set free.

My studio. My refuge. Away from the demons trawling the walls of my home. I can find peace here.

Turning to the boy lying on the table, I wonder if I am up to this last kill. I must do it. Otherwise I can never be free of the sin visited upon my family by my husband. He never would tell me why he favoured the flesh of young boys and girls over the supple tenderness of mine. I can never forgive him for that. This is the only way to atone.

Before I use the knife, I am startled by the flash of something in the boy's eyes. Then I hear the sound of footsteps outside. They could not have found this place. My beautiful ice house that Rory promised no one knew of. He took pity on me when I told him, one night after a match, of the need for space away from the domination of my husband. And anyway, hadn't I cared for our grandfather in his dotage, so maybe I should have something of his estate. The eejit had agreed. Maybe he just wanted to shut me up. I don't know and I really don't care.

I had the only key, he said. But he had another key in his hand last night. Before he stormed off in a rage. Maybe I'll have to deal with him too if I am to keep this refuge.

There it is again. Soft whispers outside. The boy's eyes are practically bulging out of their sockets. Then I realise he is trying to scream. To call to whoever is out there. I'm glad now that I stuck my painting rag in his mouth to blot out any words he might utter. Ah, that's why I could not hear what he said a few moments ago.

Now the boy is fighting me. The drug has definitely worn off. But if I try to give him another sleeping pill, I will have to remove the gag. And if he is asleep, I will not see the last vestiges of life leave his eyes. I need to see the dimming of his soul so that I can be free. So that my family is free for eternity.

'Goodnight, little one. Little Toby.'

I place my hands around his neck and squeeze.

CHAPTER SEVENTY-SEVEN

The sun slid behind thick black clouds and the humid air heralded thunderstorms. Crashing through the undergrowth with Boyd and Kirby behind her, Lottie twisted and turned trying to find where Julia could have gone.

'It has to be somewhere close by. The car is still parked up the road.'

'Slow down,' Kirby groaned.

She had wanted him to return to the station. To go home. Anywhere but here. But he'd insisted and she hadn't time to argue. Toby's life was in her hands.

'This is the way to the lake shore,' Boyd said, brushing leaves from his hair. 'Wait a minute.'

A crack of thunder halted Lottie. She stood up straight.

'What?' Boyd said.

'I'm trying to listen. Shush.'

But she only heard the flap of wings as a flock of swans rose from the lake and headed away from the path of the storm.

'Remember the map Rory Butler gave us?' Boyd said. 'There was a small building marked on it. And if I remember correctly, it's down that way.'

Lottie turned right, following his pointed finger, and immediately noticed the trampled grass revealing a well-worn path.

'This way.' She started to run, ducking and diving beneath overhanging branches. Two minutes later, she came to a halt. 'Looks like a stone hut.'

Boyd joined her, followed by an out-of-breath Kirby.

'Take a quick look around,' she instructed Kirby. He mooched off around the corner and she turned to Boyd. 'Let's go in.'

She put her hand on the handle and pushed down hard. 'It's locked.'

'Out of the way.' Boyd leaned back and lifted his leg, kicking out with all his might. The timber cracked, and with a second kick the door hung open.

Lottie stepped inside with Boyd by her side. The scene did not frighten her as much as the look of stark madness in the woman's eyes. Her hair was matted to her scalp and her skin, dotted with blood splatter, appeared translucent.

Lottie said, 'Step away, Julia.'

The woman raised a hand and in the swiftness of a blink grabbed a knife from a table beside an easel and held it above Toby.

'Get out!'

'It's okay, Julia. Look, we have no weapons,' Lottie lied, holding her arms away from her sides. Her ears were thrumming from the noise of the door splintering, and adrenaline fuelled her movements. She edged forward slowly.

'Not another step!' the woman screamed. She was dressed in a bloodied neck-to-floor cotton gown.

Desperately Lottie tried to quash her anger. The boy was bound to the table. She had no idea if he was still alive. Was she too late?

'We have Paul. Your husband. He's safe. Would you like to see him?'

Julia's lip curled upwards in a snarl. 'I couldn't care less about him now. I'm saving this boy's soul. Can't you understand that?'

'You don't have to do this. Toby has done you no wrong. Let him go.'

Julia laughed. 'He and his two friends tempted my husband into sin, into the way of the devil. I am now sending this boy back to God so that I will be able to live in freedom.'

'And Rory Butler? Did you kill him too?' Lottie was convinced Julia hadn't killed Rory, but she was saying the first thing that came into her head, anything to keep the woman's focus off Toby.

'Is he dead?' She appeared momentarily disconcerted. 'If he is, he deserves it. My own cousin, taking everything I was entitled to. Yes, I was the one who cared for our grandfather in his old age, and what did he leave me? Nothing. I talked Rory into allowing me access to this place for myself, while he retained the main house. I might be a lot of things, but I'm not greedy.'

'Rory was your cousin?'

'Yes.'

How had they not known this? But Lottie knew she just had to keep Julia talking. 'What about Hope Cotter? Why did Rory take her and tie her up?'

'How would I know? I only went over to the house because I heard the car.'

'You killed my colleague.'

'I can't say I'm sorry about that, but I am sorry it wasn't the pregnant one. How could she have shown my boy that awful photograph of the dead baby? How could she have done that? Bad enough that he'd seen the body of his bastard brother first-hand.' She paused as if musing over a thought. 'How is my boy?'

'He's fine.' What the hell was the woman talking about? Bastard brother? Was the dead baby Barry's brother? How?

'Ah, I knew he would be.' She moved as if floating, closer to Toby. 'I'm proud of Barry. He helped me take the baby from *her* and carry it to the water, where I laid it down to rest. But he never told me why he went back there. Why he caused the baby to be found.'

'Julia, put the knife down. Think of your son.'

The woman lowered her hand slightly. A furrow appeared in her brow and her eyes knitted closer together. 'Barry? My flesh and blood. Nothing can harm him.'

'But you harmed Barry's baby brother, you just said.' Lottie was still confused.

'It was no flesh of mine. Paul planted his seed in her. That Hope girl. Her spawn was tainted and had to be put to sleep. I let it float in the waters, freeing its soul.'

'After you choked his life from him.' Lottie felt the rage bulging in her chest. She wanted to slap the woman, but she needed her talking before the madness struck her dumb.

'Where is my Barry?'

'He's under arrest for abduction.' Which might be elevated to murder once forensics was completed on Rory Butler. 'He's asking for you. Come with me now and you can see him.' Lottie eased closer, Boyd's breath in her ear. She had no idea where Kirby had got to.

'Barry only did what I asked. It's all his father's fault. If that bastard hadn't succumbed to the flesh of young boys and girls, none of this would have been necessary.'

'But why kill them? Why did you kill Mikey and Kevin?'

'I knew they could not remain silent forever. If they had talked, I could have lost everything. My husband would be in jail, his job gone. I might have lost our home. Our lives would be shattered. What would everyone think of us? Our Christian faith would be mocked. I couldn't allow that to happen. I had to set them free of their secret and save their souls.'

As Julia turned swiftly towards Toby, a loud crash rang through the cramped space as a window shattered and Kirby appeared in an avalanche of glass and splinters.

The easel shuddered and fell, paint splashing across the floor, trickling towards Julia's bare feet. The woman whirled round, unsure of what had happened. Lottie took her chance, diving forward and knocking the woman flying. She hauled herself to her feet as Kirby dragged Julia upright and drew back his arm. Boyd was quicker.

He grabbed Kirby's hand. 'No, bud. We have her. She'll pay.'

Kirby's rage crumbled in a flood of tears. Boyd clicked handcuffs on Julia's wrists, while Lottie turned to the immobile boy and hurriedly released him.

'Toby?' she said. 'Toby? Can you hear me?'

She held her fingers to his throat, feeling for a pulse. Boyd joined her as he called for paramedics, shouting out instructions.

'Easy, Lottie.'

'He can't be dead!' She lowered her head to Toby's face. 'There's a faint breath. I can feel it. Jesus Christ, Boyd, help me here. We can't let him die.'

Gently Boyd shoved her out of the way, and she stood watching helplessly as he began CPR on the lifeless boy.

From the corner of her eye she saw a bundle of neatly folded boys' clothes on a shelf. Beside them, a medal on a green ribbon, and a vase of wild flowers.

CHAPTER SEVENTY-EIGHT

The clouds eventually burst and the rain fell in torrents. The path they'd taken to Julia's studio flowed with mud and debris. The paramedics found a more direct route and drove an ambulance through without trouble.

Lottie was sitting on a bench with her arm around Kirby. Julia was en route to the station, with McMahon waiting to accept her into custody.

'Come on,' Boyd said. 'We need to get out of here and let SOCOs do their work.'

Lottie let him lead her and Kirby out into the rain. She looked upwards and welcomed the freshness against her skin.

'What went on in there?' she said.

'You were there, you saw it,' Boyd said.

'I know, but before that. It must be where Julia lured the boys. Why did they go with her? Was Paul involved too?'

'I imagine they trusted her despite her husband's abuse, and got into the car with her without realising they were getting in with the devil incarnate. She then drugged them and murdered them.' Boyd put his arm around her shoulder. 'Anyway, Lottie, I think those are questions for later. Now we need to look after Kirby and see if Lynch is okay. Look out for our own.'

'And Toby, will he recover?'

'He's alive, and that's all we can hope for at this stage.'

She stopped walking, rainwater rolling down her face. 'You go on ahead with Kirby. I just need a moment to myself.'

Her two detectives left, Boyd leading a hunched Kirby, who was like a man in a trance. She pitied him the pain that was yet to come. The reality.

With her legs feeling like lead, she sank to her knees in the mud, ran her hands through the saturated earth and tightened her fingers around a clump of drenched grass.

She didn't even go home to change. Wet and mucky, she went straight to the hospital.

Lynch was lying in a cubicle wearing a gown, a conglomeration of wires and tubes snaking from her body to a bank of machines. Ben sat on a chair beside her.

Lottie stood awkwardly on the other side of the bed.

'I'm grand,' Lynch said. 'Looks worse than it is.'

'And the baby?'

'Little bugger is stronger than me. Not a bother on him.'

'It's a boy? Thought you didn't want to know.'

'They did a scan and I asked.'

'Thanks,' Ben said, 'for saving her life.'

'She didn't save my life,' Lynch said sharply. 'Gilly O'Donoghue did that. She was a hero. I need to talk to Kirby. He'll want to know what Gilly was saying before she ... before ...'

'There'll be time for that,' Lottie said. 'You sure you're going to be okay?'

'Yes.' Lynch put out a hand. 'I'm sorry.'

'It wasn't your fault.'

Lynch's eyes darted to Ben, then back to Lottie. 'I jumped to conclusions. Ben has set me straight.'

Lottie nodded her acceptance of the apology and went to the next cubicle.

Hope was sitting up in bed, Lexie on her knee. Robbie was on a chair beside them. He looked like he'd aged years. The weight of looking after his young niece and her daughter appeared to be too much.

'I'm going out for a smoke,' he said.

'How are you, Hope?' Lottie asked once he'd gone.

'I'll be fine.'

'We got the DNA results on the baby that was found in the canal.' She wasn't sure this was a conversation to be held in front of Lexie. But tiredness was eating her bones, so she went for it. 'The baby was yours and Paul Duffy's.'

The girl nodded.

'Were you in a relationship with him?'

'He got me a job cleaning at the school. We ended up together. It was a one-night stand really. He was so attentive and attractive, I fell for his charms. And he was quite persuasive. But once he'd had me, he didn't want to know me.'

'Did he know that that one night resulted in your pregnancy?'

'I went to his house one evening and told him that I needed money to raise the child, but he said he already had one kid corrupted by his mother, so he didn't want to know this one and it was best that I stayed away from him. As I turned to leave, Julia was standing down the hall behind him. I'm sure she heard everything.'

'You could've had an abortion,' Lottie said.

'I had no money for the air fare to Liverpool, let alone the cost of the actual procedure. I had no choice but to keep it.'

'Why did Rory take you to his house and tie you up?'

'He said Mikey's mum told him she thought Max might have had something to do with the boys' deaths. He came to the old tyre depot looking for Max because he knew he hung out there, but he found me instead. He quizzed me all night, but there was nothing I could tell him about the boys.' Hope hugged Lexie to her chest.

Lottie knew she was hiding something. 'You knew, didn't you? About the abuse. You told Rory.'

Hope feathered Lexie's head with a kiss, then looked up, eyes brimming with tears. 'It was something Paul said, the night he had sex with me ... He mocked me and laughed at my body and said it was nothing like what he could have. And he mentioned Mikey, Kevin and Toby. When he was finished with me, I turned over and vomited in the back of his car.'

'Did you tell anyone?'

'No, because I knew no one would believe me, an unmarried teenage mother from Munbally, over a respected doctor.'

'You could have spoken to the boys' mothers.'

'Same story. They'd have thought I wanted money for telling them. Maybe I should have tried, and then Kevin and Mikey would be still alive. Oh God!'

'You did nothing with the information then?' Lottie tried to keep her voice soft and soothing, but it was increasingly difficult.

'I tried to talk to Mikey, but he kept running away from me, avoiding me. I vowed to myself that I'd watch out for him. I would take Robbie's car every night and patrol the streets, looking for Paul. I thought I could stop him hurting those boys. But I was wrong.'

'And you told Rory all this?'

'I did, and he went mad altogether.'

'How do you mean?'

'He said if I hadn't killed my baby, maybe Paul did it. And then he started putting two and two together and said that Paul must have killed Mikey and Kevin too. Did Paul kill my baby?'

Lottie was sure that the amnesia that had gripped Hope when she'd delivered her baby had not lifted yet. Maybe when the girl was back home without the stress of thinking she had to go on the run, she would remember.

'Can you still not recall what happened?' Lottie said, trying to be kind.

'No.'

'When you came into the station that day, you said, "I think I killed him."'

'I remember waking up by the canal, my jeans beside me, my legs covered in blood. I couldn't see my baby anywhere. I thought … I thought I must have killed him.'

'You didn't, Hope. You didn't kill your baby.'

'Who did, then?'

She knew she shouldn't tell the girl, but maybe it would give her some relief to know she hadn't done it herself. 'I believe it was Julia Duffy.'

Hope clutched her daughter to her chest and cried into her hair. 'Oh my God.'

With weariness dragging her down, Lottie turned to leave. She wanted to see her own children. To wrap them up in her arms and hug them until the end of time.

'Did you find Toby?' Hope said when Lottie had one foot outside the cubicle.

'We did.'

'Is he alive?'

'I have to talk to the doctors, but yes, he is alive.'

Just about, she thought, as she left.

CHAPTER SEVENTY-NINE

Lottie ran the gauntlet of the crowd of journalists on the station steps and went to find Boyd.

After they had interviewed Paul Duffy and charged him with the sexual abuse of minors and the murder of Rory Butler, she said, 'Next on the list, Barry Duffy. Let's see what story he has to tell.'

When the teenager was seated, Lottie thought how innocent he looked. But she knew that the evidence would prove he was anything but innocent. Barry Duffy's heart had been coated with evil by his mother.

'Tell me about the baby, Barry.'

'What baby?'

'The one you killed.'

'I did not kill him. *She* did it.'

'Who did?'

'My mother. She had me keep an eye on Hope because she was pregnant with Dad's baby. I used to follow her on my bike. I saw her that night, stumbling around in the dark up by the canal. I rang Mum. We both followed her. It wasn't just me.'

'And what did you do?'

'I saw Hope in pain, lying on the ground. She was in labour. Mum hit her on the head and tore off her jeans and knickers. And then ... then the baby slid out between her legs in a pool of blood. Didn't even cry, but he hadn't a chance. Mum leaned over, wrapped her hands around his little throat and squeezed the life out of him.

She told me to put him in the canal. Said it would cleanse my soul as well as the baby's.'

The tone of his voice never changed. One long monotone. What had that woman done to her son? Lottie shook her head.

'Barry, that must have been so tough for you.' She tried to show him compassion, but all she could think about was him holding little Louis captive.

'It was. But I couldn't tell anyone. The only thing I could do was make sure the baby was found. And I did that.'

He raised his eyes and stared at Lottie, his eyes two shards of steel. She felt a shiver trickle between her shoulder blades.

'That was good thinking.' But he'd helped dispose of a body. Did he not see the seriousness of his actions? And he was just the same age as her Sean.

'You knew Mikey, Kevin and Toby?'

'I did.'

'And how did you discover your father was abusing them?'

'Mum told me. She warned me to be careful around him. I couldn't believe it at first. But I knew something was going on.'

'Why didn't you report your father's abuse of the boys?'

He shrugged. 'I tried to warn them to stay away from him. But I think they felt more threatened by me. Mum told me not to worry, that she had ways of dealing with Dad. She was just waiting for Hope's baby to be born, and then she said she would free the boys from their pain. I thought she meant she was going to go to the guards.'

'Why did you bring Sean with you to recover the baby's body?'

He picked at his fingernails. 'No matter what, that baby was my half-brother. I couldn't leave him there to be eaten by fish and rats. I thought he needed to be buried or something.' He laughed. 'And having your son with me would help prove my innocence if it came to that. It almost worked.'

The evil that stalked his mother's soul was living in Barry's heart. Lottie felt the hairs on the back of her neck prickle.

'And Rory Butler. What happened when he came to your house last night?'

'You'd better ask my dad about that.'

'We did. You had the knife, Barry. I think you killed him.'

'What does Dad say?'

Lottie knew that Paul Duffy had already confessed to murdering Rory after the younger man had arrived at his home shouting accusations. But she still felt that Barry had lost control.

'I'm asking you. What happened?'

Barry shrugged. 'Rory was accusing Dad of killing his son, Mikey. I had to shut him up. Dad was kicking the shit out of him so I lashed out with the knife.' He paused before adding, 'What killed him? The kicks or the knife?'

You're one smart little fecker, Lottie thought. She had to wait for the post-mortem results to confirm the exact cause of death, but for now, she was satisfied that father and son were equally culpable in the death of Rory Butler.

She stood. 'Boyd, add the charge of murder to his growing list of offences.'

'When can I go home?' Barry said.

'Home? You no longer have a home.'

But Lottie had, and that was where she was going. She flew out the door and ran down the corridor to the front door. She didn't even hear Boyd calling after her.

DAY FIVE

Friday

CHAPTER EIGHTY

Cafferty's was pulsing with hot bodies on this warm Friday evening. Some of the crowd had spilled over into the smoking area outside.

Lottie stood at the bar holding a glass of Sauvignon Boyd had bought for her. She watched as he sat down beside Kirby, who was nursing a pint of Guinness. He was so un-Kirby-like that she thought he could be a different person. Grief did that to you, she knew. She bit her lip so sharply, she could taste blood.

The throng was pushing against her. She noticed Cynthia Rhodes talking to someone just inside the door. That was one woman she did not want to talk to tonight. Or any night.

'Hello there. You must be Lottie. Cynthia pointed you out to me.'

Turning around, she stared into a pair of green eyes an exact replica of her own. His hair was wild, and she could see that it had once been red but was now a scorched blonde.

'Do I know you?' Confusion raced through her as she tipped her head to one side, appraising the rugged-faced stranger who didn't look like a stranger.

He held his hand out to her. Instinctively she took it in her own. His shake was slick and quick, but firm. She noticed his nails were clean and cut in straight lines, as if he filed them regularly.

'You look just how I imagined you to be in real life,' he said. 'Your photos don't do you justice at all.' A smile broke across his face, flaming his eyes with light. He ran a finger inside the collar of his shirt before putting both hands into the pockets of his navy chinos.

'I don't mean to be rude,' she said, though she knew that was exactly how she sounded, 'but who are you?' A tease of unease tickled the base of her skull. Jesus, it was like looking into a mirror and seeing herself as a man.

'I believed I had more of my father's genes than my mother's,' he said, 'but seeing you, I believe my mother's must have been the stronger.'

'Look, I have no idea who you are or what you're talking about, and I'm with company, so if you'll excuse me …' She made to move away from him, but his hand covered hers again.

'Two minutes of your time. Please? I've come a long way to meet you.'

She should just go. Leave. Walk away. But curiosity stalled her and she waited. She wanted to hear what this man had to say.

'I spoke to you on the phone. A few months ago. You wouldn't talk to me then. I was afraid I'd made a mistake, so I did some more research.'

'Research?' Immediately Lottie felt like a lab rat in a cage. His eyes were scrutinising her, travelling over her face, her hair, down to her hands. She followed his gaze, thinking that if he stared at her legs, he was getting a kick in the crotch. And then she recalled McMahon and Rose's words. And she knew exactly who he was.

He said, 'My mother was quite ill at the time. Not really my mother, but she'd imposed herself in that role, so I knew no other. While she was in hospital, I went through all her things. Her files, computer stuff, boxes in closets. I even raided her office.'

Lottie noticed that his eyes were swimming in tears, drawing in loss. She knew that look well. It was reflected back at her every morning when she washed her face.

'I'm a cop. I know how to search properly. Eventually I found the evidence.'

'I really have no idea what you're talking about.' But Lottie did know. That phone call. The day after her house had burned to the ground. Kneeling in a pool of rainwater swimming in ash, the phone locked in her hands. The same voice. His voice.

'You're Leo Belfield,' she said.

He nodded. 'Alexis believed she was doing right, separating me from my twin sister. But now I think she was just being plain selfish. She wanted a new life in the United States. She wanted a child. She took me. And left you behind.'

'Wait a minute. You have it all wrong.'

'No, I haven't. You're my half-sister, Lottie Parker. We share the same mother. With no idea of who our father was.' He dipped his head.

'I know who my father was. And I believe that this Alexis was instrumental in him taking his own life. I've seen first-hand what her madness can do. And no matter what you think you found in the stuff she hid from you, you have it all wrong. Very wrong.'

When he looked up at her, all trace of tears had disappeared. His eyes were questioning, his mouth screwed in disbelief. His demeanour suddenly became defensive as he clenched his hands into tight fists.

'I have it completely right. I've seen it all. The photographs. The documents. Don't try to deny it. You are my sister.'

'I'm not denying you might be related to me.' Why was she even having this conversation with a man she had never met before? 'But I'm not your twin. Though I will admit that it may be possible I'm your half-sister.'

His face clouded as if a shadow had fallen over it. 'I don't understand.'

'You think you have it all worked out. But nothing is as simple as it appears. Alexis Belfield spent a lifetime covering up her sordid past. She might have succeeded if it weren't for the inquisitiveness of Marian Russell, another half-sister you may or may not have found out about. She's dead by the way. Murdered. At the hands of ...' No, she couldn't shatter him this soon. 'Suffice to say, our family history is shrouded in layers of obscurity. The only people who know the whole truth are either dead or ... How is Alexis?'

'Out of her coma but unable to speak. Other than that, she's in good health.'

'Is she hospitalised?' I hope so, Lottie thought. She couldn't deal with having that evil woman on her doorstep.

'For the moment. I'm making arrangements to bring her home. But I needed to make this journey first. I had to find the truth for myself before I confronted her.'

'The truth? Ha, don't make me laugh.' Lottie snorted her derision. 'My life was built on so many lies that I'm surprised I can ever believe a word out of anyone's mouth. And I imagine yours has been the same. So don't come looking to me for answers. I don't have them. Go home and ask Alexis.'

'She can't talk.'

'I'm sure she'll be able to write out your family history for you.' She drained her wine and put down the glass. 'We're done here. Go home.'

'I'm not leaving Ragmullin until I find out everything.'

'Good luck with that, then. And don't go near Rose again.' She turned and had begun to push through the crowd when she felt her hand being grabbed. He turned her to face him.

'If you're not my twin sister, then who is?'

'You'll have to find that out for yourself.'

'Tell me.'

'Try the central mental hospital. She's incarcerated there.'

'I don't believe you.'

'I don't really care one way or the other.'

Lottie shook her head. Released her hand. Left him there. And walked over to Boyd and Kirby.

'Who was that?' Boyd asked.

Lottie put her hand into his. 'Nobody,' she said.

EPILOGUE

Three weeks later

Toby kicked the ball into the goal. He didn't celebrate. He walked slowly up to the goal mouth, picked up the ball and turned to do it again. Easy when there were no defenders. No goalkeeper. Just him and the green grass.

He reached the spot where he had stood a moment ago and put the ball down. Booted it into the goal again, then began his solitary walk to retrieve it.

'Want someone to kick around with?'

He turned. The tall, blonde-haired boy stood there. The one who had been nice to him.

'Where's Barry?' Toby said.

'No need to be scared of him any longer. My mother has him locked up.'

'What happened to you?' He noticed a stitched scar along the boy's forehead, just below the sweep of his hair.

'Nothing much. I was fighting the devil, but I won. What about that game?'

'I prefer *FIFA*,' Toby said. He saw the look on the teenager's face. 'But we could kick the ball for a little bit.'

He looked over to the wall. Hope sat there beside Max, who held his daughter, Lexie, on his knee. Max hadn't left Toby's side since he'd been released from hospital.

Toby couldn't stop the smile from spreading over his face. He put the ball down and kicked it as hard as he could.

'Goal!' He ran forward, Mikey's medal on its piece of green ribbon swinging around his neck in the evening breeze.

A LETTER FROM PATRICIA

Hello, dear reader,

I wish to sincerely thank you for reading my fifth novel, *Tell Nobody*.

I'm so grateful to you for sharing your precious time with Lottie Parker, her family and team. If you enjoyed *Tell Nobody*, you might like to follow Lottie throughout the series of novels. To those of you who have already read the first four Lottie Parker books, *The Missing Ones*, *The Stolen Girls*, *The Lost Child* and *No Safe Place*, I thank you for your support and reviews.

I would love it if you could post a review on Amazon or Goodreads. It would mean so much to me. And thank you for the reviews received so far.

You can connect with me on my Facebook author page and Twitter. I also have a blog, which I try to keep up to date.

Thanks again, and I hope you will join me for book six in the series.

Love,
Patricia

 www.patriciagibney.com

 trisha460

 @trisha460

ACKNOWLEDGEMENTS

To you, my reader, thank you for your continued support.

As a writer, I am dependent on many people, and I'm grateful to have a great team working with me. I wish to thank Lydia Vassar Smith for her tremendous editorial input on *Tell Nobody*. Special thanks to Kim Nash and Noelle Holten, for their incredible media work, organising blog tours and publicity. Thank you also to those who work directly on my books: Lauren Finger (production) and Jen Hunt (publishing), Alex Crow and Jules Macadam (marketing), Jane Selley for her excellent copyediting skills.

Michele Moran is just brilliant at bringing my books to life in audio format, so thanks to Michele and the team at the Audiobook Producers.

The writing community is very supportive of me and my work. Thank you to all who have listened to me, chatted and advised me, especially my fellow Bookouture authors.

Thank you to all the bloggers who give freely of their time to read and review and take part in blog tours. And to each reader who has posted reviews, I am so grateful.

My agent, Ger Nichol of The Book Bureau, works tirelessly, promoting my interests at home and abroad, along with her team of sub-agents. Thank you, Ger.

I wish to acknowledge the great work of libraries and their staff. Thanks also to local and national media, and bookstores.

Special thanks to Monica and Robin Parker.

Family is everything to me. Without that supportive network around me, I would not be able to pursue my writing dream. Thanks to my mother and father, William and Kathleen Ward, who have always believed in me. Thanks also to Lily Gibney and family. To my sisters Marie Brennan and Cathy Thornton, and my brother Gerard Ward, thank you.

My children, Aisling, Orla and Cathal, continue to surprise me with their determination and work ethic. As teenagers, they lost their dad to cancer, but now they are growing into superb young adults. I am so proud of you and thankful to have you in my life. Our family continues to grow. Daisy, Shay and Caitlyn have brought a new dimension to my world and filled it with love.

All the characters in my books are fictional, as is the town of Ragmullin, but real life has influenced my life and my writing.

Finally, I dedicate *Tell Nobody* to my friends. You know who you are and I am blessed to have such a wonderful bunch of people in my life.